PENGUIN BOOKS

TIME PRESENT AND TIME PAST

As a member of the Indian Police Service, Kirpal Singh Dhillon served as director general of police in Punjab and Madhya Pradesh, and as joint director, Central Bureau of Investigation, among other challenging assignments. After retirement, he served a tenure as vice chancellor of Bhopal University and has also been a hockey administrator and a human rights advocate. He is the author of *Defenders of the Establishment, Police and Politics in India* and *Identity and Survival: Sikh Militancy in India 1978–1993*, and has written essays on the Indian Constitution, human rights, minority issues and the Bhopal gas disaster. He is a fellow of the Indian Institute of Advanced Study, Shimla.

ADVANCE PRAISE FOR THE BOOK

'[The book] moves effortlessly from personal detail to the canvas of national politics . . . Readers will inevitably be drawn to Kirpal Dhillon's high-profile role as director general of police in Punjab in the immediate wake of Operation Blue Star. There is much informed insight into the upsurge of Sikh militancy, the circumstances of the Punjab Accord and the subsequent assassination of Sant Harcharan Singh Longowal. . . . [It is] an exceptionally well-written book'—Ian Talbot, professor of history, University of Southampton

'[The book is] a chronicle of events that shaped our history, our geography and our life as a nation. . . . The beauty of this book is its very precise and very economic use of words, which causes the story to move at a goodly pace. The Punjab story . . . is a story of heroism, conscientious devotion to duty and the people of the Punjab, betrayal and treachery and the stoicism and courage of the Sikhs. It is also an objective and honest narration of history. This is a "cracking good book"'—M.N. Buch, administrator, environmentalist, urban planner and writer

'The narrative, like a Russian novel, is spread across a vast canvas and encompasses events of enormous significance in South Asian history of the mid-twentieth century. . . . [The writer] journeys from his blissful but eventful childhood to the grim world of policing and then, aided by his love for literature, to a brave new world of ideas. . . . Prime Minister Indira Gandhi had summed up Kirpal in a sentence: "People tell me you are a very decent man." He eventually became a victim of his decency' —S. Iftikhar Murshed, former Pakistani diplomat and columnist

'Written in a bold and candid style, this autobiography provides, in vivid and rich detail, the unfolding political and social history of the first five decades of Indian nation building. [This] will act as important primary source material for future scholars trying to understand the personalities, events and policies which shaped India's destiny. This book [is] a great counter-narrative against those who argue that the Indian state has an inbuilt bias against the Sikhs, frustrating their ambitions and forcing them to emigrate'—Dr Shinder S. Thandi, professor, Coventry University, and founder-editor, *Journal of Punjab Studies*

TIME PRESENT &
TIME PAST
MEMOIRS OF A TOP COP

KIRPAL DHILLON

PENGUIN BOOKS

An imprint of Penguin Random House

PENGUIN BOOKS

USA | Canada | UK | Ireland | Australia
New Zealand | India | South Africa | China

Penguin Books is part of the Penguin Random House group of companies
whose addresses can be found at global.penguinrandomhouse.com

Published by Penguin Random House India Pvt. Ltd
7th Floor, Infinity Tower C, DLF Cyber City,
Gurgaon 122 002, Haryana, India

Penguin
Random House
India

First published by Penguin Books India 2013

10 9 8 7 6 5 4 3 2

The views and opinions expressed in this book are the author's own and the
facts are as reported by him which have been verifi ed to the extent possible,
and the publishers are not in any way liable for the same.

ISBN 9780143417330

Typeset in Bembo by R. Ajith Kumar, New Delhi
Printed at Repro India Limited

www.penguin.co.in

MIX
Paper from
responsible sources
FSC® C047271

To my parents,
Sardar Jagjit Singh and Sardarni Nihal Kaur

Time present and time past
Are both perhaps present in time future,
And time future contained in time past.
If all time is eternally present
All time is unredeemable.

T.S. Eliot, *Burnt Norton*

Contents

Contents

Foreword

Kirpal Dhillon, the author, a former policeman, combines the traits of an academic, a public servant and a sportsman, who has distinguished himself in every phase of his long and active career. The memoirs of such a person should be of interest to everyone.

Professor J.S. Grewal, an eminent historian, former vice chancellor of Guru Nanak Dev University, Amritsar, and former director of the Indian Institute of Advanced Study, Shimla, describing him, said: 'Mr Dhillon started his career as college lecturer and ended up as vice chancellor; in between, he did some three and a half decades of policing.' As regards the *in-between* period, the assessment of two distinguished policemen—one, his senior and the other, his junior—is highly significant. K.F. Rustamji, a doyen of the Indian Police Service, staunchly affirms that Dhillon has never done anything that can even remotely be construed as failure of duty, which he has fulfilled to the best of his ability and which he rates highly. Chaman Lal, who had worked under Dhillon as SP in Madhya Pradesh and as his DIG (Administration) in Punjab, speaks highly of Dhillon's leadership qualities: 'He supports police autonomy but with accountability—to ensure strict adherence to the rule of law.' The author's role as police chief in

Punjab in the aftermath of Operation Blue Star alone is ample testimony to this assessment. Besides, his active post-retirement involvement with the Commonwealth Human Rights Initiative for police reforms is well known.

Chapter 13 describes the most significant phase of the author's career in the police force. Its title, 'Punjab: The Ultimate Challenge', is very apt. Kirpal Dhillon was hand-picked by Prime Minister Indira Gandhi from outside Punjab to rejuvenate the demoralized Punjab police after the traumatic Operation Blue Star, which had deeply hurt the Sikh psyche. He initiated the process of revamping the Punjab police and made considerable progress till he was unjustly removed in 1985 through political machinations, leaving the task to be completed by his successor and friend, Julio Ribeiro. An official recognition of the major role he played in combating militancy in Punjab is still awaited.

Dhillon asserted that militancy in Punjab was not merely a law-and-order issue but the consequence of various deep-rooted factors—such as a feeling of injustice—which needed to be eradicated for achieving lasting peace. His message was that police brutality could not be as effective as a humane approach that factored in the root cause of hurt, and strived to gain public cooperation. This method had a positive impact and was among the core measures he employed to curb militancy in Punjab. His approach continues to have relevance in similar present-day situations, but, unfortunately, this message has not yet been fully implemented at the level of governance.

Dhillon's post-retirement activities as writer, vice chancellor, fellow of the Indian Institute of Advanced Study, Shimla, and as hockey administrator—which are described in the book—highlight his credentials in addition to those as a policeman.

In the present context, when all institutions are losing their sheen, and public service is seen as having degenerated into 'personal service', the life and career of a distinguished public servant, notwithstanding its vicissitudes, should motivate the youth and help men in public service to retrospect.

I do hope this autobiography will be received with the appreciation it truly deserves.

18 May 2012

J.S. Verma
Former Chief Justice of India
Former Chairman,
National Human Rights Commission

Preface

I suppose every writer, at some point during his writing career, harbours a lurking desire to compile a chronicle of his life and times. I am no exception. My ambition grew stronger with each passing year until, greatly heartened by the positive response to a sample chapter that I had sent to the editorial head of a renowned publishing house, I decided to write this book. Finally, it was a chance meeting with an exceptional individual, then serving as a top executive in an important UN agency in India, which proved to be the catalyst in hastening the process. Peter Delahaye, a remarkably supportive individual with a subtle blend of refinement and eclecticism, pushed and prodded me through his very entertaining daily emails, urging me to get going right away with my 'magnum opus'. He also sent me many books of the same genre—biographies, autobiographies, memoirs—from whichever part of the world he happened to be in.

A truly creative person, Peter turned everything he touched, whether a blank canvas, a stone or a piece of wood, into pieces of rare beauty. His bachelor apartments, in Delhi and Brussels, furnished with choice fabrics and objets d'art, and piles of books of all kinds strewn around, testified to his amazing sense of discernment and elegant style. I was to spend a delightful week with him a few years after he was posted to Brussels. There were several others too—long-standing close friends as well as casual acquaintances—who provided both the stimulus and the drive to make this book possible. To all of them, I express my deep gratitude.

An inevitable corollary of a writing career is the denial of a writer's time, attention and companionship to his spouse and family, and no writer can ever adequately compensate them for such deprivations. It is in this context that I acknowledge my profound sense of obligation to my wife, Sneh, and daughters, Preeti, Amrita and Sonali. Preeti, a student of English literature, suggested the title of this book. Preeti and Amrita also rendered invaluable assistance in the final proofreading of the manuscript.

This book tells the story of a life, less than ordinary in many ways, and whether it needed or deserved to be told in such detail remains uncertain. During the course of his life, every human being passes through high and low phases, which, in fact, shape and define his unique and distinctive persona. Also, no autobiographer is in a position to break up and pigeonhole these so-called highs and lows into separate sections for a fastidious reader to engage with the product as an integrated read. If at all this is to be done, it is only fair that the responsibility should lie with the reader. Also, many assumptions in this kind of writing are by nature tentative and imprecise, and a perceptive reader might often be tempted to find them questionable. Writing an autobiography is in itself a daunting task, its course marked by diverse blockages and dilemmas of conception, composition and articulacy, not to mention issues relating to the felicity of expression and holding the reader's interest. Among the more complex decisions that an autobiographer has to take at every stage in the narrative is the one which pertains to what to reveal, to what extent, and what to hold back. The disclosures, such as they are, have further to be suitably dressed in an objective and, as far as possible, judicious vocabulary, which is a far more difficult job than is commonly realized. Not all writers possess the ability to express their innermost feelings, desires and susceptibilities in an uninhibited manner. Still fewer are capable of clothing the product in an emotionally neutral terminology, which adds immensely to the value of such writing. I do not know if I have been able to meet these various criteria that I had set for myself while attempting this narrative. Nor do I need to know, I suppose. What I do know is that I have done the best I could to be true to my calling as a writer and as a person who values truth and honesty above all else.

Speaking of truth and honesty, I must admit that I have chosen not to include in this narrative some major episodes in my life, special and personal to me, which I found difficult to handle in a candid and forthright manner. Maybe, someday, I will find it in me to exorcise the ghosts of still-poignant memories of relationships which went awry, without becoming tongue-tied at the very idea of sharing my innermost thoughts and feelings with my readers. The least that I can do at this point of time is to dedicate this book to the tender memory of star-crossed liaisons, if only as a small gesture of contrition.

As I prepare to lay down my metaphorical pen to conclude this narrative, the urge to keep on writing stays strong and vibrant, and my brain continues to teem with ideas, dreams and desires. The concluding lines of T.S. Eliot's long poem *East Coker* continue to fascinate me even though the poem belongs, thematically and contextually, to a different age:

Old men ought to be explorers
Here or there does not matter
We must be still and still moving
Into another intensity
For a further union, a deeper communion
Through the dark cold and the empty desolation,
The wave cry, the wind cry, the vast waters
Of the petrel and the porpoise. In my end is my beginning.

Indeed, *in my end is my beginning*. Let us leave it at that.

Abbreviations

AC	assistant commandant
ACR	annual confidential report
ADG	additional director general of police
AIG	assistant inspector general of police
ADM	additional district magistrate
AISSF	All India Sikh Students Federation
ASP	assistant superintendent of police
BSF	Border Security Force
CBI	Central Bureau of Investigation
CM	chief minister
CP	Connaught Place
CPO	Central Police Organization
CPTC	Central Police Training College
CRPF	Central Reserve Police Force
CS	chief secretary
CSO	chief security officer
CSP	city superintendent of police
DC	deputy commissioner
DG	director general
DGP	director general of police
DIG	deputy inspector general of police
DM	district magistrate

DRP	District Reserve Police
DSP	deputy superintendent of police
IAS	Indian Administrative Service
IB	Intelligence Bureau
ICS	Indian Civil Service
IES	Indian Education Service
IFS	Indian Foreign Service
IG	inspector general
IGP	inspector general of police
IHF	Indian Hockey Federation
IIAS	Indian Institute of Advanced Study
IIPA	Indian Institute of Public Administration
IP	Indian (branch of the Imperial) Police
IPC	Indian Penal Code
IPS	Indian Police Service
JCO	junior commissioned officer
JD	joint director
LBSNAA	Lal Bahadur Shastri National Academy of Administration
MP	Madhya Pradesh
NCC	National Cadet Corps
NGO	non-governmental organization
NPA	National Police Academy
PAP	Punjab Armed Police
PM	prime minister
PMO	prime minister's office
PTC	police training college (state)
RAW	Research and Analysis Wing
RI	reserve inspector
SAF	State Armed Force
SDOP	subdivisional officer of police

SGPC	Shiromani Gurdwara Parbandhak Committee
SHO	station house officer
SP	superintendent of police
SSP	senior superintendent of police
UP	Uttar Pradesh (formerly known as United Provinces)
UPSC	Union Public Service Commission
VC	vice chancellor

1

Mai

Sometime in the seventeenth century, Baba Bhara Singh led his clan of Dhillons out of the fertile but volatile Majha tract in central Punjab with no clear idea of his destination. He and his clan were forced to leave their age-old homesteads because of the frequent periods of disorder and turmoil caused by recurrent attacks by predatory hordes from the north-west, attracted by a rich and fertile land lying on the main route to Delhi. Bhara Singh and his clansmen finally decided on the peaceful Malwa region across the Satluj River. Buttar, the village they chose, was named after Buttar Shah, a well-respected faqir. Buttar was then ruled by the Sodhis, a leading Khatri caste with family links to the Sikh gurus, a relationship that endowed them with immense power and prestige among the Sikh people. It would take many a pitched battle between the Dhillons and the Sodhis, entrenched for long in their *garhi*s, or fortresses, before the former could settle down peacefully to earn their living through farming; although, later, they would provide a large number of soldiers and officers to the British Indian army. The Dhillons also had to contend with the Gills, another Jutt clan, who had preceded them and occupied another part of the village. Family lore has it that Kahan Singh, one of the more daring Dhillons, used his muzzle-loading gun to maximum effect in the struggle against the Gills to establish his clan's claim on its part of the village. A middle school was set up in the village around 1875, and it was to prove immensely valuable for the local populace by opening a window of opportunity fairly early after Punjab became part of British India. Upgraded to a high school in due course, this school was later to become the alma mater of many civil and military officers from the region, including my grandfather, his brothers, my father and uncle. My grandfather served as a civil judge in the last quarter of the nineteenth century. His brothers, too, held what were then considered, for Indians, rather high positions in the government. Later, most Sodhi families quit the area to settle elsewhere.

The Dhillons trace their origin from the Mahabharata era and claim to be descendants of King Karna, known in Indian mythology for his valour and munificence. It is said that he would not eat any food without first donating one and a quarter maunds of gold to the poor. Swami Dayanand Saraswati mentions in his notable work *Satyarth Prakash* that after Karna's death at Kurukshetra, his kinsmen, the Dhillons, broke up into clans. Some settled down in the region around present-day Delhi and Agra, while others migrated to different parts of what is now called Rajasthan. From here, some families drifted into Bathinda in Punjab, and later moved to the central Punjab region of Majha. In a way, therefore, Bhara Singh and his clansmen were only returning to their original home when they left Majha for Malwa in search of peace and tranquillity. Swami Dayanand further states that Delhi was founded by the Dhillon dynasty, which ruled the area from 800 to 283 BC. Whether such claims have any historical validity or not, the Dhillons generally behave as though they were, indeed, a special kind of people. Though often referred to as the Dhillon

Padshas (royals) in the Indian social structure, they belong to the agricultural community of Jats or Jutts, as they are more commonly known in Indian and Pakistani Punjabs. Though they have the same surnames, they profess Sikhism in India but are Muslims in Pakistan. Some nine generations down the line from my ancestor Bhara Singh, I appeared on the scene as a rather frail child with an unusually thin neck.

My grandfather was only thirty-seven when he died, probably of cardiac arrest, which appears to have been the principal cause of mortality in the clan across generations. He died while on his way to the court in the district town of Ferozepur in a buggy—the customary mode of transport for those who could afford it before the ubiquitous motor car replaced horse-drawn carriages—leaving his three young children, two boys and a girl, orphaned. My father was the youngest, being just around three at the time. Their mother having expired soon after my father's birth, all the three children were brought up by their stepmother, an exceedingly refined, kind, quiet and gentle woman from what I can recall of her. She looked after the three siblings as well as she could, with ample support from my great-grandfather, who was still alive, and her brothers, affluent landlords in another part of the district. The loss of their father at such a young age could not but severely affect their future. In early-twentieth-century Punjab, women of her class were required by tradition to observe purdah and lead rather secluded lives, leaving most vital decision-making to the brothers and nephews of their dead husbands. This left a lasting impact on the course of my father's life and career. He fell seriously ill during the plague epidemic, which wiped out entire villages during that time, but recovered. Left to the mercy of uncles and aunts after the death of their grandfather, the three orphans somehow managed to keep going, thanks largely to their young widowed stepmother, who did not have any child of her own. In due course, the sister married into a rich landowning family of Patiala, the brother settled down on the ancestral estate and my father resumed his studies to pass his matriculation examination with distinction at the nearby town of Moga.

He also did exceedingly well as a sportsman, excelling as a wrestler and football player of repute, and he was much in demand by various well-known colleges in the province. When I started playing for my school football team, old-timers would tell each other, 'Look, that is Jagjit's son playing.' One of my teachers, Hari Singh, who had seen my father play, would often tell me that the latter used to defend his goalpost just as the Himalayas protected India from invaders. Among the colleges that he joined and represented at university-level sports were the Khalsa College in Amritsar and the Forman Christian, the Islamia and the Government College in Lahore. However, although he excelled in sports and athletics, he spent little time in studying and failed to secure a degree at the end of his college education. Despite the lack of a formal degree, he was remarkably knowledgeable and well informed, with a quiet sense of humour. We children looked forward eagerly to the evening meal time, when he was at his best, telling us fascinating stories about how his teachers and principals—the latter exclusively British in those days—pampered outstanding athletes and sportsmen.

He was particularly nostalgic about Principal Wathen of Khalsa College, Amritsar, an eminent academic of his time and a member of the elite Indian Education Service (IES). He often joined the resident students for meals in the hostel and was generally fond of mixing informally with them, conversing in fluent Punjabi. The British, who were seriously engaged in befriending the Sikhs at that juncture in Indian history, so as to keep them away from the fast-growing nationalist movement, kept this strategic objective in mind and sent their best men to manage premier Sikh institutions, like the Khalsa College. My father continued to feel guilty about not having acquired a degree and he was keen on ensuring that his children did not face a similar situation. So, when I majored in English literature with distinction, he wanted me to join a British university for a doctorate, even though that would have required him to sell a part of his estate. Finally, having made it to the Indian Police Service (IPS), I did not go abroad, a decision I always regretted.

Our relations with my father's side of the family remained strained for years as his elder brother did not give him his due share in the ancestral property. Such things are not unusual in Jutt families and at times lead to murders and court cases, thereby further depleting their resources. However, this property dispute did not lead to a serious clash between the brothers since their uncles still enjoyed enough influence to intercede effectively in the matter. I was born in my maternal grandparents' house, as Punjabi women traditionally bore their children in the familiar environs of their parental home. When my sister was born, I was reportedly very possessive of the newborn and would keep a close watch on her lest someone took her away. As it happened, she died young, leaving me heartbroken. My birth coincided with a period of heightened political activity, when the Indian freedom struggle was reaching its peak. Some two weeks after my birth, the Congress party, under Jawaharlal Nehru, at its annual session in Lahore in December 1929, passed a resolution to demand Independence (Purna Swaraj) instead of dominion status. A few months later, Bhagat Singh and his two co-conspirators were hanged in Lahore jail for sedition and their dead bodies secretly cremated on the banks of the Satluj near Ferozepur.

I spent my early childhood years with my maternal grandparents, or rather with my nani, grandmother, because my nana used to travel a lot in connection with his work, of which I knew little at the time. It was she, therefore, who was chiefly responsible for my early upbringing. I addressed her as 'Ma' like everyone else who lived with her at the time. Later, when we moved out of the village to the subdivisional town of Moga, she came to be called 'Mai', a term of respect for an elderly woman. In her youth, she must have been a strikingly beautiful woman: tall and fair with sharp, attractive features. Even in her mid-fifties which, in those days, was considered a ripe old age, she was a handsome, confident and audacious person, who severely and bluntly reprimanded men or women, whether older or younger than her, if they crossed what she considered the limits of propriety or otherwise happened to rub her up the wrong side.

She was tough on those who infringed her code of conduct. I'll relate three incidents to make my point. On learning that the teacher in the school where I was studying in class two had made me stand in the sun for some minor misdemeanour, she summoned him to our house, placed a chair in the front courtyard and, as he gingerly took his seat, took off her shoe and gave him a sound thrashing—which the luckless victim of her rage was unlikely to forget in a hurry—all the time shouting curses at him for daring to maltreat her grandson. Frightened out of his wits, the teacher promptly fled the village and never came back even to collect his luggage.

There was a large open area in front of our house, used as a community playground. It also served as an evening meeting place for the village young blades who, eager to flaunt their ripening masculinity, were prone to pepper their talk liberally with what are now known as four-letter words. Whenever the exchange of foul words became too loud and uncouth, my nani would suddenly appear on the scene, pounce on the offenders and drag them to their houses to be further chastised by their parents, who never questioned her verdict.

She did not know fear nor did she ever hesitate to do what had to be done. Once, when a gang of dacoits visited the village and fired some shots just outside our house, she went up on the roof and challenged them to fire at her rather than scare the poor villagers. We learnt later that the dacoit gang had, as a matter of fact, been hired by a prominent resident of the village in order to pressurize a rival—a common enough practice in Punjab villages. The dacoits had only wanted to make a spectacular statement; they had no interest in committing a crime.

Ours was a medium-sized village with a population of about a thousand people, almost entirely Jutt Sikhs, tilling their land; those with larger holdings, like my nana, let their property out to sharecroppers for an annual rent called *theka*. Nani had a small patch adjacent to the house for growing flowers and fruits of which she was exceedingly fond and proud. Her deep interest in horticulture was touching. When an orange tree failed to bear fruit for a couple of years, a friend advised her to feed the plant with animal blood. She promptly obtained a bottle of goat's blood from the local shepherd to empty into the plant's roots. The therapy did not work, probably because the local soil or climate was unsuitable for growing oranges.

In keeping with tradition, my nana and nani got married young—when he was about twelve and she was two years older. She often talked about her early married life: her husband, younger than her by some two years, was not greatly interested in sexual exchanges or going to bed with her, but would waste precious time playing with boys his age, while she waited eagerly for him to come home to explore the excitement of the marital bed with her. Later, when she bore only daughters, my nana killed three at birth because of the deep-seated Jutt bias against female progeny. The practice of killing girl children at birth was common to South Asian Jutts, Pathans and Rajputs, and widely practised by them until about the early 1920s, when the practice waned due to the spread of education and the strict application of law.

A variety of practices was employed to get rid of the unlucky infant. Nani would narrate to me, with tears rolling down her cheeks, how Nana had killed his female offspring: one by drowning in a bucket of water; another by smothering with pillows; and the third by administering a stiff dose of opium. I don't know whether he ever regretted killing his daughters because, from the time I came to know him, he was a fond and caring father to his surviving daughters, though he grew more and more sad and despondent with advancing age. Illicit opium was then easily available in Punjab villages to serve the needs of the addicts, known as *vellis*, who were generally looked down upon by other villagers and whom we children were forbidden to befriend. Tiloka, one of these vellis, lived all alone in the lane behind our house. I would often sneak out of the house in the afternoon to peep furtively into his room to find him in a sort of sleepy haze and I wondered when, if ever, he performed the daily functions necessary for normal existence. Tiloka was also known as *chirimar*, bird slayer, a nickname doubtless acquired during his earlier opium-free days.

Nana and Nani finally ended up with three daughters and two sons. What strange twist of fate saved the lives of the surviving daughters remains a mystery. Either Nana got sick of killing his daughters or Nani succeeded in saving them from her husband's deadly intent. In a kind of poetic justice, however, neither son survived: one died of measles at an early age, while the other succumbed, at the peak of youth, to tuberculosis after a protracted and painful struggle. During his illness, his mother carried his wasted body on her back to various sanatoriums and hospitals in the hills, before she eventually brought him back to the village to die. His last days were spent in a kind of hallucinatory spell, an event that nearly unhinged Nani. She remained in a highly distraught state of mind for several years after his death, and when I was born, my parents, alarmed at her declining physical and mental health, suggested that I stay with her for some time to relieve her of loneliness. This arrangement, however, was to last for many years, because Nani would throw a tantrum every time she sensed a move to take me away to live with my parents.

In due course, both of us got so used to each other that although my parents wanted me to move to a better school in the town where they lived, I completed my elementary studies in the village school. Nani had grown excessively fond of me and also rather possessive. She would often relate to me sad stories about the painful final days of her elder son's life, interspersed with tales of his exploits and achievements, especially as a district-level wrestler and hockey player. His first-floor room in a corner of the inner veranda was kept locked for years after his death. Once a week, she would unlock the door to clean the room and tenderly dust the various items that had belonged to him, among them his hockey stick and school bag. I frequently found her weeping silently while sweeping the room, although many years had passed since the incident. I found this surprising since she was, otherwise, a person of grit and fortitude.

Like all villages in those days, our village was quite self-sufficient. The villagers produced almost everything locally, except common salt and kerosene oil, the latter for the hurricane lanterns that a few families used to light in their houses at night. These items were sold by Harbhaj, the village shopkeeper, who also stocked various odds and ends that the villagers might need at the time of weddings and a few seasonal festivals, like Lohri and Baisakhi, which were celebrated with great gusto and joy. Religious festivals, like Diwali or Holi, were much less common; Holi was, in fact, unknown in the rural areas in the 1930s. Even the birthdays of the Sikh gurus and other hallowed events associated with them were not celebrated with much fervour, despite the fact that the village was predominantly Sikh. Special religious services were, of course, organized in the village dharamsala on the occasion of gurpurbs—events linked with the lives of the Sikh gurus. Such occasions, however, did not attract large gatherings; only a handful of elders attended while the majority of the people went about their normal chores. This was before the Shiromani Gurdwara Parbandhak Committee (SGPC), the Sikh elective parliament, took effective control of all Sikh religious places and reorganized them to function as regular gurdwaras.

In many ways, the dharamsala acted as a social and religious resource centre for the villagers. It was also the place where travellers were provided with lodging and meals for as long as they chose to stay there, in the true tradition of such institutions. Large marriage parties could be accommodated in its vast roomy precincts. These were also used as emergency housing in the event of floods and other natural calamities: once the village school had to be shifted there after severe rains had damaged the school's mud structure. The dharamsala was, in fact, by far the best building in the entire village and was managed by a two-member team, a man and a woman, both clothed in long robes and saffron turbans, although the turban looked rather odd on the woman. Like the mendicants of many religious orders, the male *sadhu*, or *sadh*, and the female *sadhni*—as they were commonly addressed, since no one knew their real names— took turns to visit every morning as many households in the village as necessary to collect food items for the day. These were used in the dharamsala to feed whoever was visiting. Needless to add, all households donated generously. Nani's house was one of the regular destinations for the sadh and the sadhni.

Not that all sadhs were so virtuously inclined. One sadh, known widely for granting fecundity to barren women, practised his infamous enterprise by preying, in a most reprehensible manner, on simple rural women who were desperate for a child. He had a cord tied around a peg in his chamber. When a woman entered his room, he would quietly ask her to untie the cord. Most rural women would be taken in by the ruse and undo the waistband of their petticoats under the impression that this was God's way of making them bear children. If a daring woman erupted in anger and outrage, the sadh would simply point to the peg with the cord, implying that that was what he had referred to. Strangely, even now, it is not only the Jutt peasantry that continues to be exploited by such unholy 'holy' men, even the more affluent classes are not immune to the lure held out by such charlatans.

Since the Jutt peasants did not need the services of a Brahmin priest to perform any elaborate rituals or religious ceremonies, Harbhaj, the only Brahmin resident of the village, had set up a shop instead. His wife, Durgi, lent an occasional hand by taking it over in the afternoon when Harbhaj went to the village well for a bath, to be followed by a nap. The rest of the time he was always there, watching over his shop, and was occasionally called upon to settle disputes between argumentative youngsters. How and why he came to be accepted as a peacemaker in such matters was unclear for he was as unlettered as any other villager. Also, he was fair game for us boys to tease and torment in many ways. I recall that some of us would gather on a dusky evening, a little distance away from his shop, choosing a spot in the road where it turned right, forming a blind corner beyond his line of vision. Harbhaj would sit cross-legged on the floor, clad only in a loincloth, his multi-layered stomach flowing over that garment, his bare hairless chest heaving like a pair of bellows in the stifling heat of August, while a small earthen oil lamp struggled valiantly to pierce the eerie darkness outside. We would briskly turn the corner, peep into the shop for a fleeting moment and chant, 'Durgi nehar wich rudh gi, Harbhaj bhalda phire.' A rough English translation would run something like this: Durgi got swept away by the flowing water of the canal and Harbhaj kept looking for her.

No one knew who had made up this couplet, but it was clearly of ancient vintage. For the so-called canal, which flowed near the village, had hardly any water, and certainly not sufficient to carry away Durgi, who was not a lean and slim damsel by any means. Harbhaj, actually unperturbed by our boyish pranks, would pretend to get up from his seat, hurling some choice rustic abuses at us and making threatening gestures. Occasionally, a small, dark, wrinkly ball would desert its companion to peep out of Harbhaj's loose-fitting loincloth, causing female customers to giggle and hastily cover their faces with their dupattas, but not before stealing a few glances at the accidentally exposed member. As for us boys, the exposure of the inert organ would work as a signal to take turns aiming a pebble at the indolent object, with the owner hurriedly trying to chase us out of the vicinity. Such was the level of social harmony in the village in those days that youthful shenanigans like this were accepted with good cheer.

Most villagers adhered to the natural cycle of day and night to finish their chores and went to sleep by sunset. However, they needed some lighting arrangement when they had to go out at night or before dawn to draw their share of water from the feeder canals to irrigate their crops. For this they used small earthen lamps, which contained locally produced mustard oil and home-made cotton wicks. Arguments among rival claimants to their share of canal water were common since rainfall was unreliable and the canal water, usually meagre. The shortfall was made up by using water from the wells, drawn through Persian wheels with two yoked bullocks going round and round to turn the wheels of the bucket chain. The ubiquitous bullock was a very useful animal indeed, being the key source of energy for every job that needed pulling or pushing, as in bullock carts and other agricultural activities. Tractors and other motorized devices had not yet reached Punjab villages. The village pond served as a swimming and frolicking pool for local lads as also for the herds of buffaloes brought there for a wash and some play. The pond was the end result of what is now known as water harvesting.

Strangely, it was the buffalo, not the cow, which was the preferred choice as a milch animal. The job of looking after the buffalo was usually entrusted to the women of the household, who tended it lovingly, feeding and bathing it with great care and affection. The other animals—bullocks, horses and camels—were the responsibility of the menfolk. An average house was large enough to provide sufficient space for the domestic cattle, usually in the outer courtyard or in a large hall at the entrance, which was high enough to let a camel enter without difficulty. For the same reason, this part of the house had to have a high roof. The outer courtyard and the hall, locally called *dalaan*, would open into an inner courtyard, which was not generally accessible to the male members of the family or to outsiders. This was the domain of the mother-in-law, where she set the rules of conduct for the younger women to abide by.

The father-in-law had to make himself comfortable outside the house during the day, generally tending to the cattle out grazing and the children who were out to play. He was served his meals and tea, twice daily, in the dalaan or outside under a tree, where he sat or lay on a charpoy. If he needed to go into the house, he had to clear his throat loudly as a warning to the daughters-in-law to cover their faces. Age was not counted in years. One was deemed to have reached old age on the day one's son got married and a daughter-in-law entered the house. Soon after that momentous event, the father would take his place outside the house and be referred to as the *burha*, or old man. Therefore, men and women aged long before their time and were treated as ancillary to the main family. This was especially so in the case of men because, strangely enough, older women traditionally enjoyed better privileges than older men. Due to the lack of sanitary facilities, everyone used the open fields as toilets, the men in the morning, and the women in the late evening to escape vulgar remarks from uncouth youngsters. While the men could bathe at the well or in the village pond, women could do so only in their homes at odd hours when the menfolk were out at work. Thus, the occasions when they could take a proper bath were few and far between. That probably accounted for the vaguely offensive smell most village women carried about them.

No medical help was available locally except what was tendered by a quack, who would cater to the needs of people who were credulous enough to be taken in by his dubious skills. The nearest hospital was located in Moga, at a distance of about three miles. But the sandy track that one had to negotiate to access that facility was so tiring that the journey was undertaken only in extreme emergencies. Whenever I had to take that road for a scholarship examination or otherwise, Nani would ask Bulaki, the *kumhar*, or potter, to bring his donkey for me to ride on, which, of course, I would simply refuse to do. So, while Nani, Bulaki and I plodded wearily, the donkey merrily ambled alongside. With the partition of the country in 1947, Bulaki, being a Muslim, suddenly became persona non grata and the option before him was to leave with his large family for Pakistan. He knew no other home and refused to adopt a new one in his old age. So he deserted the convoy of Indian Muslims who were forced out of their homes by Sikh mobs on the rampage. These Muslims had to trudge wearily along the Grand Trunk Road on their way to the promised Muslim homeland. Bulaki came back to the village of his ancestors, but he couldn't reclaim possession of his house, which was now occupied by a Sikh refugee family from Pakistan, despite intercession by the village elders. He lived a peripatetic and troubled life for a few more months and died a stranger in the village that he had refused to disown even in the face of certain death.

Sicknesses or injuries were usually treated by village elders called *siana*s, wise men, who administered concoctions and mixtures made from locally available herbs and plants or, occasionally, even the blood of birds or animals. Such medications often worked because the villagers were hardy creatures and could endure the pain and the discomfort with their innate resilience, while the natural healing ability of the human body did the rest. When I had a severe spell of coughing, which would not go away for several days, a siana suggested that I consume pigeon's blood, heated to boiling point. Nani duly prepared the concoction, but I firmly refused to swallow the brew. However, the cough disappeared soon after, which the siana ascribed to the fact that, after all, I had smelt the stuff!

If a local siana failed to affect a cure, a senior siana from another village was consulted. Thus, when two small lumps appeared on the sides of my unusually thin neck, I was taken to a siana in a neighbouring village. Nani had been advised to carry a bundle of cowries and keep scattering them along the way and wherever we halted for a meal or some other purpose. Nani followed the instructions to the letter. When we finally arrived at the siana's house, he carried out a few purificatory rituals and chanted some incantations in my ear. We retraced our steps to our village in the same manner, again dispensing cowries on the way back. The lumps did disappear after a few days. Whether this was due to the rituals conducted by the siana or something else remains a mystery.

My experience with another siana was, however, far from simple. This was when I had fractured an elbow in a riding accident while accompanying Nana on horseback to inspect his estate. The first siana summoned to set the fractured bone bound my arm so tight that in about a week's time, it visibly started to wither. So, a more reputed siana from a distant village was called. This one decreed that the arm had been set incorrectly and would have to be broken again and reset correctly. The operation was to be conducted, without any sedation, over a large tray of burning coals, which was supposed to soften the bones—a practice clearly unfamiliar to the practitioner of the craft. I was seated on a low stool while the redoubtable gentleman sat opposite me across the red-hot embers. Initially, the whole thing appeared to me as another kind of trick that such people had up their sleeves, but when he proceeded to bend my stiff arm at the elbow, inwards and outwards, by sheer force, I started howling in unbearable pain. The operation over and my elbow bandaged afresh, the siana left in some hurry as Nani was furious at him for causing her darling grandson so much pain. Somebody suggested that the child be given a dash of liquor to put him to sleep. Nani almost ran all the way to the nearby town of Moga to fetch a bottle of country liquor for the purpose. My father rushed to the village to take me to Lahore's famed Mayo hospital to consult a specialist. The slight deformity could not be put right, but we were told that there would be no lasting disability. Nani never forgave herself for this mishap.

In the normal course, boys and girls had no occasion to mix freely, socially or otherwise, except within close family relationships. The time-honoured South Asian tribal values, which still largely determined the Jutt way of life, laid great stress on rigid sexual segregation outside marriage, especially in the case of young people. However, since such strict isolation is against the natural inclination of pubescent girls and boys, some lapses did take place and were dealt with severely. And, as in all patriarchal societies, it was the girl who was the major sufferer in any such illicit relationship. She would be hastily dispatched to a distant village to allow for the controversy to die down and then get married off quietly, usually to an older man far below her social status. Having succumbed to a momentary—although a very natural—urge, she was deemed to have lost all claims to a normal future life. On the other hand, the guilty boy would be let off rather lightly. He would generally receive a severe thrashing from the wronged girl's brother or uncle, and his family would have to face social boycott for some time along with a monetary compensation to the panchayat and the girl's family. An upper-caste boy was likely to get away more lightly. It was not rare for Jutt boys to bed girls from untouchable families and not only evade any retribution but also boast about it. If, however, a low-caste male was involved in a liaison with a Jutt girl, he could even be done to death and his family evicted from the village.

Seasonal fairs and weddings provided the most common opportunities for boys and girls to meet away from the prying eyes of their elders. The much sought-after occasions for young men and women to form forbidden alliances were the long summer afternoons when they would flock to the several wild groves to pick the juicy berries that grew there. The *ber*, berry tree, in fact, forms the central theme of many romantic tales in Punjab. A mud knoll, locally known as *theh*, probably an old archaeological site that had escaped the attention of the concerned department, was another favourite rendezvous for the purpose. Older girls would create opportunities for sexual dalliance by encouraging young boys to hide with them during a hide-and-seek game or would take them into their beds under the pretext of telling stories. While the boy was intently listening to the stories of rajas and ranis of old, the girl would deftly guide his hands to explore the delicious contours of her body. Most such ventures would end in confusion as the much younger male had not yet woken up to the sensual delights and pleasures of a female body. On the other hand, homosexual practices were rife among boys because girls were mostly out of reach, and I daresay the practice was common among girls too. Same-sex liaisons were considered highly reprehensible. I received the severest thrashing of my life from my father when he found me being friendly with boys suspected of engaging in such activities.

Some names, such as Sant, Naseeb and Jagir, were common to both men and women, except that they would be suffixed with a 'Singh' for men and a 'Kaur' for women. However, the girls' names were generally changed to Santo, Seebo and Jeero. Jarnail (general) Singh and Karnail (colonel) Singh were also common male names, pointing to the strong presence of Jutt Sikhs in the Indian army. Thana (police station) Singh and Zail (an honorary village revenue official) Singh were also common, signifying the importance of the police and revenue officialdom in rural areas. Many women also carried names like Phino (flat-nosed) and Ghono (the sly one), deriving from their physical features. So did the men, with names like Lamba (tall) Singh and Nikka (short) Singh. Nani's name was Inder Kaur but she was commonly called Indi, because of her marriage to a man who ranked lower in the hierarchy of relationships in the village, where most of the men were his uncles and great-uncles. Maybe she would have been called Indu today. Later, when we moved to Moga, she came to be known as Mai Indi. Our Moga house was close to a large statue of Queen Victoria. 'Near Her Majesty's statue' would henceforth become our address, testifying to the heavy imperialist flavour of the times.

When I turned five, Nani took me to the one-teacher primary school for admission. As she did not remember my date of birth, the teacher, Kartar Singh, entered a date on his own initiative, which was a year ahead of the actual date. This innocent error would result in reducing my service tenure by a year though this proved to be a boon later, when older pensioners were granted enhanced pension benefits. The school did not admit girls; in fact, they were not provided with any educational facilities except in the nearby town. Most girls, therefore, remained illiterate and were put to learning household chores from an early age. The local dharamsala did conduct classes for girls to teach them the Gurmukhi script and some elements of *gurbani*, or the Guru's utterances. Well-to-do families, including Nana's family, sent their daughters to the nearby town for education. My mother studied in a residential school in Ferozepur. She later started a small school for girls in a part of the house and taught there for a few years before her marriage.

The most common dress for boys was a long shirt, made of homespun cloth, and a pair of shorts tied at the waist by a band, known locally as *kachh*. Much as I wished to wear the same kind of dress as other boys my age, I had to wear a standard pair of shorts with a belt, which my friends found rather funny and which they called *bundghootni*s, bum-huggers. The young men, when not engaged in manual labour in their fields, or when going out to the town or to visit a fair, wore a dhoti, known as a *chadra*, over the kachh, tied in the Punjabi style. It was a long piece of cloth, usually pink or cream in colour and worn in such a way that it trailed in the manner of a cloak, brushing the ground behind. The elderly dressed more formally, in shirts and loose pyjamas, with a shawl or a long coat in winter, especially when going to the *kutchery*, or court—a frequent enough occurrence due to continuous litigations over land—or for receiving government officials, mostly policemen, visiting the village to serve a summons or execute warrants. The girls wore a salwar-kameez combination with a long dupatta, draped to fully cover their heads as well as the upper part of their bodies. My sister had to observe this dress code strictly and, from the age of eleven or twelve, was forbidden to go up on the terrace or even stand at the outer gate of our house.

The British-era policeman was a formidable official and had enormous clout in the district bureaucracy. Just the prospect of a visit by a constable, the lowest-ranking police official, not to speak of a visit by the redoubtable *thanedar*, the station house officer, was enough to send shivers down the spines of village elders. Although a visit by the thanedar was generally a cause for concern, the village elders spared no effort in looking after him. His visits were mercifully short but even the few hours that he spent in the village kept the entire community on tenterhooks, such was the fear and terror of the police in colonial India. Our house had a large room with a separate entrance from outside, called the *baithak*—the only house in the village to boast of this luxury. This room was furnished with half a dozen chairs and a centre table but, more importantly, it had a *punkha*, a contraption made of thick cloth with an even thicker lining and embellished with frills and flowery patterns.

It was attached to a wooden pole and had a long rope tied to both ends which passed through a pulley. It hung horizontally from the ceiling and, when pulled by the rope, provided a cool, gentle breeze in summer to soothe the nerves of the occupants.

Once or twice, when the thanedar came to make some inquiries, he spent a few hours in our baithak, imparting a whole new aura of awe to our house. Later, my mother's younger sister married a policeman; this further enhanced the family's standing in the eyes of the villagers. I did not foresee at the time that I would join the service one day and head the Punjab police some fifty years later.

The village had a rigid caste hierarchy. At the very top were the Jutt cultivator-proprietors, who tilled their land themselves or employed landless labour from the lower castes belonging to the same or nearby villages. The Jutts were the principal inhabitants of the village and dominated the social and economic life of the small community. The intermediate castes—which these days would be called Other Backward Castes (OBCs)—performed a supporting role by attending to the manual and mechanical jobs that kept the village economy going. They belonged to such castes as the *chhimba* (tailor), *julaha* (weaver), *sunar* (goldsmith), *nai* (barber), *kumhar* (potter), *tarkhan* (carpenter), *lohar* (blacksmith), *teli* (oil extractor) and *karigar* (mason). All these castes were an integral part of the Punjab countryside in the 1930s and '40s since the villages had to take care of all their needs from within their own resource pool. Later, as the tractor, the tube well and the harvester entered the scene, qualified technicians were required to keep them functional, and the utility of these supporting castes was diminished. Some of the village tradesmen performed dual roles. The teli also worked as the *dhunkar*, who teased and processed old and crushed cotton pieces, called *logar*, which were used for making quilts before the onset of winter. The implement used for the purpose made a pleasant, melodious sound when the teli worked on it, and it never failed to attract us boys to the scene.

Since the Sikhs are mandated to keep their hair unshorn, the village nai was rarely called upon to try his tonsorial skills. So, he set himself up as a one-man marriage bureau. As soon as a boy or a girl attained a marriageable age in a nearby village, the nai would gather all the details and carry the information to the prospective parents-in-law. His wife, or mother, as the case may be, called the *nayan*, had free access to the ladies of the Jutt households. She was frequently summoned for massaging and fomenting the weary limbs of the womenfolk, exhausted after a long day's toil to keep their extended families well fed and the cattle well tended. These close associations also kept the nai household well stocked with vital information to be used strategically in matchmaking. Therefore, the nai and the nayan—referred to respectfully as raja and rani by the villagers—were the best-informed people in the village. This proximity to the village elite also subjected the nai household to police questioning, which could be quite brutal, whenever a crime involving influential parties occurred in the village.

Strangely, while the lohars, telis and kumhars were Muslim, all the others were Sikh. At the very bottom of the ladder were the untouchable castes, comprising mainly the *choorha*s, sweepers, and the *chamar*s, cobblers. Notionally, of course, they were not untouchable since both these castes professed Sikhism, which does not recognize the caste system and regards all human beings as equal. As Sikhs, the choorhas were known as *mazhabi*s and the chamars as *ramdasia*s. However, in actual practice, they were addressed in a far more demeaning manner. Mazhabi Sikh males worked as agricultural labourers in the village while their women helped in the households by sweeping and cleaning the cattle sheds. The Sikh Light Infantry, an Indian army regiment, consisting entirely of mazhabi Sikhs, is rated as one of the finest units of the Indian army.

Later, when the practice of untouchability was made an offence carrying a heavy sentence, and the lower castes were given reservations and quotas in jobs, the Punjab farmer was forced to import agricultural labour from the poorer states of Bihar and UP (Uttar Pradesh, then known as United Provinces). There were also some small settlements of *faqirs*, *bawarias* and *nats*, but they lived outside the village in *deras* and, strictly speaking, were not part of the village community. Faqirs earned their livelihood through casual labour and begging though some women faqirs practised as midwives too. Almost all the deliveries in Nani's house were carried out by a woman faqir. Nats were mostly nomadic people and travelled from village to village, giving gymnastic performances of a fairly high standard. Bawarias were listed as a criminal tribe and often received humiliating treatment at the hands of the police. Then there were a few families of Jutt Sikhs from Doaba, another part of the province, who had settled in the village a few generations earlier. However, they were still treated as outsiders and referred to as Doabias, so strong was the bias against those outside the close-knit local community of Jutts.

By temperament, the Jutts are generally impassive and stern-looking, but simple, individuals except when heavily inebriated which, luckily, is an unusual occurrence except at festive events like weddings. Typically, their communication skills are rather limited, though they can always make a strong point when they want to. A visit to a distant village to see a relative would go somewhat like this. On arrival at the destination, a Jutt man would be welcomed formally (to some it may even seem cold) by the relative and offered a *chhanna* (a flat metal plate) of hot milk, brimming with cream. After this, the host and the guest would exchange a few words about their cattle and the state of the crops. The host would then leave the guest to have a nap, an activity of which the Jutts are excessively fond. The departure, a few hours later, after the guest had partaken of another chhanna of milk with some home-made *pinni*s, and a final greeting of '*Achha phir, Sat Sri Akal*', would be equally formal and quiet. And the visit would come to an end. Such thrifty use of words during a visit to a close relative, involving a journey of some ten or twenty miles, is not unusual even in these garrulous times.

A postman from Moga would visit the village once a week to deliver a few postcards and, on his way back, would carry similar cards with him to Moga for delivery. The receipt of a letter was a big event, but the excitement would be somewhat diluted because there were few villagers who could read. It was usually the schoolteacher who read out the letters and also wrote replies to them, thus involuntarily becoming privy to much of the information contained in them. The letter itself began with greetings to all those who were present and listening to the letter being read out, many of the listeners being actually mentioned by name. And as each name was called out aloud by the teacher, the addressee would fold his hands and solemnly acknowledge the greeting. It was indeed a valued social event.

The village folk also harboured a strange weakness for the occult and the supernatural, with an obsessive belief in the existence of ghosts and apparitions. *Jand puja* (tree worship) and other such strange rituals, strictly forbidden in Sikhism, were much in vogue. Young women were often 'possessed' by evil spirits, which called for the intervention of a witch doctor. There was a common belief that evil spirits dwelt in old, solitary peepul or banyan trees, and we used to dare each other to visit such a tree, go around it three times and then say loudly, 'Here I go.' Needless to say, none of us ever took up the challenge. We children also believed in the existence of an eerie, scary and uncanny character, which could assume any shape, animate or inanimate, whether animal, plant, human or object. We called it the *chhaleda* and you could run into such a creature at any time, place or situation. So, the fear of the chhaleda kept us on tenterhooks all the time.

It was quite usual for the villagers to intersperse their talk liberally with oaths and swear words, and for men it was almost de rigueur to employ spicy and colourful profanities to make their point forcefully. The two commonest oaths were 'I swear by the cow' and 'I swear by Guru Granth Sahib', the Sikh holy book. In the rural version of the Punjabi language, it sounded something like *sonh gau di* and *sonh grasa di*. Later, when the Akali movement spread in the Punjab countryside, the cow became secondary to Guru Granth Sahib, but it always remained an object of veneration.

2

Montgomery

The village where I grew up only had a primary school, so I had to leave the place in 1938 to join my parents in Montgomery—

now in Pakistan—to complete my school education. Parting from my many childhood friends was sad and upsetting. When I revisited the village years later, I had grown apart in so many ways from the simple and humble people I had known that it was impossible to connect with them any more. I felt miserable at having lost forever the warm and easy bond I had shared with my rustic friends right from the time I had learnt to appreciate human relationships.

Montgomery, renamed Sahiwal after Independence, was to be my home for many years to come. The district covered a sizeable swathe of territory between Lahore and Multan, both places of considerable antiquity, featuring prominently in the history and folklore of the subcontinent. The town remains a prominent feature of my memory landscape for many reasons, but chiefly because it was against this backdrop that my value framework and attitudes to life would largely evolve. It was a sparsely populated town by present-day standards, well laid out and clean, its roads and streets sprinkled with water every evening by municipal lorries, and its sewer lines cleaned daily, a practice that fell into disuse soon after Independence. Several parks and gardens lent an air of elegance to the town, prominent among them being the famed Rana Pratap Bagh, named after S. Pratap, one of its earlier deputy commissioners (DCs).

Among the other scenic spots in the town was the race course, a beautiful meadow spread over several square miles. It provided a safe hideaway for newly-wed couples for exploring the finer points of conjugality in solitude, unthinkable in joint families. It was also the ideal setting for boys and girls to steal ardent but discreet glances at each other from a distance, or to leave hurriedly scribbled notes under the bushes, hoping that they would not fall into the wrong hands. Young people those days had few opportunities to enter into any but the most formal relations across gender barriers. I would often make for the quiet ambience of the race course to study for final examinations in the month of March, when the place would be at its best with spring flowers in full bloom, flocks of birds of myriad varieties joyfully darting from tree to tree, and the bees toiling hard to drain every succulent flower of its precious treasure.

Once every quarter, there was horse racing, a favourite British sport. It was marked by colour and pageantry, with army bands playing popular tunes and the high and mighty of the district showing up in their finest outfits, sourced from top Lahore clothiers. Once in a while, the commissioner of Multan would drop by on his way to Lahore, thus adding greatly to the status of the event. There were also the usual activities associated with fairs and festivals, such as magic and conjurer shows, street plays, prize cows and buffaloes on view and plenty of food stalls. Two cinema houses provided a welcome break from the dreary routine. The movies had simple storylines and were incredibly primitive and naive. Tales from the Indian epics and the immortal love legends of Punjab formed the most popular and handy menu for film-makers to choose from. *Raja Harishchandra* (1913) and *Puran Bhagat* (1933), both with clear moral subtexts, ran for very long. A romantic twist in the latter film where Puran's young stepmother, smitten by the boy's adolescent good looks, tries to lure him into a romantic liaison, gave it an amorous edge for the younger viewers.

Compared to the present times, there were far fewer officers in the district as well as in the provincial capitals. Apart from the top tier of DC, superintendent of police (SP), civil surgeon, executive engineer and district forest officer, all the rest were class-two- or three-category officials, almost all of them Indian, though by the late 1930s there were several Indian DCs and SPs. All senior officers lived in huge bungalows in the Civil Lines, situated along a road usually called The Mall or the *thandi sadak*, cool road, presumably because the gigantic shady trees that lined it on both sides shielded pedestrians from the intense heat. The bungalows, *kothi*s in Punjabi, had acres of canal-irrigated land attached to them, producing choice crops of grapes, oranges, Malta oranges, grapefruit, many varieties of vegetables and occasionally wheat and maize, too.

The houses were positioned at the end of a long drive and had a number of spacious rooms with high ceilings and ventilators. A deep veranda all around the house shielded it from heat and rain. The kitchen block—consisting of a pantry, a shed for odds and ends, wood or coal stoves for heating water and, of course, the kitchen proper—was located away from the living rooms, usually at the far end of a large open courtyard, where the family slept under mosquito nets in the summer months. The stables and the servants' quarters were situated away from the house but, like the kitchen block, were connected to it by a covered passage. The toilet block, usually in a corner of the inner veranda, consisted of a number of commodes—wooden boxes with a chamber pot fixed in the centre to collect the sahib log's night soil, which was carried away every morning, cleaned and reset by the resident sweeper. A highly unpleasant job for the poor man, no doubt, but then there were worse jobs which these unfortunate Indians had to perform. Urban households had rooftop latrines for the whole family. The stinking waste was collected by sweepers every morning to be carried in buckets on their heads for disposal, a practice that survived for many years after Independence despite smug promises by politicians for its abolition. It still survives although not on the same scale as before.

Needless to say, to keep the sahib and his family in utmost luxury—to which they soon got accustomed—a large retinue of servants, some ten or twelve of them, along with a butler and a cook, needed to be employed. This was not difficult as wages were abysmally low. A head cook could be had for two rupees a month and his assistants for as little as half to three quarters of a rupee, while a trained butler would be available for eight to ten rupees a month. The monthly expenses on domestic servants would never exceed thirty rupees a month, an insignificant amount when set against the thousand rupees that the DC drew as his monthly salary, a truly kingly sum those days when the rupee could stretch very far indeed. On return from work, the sahib would lazily sprawl in an easy chair while a servant squatted uneasily on the floor to remove his shoes and socks and gently massage his feet. The servant would then busy himself with preparing the bath, laying out the sahib's evening clothes, and other such ministrations. The ruling classes were thoroughly spoilt and pampered in a system that was fashioned precisely for that purpose. Nearly all senior officers owned horse carriages—called buggies, if they were four-wheeled, or tongas, if two-wheeled—for commuting. A few cars had also started to appear on the scene, but were mostly used for touring outside the town. During the War years, however, when petrol was scarce, most officers would cycle to office for work or to the club for tennis or a game of bridge. Unlike present-day VIPs, the British had no problem enduring the prevailing shortages along with their subjects.

The club was an important institution of the Raj, serving

as much more than a place merely for recreation. It was in the club that most issues of administrative or interpersonal nature were sorted out informally over a glass of beer, whisky or pink gin. If the differences were more serious, they would be sorted out with a gentle nudge from the DC, thereby reducing to the minimum formal correspondence at those levels. After Independence, the club ceased to be an integral part of the Indian administrative and social scene as governmental decision-making became hostage to the whims and fancies of the political class, newly invested with powers they did not know how to use in the larger public interest. In the event, the civil service lost its ability to discharge its functions in an open manner. Subterfuge and guile would now play an increasingly important role in the formulation of public policy.

Although Muslims outnumbered non-Muslims in the district as a whole, its headquarter town was predominantly non-Muslim. Engaged mostly in trade and business, the non-Muslims were generally affluent and had sound religious and social support systems through gurdwaras and temples. Sikhs and Hindus intermingled freely at the social level, though they often entertained acute political differences, the Sikhs largely supporting the Akali Party while Hindus were guided by the Arya Samaj. Sikhs were often the butt of jokes of Hindus. A choice titbit went something like this: '*Sikh paise da ik, Mussulman, Mussulman ik paise de char jawan and Khatri paise de batri.*' (For one paisa, you can get one Sikh, or four Muslims or thirty-two Khatris—that is, Hindus.) A paisa then was one-sixty-fourth of a rupee. Several local Hindu and Sikh leaders secured important positions in independent India. Hukam Singh, a local lawyer and Akali leader, would get elected to India's Constituent Assembly and then as speaker of the Lok

Sabha. Later still, he would serve as governor of Rajasthan. Another resident, H.K.L. Bhagat, would become a Central minister in the 1980s. Along with other Congress leaders, he was later indicted for playing a leading role in the gruesome killings of Sikhs in 1984.

The town's Muslims were generally less affluent than the non-Muslims. They were also politically and socially less organized, probably due to poverty and illiteracy. While rural Muslims generally supported the ruling Unionist Party, Majlis-e-Ahrar-ul-Islam was more popular in urban areas. The Muslim League had but a marginal presence in Punjab at the time. There was no conspicuous segregation of Muslims and non-Muslims in housing. Even predominantly Hindu mohallas would typically have at least some Muslim households. All the same, some areas in the town were distinctly Muslim in character. An isolated locality, called the *chakla*, where the town's prostitutes lived and practised their trade, was forbidden territory for us boys. Social intercourse between the two communities was sporadic though not too uncommon. I had at least three very close Muslim friends and we were constantly in and out of each other's homes, with our families on fairly cordial terms. I was particularly fond of Mobin and his family and felt thoroughly at home with them, more so with his elder sister Naseem who, in a very special way, fulfilled an important need, since I did not have an elder sister.

Despite close friendships at individual levels, interaction between Hindus and Muslims was not free from biases and misperceptions of many kinds, which tended to subvert mutually trusting relationships. Such biases took many forms. A most hurtful norm was to abstain from partaking of food cooked in Muslim households, even if they were close friends.

Those who followed religions of Indian origin commonly believed that all Muslims were unclean in their habits—a belief based on no empirical evidence—and, therefore, it was wrong to eat with them. It must be said to the credit of our Muslim friends that they continued to send uncooked food to their non-Muslim friends' houses on Eid. Such odious and unfounded prejudices against the Punjabi Muslims must have contributed in a major way to prompt them to press for Partition.

Of the three high schools, the D.A.V. School maintained a consistently high standard in academics, while the Khalsa and the Islamia were strong in sports. As usual, boys who did well in sports were poor in studies and unable to clear the final examinations for years. However, such students, known as *khalifa*s, were in high demand by all the schools for their excellence in sports. I studied in the Khalsa School and was weak in mathematics for which I often had to suffer physical punishment. Once, I was awarded eight cane strokes, four on each hand, and the headmaster chose to do the honours personally during the morning assembly. I held out my right hand for the first hit. When asked to extend the other hand, I told him rather cheekily to inflict all the blows on one hand. This unexpected response and an amused murmur from the assembly upset him and he hurried back to his office. This gesture of quiet defiance hugely reinforced my self-esteem and boosted my rating among my peers. I shifted to the D.A.V. School soon after. This greatly helped me decipher many mathematical mysteries, virtually unintelligible to me until then.

D.A.V. was an excellent school on all counts except for the obligatory recitation of the Gayatri mantra every morning, with which I, as a Sikh, was unfamiliar. But then, Khalsa School had daily gurbani classes and mandatory participation in all Sikh religious functions. I was unaware how the Islamia people safeguarded the faith of their boys. Educational institutions were routinely used to advance the religious and political interests of the communities that financed them. Politicization of the younger generation started right from elementary school. I recollect how hard the Sikh schools drove their students to join early-morning rallies (*parbhat pheris*) to urge Hindu Punjabis to declare Punjabi, not Hindi, as their mother tongue in the run-up to the 1941 Census. This strange appeal became necessary because Hindus had been recording Hindi as their mother tongue during every census for decades, though all of them regularly spoke Punjabi. Hindu and Muslim schools equally zealously propagated the causes of Hindi and Urdu, respectively, through their students. It was realized much later that it was this linguistic manipulation of their common mother tongue by different religious communities in Punjab which led to the vivisection of the geographical Punjab into many political units.

The annual inspection visit by the divisional inspector of schools was indeed a very important event. The school buildings were given a fresh coat of paint and decorated with extra care, and the students were asked to come in their best attire. The school band was put through extensive practice sessions to play *God Save the King* and other British tunes. The Boy Scouts were painstakingly coached to sing full-throated paeans to Lord Baden-Powell, the founder of the movement, as soon as the inspector came in sight. The song went somewhat like this, *Scout jhanda aalam mein, lehra diya Baden-Powell ne* (Baden-Powell hoisted the fluttering Scout flag all over the world). Well-tutored in the subject, the Boy Scouts would fluently narrate the life story of the good lord and the genesis of the movement to the visiting dignitary. Unlike these days, generalist officers were rarely invited to preside over school or college functions in order to uphold the academic autonomy of educational institutions. DCs were sometimes invited as chief guests at college functions where the principals were from the IES with whom the ICS (Indian Civil Service) DCs could feel more at home.

Harappa, a small town not far from Montgomery, sprang to world fame when excavations by the Archaeological Survey of India in 1921–22 unearthed the extremely well-preserved remains of an ancient people, later to be known as belonging to the Indus Civilization. My father often took us to see the neatly stacked relics exhibited in the museum, and the rows and rows of baked earthenware and other artefacts displayed in situ. Two especially significant events stand out in my early memory: though unrelated to each other, they were to affect critically the future political and economic developments in the subcontinent well into the twenty-first century. One was the outbreak of the Second World War in September 1939 and the other, the Lahore Resolution of 1940, commonly known as the Pakistan Resolution. Coming as they did towards the end of a turbulent decade, which had witnessed enormous changes of a far-reaching nature in the Indian political scenario, both these events were to set the course of South Asian history for decades to come. The war vastly stepped up the political tempo in the country and set in motion a whole chain of events that would eventually lead to India's independence and partition. And the many other unanticipated but highly unsettling consequences that resulted from the war would continue to colour the nature of interaction between the successor nations of British India.

The Unionist Party, which had been set up to safeguard the collective interests of rural farmers and, for a long time, was economically exploited by the urban trading classes, ruled Punjab during most of the troubled 1930s and '40s. The alliance was class- and not religion-specific, its main support base being the farming classes belonging to all the three religions—Muslim, Hindu and Sikh. The party leadership, comprising landed aristocracy from all the three religions, was led by Sir Sikandar Hayat Khan, a rich landlord, who enjoyed immense influence with the British Indian government. Being rather short for a Punjabi, he tried to add a few inches to his height with the help of a turban, adorned with a plume-like piece of muslin cloth, starched and stiffened to make it stand up, called *turra*, tucked into the top of the turban. He was the Punjab premier from 1937 until his death in 1942, a period of intense political activity in Punjab as well as nationally. He was succeeded by Khizar Hayat Khan, who proved grossly unequal to the task of keeping at bay the formidable Muslim League leader M.A. Jinnah. Jinnah was keen to co-opt this major Muslim majority province into his larger vision of a Muslim homeland, thereby validating his claim of being the sole spokesman for Indian Muslims. Since Punjabi Muslims and Jutt Sikhs made up nearly one half of the British Indian army, the province was often referred to as the 'sword arm of India'. Thus, as the Punjab premier, Sir Sikandar Hayat Khan was the only Indian politician to be invited by the imperial government to inspect the Allied troops in North Africa who were then fighting the Germans led by General Rommel.

Punjab remained largely untouched by the turmoil raging in the rest of India following the 1942 Quit India resolution. On the other hand, colourful rallies were regularly held all over the province to attract sturdy Punjabi youths to join the army in large numbers. Such spectacular events drew huge crowds of jubilant villagers, awestruck by the thrilling feats of strength put up by the army units, and various forms of entertainment, such as bullock-cart races, wrestling, *kabaddi* and other rural sports, folk song and poetry recitals, with loaded food stalls catering to the variegated taste buds of the visitors. I still remember a poem, recited by a grey-bearded Sikh, Sant Singh Sadiq, which roughly means this in English translation: 'Where is Hitler? I wish to ask him, where are all his brigades and tanks, now that they are face-to-face with the valiant Indian troops?' The poem symbolized the ingratiating style and content of such recitals at official durbars, presided over by the local DC. Impressive stalls manned by smartly clad soldiers handed out brochures containing information about the many attractions and benefits of a military career.

Such *bharti mela*s, or recruitment fairs, organized by the district administration under what was known as the 'national war front', were expressly designed to play upon the traditional Punjabi love of adventure. As it happened, while such rallies provided exciting fare for the rural people and a break from their drab existence, they also offered the British a rich source of young and gutsy recruits for their fast-depleting armies in Europe and North Africa in the war against Hitler. Despite stiff opposition from the Congress to the war effort, Punjabis continued to join in huge numbers.

Pre-Partition Punjab was distinctly isolated from the rest of India in many ways. Few Punjabis ventured outside the province to seek employment or residence. The entire region that lay beyond Delhi—then a tehsil of Punjab's Gurgaon district—was referred to vaguely as Hindustan, as distinct from their province, and all those hailing from those areas were called Hindustanis or *bhaiyas*, a term which generally referred to gardeners, dhobis and peons.

Despite the presence of a dynamic Urdu press in Lahore and some clandestine radio stations—which kept us posted about the gruesome happenings in the rest of India and the course of the war in distant Europe—the tenor of life in the province remained largely even, apart from minor incidents in Lahore, Amritsar and some other towns. I recall that I used to listen intently, and with a mixture of awe and amazement, to the news on the radio, but was unable to explain satisfactorily to my young sister the mystery of a disembodied voice emanating from a small cabinet. Except for the D.A.V. School, where some teachers did speak about the freedom movement, then in full swing in other provinces, the Khalsa and the Islamia schools were strongly pro-establishment and barred all allusion to the Congress agitation. I recollect a brief visit by Mahatma Gandhi to Montgomery, probably in 1941. An excited eleven-year-old, I was part of the large crowd waiting for him. As we gaped in admiration and wonderment, the frail old man was taken away by a policeman soon after arrival, because all public meetings were banned under the law then in force. Remarkably, however, the policeman not only paid due compliments to the Mahatma, he was also allowed to come up to the dais and stand there facing the crowd for a few minutes with folded hands. That poignant moment remains an indelible memory.

My interest in and sensitivity to contemporary political events began at an early age because my father regularly spoke to us about political events and kept us well informed about the progress of the war, when the family assembled for the evening meals cooked by my mother. All major events in India and the course of the war in Europe and East Asia were extensively covered by Lahore newspapers. Both the Congress and the Muslim League had deep political stakes in Punjab which, by the 1940s, had become crucial to the resolution of a number of complex and important national issues. They had developed extensive media networks in the country, but *Dawn*, the Muslim League newspaper, was a late arrival on the scene.

From a young age, I had been an avid reader of newspapers and periodicals, and had thus acquired an edge in general knowledge over boys much older than me. I always did well in the monthly general knowledge tests in school. This keen spirit of inquiry and curiosity about political developments at the provincial and national levels helped me develop a lifelong fascination with political processes, including the seamy side of politics that came to dominate future Indian polity.

While still in high school, I took to reading serious fiction and short stories with social and political undertones, such as the works of Munshi Premchand, Tagore, Bankim Chandra Chatterjee and other nineteenth- and twentieth-century writers. They were the principal protagonists of the Indian renaissance in literature and social awakening, which contributed significantly to the maturing and intensifying of the Indian freedom movement. A number of Russian novels, journals and other literature became available to me, thanks to my many leftist friends. All my reading was still in Urdu translations. Punjabi fiction and poetry were my next favourite fare, followed soon after by English literature, which was to remain a lifelong passion. Among English novelists, Hardy was my favourite and by the time I passed my intermediate examination, I had run through and thoroughly enjoyed all his novels as well as some of his poetry. Amrita Pritam's intensely moving poem '*Ajj akhaan Waris Shah nun*' ('I turn to Waris Shah today'), a poignant, anguished and indignant cry of despair, was occasioned by the horrifying atrocities committed on young women in both halves of partitioned Punjab. The poem invoked the memory of Waris Shah, the celebrated Punjabi poet who had rendered the immortal tale of Heer–Ranjha into excellent verse, and it brought tears to my eyes every time I read it. I graduated from Urdu to Punjabi and then to English literature in a matter of a few years. That is what finally set the course for my higher studies.

The end of the war in Europe figured prominently in the newspapers with huge headlines and pictures of a grim-looking Hitler and his colleagues: Himmler, Ribbentrop, Goebbels and others. I carefully cut out the entire set of pictures and pasted them in my scrapbook along with those of the Allied leaders: a truculent Churchill, with a cigar stuck in his mouth; a dapper Roosevelt; and a whiskered Stalin, stern and unsmiling in his trademark jacket. Out of the Indian leaders, Gandhi and Tagore among the men, and among the women, Sarojini Naidu and Nehru's sister, Vijaya Lakshmi Pandit, occupied pride of place in my scrapbook—Naidu for her poetry; and Pandit for her coiffured good looks. Also because the newspapers described her as the 'heart-throb of India', a riveting expression, suggestive of romance and mystique bound to fascinate a sensitive fifteen-year-old, awash with romantic fiction. When I finally read Naidu's poetry, I found it a huge let-down due to its brassy imagery and laboured rhymes. Jinnah and Sikandar Hayat Khan too found a place in my scrapbook, though their pictures were positioned much lower than those of the first batch of INA (Indian National Army) heroes: the trio of Prem Kumar Sahgal, Gurbaksh Singh Dhillon and

Shah Nawaz Khan. Their trial for treason in the famed Red Fort in Delhi had galvanized the entire country, especially the youth. All of us students crammed the streets to shout slogans for the release of the new national heroes, while India's many eminent lawyers, including Nehru, donned their robes to set up a formidable defence panel.

All in all, it was a heady time for young Indians and there was a distinct air of heightened expectation in the country. We read in amazement about a horrific new bomb, developed by America. Two such bombs had been enough to decimate two large Japanese cities, causing incredible destruction of life and property. The Allied victory was celebrated all over the British Empire and we in Punjab were second to none in sharing this festive spirit. Buch Stadium, named after a former DC, was the venue of night-long revelry, where the main draw were a couple of dancing girls from Lahore, who rendered some excellent, if risqué, Punjabi songs to regale an ecstatic crowd, of which I formed an intensely eager part.

Since there was no college in Montgomery at that time, in order to pursue higher studies, I had to leave the town, which had become so much a part of me. Lahore should have been the obvious choice, but deeply worrying political developments in the province, peaking in the mass agitation by the Muslim League in 1946 and the terrible riots that engulfed Punjab, ruled it out. So I was sent off to Jullunder to join the premedical course in Doaba College in order to qualify as a doctor. This was, however, not to be as the annual examinations could not be held for months due to very disturbed conditions in the province. So I had to change track and join a course in English Honours.

After some sixty years, I paid a visit to Montgomery (Sahiwal), to refresh my boyhood memories of the town. My hosts could locate my alma mater only after an extended search: being a Hindu institution, it had remained locked for some time after Partition. Luckily, the building had escaped being torched, the fate of many minority establishments during that period. After a few years, the building was put to use, first as a women's hostel and then to house a postgraduate college of commerce. My wife and I were received with effusive warmth by the principal and his colleagues and shown around the premises. I was also invited to address the students, which I did most willingly, and I fully enjoyed the experience. There were only two girls among the audience, both apparently very fetching young ladies. I use the term *apparently* because both were wearing full hijabs with only their eyes visible. The questions posed to me after the talk ranged from the personal to political, the latter being largely about India–Pakistan relations. Obviously, neither the students nor the staff members knew much about India due to the meagre coverage that India gets in their vernacular media. But I could sense a profound feeling of curiosity about many things Indian, such as its immensity; treatment of Muslims; economic progress; movies and film stars; and also, more surprisingly, their envy of Indian democracy and its strictly apolitical army. The reception that we received that morning was most unexpected, and we left the town greatly elated and fulfilled. It was like visiting long-lost friends and well-wishers. The pictorial record of that visit remains a prized possession. Since they did not have a woman faculty member, they had invited someone from the town to keep my wife company. The town itself has changed in many ways, some good, some not so good, which was only to be expected as it has grown over the years like many such towns in the subcontinent. But the Sadar Bazaar of old and many other landmarks remain largely unchanged, including the open ground in its vicinity where I had waited eagerly for a glimpse of the Mahatma one sultry afternoon back in 1941.

3

A Freedom Soaked in Blood

When the war ended in 1945, the political climate in Punjab suddenly livened up, with newspapers full of exciting things happening in Delhi, Simla and London. They also reported that talks between the viceroy and the Indian leaders were making no headway. In early 1947, the young, handsome, brash and impetuous Admiral Mountbatten, a cousin of the King-Emperor, replaced the dour and luckless Wavell as viceroy. The new vicereine, a charming and rich woman, was not averse to forming unusual liaisons. Her well-documented friendship with Jawaharlal Nehru, the new Indian man of destiny, was thought to have played a significant part in persuading the Congress, despite Gandhi's protestations, to accept Partition as a necessary corollary of Independence. Since a decision to dismantle the Raj seemed to have been already taken in distant London, Mountbatten quickly worked out the operational details, a task that he took up with military precision. The partition of the country having emerged as the only option, he proceeded to accomplish the process of dividing a centuries-old civilization in a matter of a few months. Punjab too, like the partition of the rest of the country, was to be divided on the basis of Muslim and non-Muslim majority districts. Thus, out of five Punjab divisions, three—Lahore, Rawalpindi and

Multan—were assigned to Pakistan and two—Jullunder and Ambala—to Indian Punjab as part of the partition settlement in 1947, except for Gurdaspur district where a few adjustments below district level were made. The messy manner in which this province in the west and Bengal in the east were partitioned ensured that, while the rest of India would remember 1947 as the year of Independence, Punjab and Bengal would primarily remember it as the year of Partition and the horrendous bloodbath that preceded and followed that momentous event.

To go back a little in time: elections to the Punjab assembly took place in February 1946 in which the Muslim League surprised all poll pundits by emerging as the single largest party, beating the Unionist Party. The governor, however, invited the Unionist Party, led by the luckless Khizar Hayat Khan, to form the government with support from the Congress and Sikh members. This was a God-given opportunity for the Muslim League to demonstrate its growing hold on Punjabi Muslims who, for various reasons, had grown increasingly disillusioned with the Unionists and the Congress. The League now took to the streets in possibly the first such mass mobilization of Indian Muslims against a backdrop of escalating tensions and rioting. This election was to prove a watershed in the history not only of Punjab but also of the nation. It projected the Muslim League as a powerful player—along with the Congress—in the crucial talks that were under way between the British government and the Indian political leaders to pave the way for Independence.

Governor's Rule was imposed in Punjab when Khizar Hayat Khan failed to contain the Muslim League agitation. This, too, failed to control the growing chaos. Despite opposition from some Muslim parties, the intensity of the League agitation did not abate. More and more Muslims began distancing themselves from the Congress, which now began to be seen as a Hindu party, not only by Muslims but also by Sikhs. The Punjab Provincial Congress Committee, traditionally headed by a Muslim, lost its three Muslim presidents in quick succession to the Muslim League, reflecting the fast-changing political equations in the province. I don't recall any top Muslim leader who stayed in the Congress, except Dr Kitchlew, Nehru's fellow Kashmiri, who had to flee the new Muslim homeland to seek refuge in India, along with non-Muslim refugees. Such sweeping political realignments among Muslims in Punjab were unique.

Rioting in Jullunder started in March 1947 when Akali leader Babu Labh Singh was stabbed to death, reportedly by a young Muslim man. Reports of organized killings, looting and arson against Sikhs and Hindus and shocking atrocities committed on Sikh and Hindu women in West Punjab were freely circulating in the town. The police proved increasingly incapable of reining in the rampaging mobs, and the rumour mill was busy inflating the magnitude of violence. Radio broadcasts were the only source of reliable information and one could see crowds of uneasy listeners lapping up the scanty information that came their way. Soon, schools and colleges were closed and converted into refugee camps for the thousands of Hindus and Sikhs who were fleeing their homes in West Punjab. Academically, 1947 was to be a zero year.

People living in isolated places moved to areas inhabited by their co-religionists, where they felt safer. We too moved to a Hindu–Sikh majority locality. Most shopping areas remained deserted during the day, and milkmen, newspaper boys and hawkers vanished. An eerie silence would seize the city as the evening shadows stretched out, heralding long, dark, weary and depressing nights. From the terrace, one could see entire blocks of houses in different parts of the city being consumed by flames while fire brigade vehicles rushed around frantically. Huge mobs of Hindus and Sikhs on the one hand and Muslims on the other remained on alert throughout the night to ward off any assault on their respective localities. Mutual suspicion and mistrust had driven the two communities to a state of high panic. The Muslims raised full-throated cries of *Allah Hu Akbar* (God is great), while the Hindu–Sikh mobs responded with *Bole So Nihal, Sat Sri Akal*, a war cry dating back to the days when the Sikhs were a persecuted people and victims of severe state oppression under Muslim rulers in Punjab. The occasional cries of *Har Har Mahadev*, which were first raised by the Hindus, were soon replaced by the more strident Sikh rallying call.

Soon, trainloads of Hindu and Sikh refugees fleeing from the future Pakistan became targets of Muslim mobs, as did similar trains ferrying Muslims from the Indian side. There was virtually a civil war situation in Punjab, and Jullunder fast turned into a major combat area between Muslims and non-Muslims. Since colleges were closed anyway, my parents decided to move to our hometown, Moga, deemed safer than Jullunder, since it was largely a Hindu–Sikh town. Moga was at the forefront of the effort to cleanse the area of all Muslim presence. Since trains taking the Amritsar route were being repeatedly attacked by Sikh mobs, the Indian railways diverted trains carrying Muslim refugees to Lahore via Moga. Moga residents took up the mission of finishing off the fleeing Muslims. Trains were stopped at the outer signal in connivance with Hindu drivers to enable the rampaging mobs to slaughter the passengers in cold blood. Hapless Muslims trying to escape through or hide in sugar-cane fields were hunted like quarries, as in a shikar, with triumphant cries of *Sat Sri Akal*. Typically, women and girls were treated as war booty.

With the curse of Partition looming large in Punjab and the deadline of 15 August approaching fast, both Muslims and non-Muslims were intent upon fortifying their respective claims on the putative borders between the two successor states of British India. One way to establish their claims was to stamp out the rival community from the areas they regarded as rightfully theirs. Little did they know then that the man charged with dividing this ancient land and its peoples in a matter of a few weeks would be a little-known British jurist, Cyril Radcliff, who had no exposure to Indian politics, had never been to India and had little appreciation of Indian history and tradition. Killings, plunder, arson and rapes in a frantic bid at what would these days be called ethnic cleansing continued to increase day by day as the spring of 1947 turned into a sticky summer and then a muggy monsoon.

While speaking in the Punjab legislative assembly in Lahore, Akali leader Master Tara Singh brandished his kirpan and in a fiery speech declared virtual war against the Muslim League's designs to gobble up the Sikhs in a future Pakistan. This was read as a call for battle by the Sikh masses and, as they started killing Muslims in East Punjab, Muslims retaliated with added ferocity in West Punjab. In a sinister game of tit for tat, the two communities outdid each other in inflicting appalling atrocities on members of the other community. Many otherwise decent Sikh men turned Nihang—an obscurantist Sikh sect, sporting a quaint form of attire. They disappeared for weeks and returned to normal life after doing their duty by the *panth* by slaying as many Muslims as possible, molesting their women and looting their property. To be sure, similar missions of service to Islam were in full play on the other side.

The devastation and displacement of millions of Hindus, Muslims and Sikhs from their homes in many parts of India, but especially in Punjab, continued for many months, even after the birth of India and Pakistan as separate states. In fact, the rioting mobs became even more brazen due to the impunity enjoyed by the killer gangs in the new regimes, which were no longer governed by British officers, and since the impartial boundary force to protect the minorities had been disbanded. In case of doubt about the religion of a male victim, his genitals would be examined for signs of circumcision, which would provide the clinching evidence. Saadat Hasan Manto and other writers later chronicled these ghastly tales in graphic detail and with a heavy dose of irony. Around a million persons lost their lives and over ten million were uprooted from their homes in what was to become the largest migration in human history. Expectedly, women were the worst sufferers; they were targeted for rape and impregnation so as to change the religious profile of an area. While men and boys were killed, women and girls were raped, abducted, converted and forced into marriage. Later, both countries tried hard to recover and reunite such wronged women with their families. Many women, however, refused repatriation, fearing social disgrace and loss of the babies they had had with their abductors.

Grainy photographs showing Sikh and Hindu women being paraded naked in the bazaars of Rawalpindi and other towns of West Punjab, accompanied by the beating of drums and blowing of trumpets, as bearded ruffians groped at or pummelled them, were widely circulated in Moga. Heart-rending tales of fathers and elderly relatives killing their daughters and other young women to save them from dishonour became common fare in our part of the province. Muslim women in Indian Punjab too were subjected to similar outrages. There was a timber warehouse close to our house where a number of young Muslim women, abducted from nearby villages by Sikh men, were kept in confinement. Those poor and helpless captives were often taken out in noisy processions to replicate the gruesome scenes of West Punjab and photographed. The copies were then duly dispatched to the perpetrators of the brutality in West Punjab, ostensibly as a just and deserved retaliation against the happenings there. I was aghast to see Muslim policemen at the local thana, disarmed and ready for evacuation, being beaten and humiliated, their women being molested and their houses being vandalized by Sikh mobs even as their erstwhile non-Muslim colleagues looked on. It was the same story in both the future dominions. Muslim soldiers allocated to Pakistan would randomly bayonet Sikh men, as if for sport, while leaving for Pakistan from Jullunder cantonment.

Huge convoys of famished and infirm Muslim men, women and children, numbering in thousands, escorted by Gurkha troops, passed in front of our house on their way to Pakistan. Local Sikhs traded small pieces of bread and jaggery or pitchers of water for whatever the poor refugees were carrying on their person. Among the local Muslims who joined the convoys passing through Moga for a safe passage out of their ancient homeland, I spotted the stately figure of Dule Khan, still dressed in his trademark three-piece suit, now much soiled and crumpled, trudging wearily along. Dule Khan had earned his millions while working abroad and had returned to his native land to spend the rest of his life among those he had considered his own people. Since he had no family to support, he had spent lavishly on his friends and hangers-on, none of whom came forward to help him when he suddenly became an alien in his hometown. In fact, they were the first to break open his house and walk off with whatever they could find. It is impossible to describe the pathos, misery and sheer brutality of the Partition years, when centuries-old neighbours turned against each other in the two parts of the now-divided Punjab. The Indian partition, however, did not generate even a fraction of the appalled reaction in the West as the one that was spawned by the Jewish Holocaust.

This reciprocal genocide continued until a communally diverse province was purged of its minority populations. By the end of that year, the Muslims were just over 1 per cent of Indian Punjab population while the Hindus and the Sikhs in Pakistani Punjab were even less. An entire generation of Indian and Pakistani Punjabis, longing to revisit the homes they had lost in the Partition turmoil, were forced to reconstruct their lives in an alien land. Decades later, Ishtiaq Chatha, a Pakistani scholar at a British university, ruefully told me that his old father still missed his Hindu and Sikh neighbours, who had shared his language and food habits. The Muslim refugees from UP and Bihar, who had taken their place, neither understood his language nor shared his food habits. Sadly, not even Jinnah, who was so fond of his Bombay mansion, could ever revisit his home.

The Punjab boundary force—set up to provide protection to those who were now rendered religious minorities and who were destined to be wiped out in the two Punjabs—soon lost its sense of duty in the absence of political direction and the spread of the sectarian virus. I saw Gurkha troops camping in

Moga for the night, deployed to guard Muslim convoys on their way to Pakistan, conniving with Sikh goons in killing and looting Muslim men and kidnapping their women. By the end of August 1947, the army and what remained of the police after the transfer of Muslim police to Pakistan had completely lost control. Chaos prevailed all over. The Punjab boundary force was disbanded on 1 September and its personnel sent to their own countries. This force, consisting of selected soldiers from Rajput, Baluch, Dogra and Gurkha regiments, renowned for their valour, simply lost its élan and, in the end, the urge for self-preservation obliterated its collective sense of right and wrong. We in Indian Punjab experienced no great joy on Independence Day. Nehru's midnight speech in the new Indian parliament, talking famously of 'a tryst with destiny', sounded hollow to us in Punjab, still battling large-scale disorder and the trauma of Partition.

Nothing evokes the spirit of the times more than the visual images embedded in one's memory. My memory is cluttered with sights and sounds of the carnage and the concerted efforts by both Muslims and non-Muslims to demolish forever all traces of the pre-Partition Punjabi persona. In the event, the ambience that had marked the Punjab of old lay shattered for all time to come. A visit paid by my wife and me some sixty years later to Lahore and Montgomery only reinforced the severe sense of loss with which one had long since learnt to live. It seemed to me that the people of Pakistan too shared the nostalgia. Films are a powerful medium for evoking old memories. I vividly recall the theme song of *Jugnu*—then being shown at Regal cinema in Moga, with the beautiful Noor Jehan in the lead—being relayed over loudspeakers even as the rioting mobs were doing their best to drown the enthralling melody.

I also recall another film, *Chitralekha*, introducing the doe-eyed Mehtab, who later enacted many a historical role. Then there was *Jwar Bhata*, probably made in 1944, the debut film of Dilip Kumar, who has remained an iconic actor for decades. There was also an English-language war movie being shown in Jullunder, probably in 1946, which depicted the major events of the Second World War and portrayed the three Allied leaders—Churchill, Stalin and Roosevelt—in a heroic light, and Hitler in a somewhat ambiguous style, neither a hero nor a villain, along with a host of minor characters. I enjoyed watching the lengthy *Gone with the Wind*, my first exposure to the US, its people, culture and values. Two other movies that I saw in Lahore, and that also stand out clearly in my memory, are *Kismet*, starring a thin and callow Ashok Kumar and Mumtaz Shanti, one of India's most gifted actresses, and *Prithvi Vallabh*, starring Sohrab Modi and Durga Khote, one of the foremost leading ladies of the Indian screen. Among the many catchy songs that *Kismet* made popular was the patriotic song *Dur hato ai duniya walo, Hindustan hamara hai* (Be off, people of the world, India is ours), which became the lead song at many a nationalist rally. But the film that I remember the best is *Man ki Jeet*, an adaptation of *Tess of the D'Urbervilles* by Thomas Hardy, my favourite novelist at the time, starring Neena in a short printed skirt. Nearly all the early-day actresses were Maharashtrian. A notable exception was, of course, the eminent Bengali star, Devika Rani, one of the most beautiful women of her time, who later married the Russian painter Svetoslav Roerich. Another interesting film was *Ulti Ganga*, which unashamedly scoffed at women who took up public professions, then considered a male preserve. Any such movie these days would instantly be labelled politically incorrect.

It took years for Punjabi migrants to start life afresh in alien environs and overcome the deprivations resulting from a messy partition process. Notably, while most Hindu refugees from Pakistan skipped East Punjab and spread in Delhi and beyond, most similarly placed Sikhs settled in Punjab. This turned Delhi into a Punjabi city. Bombay came to be dominated by Punjabi artistes as non-Muslim artistes fled Lahore. I often wonder why Hindus chose to bypass East Punjab to settle in Hindu-majority states. Was it because the tiny Indian Punjab just did not offer enough space to explore the vast opportunities that now lay before them for developing their enterprise in free India? Or did they apprehend some threat from the Sikhs in Punjab, even if subconsciously, at some future date? As it happened, the new Punjab did go through a shameful phase of Hindu–Sikh strife and rioting in the 1980s when a fierce Sikh militancy posed a very serious threat indeed to the Indian state.

4

Discovering Myself

Jullunder, or Jalandhar as it came to be known after Independence, where I studied for my graduation, was a town of great antiquity. Out of the two men's colleges there, I chose Doaba in preference to D.A.V., though the latter was strong in the subjects I had taken up for my premedical course. However, as no examinations took place in Punjab that year, my plans to enter a medical college came unstuck. My next preference was English literature for which Doaba College was a natural choice because Dr Ker, an eminent teacher of English, headed the English department there. Possibly another attraction for a teenager in those days of near-total segregation of the sexes was that Doaba also admitted women students. Dr Ker was an exceptionally erudite and friendly teacher and I was his only pupil in the Honours class. He covered a major part of the syllabus at his sparsely furnished home, lined with shelves and shelves of books. He must have found in me an unusually committed student, with a singular passion for learning the many subtle nuances of the English language and for savouring the richness of its literature. On his part, he ensured that I missed no chance of learning to appreciate both. He was unable to teach me much, though, in the area of pronunciation as his own intonation was atrocious, to say the least.

Some half a dozen Muslim hamlets or *basti*s, among them basti Guzan and basti Sheikhan, had grown around the town over a period of time, a legacy of the long Muslim rule in Punjab. Among the hundreds of thousands of Muslims driven out of Punjab during the partition holocaust was a young man from basti Sheikhan, named Zia-ul-Haq, who would join the army and rise to become the Chief of the Army Staff in his adopted country in the 1970s. He would go down in history for radically and permanently transforming the character of Pakistani politics by introducing a radical Islamist streak into Pakistani society and, even more importantly, into its military culture. Such radical deviation from a modern and tolerant ideology—as had been envisioned for the new nation by Pakistan's founder—would push that luckless nation more and more towards a severely regressive social and political system.

K.L. Saigal was perhaps the most gifted musician of his time, with a rich, vibrant voice that could traverse an incredibly vast range of notes, as well as a talented actor. He had served as a postal clerk in Jullunder before acquiring fame as a singer and film star. In January 1947, all of us students flocked to the nearby cremation ground, on hearing that he was to be cremated there, to have a last look at the man who had literally mesmerized a whole generation of Indians by his deep-throated voice and musical ingenuity. Sorrowfully recalling some of his popular songs, we tried hard to come to terms with the death of a legend who looked strangely inconsequential now that he was dead. The eminent Urdu poet Hafeez Jullandhuri—whose immortal poem '*Abhi to main jawaan hun*' (I am still young), so superbly sung by Malika Pukhraj, never fails to fire the imagination of many Indians and Pakistanis—also belonged to Jullunder. Sadly, Hafeez too had to flee his beloved town in 1947. At a personal level, I greatly missed my Muslim classmates, two of them women, who left us to join many other Muslim refugees on their way to an unknown land. Though clad in burqas, except when in the girls' common room, these young women had been very much an integral and fascinating part of the college scene.

The camp university hastily set up in Solan to impart higher education in Indian Punjab abridged most of the academic sessions so that students didn't lose a year. My English Honours course was completed in fifteen months instead of the usual two years, after which I joined the MA (English) course in Government College, Ludhiana, regarded at that time as the premier institution for a master's in English in the Indian Punjab. Almost all its teachers had been on the staff of renowned Lahore colleges, a city they had to leave at the time of Partition. This invested the college with a metropolitan air, facilitating easy and open interaction between men and women. The principal, a tall, handsome man and a keen tennis player, believed in free relations between men and women on the campus and contributed towards making it possible. In an address at the end of a drama festival, he told us that we were indeed lucky that real girls had acted the female roles in the plays. 'In our days, we had to make do with boys [*Sanu tan munduian nal hi kum chalana painda si*],' he stated ruefully with a straight face. When we grasped the full import of his heavily loaded statement, there was prolonged cheering and a standing ovation.

Out of some thirty students in our class, nine were women. Some of my classmates had known each other from their previous schools or colleges. So they found no difficulty in reviving their friendships across gender barriers. I generally kept to myself during the first term. It was the result of the first terminal examinations that suddenly made me the focus of attention of both my teachers and classmates. To everyone's surprise I had topped the class. Here was a quiet, shy, small-town boy, not known to be a particularly studious sort of fellow, who had beaten all his highly regarded classmates to secure the top position! This marked the beginning of a fresh new phase in my academic career. It gave me a sense of quiet self-confidence in my ability to excel in any field on which I set my heart. Clearly, my eclectic reading habits from an early age had helped in the process of developing a special aptitude for linguistic and literary sensibility. My answer books were in great demand as everyone was keen to discover the secret of my success or perhaps to verify whether my high scores were genuine. It also proved to be something of a catalyst in starting a friendship with a couple of my women classmates. They requested me to lend them my answer books, to which I cheerfully agreed. My answer books would henceforth become the entry point for long walks through the college orchards.

This was so different from all that I had known of man–woman relationships. When the socialist leader Aruna Asaf Ali had visited Moga, I had had to present her with a small bag of money on behalf of the Socialist Students' Association. The slow climb to the dais in full public view made me go red in the face. She held my hand asking me teasingly why I was blushing so hard, thus deepening my unease. Then there was the time when I used to look pensively at two Gujjar girls grazing their cattle in the grassland behind our house. They were much older, and every time they tried to engage me in some facetious banter, I would become tongue-tied, leaving them giggling. Eventually, while I continued to look wistfully at them, Gulzar, the younger sister, ran away with our syce, Sattar. But then I was at that awkward age when every young woman looked good and, although lacking the courage to approach her openly, one could fabricate elaborate plots to correspond with events in one's favourite novels and poems. It needs a grown-up individual to appreciate fully the dynamics of relaxed interaction between adult men and women. My outstanding, if unexpected, performance in the first terminal examination must have contributed substantially towards reinforcing my self-confidence to enter into and cope with such new relationships. My friendship with my two women classmates was, therefore, easy-going and self-assured, free from the clumsiness of the past. In due course, one of the two women opted out of the group, leaving her tall and statuesque friend to carry on the relationship.

Traditionally, the student who topped the first terminal examination in the first year of the master's course was appointed editor of the college magazine. This was, however, not to be in my case as the son of the professor in charge of the magazine was the other aspirant, and he eventually got the position. This unfair decision did not go down well with my college mates, thus considerably enlarging my circle of friends and admirers. Even though I failed to become its editor, I was spurred by my involvement with the college magazine to take to serious writing. I acquired, in due course, a special flair for writing English prose and, a little later, also tried my hand at verse, a pursuit that would become a lifelong passion. The college dramatic club picked me to act the role of Duke Frederick in Shakespeare's play *As You Like It*. Ish Kumar, the professor of poetry and criticism, used to call some of us home and coach us, over cups of coffee, in the finer aspects of poetic sensibility and critical appreciation, following the true tradition of British universities. It was Ish Kumar who told us that there was no such thing as bad poetry. 'Poetry is of three types,' he informed us theatrically, 'poetry that is good, poetry that is not good and poetry that is neither good nor not good.'

Dr Ker and Professor Ish Kumar were chiefly responsible for sharpening my literary sensibility and helping me acquire a heightened awareness of the structural and aesthetic intricacies of various branches of literature but chiefly of modern English poetry. T.S. Eliot became my favourite poet, and the Romantics and the post-Romantics were relegated to the background. Consequently, my poetic outpourings ended up being no more than poor replicas of Eliot and Pound. Mercifully, the realization that you can't write great poetry merely by emulating the style of your favourites came in good time and I switched to prose with far happier results. I did compose the occasional verse, though, due to sheer loneliness and tedium, especially while posted as an assistant superintendent of police (ASP) in an awfully isolated district in central India. It was around this time that I took to letter writing in earnest, seeking to convey through long letters to close friends the isolation and ennui of a virtual exile. Words would just pour out of my Sheaffer pen; many of my letters were fifty or sixty pages long and one even ran to some eighty pages.

I had developed a fondness for what was loosely termed fin-de-siècle literature, that is, the genre of English and continental writing produced around the end of the nineteenth century and generally reflecting a spirit of gloom and cynicism. This, together with my growing proximity to a few of my women classmates, led me to adopt what I thought was the Bohemian lifestyle, which my favourite characters favoured in their charmed existence. This involved living on a near-starvation diet to cultivate a lean and hungry look, which my pensive heroes would have sported so as to appear anguished and dreamy. This also meant sitting in the college café over endless cups of coffee and missing classes. When my fascination for nurturing a 'lean and hungry look' started affecting my health, it had my father greatly worried; he took me home to nurture me back to good health. It was after my marriage, however, that I finally overcame my fancy for the slim figure though I never gave up on a strict dietary regime. When I wanted my pregnant wife too to consume only boiled food to acquire a lean look, her parents were hugely alarmed about their son-in-law's mental equilibrium.

As the final examinations drew near, the college café and the girls' hostel lost their charm for most of us and the two most favoured destinations became the library and our professors' offices. The college greens were now crowded with bookworms rather than hand-holding couples looking fervently into each other's eyes. As we became aware of the very high stakes involved in securing a good grade, academic rivalry between the likely toppers heightened, which entailed furtive surveillance and spying to trace the sources of each other's notes. It was not easy to do a turnabout and suddenly get into the industrious and diligent mode, but most of us did manage to do so well in time. Despite the many distractions that had kept me busy during my two years in master's, I did very well, securing a high position in the university, though missing the first division by a few marks. But then, there had been no first division in the preceding year, and there was none that year or the following year. First divisions in MA English were a rarity those days. I scored very high marks in the essay paper, and thenceforth, that became my forte.

In comparison with mathematics or sciences, English literature was a low-scoring subject in the competitive examinations conducted by the Union Public Service Commission (UPSC), though a high aptitude in humanities and literature was considered basic to the making of good civil servants. This was before medical and engineering subjects were included in the UPSC examinations. As it happened, three of us made it to the All India Services and one to the Indian Foreign Service (IFS). I took the UPSC examination the same year as I did my MA. Considering that I had had no time to prepare for the country's foremost competitive examination, I topped in two of the three compulsory papers—English essay and general knowledge—while scoring very high marks also in the third compulsory paper, general English, and one of the elective papers, English literature. My performance in the other two subjects of Indian and British history was, however, dismal due to unfocused and casual preparation. Even then, I qualified for the viva voce test where I did the unpardonable:

I entered into an argument with the chairman, R.N.Banerjee, on a rather trivial issue.The upshot was that I failed to secure the requisite minimum marks in the interview, which at that time carried a weightage. If you failed in the interview you would not be selected regardless of how high your score may have been in the written examination.

Elitism and old-school ties were an important factor in making it to the higher civil service in those days. R.N. Banerjee had visited our college as chief guest at the Annual Day function.The sons of the principal and a senior professor had been duly presented to him at a dinner hosted by the principal. Both the young men made it to the top service shortly thereafter. Madan Bhatia, one of my brighter classmates, however, chose law as a profession over civil service and set up a lucrative law practice in Delhi. He later became well known as Indira Gandhi's advocate, when a vengeful Janata government targeted her with childish glee to prosecute and persecute her for the excesses committed by her administration during the internal emergency of 1975–77.

Not having made it to the civil service that year, I joined as a lecturer in October 1951 on the then-handsome monthly salary of Rs 175. I was to teach English literature to an assorted group of students, mostly of rural origin, unversed in the niceties of a foreign tongue and unaware of the simple rules of pronunciation, accent and syntax. I spent a couple of weeks in the beginning trying to teach them the correct enunciation of such simple words as 'little' and 'father', which soon became the source of much good-hearted mirth in the college. Despite my protracted efforts, however, the boys continued to mispronounce even simple English words. A couple of girls provided an element of glamour to the predominantly male class. They kept giggling with each other most of the time, probably feeling uneasy in a class of strapping young men. I would carry on with my lectures, pretending to ignore their soft laughter as a natural expression of femininity in a mixed class as long as it did not interfere with my teaching. But I could not remain entirely indifferent to the way they constantly tried to attract my attention, whether in the class or outside. It was a heady feeling that made me show off my best on and off campus.

I thoroughly enjoyed my new status as a teacher of a language that was still considered something of an elite branch of learning. My senior colleague in the English department, a most amiable and interesting human being, suffered from a peculiar mental ailment, probably the result of an accident. He would have sporadic bouts of unusual behaviour, when he would wander aimlessly around the town, unable to sleep or eat normally. He would often drop in at my lodgings late at night, talk literature with me over endless cups of coffee, which I made for him, and leave after some time. I deeply valued his advice and companionship during my breaking-in period. He continued to correspond with me for some time while I was doing my IPS training in Mount Abu. Like all lonely and restless souls, he too occasionally tried his hand at writing what seemed to me rather inelegant poetry.

In many ways this was one of the happiest periods of my life. I read a lot, fully indulged my passion for long walks and played a lot of badminton. However, my stay in that beautiful place lasted only five months as another college offered me a much higher salary. I did not stay in the new college for long either as the same year I made it to the IPS, then the favoured choice of young men in Punjab for the sheer allure of the uniform that went with the service. I had been selected for the Central services too but opted for the IPS simply because I knew little about other services. I look back on my brief teaching career with some satisfaction as many of my students later emigrated to teach in foreign lands while a few joined the civil service and held high jobs. Teaching was not a very attractive career option then not only due to its low salary and perks but also because teachers ranked rather low in the social pecking order. So I had continued to apply for any worthwhile job with the provincial government, including the Punjab Civil Service (PCS), for which I appeared in 1952 and came second in the order of merit. Just below me was a candidate who later occupied some of the highest posts in the Indian government, both in civil service and in politics, but who would have failed to get into the PCS if I had joined as it had only two vacancies that year.

My selection to the IPS suddenly made me a much sought-after person in Moga and I acquired a large number of friends overnight. My sisters, both younger than me by years, now regarded their brother with a heightened sense of pride and awe. My parents were justifiably happy and proud but unruffled, in keeping with the stoical nature of the family. When I left my hometown on the long train journey to Mount Abu to join the Central Police Training College (CPTC), all my uncles, cousins and friends came to the railway station to see me off. Even the railway staff joined in to wish me bon voyage.

5

Young Pups and Pregnant Ducks:
Mount Abu

Officers appointed to the Indian (branch of the Imperial) Police, or IP, the predecessor service of the IPS, did not have a dedicated central training institution. They received their induction training in the provincial police training colleges (PTCs) before they were attached to selected district SPs for on-the-job training, which was considered more important and useful than classroom lectures. This system worked well because provincial police forces functioned more or less in isolation except in bordering areas where local officers ensured the required coordination between different provincial police forces. The only Central Police Organization (CPO) was the Intelligence Bureau (IB). It was much smaller in size and functional span than the present-day IB, and was staffed largely by provincial-cadre officers, as now, except that there was no permanent seconding to the IB. Unlike the officers of an imperialist oligarchy, independent India regarded a course of centralized training for the IPS appointees essential for inculcating a national perspective and a pan-Indian vision in its police leaders to help them serve the free people of a democratic India. It was with this objective that the CPTC was set up at Mount Abu in 1947.

The long journey in October 1953 to the remote hill station of Mount Abu to join the IPS took me the best part of two days. The landscape was distinctly unlike any that I had seen so far during my travels in the plains and hills of Punjab. The short distance from the Abu Road railhead to Mount Abu was negotiated in a ramshackle bus, which had to slow down often to negotiate the many sharp curves. A fine October day greeted me in the hill town. The last half mile to the Officers' Mess had to be covered on foot with a coolie carrying my luggage. On the way, I passed the college parade ground where the trainees—a new elite class in the making—wearing what I later came to know was the infantry training (IT) uniform of khaki shorts, shirts, cross belts, ammunition boots topped with putties and sola hats, were being put through their paces by tough-talking ustads. It was a riveting sight in more than one sense. I arrived at the Mess and was deferentially ushered into my allotted room by the quartermaster, a burly Sikh with considerable clout in the CPTC set-up, as I was to learn soon, with my bearer officiously taking charge of my luggage. I became acutely aware of the vast difference that lay between the world I had left behind and the one I was now entering—a world of power and prestige in which all doors opened at the very mention of my new service. With the signing of the charge report a little later, I acquired the privilege of adding the magic letters 'IPS' after my name. This heralded my entry through the portals of a fresh new fraternity, very special and exclusive, and very jealous of its privileges and position in society.

There were thirty-seven of us officers in the batch, hailing from all over the country. One was dismissed from the IPS, shortly afterwards, under a Constitutional clause which provided for summary dismissal of government officials without holding a formal inquiry. We were stunned to see him pack up all of a sudden and leave, escorted by a police official. We learnt later that he was closely related to a senior British communist leader. Notably, it was Marxism that the Indian state feared most as a subversive ideology, unlike in later times when mainstream communist parties were fully integrated within the Indian political system. For most of us, this was our very first interaction with individuals who bore odd-sounding names and came from far-off places, and who spoke in peculiar accents with unfamiliar cultural foibles. The south Indians formed a fairly large group, and though it was impossible to tell one from the other in the beginning, they were hardly a homogeneous group, belonging as they did to different linguistic, cultural and regional groups. The Bengalis, the Assamese and the Oriyas seemed to speak the same language though they were all very proud of their distinct linguistic and cultural identities.

It was difficult for us highly educated individuals to give up our considerable intellectual pretensions and to get sucked into the semi-authoritarian culture of the new training regimen. Even so, it took no more than a fortnight for us to divest ourselves of our cerebral airs and turn into avid supporters of the new culture matrix, which we now shared with all our colleagues in the IPS. It was natural that in a group of this kind there would be a vast diversity of intellectual and cultural talent. While some of us excelled in dramatics and poetry, others focused principally on training schedules. There were also plenty of dirty jokes and lewd stories, only natural in an all-male course. So, when a law teacher's crotch displayed a rather telltale bulge, Satish Pandey promptly assigned him a moniker, Foteram—*fote* meaning balls in Urdu—or F. Ram, soon to change to a safer and more deferential Framji. Brij Saigal enjoyed teaching choice Punjabi invectives to Ponnaiah from Tamil Nadu, who then went around repeating them through the day without grasping their import. One common epithet that caused much mirth and hilarity was the Punjabi equivalent of 'Come, fuck me' that he went about repeating to everyone he came across on a certain day.

Abu was a typical hill station, strikingly British in its ambience and, like several other hill stations in the subcontinent, created by the British to feel at home in a distant land. Mount Abu was much smaller than Simla (later to be called Shimla), with which I was more familiar, having spent my summers there in the years shortly after Partition. While Simla had a vast variety of shops and stores for the rich and famous to stock their wardrobes with the latest in men's and women's fashions, Mount Abu could boast of only a modest bazaar. Its streets remained unfrequented during the greater part of the year, except during the brief tourist season when hordes of Gujarati families descended upon (or rather, ascended to) the hill town for a day or two of recreation. The sleepy township would suddenly wake up to a cacophony of noise and popular film music. Cheap eating places would come alive with a raucous and chattering clientele, enjoying its favourite Gujarati dishes. The tourist season provided us with a rare opportunity to feast our eyes on female figures, living as we did in a starkly masculine world.

On learning that an ashram, housing an esoteric religious order of women devotees of Lord Shiva, called Brahma Kumaris, was located in the town, some of us went exploring in the vicinity only to find that most of the ashram residents were rather poor samples of womanhood. Those of us with a greater exploratory drive sought more intimate physical delights in local village women, whom they accessed through their bearers, while the others had to be content with gazing longingly at quaintly attired Bhil female graziers in the meadows around the town. There were plenty of scenic spots within walking distance from the Mess, besides the famed Nakki Lake, a delightful place to spend a crisp winter day. Some nearby hillocks provided a good spot for surveying the adjoining fields and meadows or going leisurely through a lengthy novel. A number of old palaces, belonging to former princes, dotted the countryside but most of them remained locked and deserted. The Residency, once the most important address in town as the seat of the British Resident, whose writ was inviolable in princely India, remained unoccupied.

With the end of the season, life was back to normal, our days packed with classes, parades, riding lessons and games. Our day started at 4 a.m. with the bearer bringing in the tea tray and ceremoniously pouring out the brew. He would then lay out the physical training (PT) dress while the young sahib-in-the-making would repair to the bathroom for the 3S (shit, shave and shower) drill. The shave was the most important because the inspecting officer might run his hand over your cheeks to verify their smoothness. The other two functions could be glossed over with little fear of discovery except the odd rumble in the tummy, which could usually be held back with some practice. As Philip Woodruff was to write in *The Men Who Ruled India*:

If peptic noises punctuate
The flow of conversation
Politely pause till they abate.
No gentleman should deprecate
An honest eructation.

After some forty minutes of PT, which could comprise a great many clumsy contortions of the body, requiring extreme perseverance, we would soon graduate to more difficult calisthenics, like rope-climbing and horse-vaulting, all aimed at transforming the weakest among us into a true Hercules. After that, we were given just five minutes to change into the rather complicated IT uniform for about forty minutes of IT. It began with simple movements, like standing at attention, saluting, turning and marching in step, and went on to more complex exercises like rifle, lathi, company drill and bayonet training and, at a later stage, tactical exercises, like crawling, ambushing and taking cover. Following the calamitous events of 1857, the British had introduced semi-military training for the Indian police who were reorganized under the Indian Police Act of 1861 to develop into important defenders of their rule.

The change of uniforms from PT to IT involved an intricate operation: wearing putties and hose tops, and ensuring that the width and spread of the various loops and layers adhered strictly to the approved pattern. This was an easy enough exercise for our bearers, who helped us change into the various forms of apparel as ordained by the CPTC establishment. After all, they had been doing this for generations of trainees. One morning, the assistant commandant (AC), the redoubtable J.W. Roderigues, appeared all of a sudden in the gym, where the bearers were engaged in dressing their sahibs in the IT uniform, and asked all of them to leave. When he saw us hopelessly stuck in the intricate exercise, he relented and called the bearers back with a warning that thenceforth all of us would *bloody well* do the entire exercise ourselves. This scary expression was an important part of police training culture and regarded as critical to making the training process effective. Needless to say, we laboured hard that day to master the art of putty-trying and duly pulled off what had seemed, until then, to be an impossible task. This also taught us a very useful lesson: there was nothing we could not achieve if only we set our hearts to it.

We rushed back to the Mess from the parade ground for a hurried breakfast and a change of uniform and dashed to the college for classroom instruction until lunchtime. Tired to our bones after a morning of strenuous exercises, we had difficulty keeping awake. Wedged in between classes was the tea break, which was an exercise of another kind. The commandant, called the General, though we never knew what rank he wore on his shoulders for we never saw him in uniform, would join us for tea. He made a rather grand entry into the tea room, elegantly walking the short distance from his office, preceded by an equally finicky white Pomeranian. All of us would smartly spring to attention, waiting deferentially for the great man to smile and ask us to stand-at-ease. This was the signal for the more ambitious among us, somewhat derisively called KTPs (keen-type probationers), to form a half-circle around him, awestruck and spellbound. We were to view this exercise at all police gatherings until, later, we too became senior enough to attract junior officers in similar half-circles around us. The General truly cut an imposing figure, fair and handsome with the easy affability of a superior, aware of his power over the trainees, whose future prospects depended so much on the entries he would make in their dossiers at the end of the term. He never used any language except English to communicate with us, clearly enjoying the awe and deference that he almost studiedly induced all around, and went to great lengths to act the Englishman, not only in his speech and deportment but also in the way he lived.

His successor, S. Waryam Singh, a hard-boiled Punjab officer, was more grounded in reality and could outdo any of us in drill and PT. He could nimbly climb the rope—something most of us found difficult. Some thirty years later when I was the director general of police (DGP) for Punjab, I called on him in Chandigarh, where he had settled after his retirement. He recalled several interesting anecdotes of his CPTC days though, of course, he had visibly aged.

To revert to our schedule: in the afternoon, we again had two periods of IT, horse-riding or, at a later stage, fieldcraft and tactics and then games. Police games, like hockey and basketball, rather than tennis and badminton, were encouraged. It is not as if the evenings were freer. We would trudge back wearily to our rooms from the playgrounds for just about an hour to ourselves and then it would be time to dress up for dinner and for the mandatory assembly in the lounge. The prescribed dress for dinner was full uniform on weekdays and a lounge suit on holidays. You could not depend on getting even that one hour entirely to yourself. Mr Roderigues would frequently surprise us in our rooms, as we lay on our beds, often unclothed, dead tired from the day's exertions. Such unexpected visits were meant to ensure that we were mindful of the way a gentleman officer should keep his room.

By the end of the training we were expected to have acquired sufficient skills and expertise to provide leadership to a police force which was equally proficient in functioning as a civilian and as a paramilitary police. We were taught the use of rifles, pistols and semi-automatic weapons, and our deftness with these weapons was put to the test at the annual musketry practice. An elaborate riot drill demonstration was arranged midway through the course, in which some of us would act the part of rioters while the rest were the police and the magistrates. The riot drill soon became our favourite exercise because it enabled those of us who were rioters to make as much noise as we liked, unconcerned about the stern face of the AC, who was always around to check what he termed 'unofficer-like' behaviour. He would put an end to all dissent with his favourite phrase, 'There is only one way to do things, gentlemen, and that is the correct way.' And, it was always he who defined what was *correct*.

The evenings were devoted to learning basic table manners in the dining room, preceded by a brief session in the lounge, learning from the AC (who else?) how to dress properly as an officer; how to match socks and ties; the minimum number of formal and informal outfits with which we were required to equip ourselves; the colour of clothes to be worn at different times of the day. We were also meticulously coached in the noble art of making small talk at social gatherings. All this was regarded as crucial as classroom and outdoor training in the making of an IPS officer. Those of us who questioned the relevance of such superficial knowledge were severely reprimanded and told in no uncertain terms that unless we fell in line, there was little chance of our making good in the service. We learnt over the years that the ability to conform was the most prized attribute for success in Indian bureaucracy, and even more so in the police. A non-conformist IPS officer was unlikely to go far.

A lot of humour was generated by clumsy drill movements and the way defaulters were told off by the instructors. When Joseph from Kerala was asked by an ustad to do a round of the ground at the double and he said okay, he was severely reprimanded by the havildar instructor, '*Okay-pokay kuchh nahin chalega, sahib. Salute karo aur bhago.*' Pratt, the tall, handsome Anglo-Indian chief drill instructor, was often unable to tell apart two trainees bearing similar names. Thus he would shout from one end of the parade ground, 'Senapati or Kailashpati, whichever Pati you are, don't march like a pregnant duck.' It was only in the CPTC that the gait of ducks was so carefully monitored. We were compared to pregnant ducks or young pups, depending on our performance on the parade ground. The indoor staff—headed by the chief law instructor, a Bengali with the unmistakable accent of his native land and who was a veritable encyclopaedia of legal learning—had their own share of gaffes and funny anecdotes. The college medical officer, who taught us first aid, rarely touched upon his subject, very much like the ex-army-captain who was supposed to teach us wireless telegraphy. Both of them regaled us instead by telling dirty stories except that the doctor used a heavily accented Punjabi to relate the stories while the army man made use of what he thought was 'military' English.

Since, at that time, there was no foundation course for the higher civil services, the IAS (Indian Administrative Service) and the IPS probationers used to pay a week's visit to each other's training colleges. Thus, our IAS batchmates came to Mount Abu and we visited them at Metcalfe House in Civil Lines, Delhi, to get to know each other. This was considered important since these two key services were expected to work in close coordination throughout their respective careers. Prem Kathpalia and Anand Sarup from my college were then at Metcalfe House. Prem and I would walk to Connaught Place every evening, drink a glass of chilled milk at Keventers and walk back all the way to Metcalfe House. Today, it would be unimaginable to undertake such a journey on foot in the rush of traffic and the dirt and grime that characterize India's capital city.

The final examinations over, we started practising for the

passing-out parade, regarded as a striking finale to the year-long training. We also realized with some disbelief how much we had changed in our bearing and outlook over the year. The small group of indoor and outdoor instructors had indeed done a great job in converting us from intellectual snobs to stiff-necked police officers, ready to paint the countryside red with our newly acquired skills and aptitude. After the passing-out parade and with the state allotments in hand, we left the CPTC, firm in our resolution to change the way Indian police went about their business, and hugely confident of our ability to accomplish what we then considered our principal mandate: to serve sincerely and efficiently the people of our country. It is another matter that those dreams soon turned sour when we came face-to-face with an obstructive and all-powerful political and bureaucratic leadership which regarded all innovative ideas and initiatives as subversive of their authority.

If anything could truly capture the real flavour of our CPTC experience, the following poem from an anthology of my own poems that I could never put together would come very close to doing so:

We went on talking smut half the night through,
Improvised bawdy verses to fit old favourites,
Scrounged the sweeper's beedis
When the cigarettes were spent.
Then like a tight rope, hilarity broke
And all were silent, 'So long',
A final titter
And one by one we all shuffled to the lavatory.
We called on God and God was there:
'Dear God, save me from the whoring vice

'Help me save some money for mama at home.'
Then God went out and we stiffly snored
In the arms of girls beyond our reach.
Till the tongue knocked against a rancid palate
And morning cried for a cup of tea.

The next phase of our training involved a two months' attachment with the Indian army. This was to serve two ends: one, to reinforce further the militaristic traits of our training and two, to help us grasp the functioning of the armed forces, often deployed to aid civil authority in public disorder and natural disaster situations. We left Abu on a fine October morning after a night of revelry, bound for the cantonment town of Dehradun for a six-week attachment with the various battalions of a Gurkha regiment. My group of twelve officers was assigned to the 3/9 Gurkhas, commanded by Lieutenant Colonel Pant, with Captain Malik, the adjutant, in charge of our training. He treated us simply as pseudo-intellectual softies, who had somehow been allowed to wear an officer's rank on their shoulders but who were unlikely to go far in their careers. I must say that he took his mission of honing us into officer material rather seriously. The subedar-major told us bluntly that the *ragra*, physical toughening, that we had undergone in the CPTC at the hands of some incredibly sadistic ustads was nothing compared to the one they had in store for us.

In the mornings we were taught map reading, fieldcraft and tactics, and taken for long route marches by a sadistic band of trainers under the watchful eye of the subedar-major. The evenings were monopolized by Captain Malik for giving us a crash course in the finer points of Mess life and social etiquette although we were no strangers to that realm, thanks

to the extensive grilling by Mr Roderigues. The sermons that
Malik dispensed each evening were copiously garnished with
expressions like 'bullshit' and 'bloody hell', an integral part of
army lingo then as now. Since army men assess the worth of
an officer from his shoulder badges, and since we wore only
one star compared to his three, he treated us as officers barely
worthy of notice. But then that was the accepted culture of
the Indian army, and it was decades before it was realized that
the civil executive plays a definitive role in a democratic polity,
and the scale and worth of its role is more, not less, important.
Incidentally, Captain Malik landed up as a National Cadet
Corps (NCC) officer in a district where I was then the SP.
He was still wearing three stars while I wore a major's rank.

Midway during our attachment, the festival of Diwali was
celebrated with verve and élan by the battalion and we were
invited to the JCO (junior commissioned officer) Mess along
with the army officers. As the JCOs drank *rakshi*, or rum, in
enormous quantities, sang sadly of their homes in the lands
beyond the Himalayas and danced robustly to the tunes of
Nainitalo and *Dhalke dhalke*, briskly belted out by the band, we
instantly grasped the profound poignancy of their situation
and happily joined them, disregarding the barriers of vocation,
rank and nationality.

The army attachment in Dehradun allowed me to spend
some time with my aunt, who lived in an exclusive suburb
of the town, also home to several minor princely families,
left indigent due to the loss of their estates. Among them
were M.N. Roy, a pre-eminent radical thinker and one of the
leading lights of international communism, and Raja Mahendra
Pratap, a revolutionary and, for some time, president of the
first government-in-exile of free India in Kabul. Rendered

somewhat irrelevant to the younger generations of Indians, they lived there, lonely and unknown. One of the rather odd hobbies of my uncle was cutting logs of wood, which was considered by him as an ideal exercise for both body and mind. Every morning, the servants placed logs of wood in the courtyard and provided him with an axe, and he would set about his exercise in right earnest. Later, the servants would collect the hewn wood for use in the living room fireplace. His exercise over, he would ease himself into a chaise longue, placed in the deep veranda. This was a signal for me to join him for breakfast and provide him an opportunity to launch into a long discourse on Sikh religion and history, an area in which he considered himself an authority. As the sole and virtually captive audience, I had little choice but to remain a silent sufferer. His insistence that I recite the Sikh scriptures every day was later to make me question the overly ritualistic form of Sikhism.

My aunt was a sharp and vivacious woman and, having lived a carefree life, possessed plenty of what these days is called 'attitude'. Among daily visitors to the house was a swami from the Ramakrishna Mission who dropped by every evening at teatime, clad in a saffron dhoti-kurta. When she saw him approaching, she would exclaim, not too loudly though, 'There comes the Swamra,' but greet him warmly on his arrival. Soon, the servants would appear with the tea tray, a home-baked cake and cookies. Her favourite brew was Darjeeling tea from the Lopchu estate. As the servant poured out the tea, she would ask the swami if he would like some cake. His response was always 'Sakna, sakna [Can have],' uttered in a pronounced Bengali accent, and she would look at us and mutter mischievously in Punjabi, 'Hor ki karna si tu! [What else!]' While the swami continued to look quizzically at all of us doubled up with laughter, she plied him with slices of cake and other eatables, which he hugely enjoyed.

Dehradun brings back some fond memories of past visits; of lounging around in the Indiana Coffee House; making up imaginary romantic episodes and composing totally unremarkable poetry. In the early 1970s, when I was posted to Lal Bahadur Shastri National Academy of Administration (LBSNAA) in Mussoorie, I would often visit my aunt in Dehradun. Rising prices and political corruption had by then vastly changed the social structure and, in the process, the lifestyles of the older residents, including my aunt's, who had settled in the city for its exclusivity. A nouveau riche middle class with hordes of money and crass moral and ethical values now dominated the social scene. The Boulevard that had housed the Indiana Coffee House too had vanished in the flurry of the building boom.

The last part of our training involved a two-week attachment with the army in Jammu, and, once again, three of us were with a Gurkha battalion. Our day started early with the batman bringing a mug of hot tea and laying out our uniform for the day's activities. If it was to be a route march, he would also get us a packed breakfast. The day's activities in the forward areas were generally over by lunchtime, though, of course, a sizeable reserve always remained on duty for contingencies. Thus, we were mostly on our own in the afternoons, which I spent exploring the vicinity or catching up on my reading. Many service officers find field postings dreary, and many of them take to heavy drinking. Since the men too are similarly placed, problems of discipline abound. The only teetotaller in the battalion was the adjutant, Captain Srinivas Kumar Sinha. He came from a police background; both his father and grandfather had been in the IP.

Later, General Sinha (as he was then), superseded in the post of army chief, resigned his commission, joined politics and became a bitter critic of Indira Gandhi. I often ran into him during morning walks in Delhi's Lodhi Gardens around that time. He remained active in the country's public life for many years, serving as governor of Assam and of Jammu and Kashmir (J&K). The severe unrest that erupted in two regions of J&K in the summer of 2008 was ascribed by some political analysts to the debatable move to transfer government land to the Sri Amarnath Shrine Board, of which he was chairman. In December 1954, when I had met him at his house-warming party in his new *basha*, he had come across as a sober, well-read and friendly young officer.

The end of the army attachment also marked the conclusion of our institutional training. After a short break, which I spent with my parents, I set off for a remote district in central India for on-the-job training.

My batch of the IPS provided, in the course of time, two directors for the IB, one director for the Research & Analysis Wing (R&AW or RAW) and several state police chiefs and police commissioners. At one time, most Indian state police forces were led by my batchmates. Julio Ribeiro and I were specially chosen to head the Punjab police during a very difficult period, when the Indian republic was faced with a period of acute Sikh militancy. Whatever one might say about the performance of the Indian police during recent times, we did give our best to provide a sense of security to the people, but we could have done much better if Indian law-enforcement systems had not been hostage to an antiquated legal structure and medieval concepts.

In 2003, we met for our 'Fifty Years' reunion at the National

Police Academy (NPA), the successor to the CPTC. It was openly recognized and acknowledged that all this would have been impossible without the rigorous training and attitudinal reorientation in Mount Abu under the direction of the AC, J.W. Roderigues, ably backed by Messrs Pratt and Deb and several inspectors, sub-inspectors and head constables. Mr Roderigues had retired from the post of commandant general of the Home Guard in Madhya Pradesh (MP) and had settled in Bangalore. During my tours, I used to call on him and his gracious wife and enjoy their wonderful hospitality whenever I happened to visit that beautiful city. Deb returned to Calcutta to teach and do research in law at the university. He continued to correspond with me for several years, especially when I was vice chancellor (VC) of Bhopal University. As for my batchmates, sadly, only twenty-one of thirty-seven had survived the severity and strain of their working lives by the time we met for our reunion. It was also most depressing to find some colleagues, outstanding riders and sportsmen at the CPTC, walk with difficulty because of age-related physical infirmities.

6

In the Land of the Vindhyas

From Jammu I came to Moga for a short break and found that I had been posted to Chhatarpur in central India for on-the-job training. My father tried to locate the place on a railway map, but it proved futile because it was not connected by rail. Luckily, my future SP had anticipated the problem and sent me a detailed letter, telling me how to reach my new destination.

The station master and his staff went out of their way to help plan my itinerary as I had already become something of a celebrity in the small subdivisional town for having made it to a service still viewed as one of the top career options for young men. The few free days before reporting time passed only too quickly, and soon it was time to leave home for a strange and distant land and, although it was not my first journey out of Moga, it had a certain air of finality. I had chosen a career that would in time sever me from my roots, isolate me from my friends, my relatives and, indeed, from all that had been familiar and dear to me until then. It was certainly not easy for me to leave my parents and my sisters, who were years younger than me and unable to fully comprehend the subtle pain of separation; but it was far more painful for my parents. None of us, of course, voiced our feelings so as not to put a damper on the festive mood. My father accompanied me to the nearby rail junction from where I was to board a direct train to Jhansi. My father was the strong, silent type, not given to displaying his emotions openly and, though both of us did our best to maintain our composure, a certain air of sadness and unease did permeate the parting. Both of us were anxious about the many attitudinal and lifestyle changes that were in store for me in my new post. A degree of emotional gulf between my parents and me seemed imminent.

I felt quite upbeat during the journey from Moga to Delhi and looked forward cheerfully to what was going to be my new stamping ground for the next many years. However, as the train left Delhi station at night, I felt increasingly uneasy at the thought of the long journey ahead through unfamiliar terrain, and my mental state soon drew the attention of a fellow passenger. He promptly introduced himself and took matters in hand. He turned out to be the former nawab of a small state near Jhansi and quite familiar with the area. Nawab Sahib, my new friend, was a voluble talker and he soon began a running commentary on the social, historical and archaeological features of the region where, little did I know it, I was to serve for many years. What really caught my attention was his graphic description of the lush forests, swarming with wildlife, especially since the area from which I came was woefully devoid of forests. This laid the foundation of my lifelong passion for the wild and it marked my entire service career.

I was later to meet and get to know a variety of minor royalty, still doggedly clinging to their past glory, addressing each other as 'Your Highness' and expecting everyone to do the same. It took me years to adapt to princely India's royalty-obsessed ways, but I could never say 'Your Highness' to anyone. As Chhatarpur itself was a former princely state, my initiation into the fads and fetishes of the former royals was immediate. As a protocol requirement, a police guard was provided to its former ruler. When I replaced his guard as per the police manual, he vehemently protested because he played chess only with those men! Since almost three-fourths of Madhya Pradesh comprised former princely states, the functional and attitudinal styles of its bureaucracy were largely shaped by what was commonly referred to as the durbar culture. This involved excessive fawning over the powerful and manipulative dealings with equals and subordinates. Since one of my colleagues in Chhatarpur was a high-caste Thakur, I was inducted fairly early into the finer points of caste hierarchy in princely India.

On the day of my arrival, I had to wait at Jhansi the whole day to take the late evening train to Harpalpur. Mercifully, railway bookstalls still stocked good English literature and I picked up a Sartre book on existentialism for less than a rupee. The train reached Harpalpur around midnight where I was received with much deference by the reserve inspector (RI), a very correct and courteous officer indeed. However, all my attempts at making small talk with him to bridge the gap between our respective ranks and to lessen the unease of my first experience with a junior officer in the then-inflexible relationship across ranks in the police proved inadequate. My questions were met with just two one-word responses—*hukum* and *marji* (*marzi*)—which, I was told, was the standard form of response in princely India in all interaction between a senior and a junior. While both the terms roughly meant 'As you wish' and implied some degree of subordination in the rank or position of the second party, hukum was also used to refer to a senior person in the caste hierarchy among the Indian princely fraternity. The area abounded with such types and my early initiation into the hierarchical niceties of caste patterns was of great help to me later. Having failed to make much headway in my efforts to draw out the RI, I gave up and we set off for Chhatarpur in the red ramshackle jeep with two armed men to guard us against the many dacoit gangs roaming the countryside. Later, when posted to the heavily dacoit-infested Chambal valley, I learnt that they rarely troubled senior officers for fear of massive reprisal from the state.

It took us about an hour and a half to cover the thirty-odd miles to reach the Chhatarpur circuit house, which remained my abode until I was allotted government quarters. The khansama received me with old-world courtesy and conducted me to a well-appointed, in fact, rather ornate room. He asked me whether I would like to dine in my room or at the dining table, where the prescribed set of crockery and cutlery had already been laid out. I opted for the latter and soon enough an elaborate three-course meal was served to me, which I ate in solitary splendour. It was an excellent example of English cuisine, served in style, and although I was awfully tired after a long and tiring journey, I fully enjoyed the repast. It was Mount Abu relived but without the vigilant eyes of the staff watching for any slip of etiquette. It seemed to me that I was going to like immensely this new phase of my life. There was, however, no electricity and the whole place was lit with huge ornamental lamps. Power was available for only three hours in the evening as Chhatarpur was still dependent for power on the maharaja's small powerhouse, and he did not believe in sharing that luxury with his subjects. The time was past midnight on 30 December 1954.

I went to sleep in the wee hours of the morning, a relaxed man, but was woken up soon after by a knock on the door and a summons from the SP, I.J. Johar, to join him on a visit to the police lines for the general parade. This was an unexpected and rather unpleasant diktat as it meant fishing out the various articles of uniform from my huge metal trunk, shaving by the dim light of a lantern and reporting to my boss in time, for which I was plainly unprepared. But if there was anything that a year's rigorous training in Mount Abu had taught us, it was to be always prepared to take such situations in our stride. So I went through the 3S drill as of old, put on my parade dress in record time—cross belt, boots, putties, sola hat, etc.—and was at the SP's house as directed. He was pacing agitatedly up and down in the veranda and responded to my 'Good morning, sir' with a chilly 'Good afternoon'. Apparently, I was late by a couple of minutes by his reckoning. We had learnt the hard way at the CPTC that it never pays to question the boss or protest against his verdicts even by a mere look or gesture. So I kept my cool and muttered a hushed 'Sorry, sir'. My silent acceptance of his curt greeting seemed to pacify him; he visibly softened and remarked in Punjabi, 'But I thought you were a Sikh,' alluding to the absence of a turban and a beard on me. I could see that my boss was a pleasant and humorous man and our first meeting had gone off well indeed. As it was, he turned out to be an excellent mentor during my breaking-in period.

We drove to the DRP (District Reserve Police) Lines where he inspected the parade, and then visited the clothing store, motor transport (MT), the armoury and the magazine to check the many registers and files. He also went around the family quarters and the men's barracks, tasting the food cooked in the men's kitchen to check the quality. An important part of the exercise was the visit to the orderly room, for instant disciplinary and grievance redress. Minor breaches of duty and petty grievances were disposed of on the spot, giving the men who were brought before him a sense of participation. Inspection visits to all police units ensured that the SP remained in close touch with his men. While going through the MT section, he poked his finger into the innards of an old truck and, not unexpectedly, the finger came out soiled with grime. He looked severely and critically at the RI and then at his finger. The RI got the message, muttered a 'Sorry, sir' and the matter rested there. On the way back, he smilingly narrated a story about a very prim and proper woman, who wanted to buy a chicken for the table. The dealer showed her a number of birds but none came up to her standards of cleanliness as every time she poked a finger in the bird's bottom, it came out mucky. Tired of the lady's objections, the dealer coolly asked her if she herself could pass the same test that she was inflicting on the poor bird!

After the parade, he took me home for breakfast, which consisted of parathas with a pat of butter on top and a thick fluffy omelette, generously sprinkled with lemon juice, of which he was very fond. Naturally, the lemon tree had become something of a popular plant in the district. Station house officers (SHOs) vied with each other for planting lemon trees in their thanas. A senior officer's wish is no less than a command in Indian police culture. Successive generations of officers continued to enjoy the fruit of such plants until the trees grew old and died. After a substantial breakfast, we drove to a nearby thana for what in police parlance, and otherwise, is called a 'surprise visit'. Aware that all his actions and gestures were going to shape my frame of reference regarding the functioning norms and values of the force, he was extra careful about everything he did that day. After going around the police station and checking a few registers and case diaries, with me in tow, he eased himself into a chair and started grilling the SHO about his sundry acts of omission or commission, which the SHO swallowed with the long-suffering look of a man inured to such tongue-lashing. This too was part of the police culture, as was the rich fare that followed, courtesy some transporter or contractor forever reliant on the police for favours of different kinds. A minor addiction of the SP was chewing paan, forbidden while in uniform. And he certainly could not violate the dress code in the presence of an ASP. After a little while, he removed his bush shirt, hung it on the wall and happily put the paan in his mouth, without a trace of guilt.

We returned to Chhatarpur in the afternoon and the boss finally let me go back to my room for a cosy snooze after what seemed to be an eternity of train and road travel followed by concentrated training inputs to prepare me for a brave new profession. He also invited me to join him for dinner the same evening. This put me in a fix as we had been told at the CPTC that we must formally call on the SP and other senior officers before being invited to a meal. Here was my very own guru asking me over for a meal though I had not *formally* called on him. And although I would have given anything to partake of what was sure to be a very delicious meal, I had to decline the offer, bound as I was by the strict code of conduct learnt in Mount Abu. So, I said, 'Sorry, sir, I cannot accept your invitation today.' Taken aback by my refusal, he said, 'But why the hell not?' 'Because I have not yet called on you, sir.' He gave a hearty laugh and said, 'Don't be silly. You have been with me for hours. Is it not adequate compliance with whatever was taught to you at the CPTC?' And there the matter ended. My first meal with my mentor was to turn out to be a memorable experience in more senses than one.

Lieutenant Colonel Johar—who had been appointed to the IPS as part of an emergency scheme to fill the vacancies caused by the departure of British and Muslim officers after Independence and Partition—was extremely fond of the good things of life and was a true connoisseur. Dressed in a see-through bush shirt where the texture of the vest mattered as much as the outer garment and with a tin of '555' cigarettes in hand, he cut a fine figure indeed. It is a different matter that he could never convince me about the primacy of fashionable clothing over intellectual flair and elegance. We would engage in lengthy and often inconclusive arguments over the correct interpretation of the design of shoes or the width of trouser bottoms as prescribed in the uniform rules. He would finally give up in disgust and I would remain a nonconformist, both professionally and sartorially. Despite the disparity in our views, his confidence in my professional and personal aptitude was unwavering.

He was as deft in coping with an awkward situation as with handing out a witty repartee at a formal dinner. Once, a capricious governor, who was passionate about women's progress and who was particular that women should attend his meetings in large numbers, visited the district, but no women turned up to listen to him. The SP and his aides got into a huddle and came up with a unique idea. All off-duty policemen were hastily assembled, asked to cover themselves from head to foot with enormous *ghunghat*s and were prominently seated in the front. The governor was hugely impressed with such a massive turnout of whom he thought were women, and cheerfully asked them to remove their ghunghats as a sign of complete liberation. The SP, alarmed at the prospect of moustached policemen being discovered under the ghunghats, winked at the city inspector, who swiftly disconnected the power supply, plunging the entire area into darkness. The governor promptly left for security reasons, still secure in the belief that he had addressed a record number of women.

The SP was both a caring boss and a fine gentleman, lively and entertaining, and had a special flair for witty and lively conversation. Once, when I asked him whether the stylish necktie he was wearing was a club tie, he informed me with a straight face, 'Yes, an MOBC tie.' Noticing my blank expression at the acronym, he chuckled and said, 'My Own Bloody Colours.' He had an inexhaustible stock of funny stories to suit all occasions. His guidance and advice were always couched in simple and clear-cut idiom. 'Never allow your wife to meet the RI or the kotwal,' he often told me. It is these two officers in the district police set-up who mislead the wives of many young policemen into misusing their authority. When I asked him what mode of transport I should use for commuting to office and back, expecting that he would let me use the spare jeep, he said, 'Buy a cycle, son, if you can't afford anything better.' The bicycle was the common mode of transport for all officers who could not afford a car or a bike. I bought a red six-horsepower Norton, thanks to my rich aunt in Dehradun.

The collector—on whom I was required to call next—formed an important tier in Indian administration. The office retained its centrality in Indian administration despite some erosion in his powers in democratic India. When I arrived at his house, rather ill at ease in my full uniform, ready with two visiting cards, one for the collector and the other for his wife, as taught to us at Mount Abu, I found a far-from-formidable collector holding office in the front lawn of his house. I was escorted to his table right away by a couple of peons, of whom there were plenty. The lowly chaprasi (literally one who moves around to the boss's left and right, from the Persian *chap* for left and *ras* for right) wields huge clout as a medium to access the officer for whom he works. As I clicked my heels and saluted, the collector extended a limp hand, beckoning me to take a seat. Some small talk followed and I could see that he was not much used to such trivia. I too was equally uncomfortable and wished ardently to make a quick getaway except that I still had to hand over my two cards to the great man. When I tried somewhat furtively to place the cards on a side table, he asked in Hindi, 'Where is the need for that?'

He had a point there, but I was bound by the CPTC code of conduct. 'But why two cards?' he asked and tried to return one. I resolutely refused to give in and made my escape, satisfied that I had not strayed from the fine traditions of the service and that too in the face of such heavy opposition. To avoid similar episodes while calling on other officers, I took the precaution of doing so when they were out of station. Later, I often encountered the collector at the SP's bungalow at dusk, both of them paddling around in a small pond in one corner of the lawn. When invited to join them, I always declined on some pretext or the other. In any case, the pond could hardly accommodate a third body in addition to such heavyweights, both literally and figuratively. I would, instead, offer to serve drinks to the duo, helping myself too in the bargain. Soon after I joined, the SP told me that an officer must always keep a stock of liquor at his house. 'Buy a bottle each of whisky and gin and half a dozen beers, son.' He also offered to lend me his jeep to travel to the nearby former cantonment town of Nowgong and purchase the stuff from Moona Lal and Sons, long-standing dealers and contractors from the days of the Raj. The total bill came to just about eighteen rupees.

I may as well speak about Nowgong at some length as it was destined to play a key role in my life. Nowgong, formerly the seat of the Resident for central India, who was a crucial constituent of the Raj, had a special significance for the many princely states of central India, both large and small. A small army contingent, along with a central intelligence officer (CIO), was stationed there to help the Resident enforce the imperial writ. The Resident, who enjoyed vast powers of direct and indirect intervention in any matter of a sensitive or problematic nature within his domain, was indeed a much-feared man. He lived in a huge, sprawling bungalow, called the Residency, covering acres of green and well-tended lawns and gardens. He was served by a horde of retainers of various ranks and grades—from sweepers, *farash*es and *masalchi*s to khansamas, orderlies and bearers; from stewards and butlers, gardeners and horticulturalists to a tennis marker and ball boys—all of whom were supervised by a manager. Thatched roofs and deep verandas all around the bungalow kept it cool during the long Indian summers.

A large and spacious porch led through the front veranda to what was called the durbar hall, decorated with skilfully mounted trophies of tigers and panthers, shot by the Resident or his guests over the years. The heads of bison and wild buffaloes and other shikar trophies and photographs in sepia tones adorned the walls, which also carried the respective insignias of the numerous native states that constituted the Resident's domain. Then there were cannons, guns and other military memorabilia strewn all around. The sitting room had wall-to-wall carpeting and solid Victorian furniture, done in chintzy English prints. The side tables were made of elephant feet and animal bone stands. The dining room was furnished with a grand Burmese teak table to seat some twenty persons and the sideboards were equally imposing with a silver dinner service and serving bowls. Half a dozen meticulously furnished bedrooms formed the living quarters. In the centre of the front lawn was an old weeping willow under which stood an exquisitely carved bird bath. Beyond the lawns were the tennis courts and a private swimming pool. The office block and the guest rooms could be accessed both from outside the house as well as from inside through a corridor. A well-stocked library, with regularly updated gazetteers, formed part of the office.

Post-Independence, several princely states in central India had been integrated to form the small state of Vindhya Pradesh, and the Residency became the divisional commissioner's official residence. I visited that imposing bungalow shortly afterwards and my description is based upon what I saw then. Finding that I was getting more and more lonesome with each passing week, asking for leave to go back home on one pretext or the other, my SP was constantly looking for openings for me to develop attractive local links. A police guard was posted at the Residency as a courtesy to the commissioner. Since one of the commissioner's daughters had recently returned home after doing her master's in English, my SP saw a possible friendship between the two of us that would help tie me up more firmly to Chhatarpur. So he would lend me his jeep every now and then to go inspect the guard at the commissioner's house.

What began as a routine duty gradually turned into a pleasant trip to Nowgong, and an official chore became an eagerly awaited social occasion. Soon after, my attachment to the court of the district judge, then located at Nowgong, required me to stay there for a fortnight. This resulted in a deepening of my association with the family, and especially with the young woman who had an MA degree in English literature. We spent hours talking about modern poetry and various genres of art, subjects that were still fresh in my memory. She was deeply interested in painting and was learning the art from a local Bengali artist, adept in the stylized idiom of traditional Bengali art. My knowledge of the visual arts was rather limited and derived largely from what I had learnt in college. I had learnt the essentials of aesthetics as part of the English criticism paper with Walter Pater, Matthew Arnold and Herbert Read providing the backdrop to my art education. Over cups of tea and plates of pakoras, we spoke about art and poetry, and about the odd habits and foibles of the

English memsahibs, as related by the numerous retainers at the bungalow. I was also discovering new interests and attachments that would, in time, bind me more firmly to my new situation and blur old associations.

During the Raj, the winter season was marked by week-long festivities, under the title 'Nowgong Week', with the Residency as the centre of action. The many princes and princelings of the region converged on the town and held durbars and other grand events, trying to outshine each other in grandeur while also affirming their loyalty to the Empire. Cricket and tennis matches were organized for which the princes turned out in the choicest blazers and ties. Colourful cultural events filled the evenings with local numbers, such as the Bundelkhandi rai dance and the heroic tales of Aalha Udal taking centre stage. Late evenings were given to formal dinners, hosted by leading princes like those of Panna and Orchha, where the fare was outright western, complete with the choicest liquor and ballroom dancing. The chief guest at all such events used to be the Resident, much fawned upon by the Indian princely order.

As a rule, Indian princes were conservative by nature. Bir Singh Ju Deo of Orchha, for example, would discard all utensils used for cooking or serving food to a foreign guest and wash the entire premises with holy water before setting foot in the place. The hand shaken by a *firangi* was also meticulously washed with Ganga *jal* before being used again.

Nowgong Week was revived when it became the commissioner's headquarters. Although its past splendour could not be replicated, it did provide a platform for the now sorely hard-up princes to take their regalia out of mothballs and flaunt their importance once again. Strangely, the poor peasants, who had suffered untold humiliation and deprivation under princely rule, continued to regard their former rulers with awe and deference, addressing them as *anna-data*, provider of food, for decades to come.

I was just a few weeks old in my new job when Nowgong Week came round again. My SP proudly presented me to at least two former rulers, the handsome but standoffish Panna and the modestly built but cordial Orchha. He also pushed me into a revolver-shooting competition, where I stood first and duly received the trophy from the commissioner's daughter (who else?), thus adding another tier to a still-vague relationship.

At that time, Chhatarpur was seriously affected by gang dacoity, a very grave crime indeed in the Indian police lexicon. Of the two deputy superintendents (DSPs), my colleagues at Chhatarpur, one was a tough-talking, tenacious Thakur, and the other, a mild but shrewd Brahmin. This was not a mere coincidence as the postings of Thakurs and Brahmins—the principal contenders for power in those parts—were usually determined by the need to maintain a delicate balance between the two. I was assigned to the Thakur for my anti-dacoity training and to the Brahmin to teach me accountancy. Both of them were excellent mentors and I learnt a great deal from them. Shikar formed an essential element in the district training of IPS as well as of IAS officers. Anti-dacoity work and shikar were thought to be closely linked; both called for the same qualities of courage, daring and quick reflexes. Also, shikar taught the men to live under difficult conditions in villages and forests, to mix with rural people and to get acquainted with the countryside. So, a taste for it was carefully inculcated among the trainees, with colourful shikar tales taking centre stage at parties and picnics. My anti-dacoity mentor was also a reputed shikari and I joined him in many a hunting trip, learning the nitty-gritty of organizing a tiger beat, the finer details of which weapons to use and in which circumstances, and an elaborate catalogue of the dos and don'ts of the sport.

Following the trail of a tiger often led us to dacoit territory, thus running the risk of a clash with dacoit gangs. Historically, many Indian princes were known to shelter them, provided they confined their nefarious activities to the British provinces of United Provinces (UP) and Central Provinces and also shared their booty with the princes. In a way, therefore, this menace was a legacy from the past and carried the cultural and operational footprints of those times. For me, anti-dacoity work involved getting used to a whole new vocabulary as gang dacoity had ceased to be a problem in Punjab ages ago. These operations could only be planned when the presence of a gang in a given area had been established. No villager would dare inform the police about its movements for fear of reprisal. The role of an informer, thus, was crucial in this work.

Cultivating and utilizing informers to the best effect is an art in itself and not every officer becomes proficient in it. Often, informers were also double-crossers and worked for both sides. Informers normally belonged to a lower caste as it was not considered an 'honourable' job. No genuine informer met an officer except under total secrecy, usually at night and with a heavily veiled face to conceal his identity. Only after being assured that no one else was around would he speak and that too in barely audible whispers. There was also a class of professional informers, but they were to be found mostly in the Chambal region. Anti-dacoity operations were generally launched in the rainy season, which was marked by spells of heavy rains for days together. The flooded streams severely restricted the mobility of dacoit gangs. As vehicular movement was impossible in such conditions, most such operations had to be carried out on foot.

In one such operation in Bijawar tehsil, we had to camp in a part of a haveli, belonging to a local zamindar. All of us—an inspector, two sub-inspectors and about forty constables—with arms and other equipment, had to put up in that small space, run a small kitchen and improvise an armoury. I had to use the mosquito net for all the twenty-four hours as the place was swarming with flies and mosquitoes. While it was a hugely difficult situation in itself, the most awkward part was the morning trip to the nearby bushes, for which two armed constables had to escort me and stand guard, while I squatted behind a bush, to pre-empt the possibility of the dacoits seizing the ASP with his pants down—literally! I found it was best not to wear shoes during such operations as we often had to walk barefoot to cross a rivulet or to jump over a wall. I enjoyed my anti-dacoity training for the sheer thrill of it despite the hazards and hassles of such operations; and, at the same time, I was also learning to make do with whatever was at hand.

For a district town, Chhatarpur was incredibly primitive. There was no piped water, no cinema house, no bookshop and no good provisions store. Power supply was available for only three hours in the evening. One had to depend on the weekly haat to procure common vegetables, chicken and eggs. In fact, one had to get used to living virtually on poultry and eggs—a habit that proved most useful during the extensive anti-dacoity operations in the jungles of Morena and Gwalior, where parathas and omelettes formed the standard fare. The solitary clubhouse came to life only late in the evening when its members gathered after dinner to play cards. When they chose to use the English form of greeting, it would be 'Good *evenings'* and 'Good *nights'*, if they were addressing more than one person. The use of the plural noun sounded amusing though they were trying to be grammatically correct. Once when I was invited to speak at a sports function in the local college, the principal tried laboriously to anglicize my name so as to introduce me in English. He finally chose to call me Mr Dribble. This uncannily smacked of a Dickensian slip of the tongue, but I remained unruffled out of a sense of decorum. In the course of time, though, the laid-back people of my new state learnt to pronounce my name correctly.

Since no ASP had ever before been posted to Chhatarpur, the local police officials could not place me precisely, rank-wise, in relation to the two DSPs, who were considerably senior to me in age, and who wore three stars against my one, especially as the SP seemed to give me more importance. This ambiguity was resolved one day when the SP referred to me as the '*chhota* SP sahib'. One of my more interesting duties was to read and translate into English, for the SP's benefit, the intercepted Punjabi letters from a young wife to her communist husband, who was then under surveillance. I also picked up a smattering of Bundeli, which sounded particularly mellow and sweet when spoken by women, though the gender confusion in such common nouns as towel (*tolia*) and path (*rasta*) seemed puzzling. It was here that I first heard of the ubiquitous mahua tree that figures so prominently in local folklore. Mahua grew in profusion and its dark purple flowers were used to ferment a rather potent and smelly local tipple. It also earned infamy in rape and molestation cases as women were waylaid and molested largely while they were out picking mahua flowers.

The famed Khajuraho temples in Chhatarpur district attracted a number of VIP visitors but were not accessible to ordinary Indians due to the paucity of reliable public transport. I was often deputed to take visitors around the temples. Frequent visits and some focused reading on the subject enabled me to talk glibly on the history, the architectural elegance and beauty of the temples and the sculpture. The many intricate coital positions, carved on the walls of some temples, often evoked interesting comments from visitors. Once, while looking intently at a frieze of copulating human beings, a state governor's young niece exclaimed, 'But this is impossible!' Then she looked at me and blushed crimson. I tactfully withdrew from the scene for a while so as not to embarrass her further when she got to the next column, where infinitely more inconceivable coital positions, graphic scenes of bestiality, and what would be termed these days as alternative sexuality, were depicted. By far the most important visitor to the district at that time was Prime Minister Jawaharlal Nehru. Though VIP security had not yet acquired the kind of hype in India that it did later, even so, protecting him from crowds of unruly fans was serious business. As his official escort during his day-long engagements in the district, I had the privilege of travelling in his car, sitting next to his principal security officer (PSO) in the front seat while the state lieutenant governor and the chief minister (CM) sat with him at the back.

I thoroughly enjoyed my few hours' proximity to the great man, even trying to show off rather proudly whatever little I had learned by then of the art and craft of policing to his PSO, the formidable G.K. Handoo, a tall, handsome Kashmiri and, by all accounts, in Nehru's confidence. He was then a deputy director in the IB and senior to me by decades. I must say to his credit that he took my smug claims to fame with a mix of amusement and tolerance. That is not quite what one could say about most officers of his vintage. B.N. Mullik, then director, IB, had come across to me as a rather conceited officer, intolerant of dissent, when he had addressed us at the CPTC. Mullik was known to be closer to Nehru than anyone else and wielded enormous power in New Delhi. Even so, he never thought of using this power to redress the glaring disparity between an outdated police system and free India's democratic imperatives.

But, to revert to our narrative, as Nehru was getting back into the car after going around a few temples and apparently in an expansive mood, he hurt his left hand when an overzealous police official tried to shut the door before the great man could fully ease himself into the rear seat. The prime minister (PM) was suddenly transformed into a spoilt brat and ran after the policeman, displaying the famed Nehruvian temper in its full glory, while all of us watched with deep concern. Soon, the comic aspect of the episode dawned on him and he laughingly asked me to convey his apologies to the scared officer. Our next stop was a general-purpose museum that displayed a variety of objets d'art, collected from former princely houses. Here, a veritable gastronomic treat, comprising assorted cakes, pastries, cookies, sandwiches and pakoras, all sourced from the nearby Jhansi cantonment, awaited the PM for his evening repast. Though not a great gourmet, he did enjoy the goodies and settled down to smoking a half-cigarette, offered to him by Handoo, but not before the photographers had been shooed off. Evidently, he did not want his adoring countrymen to learn of his minor vices. When he casually asked the PWD (Public Works Department) minister whether the road that he had traversed that day was a highway, the honourable minister hesitantly muttered, 'No, sir, it is not very high.'

Those days, politicians, as a class, were usually simple people, who took their role in public service rather seriously. They would happily go back to simple lifestyles after they ceased to hold office, reverting to the humble bicycle and the third-class rail travel. Days after I joined at Chhatarpur, the state home minister visited Chhatarpur. I was deputed to receive him at the circuit house. Apprehensive about my very first meeting with a minister, I was uneasy and fidgety, waiting for him in my full uniform. I was on my best formal conduct when he arrived, replied in English to all his queries, which were made in the local Bundeli dialect. Soon the SP arrived to relieve me of a task that was obviously hanging heavy on me. The first question the minister asked the SP was, 'Where is this youngster from?' 'From Punjab,' the SP told him. 'Oh! That is where the *murrah* buffaloes also come from,' again in Bundeli.

My next posting was as attachment to the police headquarters in Rewa to learn the working of the office of the inspector general of police (IGP). Gian Chand, an elderly, portly and balding officer, was in overall charge of the headquarters as an assistant inspector general (AIG) of police. Having risen from the ranks, he was not a great favourite with Johar, my former boss. Indian bureaucrats have devised their own version of the caste system, which places direct recruits at the top, emergency recruits at number two and those who are promoted at the bottom. Gian Chand was thus often at the receiving end of Johar's sarcastic jokes. Once, when he found the former putting his signature on office files without untying the proverbial red tape, he remarked in a tongue-in-cheek tone, '*Gian Chand, nala tan khol liya kar.*' (Gian Chand, at least untie the waistband.)

Several local socialist party leaders were then under secret surveillance. Most of them eventually joined the Congress and ended up as ministers, two of them even serving as governors. Arjun Singh, inheritor of a small estate in the adjoining Sidhi district, was gradually gaining visibility as an up-and-coming politician. I did not then know that I would meet him again in a rather hostile context towards the end of my service.

After completing my practical training, I was posted as ASP, Rewa, and given charge of the city police and the DRP Lines. Since suitable accommodation was unavailable, I made myself comfortable in a Swiss cottage tent, pitched in the parade ground. This was fine with me as I could now regularly join my men for the evening games. The only problem was that I had to get up early enough to finish my morning ablutions before the men fell in for parade, otherwise I could face a rather awkward situation—that of standing stiffly at attention in my dressing gown with a lota in my hand on my way back from the toilet tent, while platoon after platoon marched past me with the parade commander shouting 'Eyes Right' or 'Eyes Left', as the case may be, in respect of the deference due to my rank. As an alternative, I could stay on in the toilet tent, glued to the thunder box until the men marched off after their morning schedule.

With my postbox-red Norton parked in front of my tent and the few books I had acquired during my visits to Punjab to keep me company, I was gradually getting sucked into the routine and grind of a typical police officer in a mofussil town. Interestingly, police officials were addressed in terms that bore clear geometrical connotations. The lines officer was called 'line sahib', and the circle inspector (CI), the 'circle sahib'. Quite often, circle sahibs were in fact circular and rotund. The then-Rewa CI certainly did fit the description. Further, the court inspector was called 'court sahib'; the city inspector, 'city sahib';

and the town inspector, 'town sahib'. To cap it all, the humble head constable was referred to as 'head sahib'!

Surinder Gill, an IAS officer from my hometown and posted in a nearby district, would drive once a week to Rewa in his jeep, with his wife, Satya, to spend an evening with me. He was always well up in Urdu poetry and kept me posted with current trends in English writing, while Satya added a faint but very refreshing feminine essence to my scantily furnished and severely bachelor lodgings. Their visits were always enjoyable and stimulating except that, as a happily married man himself, Surinder was forever pushing me into early wedlock, while I was strictly against getting married unless I was earning a decent carry-home salary. Undeterred by such reasoning, however, he continued in his efforts to pluck me out of my state of single blessedness as soon as possible. The advent of an eligible bachelor in small-town India enlivened the social scene in a manner unimaginable in the West. While the ladies played matchmaker, the men vied with each other in telling dirty stories using the poor griffin as target.

Surinder surprised me one evening during a football match between the DRP and the State Armed Force (SAF) teams, pulled me out of the game, informing me rather ominously that the girl with whom I had been friends in Nowgong and also in Rewa was about to get engaged. Before I could fully grasp the subtext of what he was talking about, he hurriedly shoved me into his jeep and we both drove to the Civil Lines area. The former commissioner of Nowgong was posted now in Rewa and I often visited their home to see his daughter who was still on somewhat friendly terms with me. In our social set-up, most such friendships are expected to lead to matrimony, sooner or later. When her parents had found no noticeable progress in this regard, they had decided to look elsewhere for a match. I did not fully appreciate her parents' anxiety in the matter and, in any case, I thought one should marry only after getting a regular district charge. But, faced with a now-or-never situation, I said yes to the proposition, much to the relief of my future wife, as she confided to me later. Surinder's arrival in the town that evening would thus remain a landmark event in my life—but for his timely intercession, my wife and I may never have entered into matrimony. Or, I may never have married, not being the sort of fellow who is adept at forming and nurturing close emotional relationships.

An ASP in the Indian police also serves as an all-purpose assistant to the SP. My SP, C.E. Sharp, was a true professional with a high sense of integrity. Instead of using his official car, he cycled to office and, in the evening too, he and his tall, comely wife rode to the club. Mrs Sharp was quite fond of the girl whom I was to marry. Amongst many other compliments she paid to her was that she could turn a barn into a home with mere bits and pieces of furniture. The collector, P.D. Chatterjee, would drop in most evenings at the SP's bungalow for a drink. As a young ASP, it fell upon me to fix his drinks, usually stiff shots of whisky. Every time he downed a drink and I asked him if he would have another, his response would be a vague, 'Rather, Mr Dhillon,' and it was left to me to interpret it whichever way I would. He was a heavy drinker and continued to be so until the very end. When Chatterjee headed the state electricity board, one of his drinking buddies in Bhopal, an army colonel, often referred to him as 'Cheaterjee', for reasons to which he may have been privy. Rewa has been notorious over the years for its unruly residents and mutinous politicians, whose rabble-rousing skills often led to grave law-and-order problems.

In August 1956, the minister of education, Mahendra Kumar Manav, suspected of having made money by pressurizing school principals into buying his photograph for displaying in their offices, was severely beaten up by an outraged mob inside the legislative house. This was probably the first incident of its kind in an India still learning to adjust to a system of governance so different from the feudal culture it was used to. It now became incumbent on the district administration to protect the honourable minister from mob fury, which was likely to have been fuelled by accusations of corruption against some other ministers also. I was put on duty with the CM, S.N. Shukla, a kindly but shrewd politician, to escort him to and from the legislative assembly, then in session, and generally keep an unobtrusive eye within the chamber to ensure that he was not harmed in any way. It was an interesting way to get to know the internal working of our political parties and their cultural mainspring.

In December 1956, Indore was the venue for the annual session of the Congress party. Such huge gatherings entailed a lot of work for the police as, apart from the mercurial Nehru, many of his senior colleagues also needed to be protected. Congress sessions attracted huge crowds, eager to catch a glimpse of Nehru and his men who ran the government from distant Delhi. Crowd management in India is an enormous task in itself, but with Nehru acting as a powerful magnet for the masses, the task assumed massive dimensions indeed. Nehru was also given to rushing impulsively into crowds. All this kept the police on their toes for months before and during such sessions. Poorly equipped to manage such intense jobs within locally available resources, the host police had perforce to rely on reinforcements from elsewhere. So, I was called from Rewa for special duty for the session. This was a wonderful chance for me to visit Indore, then as now the most happening place in MP. This also gave me an opportunity to meet several of my colleagues in the IPS, and to call on the IGP and some deputy inspector generals of police (DIGs).

K.F. Rustamji, Nehru's new PSO, dressed in khadi kurta-pyjama, accompanied the PM. Being in charge of the PM's security inside the pandal, I often had to interact with Rustamji, who succeeded B.G. Ghate as IGP, MP, in due course. By and large, those were peaceful times and there were no threats of terrorist attacks or of suicide bombers. The writ of the police still went a long way in keeping public places free of lawless elements. Characteristically, Ghate never wore his uniform throughout the session and appeared at the site only once for a few minutes. The rest of the time, he was busy attending parties and picnics. The death of Ravishankar Shukla, he of the bushy white whiskers, the first CM of the new Madhya Pradesh, allegedly due to corruption charges, at year's end, cast a pall of gloom over the entire proceedings.

With the announcement of general elections in February 1957, I was promoted to acting SP, Rewa, ahead of time since my SP, whose brother was a candidate in the elections, had to be transferred. Though it was unexpected, I took the promotion in my stride. The collector, M.P. Shrivastava, was a thorough and diligent officer, a good-natured and friendly colleague. We toured the district jointly to supervise the conduct of elections and had often to stay overnight at the most unlikely places in the absence of dak bungalows. Once we were put up in the maternity ward of a newly built health centre, still to be commissioned. Another time, it was a headmaster's office in a village primary school, where two benches were put side by side to serve as our beds. The place was infested with huge jungle mice, which thought we were some kind of fresh bait for them to chew upon, and, of course, with swarms of mosquitoes.

In those days, legislative elections were simple and smooth affairs. We had to manage within our resources as no help was available from outside. Village *konwars*, enlisted as special police officers and armed simply with the good old lathi, provided the only security cover at many polling stations. The elections over, a new SP replaced me as I was not yet senior enough for a regular promotion. After a couple of months, I proceeded on long leave to Moga with my wife, Sneh, in an apology of a honeymoon since my involvement with the elections soon after our marriage had left no time for a honeymoon—the source of many a heated argument between us for years.

This was Sneh's first glimpse of a part of the country she had never known and, as was to be expected, it required considerable mental effort for her to adjust to what must have seemed to her our rather bizarre habits, behaviour and orientation. While I happily enjoyed meeting my many old friends, she tried her best to come to terms with a very different milieu and culture that seemed to her rather outlandish and so unlike everything to which she was used. The sight of a buffalo, sprawled contentedly in the courtyard—something taken for granted in a household which was still rooted in its rural past—had left her shaken for weeks. Sneh could never get over a nagging fear as to what might happen if the buffalo some day managed to break the chain, although we kept telling her that the gentle animal was fully domesticated and there was little danger of a mishap.

Finally, it was the ever-cheerful and witty Dharam, my cousin and childhood friend, who helped me allay her uneasiness and misgivings and to make her feel at home. He was a source of lively company for us for many years. After doing his MA and law, he set up a thriving law practice in Moga but left home soon after when his father did not allow him to marry his Ceylonese girlfriend, Gita. Both of them finally made it to the US where, after years of hardship in a foreign land, he secured a senior position in the World Bank. His magnetic charm made him irresistible to women. Though we visited him twice in the US and he often came to see us wherever I was posted at the time, his immigration deprived us of his company long ahead of time. The loss was compounded many times over when he died of several illnesses from which he suffered during the last years of his life. For someone like me, who finds it very hard to form and sustain close relationships, Dharam's death was an irreparable shock.

Early that year, the Union government decided to make emergency recruitments to the IAS due to a growing need for generalist officers to handle the many new social and economic obligations of the state. Many IPS officers took the opportunity to enter the IAS which offered greater mobility and better prospects. I too appeared for the initial examination and in time was called to Delhi for an interview while still on long leave. Ultimately, I did not join because if I had, I would have lost seniority by three years and, in any case, the rigid civil service 'caste system' would never have let me feel an integral part of the elite group. My IAS father-in-law was understandably unhappy with my decision but I never regretted it.

I was posted as SP, Khargone, at the end of my leave. Once again, I found myself posted to a district unconnected by rail. This time, it did not really matter because, in any case, I had to go back to Rewa before proceeding to Khargone. Those four months in a rustic setting in Punjab had been a veritable journey of exploration and discovery for Sneh. It was hardly possible for her to have fallen in love with our way of life but it had offered her a canvas on which to draw the broad contours of her husband's cultural anchor, and had provided her with a keyhole view of his formative years, as well as his social and emotional roots. It requires enormous effort and flexibility for individuals to make an unqualified success of marriage across cultures and lifestyles.

7

Coming of Age in the Police

My three district charges as an SP were mid-career positions in the IPS. A district charge offered a young officer a learning platform to come of age in the service and a chance to prove himself in an assignment which is regarded as central to maintaining peace and order in society. The selection of districts where an officer was to be posted was largely determined by his aptitude and integrity. An officer considered as good leadership material was carefully evaluated by posting him in districts that posed increasingly tougher challenges. This involved three district postings, ranging from a class-three to a class-one district, classified on the basis of their importance from a policing angle. On the successful completion of a term that generally lasted about three years in each such district, he would be tried in a staff job in the headquarters. After about fifteen years of service in the districts and the headquarters, an officer would normally get promoted to selection grade.

His expertise could now be put to good use to head the state PTC. After a few more years, he would be due for promotion to DIG, if a vacancy existed, or for deputation to the Union government to serve in a CPO. Such career planning models ensured that the state would never be short of capable officers to staff the many leadership positions in the department. Similar career planning was adopted in the IAS. Such training patterns were later severely compromised due to rampant politicization and other factors.

Khargone district covered a vast area and the Narmada River—known as Nerbudda to the British—flowed through some of its picturesque parts. The dense forests and hilly tracts, dotted with charming rest houses, were my favourite haunts during the summer months. A lovely dak bungalow at Sirvel, a remote tribal hamlet deep in an inter-state hill range, offered an ideal retreat if one was prepared to make do with whatever fare was locally available. The Niwali rest house, located on a hilltop near the Sendhwa–Khetia road, was a better choice, and I often went there to unwind with a stack of books to keep me company. The Barwani Club had a well-stocked library with several English classics, including the complete works of Dickens and Thackeray.

Within days of my taking over as SP, I had my first experience of the prevalent police culture of manipulating investigations to favour friends and those in high places. While visiting a thana on the Agra–Bombay road, I found that a charge of rash and negligent driving was pending disposal for several months. Two young women, travelling in their car from Bombay to Indore had run over a man, who later died of injuries sustained in the accident. Such cases should normally be cleared within a week; any undue delay is a cause for suspicion. When questioned, the SHO admitted that he had been instructed by a DIG in Indore to go slow. Although the investigation had been concluded in time, no further action was taken as the women belonged to an influential family in Indore. When I pulled up the SHO, he promptly arrested both women. This raised a big storm in Indore. Since I was still an unknown entity, the affected family thought it prudent not to pull strings but approach me directly. So, the next day, I found a well-groomed gentleman waiting for me when I came home after a game of tennis. He greeted me somewhat uneasily but came to the point right away. He was the brother of the two women accused in the hit-and-run case. I assured him that I would look into it but warned him that the law would have to take its own course. He went away, seemingly satisfied. What really impressed him, he told me later, was my courtesy and candour along with my commitment to the due process of law. His old father expressed a wish to see me as, according to him, upright and courteous policemen just did not exist. When I did visit the old man, I found him extremely keen to learn more about the new generation of IPS officers. His son and daughters remained lifelong friends of mine.

The collector, Birbal, alumnus of the famed St Stephen's College, known for his flair for mathematics and astrology, was charmingly eccentric in many ways. He would hold his cigarette between his ring finger and little finger, and often wave it vaguely in the air, causing it to land in a neighbour's lap. This happened once to the AC, Vinay Malik, also a Stephanian, posted in Khargone for district training. Already disoriented in body and mind due to the primitive surroundings, the flying cigarette butt unnerved him further. However, Vinay soon made the needed adjustment that all of us from vastly different backgrounds were required to make when serving in unfamiliar lands. He was a keen gardener and fine cook, two hobbies he shared with my wife, and thus became a constant companion in that uncongenial place. He and I shared a passion for literature and a love for forests, so we often went wandering in the fabulous forests of Barwani. Vinay's wife, Sheila, a pretty Maharashtrian, who had fallen in love with the handsome Punjabi in the agreeable environs of Delhi University, complemented him in many ways. The two of them brought a welcome breath of fresh air to the very pedestrian town, where a solitary cinema house was the sole source of entertainment. Two deputy collectors, named, respectively, Kale and Gore, were the collector's other aides. Ironically, the man called Kale was fair-complexioned while Gore was dark as the night.

Birbal's successor, K.L. Agarwal, was a total contrast to the former. Born and brought up in Chhatarpur, my very first point of entry in MP, he was a true son of the soil, utterly uninhibited and unspoilt by urban upbringing and, professionally, pragmatic and down to earth. He was the quintessential field officer and later held some very important charges. His four sons, ranging from three to nine years in age, attired in ready-to-wear checked shirts and shorts sourced from the local bazaar and usually a size too large for them, were always present when he received visitors. The elder two, Suresh and Ganesh, often accompanied him on tours. Usually quite fond of meat, he surprised me one day by flatly refusing to touch a juicy chicken leg at a rest house. I was taken aback by this strange behaviour, but my DSP soon caught on to the mystery and immediately took the collector's two sons away, promising to show them a movie. After their departure, he explained his earlier refusal to eat meat and had a hearty meal. His sons would have told their mother who, like many Indian wives of a certain class and age, consider their husbands to be paragons of virtue.

K.F. Rustamji, forty-two years old with only about twenty years of service, succeeded B.G. Ghate, ten years his senior, as IGP, MP, in June 1958. In many ways, this change marked the end of colonial-style policing and the beginning of a modern approach to policing and law enforcement. Rustamji had been on deputation with the IB for several years and had also served as PSO to Prime Minister Nehru, a position that had enabled him to travel extensively in India and abroad. With the passion and energy of youth and the self-assurance of an officer on first-name terms with the high and mighty in Delhi, he was uniquely qualified to transform radically the way the MP police had functioned until then. In the seven years that he headed it, he altered, modified and reorganized every facet of policing and law enforcement in the state, thus upgrading a medieval police into a highly respected modern force. The values and concepts that he instituted in the force continued to define the MP police for decades to come. His journal, published posthumously, reveals a man of extraordinary sensitivity, imbued with a deep sense of humanism and an unquenchable thirst for knowledge.

Shortly after I joined Khargone, Rustamji visited it for inspection, along with the range DIG, a former teacher of physics, who had joined the IPS as an emergency appointee. He spent three days in the district, inspecting the various units. He would also stop at wayside tea shops and small village markets to get a general sense of what the people had to say about local police officials. Unlike most officers, his interaction with the police rank and file was warm and friendly and it did not go unappreciated by the latter. Having taken over only recently as the IGP of the sprawling state after a long tenure in the IB, he seemed to be himself engaged in a learning process. Incidentally, he was the only police chief to visit every district and most police stations in the state. This was in sharp contrast to his predecessor, who had confined his visits to those forest districts that had plenty of shikar and picnic spots. According to protocol, I invited him for lunch at my house to which he happily agreed provided it was a small affair.

He enjoyed going around our incipient garden with my wife, sharing with her many stories of his own early life as a young SP at Khandwa, just starting to raise a family. In the process, he offered her bits of advice on gardening and running the household, while I kept the other guests company. The hospitality was not one-sided. The IGP invariably reciprocated the gesture whenever the SP visited the state capital. In contrast, these days, huge and expensive parties are arranged at the local circuit house for visiting officers, where the SP is notionally the host, but the expenses are met from funds raised by subordinate officers through some very dubious means. Rustamji also told my wife that, when he returned to Khandwa with the Bombay girl he had married, his officers had engaged a local band to play the then-popular Hindi movie song *Main Bombay se dulhania laya re* (I have brought back a bride from Bombay). He followed my later career with fond interest and was particularly supportive of my performance in the critical years when I held charge as the DGP in a militancy-ridden Punjab.

No description of a district inhabited by the Bhil tribal people would be complete without speaking of their colourful *bhaguria* fairs during Holi. A carefree people and very fond of dance and music, the Bhils celebrate Holi with great abandon, getting drunk on a potent locally brewed liquor. The celebrations last a week with village fairs and haats attracting hordes of brightly clad young men and women, showing off their finery and, more importantly, their youthful and lithe bodies. While the women gaze bashfully from behind their scarves at the men, the latter break into wild dances to the beat of drums, displaying their physical agility. When a man and a woman feel attracted to each other, they smear each other's faces with *gulal* (red colour). This gesture is a prelude to marriage. They then take off to the forests for what can only be called a prenuptial honeymoon, after which they settle down as husband and wife, except that the bridegroom must recompense the bride's parents in the shape of goods or physical labour. The Bhils are a highly volatile people and, therefore, require a heavy police presence to keep the peace though, of course, they are not criminal by nature. On the contrary, they are a charming and loveable people.

A regular and detailed inspection of police stations—the basic unit of service delivery to the people—is an important part of an SP's functional charter. No other administrative unit is so often and so thoroughly put through a process of scrutiny and appraisal as an Indian police station. The annual inspection by an SP is indeed a trying experience for the SHO, whose further advancement in the service depends on the former's assessment of his professional competence. So the latter does all he can to satisfy the boss not only by his performance but also by looking after his creature comforts. Police stations, which are otherwise notoriously dirty, unkempt and ill-equipped, are scrupulously dusted, scrubbed, whitewashed and painted, courtesy an obliging contractor. Furniture, crockery and cutlery are taken on loan. The inspection starts with a parade and some drill exercises by the few men present, after which the inspecting officer goes around the police station building, randomly checks a few registers, then takes his seat and picks up a register from a pile neatly stacked on a side table. While the SP is busy looking into these tomes, the SHO and most of his staff disappear, soon to reappear, walking in single file, led by the SHO, with trays laden with biscuits, pastries, samosas, fruit and, most importantly, cashew nuts, called 'promotion nuts' in police parlance.

I was to witness this elaborate drill so many times that I finally learnt not to get impatient but to take it in my stride. I would just wait for the ritual to be over before getting on with the job though I would often tell my officers that my visit was meant to assess the quality of service they provided to the community, not their hospitality. Even more awkward was the settlement of expenses incurred at the end of the visit. While the SHO would insist that there were no dues to be paid, I would ask for a detailed bill, which, when finally produced after much discussion, would amount to a ridiculously low sum. The officer may well be right in claiming that no payment was due because the provisions were in all likelihood sourced gratis from the local baniya in return for favours, past or future. I found such situations both funny and awkward. Perhaps some officers did actually like such lavish hospitality and the poor SHO did not want to be caught on the wrong foot. Having failed to convince my staff that I truly did not want all that *khatir tawazo* (lavish entertaining), I started carrying a lunch box with me on tours. My driver would produce a reasonably appetizing meal, which he and I would consume with relish, though it caused much glee and amusement among my colleagues and subordinates.

After about two and a half years in Khargone, I was

nominated to attend the first advanced six-month course for IPS officers to be held in the CPTC at Mount Abu from June 1960. This course had been conceived as a mid-term refresher-cum-advanced-course for SP-level officers to enable them to pick up new ideas and practices in the fast-developing sphere of policing and management sciences. Although it was like going to school again, I looked forward to visiting my old haunts in Mount Abu. The flip side was that we had to vacate the SP's house and find a place where my wife and daughter could stay because families were not allowed at the CPTC. My wife finally parked herself in Delhi with her sister. Arriving at the CPTC, I was pleasantly surprised to find nine of my old batchmates in the course, and we happily sat up late into the night sharing our experiences of the intervening years.

In the six years that we had been away from Mount Abu, much had changed in the CPTC as well as in the town. The entire senior staff had been given new designations: the commandant was now the director. His next in command was Deputy Director Eric Stracey, who looked after all training courses, including ours. The posts of the chief drill instructor and chief law instructor had been upgraded to assistant directors (ADs), outdoor and indoor, respectively. While the good old R. Deb continued to look after indoor training, the portly but jovial Davenport was the outdoor AD. Stracey and Davenport, both Anglo-Indians, now virtually handled all the various tasks that the matchless Roderigues used to do. Davenport had a quiet but incisive sense of humour. Once when he found the short-statured Kailashpati holding his rifle dangerously close to his groin, he gently cautioned him to watch out lest he damage a vital and irreplaceable part of his manly equipment. Davenport's daughter, Elizabeth, a pretty, outgoing girl and a national-level athlete, provided a much-needed glamorous touch to the drab all-male environment. The director was G.K. Handoo, the tall and handsome Kashmiri who had accompanied Nehru on his tour of Chhatarpur district, where I was then the ASP. He was famous for his shock of silvery-white hair, and, with his exceptionally lithe body, he was as energetic as ever and could out-dance any trainee on club evenings. He was soon to leave for Goa to join the high-powered team then engaged in planning military action against that Portuguese enclave on India's west coast. Bahadur Singh, the much-loved riding master, had left and so had the doctor of the dirty-stories fame; the army man was still there but somewhat reticent now in his relations with us, presumably because of our seniority.

As for the town, which was a part of the tourist-friendly state of Rajasthan, it now received many times more visitors than before, thus adding considerably to the number of lodges and eating places. One of the very few coffee shops at which some of us used to hang out back in 1953—not so much for a cup of coffee as for a chance to flirt with the shop-owner's daughter—was no longer in business; the father had died and the girl had married a local trader. What a let-down, many of us quietly grumbled! The rules and etiquette for the Mess were also more flexible, allowing non-IPS officers to be invited to its functions. The local club had been activated and attendance was made compulsory for CPTC trainees. We were lodged in a separate Mess and mercifully did not have to observe as many restrictions as the probationers. We were now required to engage in individual research work, write book reviews and hold discussions on topical police subjects in peer groups. I chose the popular novel *Lolita* by Vladimir Nabokov for the review, and I still recall the assortment of suppressed giggles it caused among my listeners. We often had night-long sessions of telling dirty stories as is common in courses comprised of single men. This was long before women were admitted into the IPS.

Midway through the course, we set out on what was called 'Bharat darshan' to visit police institutions and meet police chiefs and their colleagues in several states. This notably included the cities of Delhi, Bombay, Bangalore, Madras and Calcutta. In Delhi, we were presented to the high and mighty of the land—the president, the vice president, the prime minister and the redoubtable B.N. Mullik, the all-powerful director of the IB. Typically, we were expected to stand at attention and avidly lap up all the wisdom dispensed by the great men. As we had been taught strictly to avoid talking about our colleagues, we were taken aback to hear the philosopher-politician S. Radhakrishnan, the vice president, talking adversely about the way Nehru handled the Kashmir issue. As for Nehru, reputedly a voluble speaker, the great man was amazingly unfocused and off colour while addressing us. Perhaps, he had not been properly briefed by his advisors, or, perhaps, IPS probationers did not rank very high in his scheme of things. President Rajendra Prasad was agonizingly uncommunicative but the food served was marvellous.

Train travel through the length and breadth of this vast land can be fun except that we were expected to perform the customary 3S drill before we detrained at the other end, and this could be taxing, given the state of hygiene in railway toilets. For some of us north Indians, it was our first sight of the sea and for many, the very first visit to a nightclub or a striptease joint. Bangalore was still largely an old-world bungalow town with leafy streets and verdant gardens, where one could do the sights of the city on foot. Madras had a distinctly civilized flavour that north Indian cities lacked. Calcutta offered amusements of a different, and more tantalizing, kind. But it was the time-honoured Bengali penchant for intellectual disputations over excellent coffee, which remained etched in my mind for many years. A brief visit to Sonagachi, the well-known Calcutta red-light area, at the suggestion of a friend, who was apparently quite familiar with such beguiling diversions—including the precaution of buying, from a corner shop, a prophylactic, then called an FL for some strange reason—was eminently forgettable. This was long before the term 'condom' became common in a more liberated India.

After completing the course, I was posted as SP, Bhilai, an up-and-coming industrial town in eastern MP. It was typical of Mr Rustamji to look far into the future and carefully work out a different policing structure for the area, comprising a city-centric system, distinct from the one based on the Police Act, 1861. He visualized a structure consisting of specially trained, quick-reaction police contingents, ready to move in at short notice and deal with situations of labour and industrial unrest, and of a modern, technology-driven control room, directing and controlling the operations. The SP was to be relieved of all routine duties that kept him bound to his office. This bold departure from the prevailing model did not last long because the civil bureaucracy saw in this initiative an incipient police commissionerate system, always an anathema to them. Mr Rustamji realized that a futuristic police service had to be officer-oriented rather than a force relying mainly on constables, who at that time constituted over 95 per cent of its numbers, although a constable had no real powers under the law and served merely to provide muscle and coercive power.

He proposed that an adequate number of posts of assistant sub-inspectors be created to take over city police duties from constables. This far-seeing proposal, however, failed to find favour with a hidebound bureaucracy, thereby perpetuating the old and antiquated system of policing.

In February 1961, Jabalpur and its adjoining districts were racked by serious Hindu–Muslim riots. Originating in Jabalpur over an alleged incident of the rape of a Hindu girl by a Muslim man, incidents of killing and arson by Hindus and Muslims against each other spread rapidly to a large swathe of territory in central MP, taking a heavy toll on life and property. This was the worst carnage the state had experienced so far and it took nearly two months for the combined efforts of the MP police and the Central forces to bring the situation under control. In June 1961, I was moved to Sagar, one of the more severely affected districts. Having earlier served only in princely India, where people were excessively servile to the ruler but rude and hostile to his officials, this was my first posting to a district which had formerly been a part of British India. Here, the SP was treated with due deference, and visitors rarely came calling without prior appointment.

Some of the most eminent IP officers had served as SPs in Sagar, an important district in British India. It had been badly affected by the menace of gang dacoity, originating in the neighbouring princely states that were notorious for sheltering them. I would listen spellbound as groups of villagers would speak excitedly about the heroic deeds of Quinn Young, who was SP, Sagar, for seven long years until he opted to go back home in 1946. He would rush to the scene of crime in his old Ford Model T, accompanied by a couple of men hastily picked up on the way, as soon as a report of a grave crime was received, and he would not leave the scene until the offenders were nabbed or operational plans and strategies had been put in place for the purpose. Since there was little hope of obtaining armed police assistance from the headquarters, he would raise patrol parties of young villagers, armed with locally available muzzle-loading guns and lathis, and lead them to comb the forests in search of the offenders. Evidently, he put up with the primitive living conditions out of a deep sense of duty. I would have found it impossible to survive for more than a day in those conditions.

Sagar or Saugor, as the British called it, was situated along the old trade route from north India to the Deccan, and had been turned into a district in the second half of the nineteenth century. It formed part of a region seriously afflicted by the menace of thuggee and dacoity, and thus had a lot of history behind it, including a brief association with Sir William Sleeman, who is credited with the eradication of these two pernicious forms of crime. Sleeman operated from the town for a couple of years before his office was shifted to Jabalpur. Imbued with a keen sense of history, Mr Rustamji would often talk at length about Sleeman and his times. It was at his suggestion that I located the now-dilapidated house on a hilltop, which had been occupied by Sleeman during the late 1820s. Sleeman was to spend the next few years of his remarkable life in Jabalpur, collecting and collating intelligence about the many deadly gangs of thugs and dacoits, which were then operating with impunity in large tracts of central and western India. It was an unusual situation that needed special responses to contain and eliminate the menace. Sleeman rose to the occasion and often functioned as investigator, prosecutor and judge, all rolled into one, to bring this evil fraternity to book.

Sagar was still defined by its rolling hills, dense forests and its old-world rest houses from the Raj days, and it exuded an air of quaint charm. The local zamindar came calling with small offerings of local products, as he used to do in the days of British rule. Shikar camps were a regular feature every winter as were the tented winter tours of district officers. The novelist John Masters had done a posting in Sagar for training in jungle warfare before moving to another MP town, Chhindwara, for advanced commando training. No wonder then, that his early novels evoke so faithfully the local landscape. This lent a special aura to the place and I often wandered around the jungles of Malthone and Lalitpur to explore the many landmarks that form the backdrop of his early work. Konpara, a small village in Sagar, forms the backdrop to *The Venus of Konpara*, one of the last of Master's Indian novels. When Sleeman finally moved to Simla from Jabalpur after the successful completion of his thuggee operations, he travelled in a large convoy, consisting of horses, camels and bullock carts, through the Sagar countryside. He wrote a fascinating account of his long and adventurous journey through some of the most dangerous territory in central India. This very evocative travelogue, published under the title *Rambles and Recollections of an Indian Civilian*, is now virtually unavailable, except a copy in the Police Academy at Sagar or with the IB in Delhi.

Soon after I moved to Sagar, Rustamji made a visit to take stock of the post-riot situation. This was only the first of several visits that he was to make to Sagar, of which he was rather fond, having had his district training there in 1939 as a young IP officer. As he put it in his usual crisp style, my principal mission in Sagar was to re-establish normalcy in the working of the police and to restore the morale of the force, shattered so badly during the riots. He also wanted me to prepare an expansion plan for the city police, which had stayed frozen to its pre-Independence levels of just two police stations, to serve the city's growing population. The government had sanctioned an overall increase in the police of 11 per cent across the board, and it was up to the IGP to distribute the resultant accrual among the affected districts. Sagar city got two more police stations, the first-ever expansion in its police strength since its formation.

The towns of Sagar and Jabalpur were notorious for hoodlums, toughs and bullies—goondas in police parlance—who made their living from the sale of illicit liquor, gambling, extortion, blackmail and disposal of stolen property. Not having adequate faith in the ability of the police to protect them against such gangsters, local businessmen readily paid protection money to these gangs to be allowed to carry on their business, unmolested by petty criminals. The police chose to turn a blind eye to such lawlessness because the hooligans enjoyed political patronage. One such ruffian even published a rag of a newspaper, mainly to blackmail prominent citizens and junior officials. The reigning gangster of that time was a short, wiry man of indeterminate age, who wore a silk dhoti-kurta and a huge turban on his head for increased effect. Soon after I took over, he visited me one evening to assure me of his support and total cooperation to my staff in whichever way I required. This was a rather strange offer though I had been duly briefed about the man. I told him plainly that my officers were strong enough to enforce the law in the full sense of the term. He got the message. Some self-styled activists used to write, on a board in front of the kotwali, the so-called 'news' of the day, naming some businessman or government official for purposes of blackmail. We seized the display board repeatedly until the practice stopped.

Besides being afflicted by the scourge of gang dacoity and gangster-ism, Sagar was also the seat of the state's oldest university with a large student population, which needed careful handling during spells of student unrest. There was a sizeable presence of the Indian army in the cantonment, and the SP had to use considerable tact in maintaining a delicate relationship between the army and the police. As SPs wore only a state emblem on their shoulders, the army people ranked them rather low in the hierarchical order, and it took them some time and a couple of mishaps involving their officers, to realize that the SP did indeed enjoy more administrative clout than an army major. All these factors added considerably to the importance of the district from the policing angle. Sagar was also a major training district for young IPS and state service officers. Some of the officers trained during my time rose to occupy top positions in the state and Union governments.

The British found Sagar an appropriate place, strategically and climatically, to base a large cantonment there early during their rule. After Independence came the need to guard the new frontiers with Pakistan, so, most of the army fighting units were moved out, but the Mahars, one of the oldest regiments, held on to their regimental centre in Sagar. The MRC (Mahar Regiment Centre) Mess, housed in a massive nineteenth-century building with lime and mud walls, some ten feet thick, was a heritage building of note. Since prohibition was in force, this Mess was a favourite watering hole for the collector and me. Indian army authorities, generally dismissive of civilian officers in matters of professional competence, are nevertheless gracious hosts at a social level. A visit to the MRC Mess, under its gracious commandant Colonel Man Singh, a veteran soldier from Patiala, was indeed a most pleasant experience. As frequent guests at their Mess functions, we were looked after very well indeed, with the Mess secretary always close at hand to offer us refills. B.P. Pathak, the collector, who had an infinite capacity for consuming liquor without any visible effect, would gleefully inform our hosts that all the liquor they poured in his glass made its way straight to his stomach without passing through his head!

In early 1963, after the brief India–China war, Sagar's sedate social life suddenly brightened up with the arrival in town of a battle-weary infantry brigade for training and recuperation. Brigadier Barua, the commander and his staff officers, Vohra and Mann, made the best of their short stay at the peace station and painted the town red. The army wives too—as is their wont—did not let their men down in the enterprise, with the tall and stately Janak, Vohra's wife, leading the pack. A fresh new spirit of liveliness swept over the dull social scene in the cantonment town with sports functions, dance evenings at the newly renovated local club, and picnics galore. Sadly, this festive break did not last long and the town returned to its staid self when the brigade moved out as suddenly as it had arrived. I ran into Vohra decades later, now a major general and posted as chief of staff with the Jalandhar Corps, when I was DGP, Punjab.

D.P. Mishra, VC, Saugor University, as it was still called, had had a long political career. He was the first home minister of Central Provinces after Independence. However, he had to quit office in 1951 when he offended the egotistical Nehru by siding with P.D. Tandon, who had been elected Congress president against Nehru's wishes. It took him twelve long years to be reinstated in the party in 1963 and to take over as CM of MP.

As a former home minister, D.P. Mishra was still held in some awe by Sagar officialdom. He transacted his official business mostly at home in a large room, half of which was occupied by an enormous divan, swathed in white sheets with huge Indian-style cushions to recline on. It was here that he received me when I called on him formally. I found him in a relaxed mood, half-lying and half-sitting on the divan, with his trademark cigar in the ashtray beside him and a thick book lying face down nearby. I remember these details because this is how I always found him several years later when he finally settled down in Jabalpur, after quitting active politics, to write the story of his life in two volumes titled *Living an Era: India's March to Freedom*, a fascinating account of a crucial period in Indian political history. There was always a cigar in the ashtray and a book forever open and lying nearby. Incidentally, he never forgot to present me a fine Havana during my visits to Jabalpur.

I was in uniform and saluted him stiffly when ushered into his presence. He half got up to shake hands with me and motioned me to take a seat, which I occupied as expected of a junior officer in the presence of a dignitary, that is, on the very edge of the chair. Soon the telephone rang and while he was speaking to the caller, I surveyed the garishly furnished room. He spoke to me in a soft, unhurried, husky voice—as would a man who was assured of being listened to—about the few problems that the university presented. But he was much more forthcoming on the history and politics of the freedom movement, delicately avoiding any reference to Nehru, though he did mention his association with his father, Motilal. He also mentioned, rather deprecatingly, that most visitors, including senior officers, insisted on touching his feet, much as he disliked the practice. This raised him greatly in my estimation. Presently,

B.R. Mandal, the collector at that time, and the principal of PTC turned up, the latter in uniform. Both of them proceeded to touch the great man's feet, a practice he had deplored just minutes earlier. Far from showing any disapproval of this form of obeisance, he seemed quite pleased with it.

G.P. Bhatt, a former high court chief justice, who had succeeded D.P. Mishra as VC, was so fond of his own voice that he never let go any occasion where he could speak endlessly on mostly inane subjects. Having had to keep his mouth shut for so long, the judge was probably making up for lost time.

B.P. Pathak, who succeeded Mandal as collector, Sagar, had joined as a deputy collector but rose rapidly in service by virtue of his intrinsic common sense, helped considerably by the correct caste and political affiliations. He was a hugely popular district magistrate (DM) with his police colleagues because of his matter-of-fact approach to law-and-order issues. Once, a suspect allegedly died in police custody in Behrol police station and my DIG insisted that the SHO be placed under suspension without waiting for the result of the magisterial inquiry. Pathak told me to inform my DIG that he himself, as DM, would personally inquire into the incident, pending which, any action against the SHO would be improper. 'Your DIG is a *baccha*. He does not realize the full implications of the case,' he added and asked me to set up an inquiry the following day. Early next morning, we reached the police station where the DM proceeded to examine the witnesses, who were already assembled there. When I asked him why he was not recording the evidence, he told me, 'The DM does not have to record the proceedings; he only gives his finding on the overall sense of evidence.' In the end, he found all the allegations against the SHO and his staff baseless.

The MP PTC, set up for induction training of police sub-inspectors in the early twentieth century, as part of the overall reorganization of the Indian police, was housed in an ancient fort in Sagar. During the Raj, training institutions were staffed by the very best officers. After Independence, however, training jobs, which lacked the creature comforts of the district charges, lost much of their attraction. Relations between the PTC principal—called the 'Qila Kaptan'—and the SP—called the 'Zila Kaptan'—often came under strain as the former was totally reliant on the district for orderlies and vehicles. The ingenuity of both officers was severely tested by a proper management of interpersonal relations. An important event in the PTC calendar was the annual passing-out parade of sub-inspector cadets, in which the state police chief traditionally took the salute, but later, the privilege was extended, improperly to my mind, to the CM. This was also the time for the police chief and his senior colleagues to take stock of police performance in the year gone by and to plan for the future in a relaxed environ, away from the prying eyes of politicians and the media.

A festive spirit prevailed during the week-long event, called the College Week, which consisted of sports competitions, dinners and *burra khanas* galore. A tented township was set up in front of the circuit house to accommodate visiting officers, including the DIGs, then a powerful rank, next only to the chief. Given the piteously meagre resources, the local police had to beg, borrow or steal most items of furniture, such as commodes, buckets, bedsteads, side tables, carpets and tea sets, from the town, to set up this temporary township. Police officers can be awfully mean in demanding the best amenities. One particular DIG made it a point to carefully check the furniture in other tents to see that his tent was as well furnished as the others. Older residents of the town recalled the British-era College Weeks with unabashed nostalgia. Oddly, however, it was the principal who received all the praise and thanks, not my officers who had made it all possible.

The police had come to play a crucial role during the last few years of British rule as the Indian freedom struggle peaked. The new rulers of independent India, however, were not very fond of the police, and the early post-Independence years witnessed a substantial downgrading of the service in decision-making processes. A few decades down the line, though, when the security situation in the country deteriorated badly, the IPS regained some of its earlier clout with the government. But in the early 1960s, a visiting CM would hardly look at the SP before going off with the collector to attend some function in the town or the countryside. Dr K.N. Katju, almost senile and very absent-minded but close to Nehru like many other Kashmiri Pandits, was then the CM. He once mistook the city superintendent of police (CSP) of Indore for the DIG of Jabalpur, merely because both of them were Sikh. In another instance, when a junior minister in his cabinet met him in Jabalpur and told him that he was Dashrath Jain, the CM innocently remarked that there was also a minister in his cabinet by the same name.

District officers were not expected to dance attendance on government ministers during their tours. What is more, the latter seldom held it against the officers if they did not turn up unless specifically sent for. Once, when a senior minister, Mathura Prasad Dube, lost his temper for not having been provided with a pilot vehicle to escort him into town late at night, I walked off, telling him plainly that there was no provision in the budget for such duties and that I would not have anyone make unreasonable complaints about my officers. What had really upset the minister was the fact that his car had been stopped for checking just outside the town by Central Excise, as they had information that a large consignment of opium was to be illegally transported in a big car, and the minister was travelling in just such a car. And since the excise officials were in khaki uniforms, he had presumed they were policemen, while they refused to listen to his claim that he was a minister. A couple of months later, by which time he had understood the situation, he was gracious enough to apologize to me when he came to Morena, my new district charge.

Sometime in June 1963, when I had barely completed two years in Sagar and looked forward to another year in that beautiful district, Rustamji called to tell me that the government planned to post me to Morena, then severely affected by gang dacoity, and wanted to know if I had any reservations. 'None whatsoever, sir, except that I would have to take my four-year-old daughter out of the school that she has recently joined. But that can be managed.' I also added after a pause, 'Sir, officers have often moved from Morena to Sagar, this must be the first move in the opposite direction.' The IGP merely gave a delighted chuckle. This kind of exchange between an SP and a police chief would be unthinkable these days but, in the good old days, it was normal to sound out an officer about an untimely or inconvenient posting. I was not too happy to leave a place with which I had virtually fallen in love, and also because the move involved putting our child into the school hostel. This arrangement did not work for long and we had to deprive our young daughter of decent elementary schooling during my Morena posting. But that, of course, was part of service protocol and I never held it as a grudge.

We arrived in Morena one hot June afternoon by road from Sagar. The change from the green, rolling hills and dense forests of Sagar to the drab, dreary, dusty and scorching landscape of my new district could not have been more unsettling. But I had a job to do and nothing else mattered. The SP's official residence was situated adjacent to a grain godown, overrun with rats grown to a monstrous size, thanks to the plentiful supply of food. When they got fed up with devouring raw grain, they would turn their attention to the SP's kitchen and pantry. We found to our dismay that the moment we left the table after meals, swarms of rats would take over. It was impossible to sleep at night because of the forays by curious rat families into our bedroom. As we were located close to the district courts and the main market, there was never any respite from the din and filth of an overgrown village, which the town in reality was. Then there was the stench of bird droppings from the flocks of birds of all kinds that populated the many trees in the front courtyard. The difference between this and the Sagar house was hugely depressing.

The IGP called up the next day to ask me in a lighter vein about the very same rats and promised to find a way out. As it happened, a house built for the collector had remained unoccupied since he did not wish to move there for some reason. So, the new house was allotted to the SP and we happily moved out of the rat-infested and stench-ridden house to our new abode, thenceforth the official residence of the SP. This provided my wife with the chance of a lifetime to plan the garden of her dreams for the new house. It took her some time to feel at home in an environment of fear and insecurity, typical of any dacoity area. She told me later that she used to keep a pair of scissors under her pillow at night as a weapon of defence in case of any mishap! Anti-dacoity work is demanding but not without its thrills. Mr Rustamji used to say that a dacoity-area tenure is like attending a staff college course in the armed forces: it promotes professional maturity, agility of mind and body, and instils a dynamic vision in the officer.

Morena district, a thin slice of territory, stretched from the north-east to the south-west. It was all length and little width, for the most part lying along the Chambal River, which formed the boundary between MP and Rajasthan, and was a strange amalgam of three different kinds of terrains. The three eastern tehsils were like the adjoining district of Bhind: fertile farming country but criss-crossed by ravines that had for long served as hideouts for the many ferocious dacoit gangs active in the region. The central segment was comprised of dense forests, hillocks and streams with miles of impassable paths, called *khos*, between them. During the rainy season all such places became inaccessible except by an extended and punishing journey on foot. The Sheopur subdivision in the extreme south-west, some three hundred miles from Morena, was part forest and part farming country but akin and much nearer to Shivpuri than to Morena. Several police stations were easier to access from Gwalior or Shivpuri. So, I sent up a proposal for the dismantling of the district by parcelling it between Bhind, Gwalior and Shivpuri districts. Some friends thought it was a ploy to get out of a difficult posting.

Anti-dacoity operations are especially complex in areas lying along interstate borders due to the differing functional styles and strategies in the individual states. Across the Chambal River lay Dholpur, a subdivision in Rajasthan's Bharatpur district, of which Narain Singh, a much-decorated DSP, was then in charge. His nameplate mentioned in detail all the various decorations that had been awarded to him during his long service. A typical anti-dacoity specialist, Singh believed in eliminating dacoits rather than the crime of dacoity and, in this, he enjoyed the full support of his senior officers. Our state, on the contrary, disapproved of any unlawful approach to anti-dacoity work, though some dubious deals did take place on the sly. My firm aversion to police brutality and the illicit killing of alleged criminals marked the way I functioned in MP. This stayed inviolate even when I was posted, two decades later, as DGP, Punjab, then torn by a vicious wave of Sikh militancy. Beyond Dholpur lay the Agra district of UP, where the police were known to turn a blind eye to crime, so long as their areas remained unaffected. Although the DIGs of Agra and Jaipur were both very cordial towards me, the clash of basic principles remained unresolved.

Gang dacoity and banditry are endemic to the Chambal valley. The feats of SP Freddie Young in battling Sultana Daku are part of village folklore in the regions from Agra to Gwalior. In village *chaupal*s, local residents speak with awe of the audacity of successive generations of dacoits. The last of these legendary dacoits was Man Singh of the enormous white whiskers, who had acquired a Robin Hood–like image of chivalry and munificence over the several years during which he had operated in the area. He was shot dead in 1955 by a crack company, of about 130 officers and men, commanded by Bhau Sahib Shinde of MP SAF in the Chambal ravines in Bhind district. When Man Singh's dead body was brought to Bhind town for post-mortem formalities, thousands of curious spectators from far and near thronged to get a glimpse of the dreaded dacoit. After his death, the problem grew worse as his gang split into two along caste lines, a Brahmin gang under Roopa and a Thakur gang under Lakhan Singh. The bitter rivalry between these former members of Man Singh's gang enabled the police to liquidate them one by one. However, this too failed to put an end to the menace as the residual gangs split further into several caste-based gangs. When I joined as SP, Morena, thirteen major gangs, each representing a caste or a sub-caste group, roamed the district.

The most fearsome was the Gujjar gang of Mohar Singh, consisting of some ninety members, while Madho Singh, Nathu Singh and Chhida–Makhan led smaller but no less fearsome gangs of Bhadoria, Tomar and Sikarwar Thakurs, respectively. Backward castes, like Kachhis, Kurmis and Jatavs, too had their own dacoit gangs. All these gangs received ample support from their caste-fellows in a mutually beneficial arrangement. A caste group not backed by a dacoit gang was virtually defenceless in village feuds and land disputes. Much like tigers, major gangs refrained from operating in territories that were apportioned to other gangs under a long-standing rule of thumb, although inter-gang rivalries and clashes were not unknown, which the police fully exploited for operational purposes. To maintain secrecy, dacoit gangs were allotted code numbers, priority being accorded to their *seniority* as dacoits or the degree of severity of their crimes. Thus PE1 (Public Enemy # 1) would be the most dangerous, followed by PE2, PE3, and so on. When PE1 was eliminated, PE2 would be *promoted* to the first place. I often received indignant letters from gangs, who had been listed lower down in this roll of infamy, threatening to carry out a spate of murders if they were not immediately *promoted* to a higher category!

Princely India had had a rough and ready solution to the

dacoity problem. Gwalior rulers would just have the suspects rounded up and publicly hanged from time to time. They had no use for due process or the rule of law. This had not ended the menace and the crimes had continued to grow. Systematic and organized anti-dacoity operations really began when K.F. Rustamji took over as IGP, MP, in mid-1958. He made an in-depth study of the problem and how it had defied all efforts of eradication. Departing from conventional wisdom that only hardened SPs, risen from the ranks, could handle dacoity districts, he posted young IPS officers, hailing from outside MP, as SPs, with remarkable results. In 1959, a former army general initiated a move to bring about the surrender of dacoits. A few dacoits did surrender, Man Singh's sons Tahsildar Singh and Lukka Brahmin among them. Vinoba Bhave, the noted Gandhian, embarked on a walkathon in the area in support, raising grave issues of security for him and his companions. Rustamji was firmly opposed to conditional surrenders by hardened criminals since the process seriously undermined both the rule of law and police morale. He publicly questioned the very idea of such surrenders and the move was hastily abandoned, enabling the police to resume anti-dacoity operations.

Narsingh Rao Dixit, the powerful deputy home minister, called me shortly after I joined in Morena to tell me that he was delighted to have me as the SP of the most important district in the region. He promised me all help in my efforts to deal with the problem, also obliquely asking me to transfer some SHOs for various reasons. I thanked him for the many good things he had said about me but, as for the transfers, I politely asked him to speak to the IGP or my DIG as I took orders only from those two officers. He grasped the gist of my reply right away and never again intruded in my sphere of work. What is more, he did not hold it against me and remained a lifelong friend. Later, when both of us had retired from our respective careers and settled down in Bhopal, he regularly dropped in at my house once a month for a cup of tea. Which present-day politician is so broad-minded and tolerant of dissent?

Madho Singh was the shrewdest, and Mohar, the most brutal, of the gang leaders then operating in Morena. The dacoit gangs preferred kidnapping for ransom—which was far safer and more lucrative—to dacoity. The kidnapped person's relatives would beg, borrow or steal to raise the huge ransom amount while, in a dacoity, the criminals could carry away only whatever was readily available. Living in jungles all the year round was hard, so some gang leaders would shift base to safe houses in other areas during severe weather conditions. Madho Singh told me later, when I was DIG, Gwalior, that he had often stayed in Delhi and Bombay with his girlfriend, Katori Bai, in hotels or rented lodgings. Madho also often sent letters, written in rustic Hindi, threatening me with dire consequences if overzealous police officers did not stop harassing his supporters. Once, he sent word to me that the new collector tended to stray deep into the forests in pursuit of game and was thereby exposing himself to serious risk. J.N. Kaul, a young, handsome Kashmiri Brahmin, who joined in Morena soon after I did, was an avid shikari and often combined his tours with a bit of sport, a common enough practice those days. Kaul was a welcome change from his predecessor, a rather conceited officer, too conscious of his status to mingle with other officials.

Morena forests were rich in game, both big and small, such as tigers, panthers, bears, black buck and many other types of deer. The area abounded in birds, both indigenous and migratory. The fierce and vicious wild dogs, which hunted in packs, taking on even tigers and panthers, and the Great Indian Bustard, soon to become extinct, were found there. Partridges and other table birds were in abundance all over the place. Whenever you needed them, you just drove out a few miles and brought back a bagful, just as though they were stored in your refrigerator. The presence of so many formidable dacoit gangs had effectively turned the area into a sanctuary for wild animals and birds. Only senior district officers dared enter the forest for shikar. This dubious privilege also extended to state guests who were fond of shikar. It was then for the collector and the SP to ensure that the guest returned happy and satisfied with the shoot, carrying plenty of trophies.

One such VIP visitor was King Mahendra of Nepal, eager to bag some black buck, a handsome but rare species of deer, found aplenty in Morena district. His Majesty was to drive directly from Gwalior to Gaswani forest, earmarked for the shoot. Indian district officers are expected to perform all types of jobs, official and unofficial. So, Collector Kaul and I, charged with making arrangements for the king's shikar trip, reached the spot hours in advance to ensure that everything was in order. While we anxiously awaited the royal arrival, His Majesty was being leisurely massaged and bathed by retainers in Gwalior as we learnt through patchy reports via an antiquated wireless set. The convoy of cars, carrying the royal party, including two expert shikaris, DSPs Ram Singh and Madho Singh, finally showed up at dusk and drove into the forest after a short halt. The king was accompanied by B.N.Verma, ICS, commissioner, Gwalior, and M.K. Rasgotra, the Indian envoy to Nepal, a few years senior to me in Government College, Ludhiana. Rasgotra, who had started pronouncing his name as 'Raasgoutra' after his selection to the IFS, did not so much as look at Kaul and me. We did not, of course, expect the king to notice our presence. In confusion, Kaul gave a smart salute, although, as a civilian, he was not expected to. Only Verma spoke to us briefly. As it happened, all the shots fired by the king from his expensive weapons missed their targets, but Madho Singh and Ram Singh, well-versed in the art of keeping VIP guests happy, did not fail to applaud the shooting skills of the king every time he fired. It is another matter that they had to pay another visit to the area early the next morning to make up for the royal failure and collect the carcasses of several black buck, supposedly shot by His Majesty, and duly present the trophies to him before his departure.

I was not a great shikari, though I loved driving around in the dense forests that dotted the district, accompanied by my driver and orderly, both good shots and keen shikaris, with just three rifles between us. If I happened to hit an animal, the driver, Rahim, a plumpish, pious Muslim, would run at top speed to the wounded animal to administer the final slash with his knife, while reciting the holy Kalima, to ensure that the poor soul did not depart from this world an infidel. Dirt tracks and forest roads that linked many remote police stations were familiar territory to me and I could drive from Pahargarh to Sheopur through Vijaypur, Palpur and Kuno without hitting the main road. This enabled me to visit some of the remotest parts of the district, which the district officers had virtually left to their own devices. Even the IGP and two senior DIGs once drove with me through the forest taking one of those routes and greatly enjoyed the experience. The district was swarming with dacoits, and it was not unusual for an SP to get lost for days in the jungles. I too would make for my favourite forest retreats, such as Palpur or Pahargarh, to dodge awkward queries from faceless babus in the state secretariat and to avoid trying to explain to them that dacoity was a long-festering problem, and that there was no instant solution that I or anyone else could deliver in a short span of time.

Palpur, situated on the banks of the placid Kuno River and unreachable except by a dilapidated forest road, was my favourite hideaway. There, a massive garhi, belonging to the former raja, possessed enough defence to guard against any attack by the many dacoit gangs roaming the area. A fairly comfortable room, overlooking the river, would be my temporary abode and my orderly could rustle up a good meal of chicken and jungle fowl. My only contact with the outside world was through a transistor radio and a wobbly wireless link with other police units. It was at Palpur, via my modest radio set, that I learnt about President John F. Kennedy's assassination and Prime Minister Nehru's death. It was also at Palpur that I had a chance run-in with a tigress, which happened to cross our path, while we were driving back to the garhi after a day's tour of forest villages. The animal ran across the narrow path into a dense grove like a streak of lightning in the failing light and I had just an instant to fire. There was a brief crackling sound in the dry bushes to the right but no further indication of what could have happened to the animal.

We waited for some time and, presuming that the animal had got away, drove back to the garhi. It is always wise to look for a wounded tiger after such an episode. So, we duly sent a search party next morning to find out what had happened to the animal. And, they did find the tigress, dead in a nearby thicket, shot clean through the heart. A chance shot indeed! Needless to say that there was much rejoicing in the camp. The elimination of a predator is celebration time in the insecure rural areas where people fail to understand why the government should show such deep concern for tigers and other killer-animals of the forest, which prey upon their cattle and otherwise make life difficult for them, and spend large sums of money to save them.

Another such episode might indeed have had a tragic end but for the presence of mind of my ASP, Pratap Singh, a skilled shikari. This happened in the Vijaypur forests during a tiger shoot with hordes of beaters making a huge racket with drums and other such tools to drive out the tiger from a nullah. Two machans, overlooking the tiger's probable escape route, seated four of us shikaris. Initial beats drove out only small game. It was towards the evening that a tiger, annoyed by all the noise and clamour, rushed out angrily, determined to teach a lesson to the intruders. Two of us in separate machans fired at the same time and the tiger retreated into the bushy undergrowth in the nullah. We climbed down and, on inspecting the spot, found telltale signs of a wounded tiger—a thick trail of blood and pieces of bone, all indications that the animal was seriously wounded. A friend and I foolishly leapt into the nullah to follow the wounded animal as dusk was settling down. Pratap, acting on an instinct born out of his long experience that a wounded tiger could be an extremely dangerous quarry, went up a nearby tree to have a commanding view of the site. As we entered what was obviously the tiger's lair, it leapt at us in outrage and wrath. We would both have been dead meat but for Pratap's presence of mind. He promptly fired and got the tiger in mid-air. We often recalled the incident light-heartedly though it could have easily ended in disaster. Pratap went on to head the MP police.

Sunil Dutt's film, *Mujhe Jeene Do*, a romanticized account of the dacoit gangs that infested the badlands of Chambal, brought them to public notice all over the country. Since a large part of the film was shot in Morena, I became an instant celebrity with my friends and relatives in distant Punjab who, until then, had thought of me with pity, as someone who was lost in an unknown, poor and backward state. I was often grilled by curious army officers why a few hundred dacoits could not be eliminated by the hundreds of policemen, who had been engaged in the task for decades. I could never convince them that fighting a war against an enemy and carrying out anti-dacoity operations were two very different things. In the latter, there were no enemies, only criminals to be apprehended and brought to justice through due process of law. We were under orders to operate strictly lawfully, though many officers, including some in the IPS, did act illicitly in league with their subordinate staff. Unable to prevent or unearth gruesome offences, we were often tempted to go for the dacoits' families, who lived unguarded in villages and towns nearby, but an unwritten code of conduct always held us back.

An infusion of massive funds stimulates significant economic activity and leads to huge employment potential. Similarly, in insurgency-afflicted areas, dacoity—a concept defined as conflict economy—had become a kind of industry in the region because so many sections of society had acquired a vested interest in its continuance. This included lawyers, arms dealers, petition writers and, of course, the politicians, who relied so much on dacoit gangs during elections. Even police departments were not averse to exploiting the situation. For one, it enabled the police to obtain enormous funds, manpower, vehicles, police stations and other such services but, above all, it brought recognition to police officials in the form of a rich haul of medals, whether genuine or fake. Dacoity-area SPs soon got used to being treated as a special breed and could usually be recognized by their swagger and affectations. Years later, during a study visit to New Scotland Yard in London, I found police commanders in charge of the more notorious London suburbs affecting a similar air of snobbery. It would appear that the status of a police officer among his peers is defined by the degree of notoriety of the area managed by him.

The quest for medals in the dacoity area takes many forms, the most contentious being 'encounters', real or fake. While real encounters were not unknown, most of the successful operations in anti-dacoity were carried out through what was called *hikmat amli*, intelligent planning, rather than open clashes with the gangs. In many cases, informers killed the dacoits in their sleep or poisoned an entire gang, and the police then came on the scene in strength to claim the dead bodies. An elaborate plan of action would then be drawn up, detailing the sequence of events from the time the information was supposed to have been received by the SP. All these various details had to be dovetailed with the requisite entries in the many registers kept at the concerned thana—an intricate process but necessary to forestall future inquiries. Police subordinates with long tenures in the area excelled in drafting encounter reports that were difficult to fault unless senior officers had had personal experience of the nitty-gritty of anti-dacoity work. Some SPs even *set up* an encounter so as to receive the news about the killing of some notorious dacoit in the midst of a conference in Bhopal, thus earning compliments aplenty from the IGP and other officers. Shrewd SPs would also include their DIG in the reward report, thus minimizing the chances of exposure. Occasionally, however, when such actions went wrong through lack of tying up all the loose ends, the police would indeed land in serious trouble.

A DSP in Morena once had to face murder charges when he killed some suspects, who had been kept in illegal custody in a thana and provided with daily meals by relatives.

By the 1960s, the award of a medal or two, whether fake or real, had become a normal office perk for dacoity-area SPs and the practice had gained acceptability among top officers. Encounter reports were only loosely scrutinized to let even patently specious medal proposals go through. Subordinate officers would carefully set up an encounter situation in which the SP could be shown as having exhibited exceptional courage so as to deserve a medal, without having been exposed to any real danger. A common ploy was to carry the officer's cap to the site of the encounter. A bullet-riddled cap was evidence enough to prove the officer's outstanding bravery in a fictitious encounter. Sometimes, encounters had to be staged for other reasons too. Thus, when Madho Singh seized the uncle of the Congress MLA Nawal Kishore Garg in 1964, expecting a huge ransom, the MLA pestered the IGP so much that he told me to do something urgently. I asked all my officers to get the old dear released by whatever means. Sub-Inspector Dixit, an old anti-dacoity hand, and SHO, Pahargarh, persuaded the gang to release the old man without ransom, using all their contacts in gangland. A release could, however, be made possible only through the payment of ransom or an encounter. So, an elaborate plan was chalked out to stage a dramatic encounter in the jungles of Pahargarh where the SP himself had to be present to reclaim the MLA's kin. I had to participate willy-nilly in the charade but, to my subordinates, who had so cleverly plotted the whole episode, the occasion was tailor-made for yielding a number of gallantry medals, if a clever-enough encounter report were prepared.

Not one to dissemble, I promptly spilt the beans when the DIG called to congratulate me on the basis of the wireless message flashed by my deputy, thus putting paid to the hopes of my staff. Even if an informer was able to give foolproof information—which was rare—and the police parties reached the spot in time to lay siege to the fast-asleep gang, an untimely sneeze or cough could alert the gang and the dacoits would be gone in an instant, at times leaving behind cooked food and booty. In one such botched operation, as the policemen fell upon the abandoned fare, the slain dacoit Lakhan Singh's elder brother, Firangi Singh, who had climbed up a tree in the melee, jumped down and fled for all he was worth.

Kaul and I often went out for night drives when touring together. While most such enterprises ended up as plain shikar trips, one such outing turned out to be rather awkward when we were returning after a night drive in Sheopur. We heard loud cries and shouts from a nearby village and the commotion sounded like an act of dacoity. So we promptly headed for the scene of crime, as is expected from the district top brass. Since Kaul's white shirt was a sure giveaway, Rahim, my driver, hurriedly took off his uniform shirt to be donned by Kaul while Rahim remained bare-chested. By the time we reached the village, the dacoits had gone and we found a few huts on fire. Soon, word went round that we too were part of the same gang. This was an unexpected turn of events and we quickly perceived the danger inherent in the situation. So we hastily took to our heels and returned post-haste to Sheopur, believing that our presence at the site had gone unnoticed. Politically, Sheopur was a highly volatile place where prominent events of the day were depicted neatly on a blackboard kept in the main bazaar. The previous night's episode duly found a prominent mention therein though, mercifully, our role in it remained unmentioned. It was only a matter of time, however, before the juicier parts of the episode came to public notice. Somewhat amused at the unease visible in our bearing, the local SHO assured us that he would manage the situation, hinting that it might be best if we left the place, which we promptly did.

I had now been in this very difficult charge for well over two years and it was time that I got a lighter district for rest and recuperation. Even more than me, my wife was very keen that we moved out of Morena because my daughters were being deprived of proper schooling. In a move that Rustamji called a change of batmen, I was posted to Damoh. Though a considerable comedown from my previous charges, I was not too unhappy because Damoh, one of the most picturesque districts of Bundelkhand, offered plenty of leisure, thick forests and ample game. Gang dacoity, a major problem till the recent past, was now firmly under control. My predecessors used to work only from the bungalow office. So, the district office had no office room for the SP.

When I landed at the district office one day, I found an unusual commotion there as the DSP had had to vacate his room hurriedly, leaving from the back door while I was ushered into his room. That was the last time I visited the district office. Along with a sprawling bungalow, I also inherited a first-rate cook since my predecessor had been exceptionally fond of the good things of life. Unfortunately, my stay in that charming district proved to be short. Before demitting office as IGP, MP, to join the Union government, Mr Rustamji had left a note suggesting that a new force, Border Security Force (BSF), be raised to man the Indo-Pak borders, and that I be given an important assignment in view of my bright record. I was accordingly posted to Bhopal as AIG, SAF. As it was, I spent some six years in Bhopal, first as an AIG and then as SP, Bhopal.

8

Bhopal: The City of Lakes

I took over as AIG, SAF, at Bhopal in October 1965. The two things that define Bhopal are its lakes and the composite Hindu–Muslim culture, shaped by its many begums and their Kayastha ministers. While it still had a long way to go to acquire the various attributes of a city, it offered amenities unthought-of in my previous stations. An elegantly furnished cinema house showed excellent English films, where one could relax with a cup of coffee after a hard day's work. A couple of fine restaurants served as a civilized person's watering hole and, to top it all, there was a well-stocked bookshop, the Lyall bookstore, a sister unit of the one I had known in Ludhiana as a student of English literature, and the famed British Council Library. Ten years ago in Chhatarpur, a doctor friend of mine used to tease me that when Bhopal became the capital of MP, I would surely marry a Bhopal princess. That probability had, of course, long since vanished but I did fall sufficiently in love with the place to settle down there eventually.

At that time, the SAF, armed reserve of the state police, consisted of twenty-one battalions, four of which were deployed in north-east India under army command to combat Naga insurgency, while the rest were located in the dacoity area and big cities to aid and assist the district police as and when required. The command and control functions of the SAF were vested in the DIG, SAF, backed by an AIG and the requisite ministerial and other staff, known as the SAF headquarters, which also controlled motor transport, training and welfare, police radio, mounted police, dog squads, sports and protocol, besides other assorted duties, not specifically allocated to any other section in the police headquarters. As compared to this, now, several ADGs (additional directors general of police), IGs and DIGs handle the same tasks. No doubt, state police commitments in various areas have grown greatly, but a reckless break-up of integral tasks, merely to find berths for a growing cadre of senior officials, is not good for either discipline or morale.

The post of AIG, SAF, was a much-prized posting as he was the only AIG to whom an official vehicle was allotted for carrying out his duties, which included visits to field units and receiving visiting dignitaries on behalf of the IGP. In J.W. Roderigues I had an excellent boss, having known him as a hard taskmaster at Mount Abu where, as the AC, he had virtually initiated us into the IPS. My new job brought me into contact with the men and officers of the SAF, a large section of whom came from the former state armies of Gwalior, Indore and Rewa. They brought with them a cultural baggage that set them apart from the general run of policemen. They spoke a lingo which was liberally strewn with army jargon and soldierly slang, uncharacteristic of a civilian force. Not ordinarily required to deal with criminals, they were relatively free of the wiles and cunning of the thana police. The tradition of a service Mess, unknown earlier in the police, was a welcome legacy of the state armies, inherited from the princely states of Indore and Gwalior.

No account of the MP SAF would be complete without a reference to B.A. Sharma, a former Indore state officer. Also known as Tom, a moniker he had picked up during a brief army attachment a long while ago, Sharma was a compulsive talker about dacoity and shikar, two subjects in which he claimed special expertise. Like Coleridge's Ancient Mariner, he let go no opportunity to buttonhole any listener, willing or unwilling, to ply him with endless tales of his anti-dacoity skills while serving in the Chambal region, where he had been posted for ages. If dacoits were not the subject of his assumed exploits, then it would be tigers and other big game. Among the many yarns that he used to spin with great delight was one of a chance encounter with the wily dacoit Amrit Lal, who occasionally dropped in at the Kuno rest house, where Sharma often made night halts. He had preceded Roderigues as DIG, SAF, and many office files carried telltale marks of his odd functional and linguistic whims. He prided himself on his flair for dictating anti-dacoity operational orders but, to do so, he always needed a pack of Simla cigarettes to puff on and a group of junior officers to applaud him. If his favourite fags were unavailable, no operational orders could be dictated and any planned anti-dacoity action had to be aborted. In 1967, when D.P. Mishra's government was toppled by Congress defectors joining hands with the opposition Bharatiya Jan Sangh (BJS) party, Sharma replaced B.M. Shukul as the IGP. This was the first-ever capricious transfer of a top official in MP though the practice was later to become only too common, thus gravely damaging administrative norms. Mercifully, Sharma's not-too-glorious tenure lasted just over a year but it was long enough for him to weaken critically the core values of the state police which could never be salvaged in full measure.

B.M. Shukul, BM to his friends and admirers, who succeeded Rustamji as IGP, was a remarkably supportive boss.

All those who came in contact with him, even briefly, would instantly become BM fans. It was rare for any person not to be impressed by his sincerity and helpfulness. To us junior officers, laboriously toiling away in remote dacoity districts with meagre resources or trying to cope with complex law-and-order situations in the cities, a telephone call from BM was a most prized event. For he would not only listen attentively to our difficulties but also do his best to help out with resource mobilization from every possible source. As an old hand in the police headquarters, BM was the right-hand man of whichever IGP was in office at that time. When promoted as IGP in 1965, he handled his formidable charge with consummate skill, poise and fortitude. He was to prove a source of enormous strength to me a couple of years later, when my immediate boss turned against me for some petty reason. A most remarkable human being and a policeman par excellence, BM did not forsake his customary cool and good cheer even when he was gravely ill with a serious disease.

R.N. Nagu, the quintessential man for all seasons, held the key post of DIG, administration. Possessing a rare ability for forming and retaining close friendships across all sections of society, he radiated a keen sense of warmth and affectionate charm that could not but win over even the most sceptical individual. His fabulous personnel-management skills set him apart from his peers. The police rank and file firmly believed that he would never deny a legitimate and, often, even an illegitimate request. His *durbari* style of grievance redress had a rationale of its own and, though many of us younger officers looked with some amusement at his way of dealing with supplicants, his popularity in the force was legendary. It was widely believed that no one who approached him with a grievance, especially one who had received the choicest invective from him, would come away unsatisfied.

Although he was not my immediate boss, many of my files landed on his table. We in the SAF were an autonomous unit though, while under Nagu's charge, we had to guard constantly against intrusions by the general branch (GB). Once, we had to oppose strongly the transfer of the post of police welfare officer from SAF to GB. Finally, when the proposal was dropped, I noted on the file, 'It is gratifying to note that the status quo ante has been restored.' Nagu summoned me and asked me why I could not say, simply, 'I am grateful.' I said, 'I only find it *gratifying* to note; that is not the same as being grateful.' 'But what is the damn difference?' he asked, looking intensely at me over his half-spectacles. I thought it was a good chance to show off a little. I said, 'Sir, the difference is the same as that between Tweedledum and Tweedledee.' This foxed him somewhat but he soon regained his usual aplomb and dismissed me. I was sure, though, that thenceforth, my file notings would be read with renewed interest by the all-powerful DIG. That was typical of him—to not let such good-natured retorts stand between friends. The last time I met him was a few days before his death. On learning that he was critically ill, I flew to Bhopal to see him. True to form, he tried to perk up and act his natural old self. He called his son and asked him to get me my usual drink, which he graciously remembered every time I visited him. It was not an occasion for a drink, moreover because he himself would have been unable to join me, but he would accept no excuse. That was the greatness of the man. I returned to Jabalpur deeply troubled and saddened, only to rush back within a week to attend his funeral. Another warm-hearted and kind human being was gone.

As the chief sports officer of MP police, I was responsible for promoting sports in the force and organizing sports events from time to time. We had a fairly strong hockey team and often finished near the top in the All India Police Games. One of our players, Daud Mohammed, who did remarkably well as a Left Out in the Indian national team, then on a tour in Japan, was given an out-of-turn promotion. It would thenceforth become a normal practice. I accompanied the MP contingent for the police games as manager all the three years that I remained posted in the SAF. The most memorable of those outings was to Lucknow in 1968, when we defeated the redoubtable BSF team in the hockey finals. Our boys fought valiantly against the sturdy Sikhs of the BSF, which had contributed several players to the Indian national team, while the brawny H.P. Tiwari, our Right Full Back, put up a Himalayan defence against the BSF's repeated forays into our goal. The previous year in Jalandhar, I had come to know Ashwini Kumar, an iconic figure both in the Indian police and Indian hockey. A few years later, when he visited Bhopal, I somewhat diffidently invited him for a drink at my house, which he readily accepted. This started a friendship that finally led me to the lofty portals of the Indian Hockey Federation (IHF).

I have always found old files and manuscripts of special interest and there was plenty of such stuff in the record rooms of district offices and thana *malkhana*s. The files of the police headquarters remained 'alive' for long periods, silently holding up a mirror to the thought processes and linguistic quirks of all those who had made entries in them from time to time. I wonder if all those who had access to official files were aware of the risks they ran while heedlessly filling up note sheets with what they considered literary masterpieces. All old files carry a unique flavour about them, ready to be unlocked by an inquisitive mind. One such eye-catching file bore the intriguing caption 'A Mount for Prince Cyrus', initiated by B.A. Sharma, around the time IGP Rustamji had become the proud father of a son, Cyrus. Received Indian wisdom says that the route to a boss's heart is through his progeny. Therefore, many officers of the headquarters vied with each other to do something special to please the boss, among them B.A. Sharma, who came up with a unique proposal that the MP police should set up a stud farm to breed horses. And since mares are not the most cooperative of animals in such matters, it was necessary to acquire what is called a teaser in the horse breeder's lingo. It is the teaser's job to stimulate the mare to get her into the right mood for the mating to take place. Now, as teasers are small animals, one of them could serve as a mount for Cyrus, while not engaged in the noble act of *teasing* the mare. Sharma must have been mighty pleased with this masterly coup. Sadly for him, though, the bizarre plan had to be dumped because the IGP would have none of it and, in any case, he left the state before Cyrus was old enough to ride.

Some six months before the general elections of 1967 were due, the state government asked the police headquarters to eliminate a man-eating tiger in the far-flung hills and forests of Abhujmarh in the tribal district of Bastar, because fear of the animal was likely to keep voters away from polling stations. Abhujmarh, which literally means 'the great unknown', acquired prominence because of very vivid tour notes recorded by R.P. Noronha of the ICS, who was collector of Bastar for seven long years and who famously even declined a promotion so as to continue in that position. The task of organizing a hunting party fell within my sphere of duties. I proposed a six-member team to be headed by G.W. Deshmukh, an eminent police officer and seasoned shikari, widely known for his penchant for being a bit too quick on the draw to quell riotous mobs, but otherwise an agreeable person. I offered to accompany the team as a sort of operations manager as I just could not let this opportunity pass. I had heard so much about Abhujmarh that I simply had to go. And then there was the sheer thrill of big game hunting that had all but gone out of my life after Morena. My proposal was approved right away and the decks cleared for the mission. A camp was set up at a charming little dak bungalow just outside Abhujmarh, and we all agreed to meet there by a certain date. I did not forget to carry with me enough reading material and, even more notably, a set of Scrabble as there was precious little to do in those backwoods except shikar and night drives. The lack of electricity and running water did not matter as the weather was good and the well water was eminently potable. No fresh vegetables were available but plenty of poultry and eggs could be had. Escorted by a local official, we would drive each evening into the remote hills and dales of the area to the spot where the tiger had been sighted the previous night.

We would return to the camp early the next day for rest and recoupment unless the tiger had made a kill, or a buffalo calf tied as bait was found mauled, in which case we would climb into the machan and wait for the animal to reappear to reclaim its kill. On a few occasions when we did see the tiger for a fleeting moment, it vanished into the undergrowth like a flash of lightning and we had to hold fire. Obviously, it needed a lot of patience and many more days of stalking before the mission could be accomplished. Neither Deshmukh nor I could afford to stay away from our desks for long. We had studied the terrain and made a fair assessment of the tiger's movements and habits. Based on this appraisal, we prepared a detailed plan of action and sent another team soon after, which was able to complete the task.

Abhujmarh tribals had had little contact with the outside world and, despite their abysmal poverty, lived a most relaxed life, full of dance, fun and cheer. The community dormitory, the *ghotul*, located outside the village, where young unmarried men and women could gather to form and nurture sexual liaisons before getting married, still retained an air of mystery and intrigue for outsiders. As it was, a few decades down the line, this entire idyllic and peaceful area was to get seriously mired in the Naxalite insurgency. Peace and serenity—the hallmarks of the region for ages—would perish, the huge district of Bastar would get sliced into smaller districts, and thousands of paramilitary personnel would remain deployed there to battle the Naxalite uprising.

Never very fond of me, B.A. Sharma wanted a pretext to ease me out of the police headquarters. As whimsical transfers of senior officers were then most unusual, he had to find a plausible enough reason for the purpose, especially as I had already done my quota of districts. He finally came up with the proposal that officers below forty-five years of age should not be posted in the headquarters. The state secretariat had long since lost the special aura that the British rulers had so carefully woven into its functioning. Virtually all files and note sheets in the secretariat could be accessed by anyone interested in them. All that he had to do was to cajole or bribe the concerned babu. Adverse ACR (annual confidential report) files could be made to disappear and dates of birth could be changed for a consideration. Since I had a genuine enough reason to resist

Kirpal Dhillon's mother, Nihal Kaur,
and father, Jagjit Singh, Rewa, 1956.

Kirpal Dhillon with his wife, Sneh, Rewa, 1957.

Dhillon with the then prime minister Indira
Gandhi, LBSNAA, Mussoorie, 1972.

PM Indira Gandhi at LBSNAA after a riding demonstration,
1972. (Extreme left, standing) Home minister of state R.N.
Mirdha; (third from left, standing) riding master, Naval Singh;
and (extreme right, standing) Dhillon along with IAS trainees.

Dhillon (centre) with participants in a conference on higher specialization in police, Messina, Italy, 1981.

The widely publicized surrender of notorious dacoit Phoolan Devi, aka 'Bandit Queen', Bhind, 1981. (Left, standing next to Phoolan) DIG, Chambal police range, Mahesh Sharma, and (extreme right, seated) the then MP CM, Arjun Singh, along with the officials of the district.

Dhillon addressing sarpanches on the perils of militancy, Ferozepur district, Punjab, 1984.

Sarpanches of Ferozepur district listening to Dhillon's message of peace, 1984.

Dhillon (extreme left) with the then MP CM, Dr K.N. Katju, who was visiting the district police lines, Khargone, 1958.

Dhillon with the then President, Giani Zail Singh, Rashtrapati Bhawan, New Delhi, 1985.

Dhillon addressing a conference on global trends in crime, Nicosia, Cyprus, 1990.

The Indian hockey team on a tour of Europe, 1992. (Standing, extreme left) S.S. Bhuller, liaison officer, International Hockey Federation; (second from right) former Olympian and coach of the team, Balkishan Singh; and (extreme right) Dhillon.

Dhillon's visit to his alma mater, D.A.V. School, now Government College of Commerce, after sixty-two years, with the principal (right) and his wife (left), Montgomery (now Sahiwal), Pakistan, 2008.

The D.A.V. School in Montgomery was locked for some time after Partition, then used as a women's hostel and is now the Government College of Commerce, Sahiwal, Pakistan.

Commandant General, Home Guards–cum–Director,
Civil Defence–cum–DGP, MP, Kirpal Singh Dhillon,
Bhopal, 1987.

Dhillon at his residence after retirement, Bhopal, 2004.

a transfer out of Bhopal, my friends in the home department helped me avoid an unfair relocation—once to Ujjain and then to Raipur—so that my daughters were not deprived of proper education once again. Therefore, I was posted as SP, Bhopal. B.A. Sharma got his favourite officer as AIG, SAF, and my daughters' studies remained uninterrupted. We did not even have to shift house, where my wife had enthusiastically cultivated a beautiful garden and made our home suitable for gracious living in many small ways.

I had been happy enough as a staff officer in the headquarters and not particularly keen to go back to a district. However, I soon realized that the police chief of the capital city enjoyed a special status. Many leading lights of the city suddenly grew very fond of my wife and me, and we now figured in the invitation lists of almost the entire smart set of Bhopal. At New Year's Eve festivities and beauty contests, my wife headed the panel of judges and I was given the honour of the first dance with the lady chosen as the beauty queen. A very hospitable DIG, who used to often pass me by, carrying a boxful of cigars for an IAS friend of mine, when I was a mere AIG, now brought out his best whisky and cigars for me.

Holding office for the first time, the BJS ministers were novices in matters of protocol and office procedure, and thus heavily dependent on their secretaries. The Congress defectors, on the other hand, knew the tricks of the trade rather too well. C.M. Govind Narain Singh, a Congress defector, conducted the affairs of the state as a personal fiefdom, mostly camping in forest rest houses for shikar. A notable exception to the general run of ministers was Deputy CM and Home Minister V.K. Saklecha of the BJS, who often called me in the evenings to consult me on various aspects of policing. He was a rather handsome man with a winsome smile, but one rarely saw him smile in public, where he came across as a rigid and severe person. Generally attired in a cheap camel-coloured *bandh-gala* suit and laced Bata shoes without socks, Saklecha epitomized in his person the austere culture and ethos of the ultra-rightist Hindu set-up, the Rashtriya Swayamsevak Sangh (RSS), which he had joined at an early age. Shortly after taking over office, he had to attend a formal police function, where he came clad in his trademark bandh-gala. When he was introduced to the police brass gathered at the function, he responded with an equally smart salute to emulate the officers. He seemed still untouched by the professional and personal weaknesses of his colleagues. A decade later, though, as MP CM in the short-lived Janata government, he got embroiled in many unsavoury scandals. He died an unhappy man, mired in many corruption cases, expelled from his party and denied a party ticket to contest elections. Sunder Lal Patwa and Kailash Joshi, his two rivals for power in the late 1960s, were still around in 2012. Patwa has fought many a political battle, flaunting his seniority in the party and chastising younger colleagues.

My immediate boss was a former Indore state officer. The cousin of a minor raja, he had risen high in the service in a climate of durbari-type sycophancy. I had served briefly with him as SP, Morena, a few years ago and remembered him as a somewhat eccentric individual. But now, as the most powerful DIG in the department, enjoying the confidence of the CM and the IGP, he came across as a much more self-assured man, easy to get along with as a boss. He often asked me to drop by at his office on my way home in the evening to talk about some problem area, relating to my district. I had asked for a few pick-up vehicles to be allotted for patrolling in the fast-growing city of Bhopal. When I reached his office one evening, after a cup of tea, he told me to watch carefully while he literally enacted a scene, wherein a suspect was lurking near a house under suspicious circumstances. And, presently, the DIG himself becomes the suspect. While thus preparing to commit an offence, the suspect sees an approaching motorized patrol. He hurriedly opens his fly and sits down by the drain. After the police vehicle passes by, he gets up and approaches a house and breaks open the lock. All these various actions by the supposed suspect and the police were actually performed by the DIG, playing the part of the suspect one moment and that of the police patrol party the next. While acting as the police patrol party, he actually mimicked the sounds and movement of the vehicle. The message that he wished to convey was that motorized transport was the wrong way to patrol a city street.

Within weeks of my posting to Bhopal, non-gazetted employees of the state and the Central governments went on strike to seek fulfilment of their many demands. With the state secretariat and a number of Central government offices located there, Bhopal had a large babu population. While the Central employees' unions had a long experience of collective action, the state employees were novices and were thus more likely to create law-and-order problems, requiring police intervention; heavy police deployment was, therefore, necessary. It was a tricky situation as use of force close to the nerve centre of the state administration could prove counterproductive. Besides other things, this also required taking the employees' leaders into confidence. The strike lasted around three weeks before a settlement could be arrived at. We managed to prevent any major mishap and were able to avoid the use of excessive force.

A few days before the strike was called off, my father suffered a serious heart attack. I had to wait for the situation to normalize before rushing to Moga. He remained in hospital for some three weeks but did not recover. On the advice of his doctors we took him home where he died peacefully in his sleep, an end befitting a good and noble man, but this left me with a deep sense of distress and regret. The loss was all the more poignant as I had been unable to visit him during all the months that he had not been keeping well because of some problem or the other cropping up in Bhopal. My mother was utterly devastated and stayed with us for several months before she could recover from the shock and return to Moga. She found it extremely difficult, however, to manage the family estate and other obligations by herself. This necessitated my visiting Moga much oftener to attend to many hitherto-unfamiliar chores.

An interesting part of my new obligations was to keep in touch with the village *patwari*, a minor but powerful revenue official, charged with the annual survey and mutation of landed properties. This opened huge windows of opportunity for him to make money. It was necessary for an absentee landlord, therefore, to keep on his right side. I had to visit my village every year in April at the time of the annual mutation operations to invite the patwari to a meal, complete with a bottle of home-brewed liquor, procured by a cousin from sources that he was prudent enough not to reveal. This ritual remained unbroken even as I continued to rise in the police hierarchy, until I persuaded my mother, very much against her wishes, to dispose of, at prices far below the market rates, the sizeable estate that I had inherited.

It took only about fifteen months for the ragtag coalition

government in MP to break apart, bringing its inglorious innings to an end. The collapse of this ignoble experiment was accelerated by a series of rallies by the Congress party. Among these was the *padyatra* from Sagar to Bhopal by the veteran Congress leader, D.P. Mishra, in violation of the prohibitory orders in force there. This was a delicate matter as we could neither allow the old man to infringe the law nor deal harshly with him and his followers. So we put up spacious tents in the Lal Parade Ground just outside the restricted area and furnished the tented accommodation with mattresses and pillows. This facility was then notified as a temporary jail by the DM. The DM and I politely asked D.P. Mishra not to let his party violate the prohibitory orders and warned him that if they defied the orders they would be arrested. On their refusal, they were arrested and escorted to the 'temporary jail'. A magistrate duly remanded them to judicial custody for the day and Congress party workers were allowed to serve cold drinks and food to the detainees. As the day ended so did their custody. Soon after, the Congress regained its majority in the legislature and was invited by the governor to form the government.

I recall the unruly scenes at Raj Bhavan when upset leaders of the ruling party noisily demanded registration of criminal offences against the Congress leader Shyama Charan Shukla for abducting their legislators. Such political wheeler-dealing was fairly common in those days, and the deviant legislators had to be carefully guarded by their parties from being lured away by the Opposition. This often involved ferrying the honourable legislators to various places of tourist interest, lodging them in expensive hotels and entertaining them lavishly, right up to the time they turned up to vote for their benefactors. And those worthies certainly did not mind being treated as merchandise!

'Trafficking' in the honourable members of India's parliament and state legislatures became a regular practice later in an increasingly unstable political environment.

Shyama Charan Shukla took over as the new CM and immediately set about restoring a degree of propriety in the administration, which had been hit hard by a wayward coalition. B.M. Shukul was brought back as IGP and B.A. Sharma consigned to an obscure post from where he retired in the course of time. He settled down in a congested locality of Indore, dolefully recalling his days of glory and growing increasingly lonely and forlorn with age. Shyama Charan was a tall and handsome man and he knew it. Like all those born into affluent political families, he could be arrogant and aloof as well as amiable and accessible. An aristocrat by disposition, he would gladly lap up all praise—even outright flattery—especially for his looks and dress sense. He routinely kept late hours and his appointments could run from midnight to early morning. When he was in Bhopal, his house remained packed with visitors, who swarmed around, on the lawns, in the verandas, lobbies, bedrooms and even outside his bathroom—the site depending on the importance of the visitor or his claimed proximity to the CM.

As the SP of the capital city, I had free access to him and often accompanied him to the airport when he was flying out of Bhopal, which was quite often. Bound by service etiquette, I never initiated a conversation and usually kept quiet except when spoken to. Once he asked me if I would like to be allotted a Fiat car out of the government quota and, sensing my need, promptly allotted me one. This gracious and thoughtful politician was markedly different from his younger brother, the political turncoat Vidya Charan, once a Gandhi loyalist, who later gained notoriety for switching parties every now and then. Both brothers figure prominently in the story of my life.

Ganga Ram Tiwari, a senior Congress leader from Indore, was the minister for labour. A man of frugal habits, he lived alone in Bhopal, travelling often to Indore, which remained his first love. Since cabinet ministers and politicians were not given to flaunting their position too much those days, one did not know very much about them. So, Ganga Ram was far from my mind when the city ADM (additional district magistrate) and the CSP walked into my house one morning to report that the honourable minister had been caught literally with his pants down in a nurse's flat in the BHEL township. The minister, feeling lonesome in his huge bungalow, had taken to visiting the lady from time to time for a little light-hearted fun, to put it mildly. She also had a much younger and livelier boyfriend. At some stage in their relationship, the young woman and her boyfriend decided to capitalize on the politician's weakness and hatched a plan to blackmail the minister, who fell into the trap only too easily. The two caught the minister's frolics with the lady neatly on camera and threatened him with exposure if he did not pay a large sum of money. They also possibly made some other demands that he did not reveal.

This was an unexpected turn of events for the hapless politician but he held out valiantly until he got a chance to escape, in a half-clad state, sometime in the early morning, to the balcony overlooking the street, and started wailing and yelling loudly that he was Ganga Ram Tiwari and was being held forcibly by miscreants. Somebody informed the police, who rescued the minister and escorted him home. An offence under Indian Penal Code (IPC) was registered against the nurse and her friend. Mercifully, there were no television channels those days to sensationalize what was, all said and done, a hugely shocking event. On learning about the incident, the IGP called me to the CM's office to apprise him of the incident. The CM listened quietly to the string of events and asked me to deal with the case according to the law. Before leaving, however, I ventured to suggest that the minister should resign to save the party from embarrassment. Somewhat amused, he looked at the IGP, smiled and said, 'Mr Dhillon, you handle the investigation. Leave political management to me.' That was a lesson I needed to learn to prevent my youthful exuberance from trespassing on alien terrain. Next, I called on the luckless minister and found a deeply shaken man, who related his version of the affair, requesting me to save him from the evil designs of the nurse and her boyfriend. He left for Indore post-haste and stayed put there till the scandal faded out of public memory. The Congress managed to tide over the discomfiture, though the minister did not escape unhurt, acquiring, in the process, a nickname—'Nanga' Ram, the naked one.

As expected, the new government replaced the head of the intelligence branch, with J.S. Kukreja, who was charged with the collection and evaluation of political intelligence, a job that had acquired additional importance because of the growing tendency among legislators to change loyalties. As DIG, intelligence, was also my DIG, he became my immediate boss. This created an awkward situation for me as Kukreja had been nursing many biases against me from the time we were together in Sagar, he as principal of the PTC and I as the SP. He made nitpicking over my work a routine. Even when the crime and public order situation in the rest of the state was grave, while Bhopal remained an island of peace, he would find some pretext to make critical references to my work in crime meetings. Frequent pinpricks in the form of snide comments and demi-official (DO) letters tested my habitual poise to the utmost. The breaking point came when he made an unfair entry in my ACR.

I sought an appointment with the IGP and requested a transfer. The IGP, who had known Kukreja for a long time, assured me that I need not fear and that my interests would be fully safeguarded, which he did most scrupulously. With this problem out of the way, I settled down to a long tenure in Bhopal. The town was well known across the country as a major centre for hockey. In my position as district SP, I had ample opportunity to interact with the local sports community, which often sought my help in different ways. Vidya Charan Shukla, a devious politician, later to become president of the Indian Olympic Association, was a frequent visitor to Bhopal and we often met at sports functions. He led me to believe that he would like me to get into the IHF. And yet, when just such an occasion arose, he worked hard to sabotage my chances of success.

In early 1971, Madho Singh, who has already figured in this narrative as a shrewd dacoit leader, sent word to me that all the major gangs had decided to 'surrender'. Also that he had already sounded some senior politicians—including the then-iconic figure, Jayaprakash Narayan—and that their response had been positive. P.C. Sethi, the MP CM, too had been brought on board. As a part of the procedural details, he wanted the state government to post me to Morena, where the surrender ceremonies were to take place, because the dacoit gangs did not trust the local police under the incumbent SP. I refused to have anything to do with the deal as I did not believe in surrenders as a mode of tackling crime. I did, however, talk to the IGP and introduced Madho Singh's man to him to take whatever action he deemed fit.

In August 1971, I left Bhopal on transfer to Mussoorie. The surrenders took place in February 1972 with much fanfare and in a blaze of publicity. The entire world's media was present to cover this most unusual phenomenon in a remote dak bungalow at Pagara in my old district of Morena. The surrender ceremony comprised groups of outlandishly attired, fierce-looking outlaws emerging from the forest, holding their firearms aloft and shouting full-throated slogans in praise of the Hindu goddess Durga and, strangely, also of Mahatma Gandhi, to lay down their arms at the feet of a huge portrait of the Mahatma. Then they sought the blessings of the CM and other notables present at the site, after which the police took them in custody. The gang leaders and 'senior' dacoits were the last to surrender after making sure that the authorities would not go back on their promises.

According to the terms of surrender, the dacoits were to undergo summary trials in special courts, where the prosecution would not plead for capital punishment in any offence against them; where the convicts would be lodged in specially created open jails; and where normal prison rules regarding parole and remission of sentences would be substantially relaxed. They were also allowed to eat from silver plates in deference to their claimed special position. In the end, all of them came out of their supposed incarceration hale and hearty, after serving much shorter sentences than their long careers in crime merited. This was not unexpected in this parody of justice, devised by a political class devoid of vision and a deeply politicized police leadership. No wonder, then, that the move failed to end the menace.

My tenure as SP, Bhopal, was marked by a profound sense of fulfilment for having been able to navigate through some highly sensitive policing problems. It had required close personal and professional interaction with many senior politicians and civil servants, generally inaccessible to officers of my rank. The interactions had helped considerably in enhancing my professional and interpersonal skills in many different ways. In the process, I also gained valuable experience in urban policing and developed close friendships with several civil servants and politicians, often much senior to me in age and position. My wife and I had received enormous warmth and affection from our friends during the six years that we spent in Bhopal and, when we left for Mussoorie, we had the honour of being invited to a whole array of farewell functions, some attended by top state officials, including Chief Secretary Noronha. I felt deeply touched and honoured by his gracious gesture.

We left Bhopal one rainy August morning in 1971, carrying with us fond memories of a somewhat laid-back lifestyle in a very beautiful town. Many of my friends and colleagues settled down in the same area in Bhopal after retirement, while some of us served together in other parts of the state. An IAS batchmate, Manohar Keshav—of the phenomenal memory—and I met again in Jabalpur and Gwalior, where he served as chairman of the state electricity board and member of the revenue board, respectively. Despite the growing coolness between the IAS and the IPS, their shared experience in managing their charges in a complex political environment still serves as an important binding factor. My Mussoorie tenure, where I came in close contact with IAS trainees in the formative years of their service, further enhanced my understanding of the value structure of my IAS colleagues, which helped me greatly in my future career.

9

Among the Crème de la Crème: Mussoorie

We had lived in Bhopal for about six years and although it had been a great place to live and work in, it was time to move on. A number of options were available for an officer of my seniority. Mr Rustamji, now DG (director general), BSF, wanted me to join his force, but before I could say yes, a very attractive option came my way which I literally grabbed. It all happened at a chance meeting with D.D. Sathe, then director LBSNAA, Mussoorie. Besides serving as the premier training institution for the IAS, LBSNAA also conducted a foundation course for all higher civil services. Mr Sathe considered it important that his senior colleagues at LBSNAA should possess high intellectual and social attributes, a trait he shared with many ICS officers, who had grown up in the service in an apolitical setting.

He used to visit various states during the winter break to select officers who would fit into his framework of values and skills, for posting to LBSNAA. And that is what brought him to Bhopal in December 1970. Being a gracious host, he had many friends all over the country, including General Habibullah, the scion of an aristocratic Lucknow family, who owned a stud farm on the outskirts of Bhopal. It was at a dinner hosted by the general for Mr Sathe that I first met my future boss. As the evening advanced and conviviality levels rose, he seemed to have found me eminently suitable for posting as a deputy director in LBSNAA. When he made the offer, I accepted readily, mainly because I have always loved the hills. He promptly spoke to the chief secretary and the IGP, both present at the party. IGP B.M. Shukul asked me if I indeed wished to leave the key position of SP, Bhopal, for a teaching job in LBSNAA with fewer perks and creature comforts.

I felt a little uncertain as Bhopal was certainly a major posting, I had enjoyed the full trust and support of the IGP and the state government and I knew they did not want to let me go. But the irresolution lasted only a moment and, before the end of the evening, I was on board for the academy posting. Also, my daughters' schooling would be taken care of as Mussoorie had some of the best public schools in the subcontinent. My decision found instant favour with my wife and daughters; they had picked up from the books and journals they read some rather inflated notions about Indian hill stations and the many delightful diversions they offered—the sort of lifestyle unimaginable in backward MP though Bhopal had been a happy experience.

There was no further word from LBSNAA for some time and, just as I was getting reconciled to staying on in Bhopal, Mr Sathe called to tell me that the mandarins in Delhi were doubtful if an IPS officer would be of much use at LBSNAA. My posting seemed to have become a victim of the usual IAS–IPS squabbling. Matters might have rested there except that, during a seminar at the Indian Institute of Public Administration (IIPA), Delhi, I happened to meet B.C. Mathur, joint secretary, personnel, who was responsible for such postings. Having seen my performance at the seminar, he seemed to have revised his opinion about at least one IPS officer. He asked me whether I was really keen on the LBSNAA posting. 'Yes, of course,' I said, and my posting was soon cleared. I joined as deputy director (senior)—DD (S)—at the LBSNAA soon after, a landmark event in my career and a refreshing break from the dreary routine of policing, which I had already followed for some eighteen years. A boxful of music cassettes, gifted to me by my friend Baker, the chief pilot of the small state air fleet, formed an important part of my luggage.

Initially, the LBSNAA posting seemed to be a considerable let-down. They really had no clue as to how and in what capacity to utilize my services. I was given charge of a section called Services and Supplies (S&S) and of the rifle club. In the police, such tasks are entrusted to the RI or the adjutant, and I felt it rather demeaning to perform such petty jobs. It did not take long for Mr Sathe to realize that I was not happy with the minor role assigned to me as a DD. He called me for drinks one evening, possibly to assess my ability to handle the various jobs that needed to be done in the academy. Seemingly satisfied that at least some IPS officers could have more to offer in a generalist training institution than was generally believed, he allotted me a range of duties—teaching, co-curricular and organizational—and, more importantly, also made me course director for the foundation course. My new charter of duties required me to grow out of the rigid mindset that stereotypes policemen, a process I was able to negotiate without much difficulty.

As course director for the foundation course, I had to handle two batches, one on the main campus and the other at the local Savoy Hotel. Once I had to handle simultaneously three courses, two in Mussoorie and one for central technical services in Nagpur. In addition, I directed several in-service and specialist courses; had charge of administration, library and the officers' Mess; edited the academy journal; and also taught some subjects. There were many creative persons among the probationers—poets, artists, dancers and photographers—so we set up a fine arts society and brought art teachers from nearby Dehradun to help them refine their talent. Mrs Sathe and my wife were the prime movers of these activities, which soon attracted a number of keen probationers, both men and women. We launched a literary journal, mainly for poetry, called *Expressions*, with B.K.S. Ray, a gifted poet in English and Oriya, as editor. One of my duties was to coach the trainees in protocol, ceremonials, manners and etiquette. We invited batches of trainees to dinner to familiarize them with formal eating etiquette. I even wrote a small booklet on the subject, which remains part of the academy handouts in each course. All this helped me grow intellectually and academically in a manner that would have been unthinkable in a police career. It also gave me an enormous sense of confidence and fulfilment.

The Sathes were an extraordinarily warm couple, extremely hospitable and friendly and, in the true tradition of the ICS, totally free of narrow service biases and allegiances. In the ACR recorded by him on my work, he devoted half a page to my wife, who was an honorary warden of the women's hostel and helped Mrs Sathe in some academy activities, including running a primary school on the premises. Their departure for Maharashtra in the summer of 1973, where he took over as CS, left a huge void in the social and cultural life of Mussoorie, but they kept in touch with us for many years afterwards.

One of the perks offered to officers posted to the LBSNAA was a study visit abroad. Accordingly, I was nominated for a six-week study visit to the UK on a Ford Foundation Fellowship in collaboration with the British Council. This was my first exposure to the administrative and police systems in a mature democracy. Fascinated as I had been with British history and literature right from my college days, the prospect was immensely exciting but I did not want the visit confined only to the police, which seemed to be the initial aim of the fellowship. I wanted it to be more broad-based. A combination of circumstances helped me achieve precisely that end. Our High Commission could not draw up a programme for me as it had no education officer then. It had, in fact, asked the ministry to defer my visit. Fortunately for me, B.C. Mathur, the joint secretary in charge, just sat on the telegram until after I was safely out of India, as he told me later.

When I reported at the High Commission, they asked me to draw up my own training programme in consultation with the British Council. The kind old lady there cooperated fully with me and I drew up a programme that allowed me to divide my term equally between the police and the civil service. So, I got a short attachment with the London Metropolitan Police Service, the Police Staff College at Bramshill and a constables' training centre. And I also got attachments with the Royal Institute of Public Administration, the Civil Service Staff College and Whitehall, the administrative centre of the government of the UK. In between, the local police made arrangements for me to accompany beat patrols and investigation teams. They cautioned me, however, not to visit the seamier parts of London and offered to escort me if I did wish to go there. The police commissioner invited me to sit in at one of his periodical meetings with the commanders of the nine city districts. Interestingly, it was the commander of the most criminal district who hogged the limelight and he was mighty proud of the fact that he was handling a notorious neighbourhood. His swagger reminded me of the pretentious airs of dacoity-area

SPs back in Madhya Pradesh. I was soon to find that police attitudes all over the world are similar in many ways.

After completing my engagements in London, I travelled by train through a picturesque part of England to reach a small wayside railway station, where a loquacious policeman met me and drove me to the Bramshill Staff College. On the way, we passed a gypsy settlement and, when I showed some interest in the peripatetic people, my companion dismissed them out of hand as thieves and swindlers, cautioning me never to rely on a gypsy woman. The tall and handsome John Alderson, an authority on democratic and principled policing, headed the college in the rank of a chief constable. He received me with old-world charm and visible warmth; we took to each other instantly and have stayed lifelong friends. We were to meet again in Italy, Cyprus and the US during conferences. He wrote the foreword to my book on South Asian police and reviewed it for an American journal. The impressive Bramshill Castle, that forms the core structure around which the staff college has been built, was located on the vast estate of Earl Mountbatten, the last British viceroy of India. The annual dinner hosted by the staff college that year coincided with my brief stay there and, as luck would have it, the earl himself was the chief guest. Though much older now than what one remembered of him as a young, handsome viceroy, he had lost none of his charm and elegance.

The menu card mentioned Madras Curry as one of the courses and though I found nothing Indian about it, my hosts insisted that it was an Indian dish, placed on the menu due to my presence. I visited the staff college twice again for lectures on South Asian police. John Alderson was held in such high esteem by an entire generation of police officers that the mere fact that he was my friend would be enough testimony to my credentials as a police officer of note. When an Australian university wanted a critique of the 1984 Bhopal gas disaster for use as a case study in one of their courses, John asked Professor Seumas Miller to contact me. On his request, I prepared a case study of the tragic episode to be presented at a seminar in Delhi; it was later published as a lead article in *Australian Journal of Applied Ethics*. The last time I met John was some ten years ago, when I was his guest in Exeter, where he had settled down after retiring from the police to write and lecture on his favourite subject of democratic policing.

In 1972, London was still an inexpensive and affordable place for visitors with modest resources, and my daily allowance was more than adequate for a comfortable stay. I rented a snug little room, close to Baker Street tube station, with en suite facilities and a full English breakfast for just four and a half pounds a day. My expenses on food and travel were minimal. Many well-off Punjabis in Southall and Slough happily entertained me as a sort of investment for the future as I still had many years of service in the Indian police. Such 'investments' in the form of gifts and hospitality to influential visitors are normal among South Asian expatriates. They took me sightseeing on weekends to various places outside London. They also tried to lure me into the dubious pleasures of London's shady nightlife, which ended rather disastrously, when a streetwalker walked away because I spoke a quaint form of English.

My initiation into the London pub culture was, however, happier and more engaging. In fact, it become a lifelong passion, much to the dismay of my German son-in-law, an Oxford don, who regards such indulgences as rather plebeian. I often travelled to the countryside and came upon some of the quaintest pubs, not far from London, which claimed past associations with kings and queens, poets and novelists, familiar figures to me from my study of English literature. The London suburb of Southall, teeming with still-unrefined Punjabis, provided a familiar cultural and linguistic backdrop. While shopping for a jacket at a clothier's, however, I drew only blank looks from the Sikh salesman when I addressed him in Punjabi. Sensing my discomfiture, the English proprietor quickly took over and, in chaste Punjabi, apologized for his assistant's unhelpful attitude! The salesman, it turned out, was a migrant from East Africa and had had no contact with the language for generations, while, to the owner, it made sound business sense to be proficient in the language of his patrons.

During a weekend visit to Glasgow, while I was on my way out of a pub, a garrulous Scotsman accosted me warmly, excitedly exclaiming 'Gandhi! Gandhi!', and proceeded to draw me into a tight embrace. It was a heady feeling to find a total stranger so admiring of at least one attribute of my country. Several Indo-Pak restaurants dotted the streets of Glasgow, which was rather strange in view of the hostility between the two countries back home. Evidently, this was meant to attract nationals of both countries, who had so much in common. Among the several plays then running in London, I found *Oh! Calcutta* hugely interesting and not only because the actors appeared in the buff all through—a first of its kind for mainstream theatre, I suppose. In the queue at the ticket window, I found at least two Gandhi-capped Indians, with evident political links. They visibly squirmed when they found me looking at them with some amusement.

While in London, I took time off for a brief visit to Paris. I took an early morning train from Victoria to Dover, crossed the Channel by ship and then got on to a French train for the rest of the journey to Paris. Being ravenously hungry, I stuffed myself with whatever eatables were on offer on the ship. I had to pay dearly for the indulgence as the sea was unusually choppy and I had no previous experience of such travel. So, I had to stay locked in the bathroom the rest of the time, painfully throwing up all that I had eaten a while earlier. When we touched the French coast, dishevelled and woebegone as I was, I could not locate the ticket counterfoil to be submitted at the destination. Presently, the captain himself came to my rescue, telling me genially to look inside my breast pocket, where 'the tall, dark, handsome gentleman had put the ticket at embarkation'. And that is where the elusive piece of paper was, nestling happily, and I departed, lugging my suitcase amid much mirth and good cheer to board the French train close by. After a while, two rotund, unshaven policemen, dressed in shabby, crumpled uniforms, looked into the cabin to check passports. They looked casually at some documents and walked away. An American and a Yugoslav were sharing the compartment with me and other passengers. They asked me the weirdest questions about India, such as how do people drive through herds of cows blocking our city roads? Or, how do we keep snakes out of our beds?

Detraining at Gare du Nord, I was instantly drowned in a sea of French speech. No one would as much as acknowledge my presence unless I spoke in French, which I did not know. There were other problems too. Even proper nouns were sort of 'Frenchified', so London became *Londres* and England was *l'Angleterre*, or some such thing. Finally, I located a tourist centre, where a pretty, young woman helped me call a taxi and book a hotel room in the famed Latin Quarter, where I deposited my bags. These essentials taken care of, I relaxed, dreaming of the many titillating delights that the city offered. I took a tourist bus to savour the nightlife of the one city that had become so much a part of my imagination. The bus made a round of several well-known nightclubs, at each of which we spent an hour or so, enjoying the sumptuous fare on offer and the complimentary glass of champagne. The generous display of female flesh in the Paris nightspots was indeed a riveting sight for my very Indian eyes. Not used to such heavy drinking, I was quite sozzled by the time I returned to the hotel past midnight.

Having eaten nothing at all since morning, I was not only inebriated but also voraciously hungry, but found no proper repast at that unearthly hour except a pair of huge plantains in a corner store. I hungrily devoured the fruit and slept like a log that night. I had planned to explore the city by metro and bus next morning, but found it difficult either to pronounce the names of the places or to count out the exact fare for the tickets. So, I held out in my palm what I thought to be sufficient change at the ticket counter and to indicate my destination with the help of the tourist booklet. I had an uneasy feeling, though, that the girls at the counter often cheated me but with a smile. When I boarded the train for the journey back to London, I heaved a deep sigh of relief on hearing English voices for the first time in three days, which I had spent in trying to break through the pride the French have in their language. But, of course, Paris can be a hugely thrilling experience when one is young and adventurous. In my subsequent visits, I came to know enough of the city to find my way around both by metro and on foot. The latter mode was always my preferred choice for exploring places all over the world.

I returned to the academy, refreshed and full of new ideas, only to find that a change of command at the LBSÑAA was imminent. D.D. Sathe had reverted to his cadre as chief secretary. Signifying something of a watershed in the history of the academy, and marking a transition from the ICS to the IAS, the next director was from the IAS. This changeover was, in fact, to prove a defining moment for the entire cultural and academic template of the LBSNAA. For one thing, the trainees no longer looked for their role models in the apolitical mandarins of the ICS. Rajeshwar Prasad, who took over from D.D. Sathe, was markedly different from his precursor in many conceptual, functional and cultural aspects. Right from the word go, he set about 'Indianizing' the entire training curriculum and to root out any vestiges of a western mindset that he thought had determined the training inputs in the LBSNAA till then. This took many forms, among them, the observance of Hindu religious festivals which he thought symbolized Indian culture. Thus, the celebration of Diwali, Dussehra and Janamashtami became important events in the academy's cultural calendar. Colourful and ornate sets were prepared for staging *Ram Leela*, in which the petite Anshumala, the director's daughter, played a bashful Sita, and the tall Deepak Vohra of the IFS was Ravan, while Mr Prasad sang the accompanying verses on the harmonium.

Prasad, a great admirer of Lal Bahadur Shastri—Nehru's successor as prime minister—had the academy named after his idol. He also introduced *shramdan* (voluntary labour), along with its add-on song, *Chal dana dan phaode*, as a regular feature of all training courses. All of us from the staff were expected to do shramdan and sing the phaode song, which, in fact, became a point of reference to link successive batches of probationers. A notable high point of that time was the visit of Prime Minister Indira Gandhi, for whom we put up an impressive horse show, a sort of first for the IAS probationers, with Naval Singh, the Haryanvi riding master, also participating. My wife showed Mrs Gandhi around the academy primary school that she supervised. It used to be fun visiting each other except that drinks could be served only behind drawn curtains what with Rajeshwar Prasad lurking around.

As course director for the foundation courses and in charge for the officers' Mess and club, I have vivid recollections about many probationers. One could sense the makings of an astute politician in the ever-smiling Ajit Jogi, who became chief minister of Chhattisgarh. But it was difficult to see future foreign secretaries in the quiet and aloof Shivshankar Menon, who later went on to hold the crucial post of National Security Advisor, and the comely but shy Nirupama Rao, who would head the Indian embassy in the US. Hardip Puri won over the beautiful and very talented Laxmi Murdeshwar, a classical dancer of repute, within days of joining the academy. He blossomed into a distinguished diplomat in the course of time and held many key appointments, including a term as India's permanent representative to the UN. The extremely shy but scholarly Najeeb Jung would one day make a distinguishedVC of Jamia Millia Islamia.Vijay Singh, who should have risen to the post of Union home secretary like his father, succeeded Shekhar Dutt, another of my probationers, as defence secretary. The charming Nina Singh of the IFS would marry senior Supreme Court lawyer Kapil Sibal. Nina also wrote a very readable, and apparently autographical, novel on India's partition. We last met Nina at a Diwali function at the Indian embassy in Cairo, where she was the deputy chief of mission. Sadly, she died early.

Meera Shankar (née Chowdhary), a fetching young woman,

achieved the ultimate for a career diplomat by becoming India's ambassador to the US. Veena Sriram of the IAS, also from an army background like Nina and her constant companion, disappeared from my radar soon after I left the academy. P.S. (Pampi) Gill, from my hometown, and his troupe put up a most memorable bhangra show at a cultural function in the academy. Pampi later headed the Punjab police, a post that I too held at a very critical stage in the history of Punjab. Satwant Sidhu, attired invariably in salwar-kameez, would find time to speak to my mother in Punjabi, which pleased her no end. Then there were the princes—one from Sikkim and the other from Manipur—who mixed freely with the academy community and never flaunted their princely status. I lost touch with the Sikkimese prince, but Falguni Rajkumar, the one from Manipur, did surface from time to time. Chandralekha of the Tamil Nadu cadre made history when she joined politics and tried to take on the redoubtable Jayalalithaa.

Days before Meira Kumar, Union Minister Jagjivan Ram's daughter, was to arrive in Mussoorie for IFS training I was flooded with phone calls from her father's staff, insisting that special lodgings be earmarked for her. I firmly rejected all such requests as being against the rules. When she did arrive, however, she appeared unaware of all the fuss that was made on her behalf and conducted herself with quiet dignity. She left the IFS midway to join politics and ended up as the first woman Speaker of the Lok Sabha, India's lower house of Parliament. Kiran Bedi came to the academy, insisting on joining the IPS and no other service, defying the then official policy, thus holding up service allotments of the entire batch for months. She finally achieved her aim and thus became the first woman IPS officer in the country and acquired an iconic status. Tajwar Rehman, a modish young woman of exceptional charm and vivacity, married Rakesh Sahni, a future MP chief secretary. Unfortunately, Tajwar died early. When I took over as DGP, Punjab, in 1984, almost all the DCs and SSPs (senior superintendents of police) in Punjab were my former probationers. R.I. Singh, then DC, Amritsar, went on to hold the posts of CS and chief information commissioner, Punjab.

Among my probationers, there were also many future secretaries to the Union government; state chief secretaries and police chiefs; heads of mission in many countries; chief commissioners of Income Tax and Central Excise; and heads of various other departments. Deputy Directors Dhanoa, Kohli and Bagchi left shortly after I joined. A.K. Mitra continued his study of Tibetan so as to impress the Dalai Lama one day. Srinivasan from Tamil Nadu, married to a Maharashtrian, hated the Mussoorie cold and complained every morning that he was slowly, slowly, dying. Professors Gurumurthy, a former judge, and P.C. Mathur were erudite and amiable gentlemen. S.N. Sadasivan compiled an excellent study of India's caste system in 2000 under the title *A Social History of India*.

Many turned up unexpectedly at far-off places in India and abroad, evoking nostalgic memories of a treasured past. Pradeep Bhide and his comely wife, Sheila (née Thakkar), arranged a most delightful get-together in Washington where my wife and I were on a month-long visit in 1988.

The LBSNAA posting was a turning point in my career in more senses than one. It exposed me to an entirely different environment from the overly regimented service traditions of the Indian police. It helped me cultivate new functional skills and develop an aptitude for originality and creativity. It gave me the courage to stand up for my views, even when at odds with accepted wisdom. It offered my daughters an educational environment they would never have found in MP. Mussoorie was then a rather unspoilt hill station and the ambience was aesthetically pleasing and fulfilling. It was also the ideal setting to satisfy my passion for long walks. Every Sunday morning, I would set off for long solitary walks in the hills, wandering along the crest of a major hill, dotted with old, dilapidated bungalows, once peopled by fun-loving white men and women. My walks invariably ended up at Whispering Windows, a quiet, well-stocked restaurant at Library Point, for a beer and a plate of real sausages, not the ersatz ones you get these days. I played great tennis and often joined Naval Singh in cross-country riding.

Apart from conducting the foundation courses, I was also the course director for many in-service courses, and a member of a number of committees, which enabled me to meet and interact with many distinguished persons, both in government and academia. One of these committees, set up to draw up a new syllabus for the Indian Economic and Statistical Services, was chaired by Dr Manmohan Singh, then the chief economic advisor to the Union government. D. Sen, a promoted IPS officer from UP and, at that time, director, CBI, came across as a petty and devious officer. He held up my case for award of a medal because he declared as too lavish for my means an official dinner which I, in my capacity as the course director, had arranged for the participants of a vigilance course—where, by the way, he had gorged on every dish on the table—overlooking the fact that it was paid for by the academy and that I was only notionally the host. Sadly, such petty malice is not uncommon in Indian police cadres, or indeed in other services.

By August of 1974, I had completed three years in the

academy and it was time to move on. I had enjoyed my job immensely due to its vast potential for intellectual growth and the scope it offered to interact with some of the best young minds in the country. My office room, glazed and sunny in the bitter cold of Mussoorie, was a favourite rendezvous for groups of probationers who enjoyed spending a few leisurely and relaxing moments with a member of the directing staff, who was both friendly and helpful. My wife and daughters too were happy, living in an ambience of intellectual stimulation and good cheer. However, it was necessary to re-establish my links with my parent service. That is what ultimately made me decide to leave the LBSNAA, which had become so much a part of me. Luckily, I also received my posting orders to Jabalpur as the range DIG. I had always loved that town and on no account would I have missed the chance of running an interesting police range. The director was not too happy to let me go but relented on the condition that I complete the ongoing courses. At my request, he wrote to the MP government not to fill up the Jabalpur post until then, to which they graciously acceded. I stayed on for another three months, and left the academy at the end of November1974 for Delhi on the way to Jabalpur.

10

Going Up the Ladder–I: Jabalpur

During my time, promotion to higher ranks was not time-bound but depended on vacancies. IPS and IAS officers continued to serve in districts or in equivalent posts until a clear vacancy arose in the next higher rank. As DD (S) in the LBSNAA, I was notionally equated with a DIG of police, though I could not wear that rank, a privilege to which I became entitled as DIG, Jabalpur. Besides, as DIG of what had been a major police charge in British India, I inherited a decades-old position, represented by a long line of distinguished officers. In 1817, the British had set up Jabalpur as a cantonment. It had a significant presence in central India and housed several army units, the oldest of which is the Indian Army Corps of Signals. Nerbudda Club, one of the oldest in central India, though not as well-run as some others, is still counted among the best in the region. Its tennis courts and well-stocked bar provided a welcome retreat from the office routine. The local army units were actively involved in managing the club activities, which they did with characteristic finesse and aplomb. Although my job and touring kept me fairly busy, I always turned up for a game of tennis when in town. Chief Justice P.K. Tare of the MP High Court invariably showed up at the tennis courts, leaving his case files aside for the evening, as did P.C. Rai, a former DIG of mine and as hard a taskmaster as ever. My love for the game prompted many of my SPs to freshen up their own game and reactivate the district clubs. My visits to the districts always included an evening at the local club and a game or two of tennis. In those good old days, such small distractions were accepted gracefully by public and politicians alike. Mercifully, there were no television channels vying with each other to snoop on senior officers and no petty rags to play up the occasional mishap in official life.

A British-era DIG of police had no direct responsibility and no regular office except a stenographer and a crime clerk. Basically, he represented the IGP in his range. This arrangement remained unchanged for many years after Independence. The

British had intended a DIG to act as a friend, philosopher and guide to his SPs and had intentionally not burdened him with too much office work. This left him free to visit his districts as often as he needed to offer advice and support to his officers. Having already done heavy district charges, a DIG had no great desire to intrude into the domain of his SPs. Later, as ranges became smaller, often comprising no more than three or four tiny districts, and since most DIGs had never held a major district charge, the post lost its lustre. Many DIGs now tended to act as super SPs, forever interfering in the work of their SPs, thus making them ineffectual, and the DIG, a contestant, not a supervisor. A mature DIG prized his autonomy and exercised it in a balanced manner, providing guidance and counsel to his SPs and keeping the IGP fully posted on the developments in his range. Range DIGs were required to uphold the dignity of their offices vis-à-vis other divisional-level officers of Central and state governments. Evolving a proper equation with the revenue commissioner was a delicate task. The Indian Police Act, 1861, accorded the revenue commissioner no role in policing except through his DMs. However, over the years, the IAS bureaucracy had successfully inducted the commissioner into the scheme of policing through an executive order, itself a violation of the Police Act. Since no one contested that order, it became the accepted practice. Fortunately for me, none of the commissioners with whom I worked in Jabalpur and Gwalior over-exercised his assumed supervising role, and the equation worked well.

On 1 January 1975, IGP K.L. Diwan died in a plane crash along with Home Secretary R.C. Roy and the young pilot Noronha, son of the then chief secretary, while flying to Lucknow in the state government's poorly maintained aircraft.

The sudden vacuum at the top set off a messy tussle for the top job among those in the zone of selection. Intense political lobbying was resorted to, compromising time-honoured norms of promotion and thus gravely vitiating the process. H.M. Joshi, now the most senior IPS officer, did not possess a sound record, having been embroiled in unseemly controversies right from his days as an SP. He was thus generally thought to be out of reckoning for the post. Yet, that is precisely what did *not* happen, to everyone's surprise. Confronted by sordid lobbying by some politically aligned officers, the government played it safe by promoting Joshi. This deeply upset a couple of ambitious contenders, who now began subverting Joshi's position vis-à-vis politicians and bureaucrats, carefully cultivated for years by fair means or foul. The controversies surrounding the office of the IGP—a key state institution—trivialized it in the eyes of the public as well as within the force. Coarse and indecorous jokes about top police officers now became common talking points within the police and outside. Soon, cliques formed around them, dividing the state IPS cadre into hostile factions. This became more or less a permanent feature of the state police, destroying the esprit de corps and promoting high levels of politicization. Senior officers now needed to cultivate a powerful politician to watch their service interests. Politicization affected other departments too but the police were the worst sufferers since politicians were more interested in exploiting the coercive power of the police.

Essentially a decent man with a phenomenal memory, Joshi could be unusually erratic at times. As he was highly susceptible to flattery, clever subordinates often took advantage of their claimed proximity to him. The SP of a small district near Jabalpur collected some extracts from Joshi's articles and got a booklet printed on expensive paper, a costly enterprise obviously financed through dubious means. The pricey booklet was presented to Joshi at a public function during his visit and circulated all over the state. This pleased him immensely but it also gave ideas to other SPs. While touring my districts he found every police station flush with quotes from his speeches and articles. In the Chhindwara police lines, there were even stones engraved with his ideas and thoughts like the pillars of Ashoka. While I kept resolutely silent on this vulgar display of sycophancy, he grew increasingly uneasy, partly, I suppose, because he sensed my deep dislike for such coarseness. He was well and truly displeased with the SP, Chhindwara, and turned down his invitation to dinner which, by tradition and etiquette, an IGP never does.

In early 1975, a grave law-and-order situation erupted in Balaghat, one of my districts, when a detainee died in police custody. Death in police custody is viewed as a major failure or oversight by the SP, and rightly so. Police manuals prescribe severe punishment for such a lapse, though supervisory officers often discreetly tend to help an errant subordinate to help him escape retribution. Several errors of judgement and the casual approach of the DM and the SP to the developing situation led to the utter collapse of the local law-and-order machinery in Balaghat. The result was that three police officers were burnt alive by a riotous mob in the thana lock-up, the SP was assaulted and the DM, made to wear a garland of shoes around his neck, was forced to walk with the unruly mob. The commissioner and I reached Balaghat by evening and promptly got down to restoring normalcy, starting with the police station, which was soon fully functional. The supremacy of the district executive, so highly prized by the British rulers, is still accorded prime importance in democratic India though political concerns do sometimes dilute such priorities. State governments ensure that the dignity of the office of the DM and the SP is never undermined. Balaghat was witness to the ultimate in state humiliation, unacceptable even in a democratic polity.

There had been law-and-order episodes in my other districts too, which were handled with tact and caution. But Balaghat was a major conflagration. Disorder can result from the actions of any of several government departments, which are perceived as unfair by different segments of society, such as by students, employees, lawyers, tribals or slum-dwellers. When they come out into the streets, it is left to the police alone to deal with them as best as they can. The system of criminal justice, dating back to the mid-nineteenth century, has all but broken down. Hamstrung as they are by many inhibitive factors—systemic, procedural or personal—policemen usually end up at the receiving end of the blame, either for overreaction or under-action. This, in turn, makes them overly defensive in the performance of their duties, a feature that is mainly to blame for the dismal failure of the Indian police to gain and retain community trust.

A.S. Bal, SP, Jabalpur, handled his very sensitive charge with aplomb and confidence. He often had to deal with student unrest, especially frequent clashes between two groups of students in Jabalpur University—the city group and the rural area group. Controlling students is a serious matter because they are deftly cultivated by political parties as a fertile vote bank. On finding that the police were less than firm in dealing with the rowdy students, I asked the SP to get cracking. Soon the local police raided the university hostel and seized a truckload of lethal weapons, including firearms, and took the leaders of the two factions into custody. True to form, the entire political establishment and the press were up in arms against the police for their action. We withstood the criticism, mainly because the IGP and the CM had been kept fully in the picture. I invited Sharad Yadav, the leader of the rural group, to my office for a talk, during which I casually mentioned that he was far too intelligent to waste his time in small-town politics while there was an acute shortage of young politicians at the national level. He took my advice seriously and contested a by-election to the Lok Sabha from Jabalpur and routed Ravi Mohan, the scion of a leading political family in the state. He never looked back and went on to occupy several ministerial and political positions.

On 25 June 1975, a series of critical events in the country led to the enforcement of internal emergency by a beleaguered Indira Gandhi. That fateful evening, Kiran Shrivastava, a young IAS officer, who had done her police training with me in Bhopal and was now posted as ADM, Jabalpur, was visiting at our house, when I received an urgent message from the police headquarters to order a general alert in all my districts and await further advice from the IGP. The latter was soon on the line to brief me about the developing situation and to ask me to take the various actions specified for such emergency situations in all districts of my range. As the DM was on leave, Kiran had to hold the fort till his return. Leaving our tea unfinished, we rushed to the police control room, where all senior police officers and magistrates had been summoned to draw up a plan of action that incorporated a number of steps as directed by the state and the Central authorities.

Nothing stirs the Indian bureaucracy like an emergency situation. Then it is at its best, arresting Opposition leaders, agitators and troublemakers, enforcing prohibitory orders and activating intelligence units to keep their ears glued to the ground. Along with the Emergency, Indira Gandhi also initiated new social and economic measures, called the Twenty Point Programme, to be closely monitored by her wayward son, Sanjay. Given the highly personal managerial style practised in India, the state and district administrations fell over each other not only to meet but also exceed the targets set under Sanjay's dictates. One of his favourite schemes was family planning through mass vasectomies, and everyone, from CMs to collectors, vied with each other to exceed their targets in this and other programmes. Groups of indigent men would be picked up at random by subordinate staff, taken to a nearby shack and sterilized with or without their consent for a small monetary reward.

Setting targets in sensitive matters—like sterilization—can be highly dangerous, especially as it largely affects the poor and the powerless. I refused to allow the police to get involved in the matter. My colleague, the commissioner, an elderly promoted officer, however, had no such scruples and visited all his districts twice a week to check the progress in this regard. The Emergency ended in 1977 and Indira Gandhi lost the elections. The many unlawful acts and atrocities of the Emergency years, exposed by the Shah Commission of Inquiry, became the focus for disciplinary action. The same commissioner went around his districts with equal zeal to now chastise his subordinates for having so earnestly implemented the programmes. When I casually asked him how he could castigate his collectors for merely having carried out his orders during the Emergency regime, he only shrugged. Perhaps the finest legacy handed down by the British was an honest, impartial and apolitical administration, but this great institution did not remain unsullied by political corruption for long. By the late 1960s, there were clear signs of decay in the moral and intellectual fibre of the civil service. Indira Gandhi's Emergency signalled the demise of civil service autonomy and neutrality and the dawn of an era of commitment to the ruler rather than to the rule of law and due process. The decline in later decades was to be even more marked and unrelenting.

Jabalpur had an outstanding record in sports, especially in hockey, and several local players had made it to men's and women's national teams. Pre-Independence Jabalpur had a sizeable population of Anglo-Indians. While the women served British households, the men occupied many middle-level slots in the Indian railways (remember John Masters's *Bhowani Junction?*), the army and the police. These departments, thus, had become nurturing grounds for talented players. Independence led many Anglo-Indians, among them some well-known hockey players, to emigrate. While the army distanced itself from local hockey, the police and the railways kept up the links. The Jabalpur SP regularly joined the men for games and helped talented players excel in their field. In 1976, some hockey enthusiasts suggested that I contest for the office of the president of the Madhya Pradesh Hockey Association (MPHA), and I agreed most willingly. My opponent was the portly J.N. Awasthy, the state education minister, who let it be known that he enjoyed the CM's support and that I would soon be asked to stand down.

This was not quite the case: CM Shyama Charan Shukla, who knew me well enough from Bhopal, not only fully approved of my candidature but actually wished me success, saying, 'What will that *motoo* [fatso] do in the MPHA?' When no government directive came asking me to withdraw, Awasthy asked the DM, Vinay Shankar, a cool and competent officer, to disallow the election for fear of breach of peace. Vinay dropped in to ask for my advice in view of the minister's direction. I told him that it was for him to take the final call, but there was no imminent threat. He did not interfere, the election proceeded smoothly and I was duly elected president, MPHA. Awasthy got just three votes. I headed the MPHA for two terms, even after my transfer to Gwalior and then to Delhi. We organized a number of national and international events and several of our players were selected to play for India. At the end of my two terms, when I finally left the MPHA, I felt happy and proud on being elected president of the Punjab Hockey Association (PHA) on my posting to Punjab.

Though I had always been an upfront officer, my Mussoorie tenure had further reinforced my belief in the autonomy of thought and deed, something contrary to the prevailing culture in the police, where any deviation from the course of action set by superior and supervisory officers was considered akin to heresy. My style of functioning was defined by an attitude of healthy and reasoned dissent. Thus, when a minister in the home department called me repeatedly to transfer some sub-inspectors, I not only flatly refused to carry out his wishes, I also complained against him to CM P.C. Sethi. It was the kind of bravado rarely seen in police departments then and even less so now, but the CM's response was surprisingly positive and gracious. He promised to caution his colleague, which he probably did to good effect as the minister never approached me again.

In early 1976, the Jabalpur area commander and I organized a National Horse Show, where the Chief of the Army Staff and the IGP were the chief guests. The event went off very well indeed except that an NCC horse that I was riding decided to negotiate a compound jump without me. A small bone in my right ring finger got fractured, proving once again that I was particularly vulnerable to fracture injuries. The local Nerbudda Club had arranged an impressive cultural programme the same evening, which included a beauty contest. As it happened, the judges picked my daughter Amrita as the winner.

Army officers sometimes create awkward situations for themselves out of sheer naivety. Thus, when the Chief of the Army Staff was to retire, the Jabalpur army station decided to present a unique gift to him. A recce party discovered an ancient idol in a nearby village, just the gift they were looking for. So, the idol was removed from there in the dark of the night, nicely packed and dispatched to Delhi for presentation to the chief. When the villagers discovered the loss of the idol, a big hue and cry ensued and the matter was reported to the police and the archaeological department. On seeing that the matter had taken such a turn, a rattled brigadier came to me and related the full story. I asked him to get the idol quietly placed back at the same site. The next day, when the villagers saw the deity back, safe and sound, they celebrated the event as a divine marvel.

In mid-1977, J.S. Kukreja replaced Joshi and immediately proposed my transfer to the minor post of chief security officer (CSO) in the MP Electricity Board, Jabalpur, usually occupied by officers with poor records. He sought to justify his proposal on the ground that *my daughters were in school in Jabalpur.* This was incorrect as two of my daughters were studying in Delhi and the youngest was in a Central school and could easily move to any other such school. Luckily for me, the CM, who was to clear the proposal, was well acquainted with my professional ability since the time I had been SP, Bhopal. When he asked Kukreja why he wished to consign me to a minor post, Kukreja cited the argument about my daughters' education. The CM called his bluff by calling me up to find out the truth and suggested that I be posted to Gwalior. Kukreja did not relish the implied slight and asked me to proceed to Gwalior without availing of joining time. I had no problem in doing so except that I had to refuse several invitations to farewell functions from my friends, both in the government and outside. His ill will towards me was of long standing and became even more marked over time due to some imaginary slights of which he often accused me.

He was soon replaced by K.K. Dave, an upright and level-headed officer, posted at that time in Delhi. He had been mostly in the police headquarters and thus lacked adequate district experience. Unable to cope with the many political pulls and pressures, he resigned from the IPS over a minor matter. This bold step, however, proved futile in curbing the growing political intrusion, mainly because his move was ill timed and ill planned. P.R. Khurana was now brought back from the Centre to replace Dave. Khurana was an old friend and shared with me a deep interest in English literature. He too was shifted out soon as the topmost police post became hostage to the whims and fancies of wayward and venal politicians all over the country, which was severely damaging the discipline, morale and professional efficacy of the force.

11

Going Up the Ladder–II: Gwalior

In June 1977, I found myself once again journeying by road to the hot and dry climes of north-western MP with my wife and youngest daughter, the other two girls being in college in Delhi. Some fourteen years ago, I had traversed the same road from Sagar to Morena. Jabalpur was not easy to forget, but it was only a matter of time before Gwalior won us over with its warmth and openness. Morena had indeed been a difficult charge in 1963 with the dacoity situation at its worst. By the 1970s, however, dacoity in the Gwalior range had been all but contained and, barring one or two, I had a good set of SPs. The DIG bungalow, formerly the residence of the IGP of Gwalior state and located on a beautiful tree-lined road, was probably the best official house I had ever occupied. Also, thanks to my predecessors, the house was very well furnished. There was even a cattle shed where a milch animal could be housed, which made my mother hugely happy as it reminded her of her life back home in Punjab. This also gave her something satisfying to do during her occasional visits to Gwalior.

One could even turn a farmer since the house had a large patch of land and a tube well for irrigation. A large forest of timber and beautiful flowering trees greeted you when you entered the house. Regrettably, one of my successors tore down this lovely woodland that had taken decades to develop. My wife could now indulge in her passion for gardening to her heart's content as the soil was productive, water and help was plentiful and the climate was just right. Gwalior was familiar territory; among many links with my Morena days was Fahim, my personal assistant, a very capable hand. Then there were Madho Singh, Mohar Singh, Nathu, et al., the dreaded dacoits whom I had chased in Morena during those exciting anti-dacoity operations, now free men after the 1972 mass 'surrender'. They visited me regularly and talked about the old times and the many near-encounters we had had in the impassable forests of Morena. Madho, the man behind the entire process that had led to the mass surrender, was easily the most articulate of the lot.

Gwalior figures prominently in the very readable memoirs of General Sleeman, chiefly responsible for stamping out the curse of thuggee and dacoity in central and western India in the 1830s. When posted to Simla, he made a brief stopover in Gwalior, where he stayed in a huge camp in a *phool bagh*, specially set up for him in keeping with his status as a leading British general. Ironically, the huge brass bell kept at the quarter guard and several other costly items were stolen a day before his arrival. This deeply upset the general, especially on learning that the thieves enjoyed royal patronage. Here was a celebrity, who had wiped out the age-old bane of thuggee and yet he could not elude petty thieves, who had filched many valuable items from under his nose, as it were. The episode often came in handy for me when local politicians and media men grew too critical of police performance in the range. I only had to draw their attention to that episode. It usually worked.

The erstwhile royal family of Gwalior wielded enormous influence and the royal palace was still the hub of social and political activity in the region. Government officials, too, by and large, observed the durbar etiquette when calling on Rajmata Vijayaraje Scindia, who had acquired a heroic image for having toppled the Congress government of D.P. Mishra a few years earlier, and who was now an iconic leader of the BJS, later to be renamed Bharatiya Janata Party (BJP). Her only and estranged son, Madhavrao, was, however, in the Congress and thus politically opposed to her. For his part, the young maharaja often called some of us officers to dinner and we looked forward to such events, which were always marked by style and good taste. The major cause of friction between mother and son was the malevolent influence that a prominent courtier, Sardar Angre, wielded over the Rajmata—strongly reminiscent of medieval-era scandals in royal households—which the son strongly resented. Angre also enjoyed considerable clout in the BJS-ruled state government because of his proximity to the Rajmata.

Madhavrao, recently returned from Oxford with a postgraduate degree, was a forward-looking and companionable person, and it was a pleasure interacting with him though I had a problem addressing him, or his mother for that matter, as Your Highness, the common mode of address which they were used to. Thus, when I had to write an official letter to him, I found it impossible to address him as Your Highness. Finally, I would shoot off the letter with the standard 'Dear Mr Scindia'. Although something of a sacrilege in those royalty-obsessed days, he never held it against me. On the contrary, I always found him extremely considerate and helpful even when he was an important Union minister. When I visited him in Rail Bhavan in Delhi many years later to intercede on behalf of my daughter—then a railway officer who had been denied permission to proceed on study leave to the US (her rightful entitlement under service rules)—he readily helped her beat the bureaucratic red tape.

At that time, he was looking for someone suitable to head

Gwalior University, then in major turmoil. He sounded me out for the job, adding coolly that I was likely to lose the few hairs that still adorned my scalp if I did land the VC's job. I finally landed up in Bhopal University, but that is another story. His untimely death in a plane crash cut short a very promising career in Indian politics, endowed as he was with the singular qualities of head and heart. Rarely have I met an Indian politician so intellectually gifted and professionally competent, with a keen sense of right and wrong and a sound vision for the future. We learnt about his death while on a holiday in Shimla. My wife could not control the tears she shed as though we had lost a family member.

One of the prized possessions of the palace museum was a miniature silver train, acquired by Madhavrao's grandfather. During state dinners, the train ran on the huge dining table, carrying food and drinks for the guests at the table. Evidently, the train was meant to flabbergast his British visitors, though street gossip had it that the wily maharaja, who held the controls, would often playfully make the train move on before guests had helped themselves to the fare. Indian princes have been known to indulge in even weirder pranks in their dealings with the British. This train, though no longer in use, had become a cherished heirloom of which Madhavrao was very proud. Around five o'clock one morning, a hugely upset maharaja rang up to inform me that the silver train was missing from the museum. I asked Mahesh Sharma, SP, Gwalior, to proceed to the spot urgently and I followed soon after. Our investigators were soon on the job so as to not lose valuable time and clues.

As it happened, the crime was solved within hours and the missing relic was recovered from the palace forest. A retainer had conspired with a gang of smugglers to steal the artefact—worth a fortune on the international market—hand it over to them and earn a handsome profit in the bargain. The maharaja was thrilled at the retrieval of a prized object and deeply appreciated the police achievement. It is rare that policemen receive such fulsome praise from persons in positions of power. As a small gesture of gratitude for honouring my officers, I invited the maharaja to dinner at our house. Such was the affability of the man that he would always mention the event and compliment my wife whenever we met later in Gwalior or Delhi.

The region abounds in sadhus and swindlers of various kinds, who openly exploit its simple and credulous people for their own ends. As an agnostic, I consider myself immune to the wiles of such charlatans. Yet, just such an impostor, with many strings of *rudraksh* beads around his neck, did derive some mileage from his presumed access to me. He would park himself outside my bungalow office for all my visitors to get the impression that he was my guru. Soon after, he met me and offered to read my hand. I let him do so, half in jest. Gradually, he gained my mother's confidence and was in and out of the house whenever I was away. This was enough for him to catch the attention of the public who sought favours from my officers and police officials who were under inquiry. One day, SP, Shivpuri, called me up to disclose, rather hesitantly, the criminal history of the man he, too, believed was my guru. I asked him to take the swindler into custody right away and dispatch him to the place where he was wanted, which the SP promptly did. The search of his ashram yielded many official documents, such as orders and appeals in disciplinary inquiries against subordinate police officials as well as from litigants in revenue cases. The latter were to be taken up with a member of the revenue board, who had truly been taken in by the cheat.

Towards the end of the 1970s, the Indian police force was rocked by a series of agitations by men of all ranks for better pay scales, improved conditions of service and, even more importantly, for an effective mechanism for grievance redress. It was a rather unusual event in Indian police history and, not unexpectedly, state bureaucracies found themselves at sea in coping with the many social and political implications of an agitation by the state's principal law-enforcement agency. Apart from dismal service conditions, a sense of discontent and restiveness had been building up in the Indian police for quite some time due to the humiliating way in which they were treated, both by the citizens and their own officers. Right from the days of the Raj, subordinate ranks in the police were denied even the basic courtesies by their officers, which deeply hurt their self-esteem and sense of dignity. While most of them made up for such degrading treatment by venting their ire on members of the public, a sense of collective hurt had gradually seized the rank and file, especially when educated persons started joining the police. A major cause of discontent was the degrading manner in which the policemen who were posted as orderlies to officers, to assist them in official work, were treated.

Typically, state governments chose to ignore the portents of the looming crisis as well as the advice of their police chiefs and allowed the situation to drift. By 1978, a wave of unrest and discontent had gripped the constabulary in several states and some CPOs. There was no evidence that these agitations had been led by or instigated by their officers or that they were actively supported by mainstream political parties, though maverick politicians did try to fish in troubled waters. Middle-level officers generally kept away from active involvement and showed no disinclination to comply readily with directions to deal firmly with the agitating policemen, though, of course, they could not but feel sympathetic to the demands voiced by the agitators. The stir in MP police started in Bhopal and soon spread to the SAF and the district police. IGP P.R. Khurana suggested an eminently workable line of approach to defuse the situation well in time to pre-empt the likelihood of uniformed policemen taking to the streets. He and I called on the home minister to plead strongly for at least a token gesture to resolve the deadlock peacefully. The minister, true to form, refused even to consider the formula suggested by us. And yet, as soon as the first batch of policemen took to the streets, the government quickly gave in, but it was a case of too little, too late. The agitation spread rapidly to the whole state once the initial hesitation that had held the men back from defying their officers weakened. In my range, Gwalior was the worst affected as it had a sizeable SAF and district police population. To avoid a deepening of distrust, SP Mahesh Sharma and I visited the kotwali to address the men, and though a distinct feeling of disquiet was noticeable, there was no open defiance, which was clearly a positive sign.

We were soon able to contain the unrest though the Home Guards created considerable trouble while on duty at the annual Gwalior fair. The Home Guards are a volunteer force in uniform, trained and mandated to assist the district administration in law-and-order and civil-defence duties but paid a measly allowance. A feeling of discontent had been building up among them for some time, and they too took to the path of agitation for the redress of their grievances. Those were indeed trying times for the police leadership. IPS officers, responsible both for controlling the agitation and articulating the grievances of their men before the authorities, found it a delicate and ticklish job. For ranged against them was not only the political executive but also the IAS bureaucracy, who saw in this situation a most plausible argument against the growing demand for autonomy in police work. A service, which was unable to provide effective leadership to its own officers, could not claim to be treated on par with the IAS, it was argued. In the process, the IPS lost considerable ground in its struggle to gain more respect and support from the establishment.

The police unrest had a positive effect too; the lower cadres, always a neglected lot, gained recognition as a crucial component of the force. No longer would state governments arbitrarily disallow proposals from police chiefs to improve emoluments, allowances, house rents and leave entitlements for policemen. Although sporadic episodes of unrest and agitations in the Indian police were not unknown, the late-1970s chapter of police unrest was all-pervading and exposed the many drawbacks of the outmoded personnel management practices in the force. The level of unrest had not been uniform in all the districts of a state or among all the states. It had varied widely, depending on the leadership qualities of SPs and their rapport with the men. Similarly, those IGs who kept in close touch with their officers and men, and regularly brought their grievances to the notice of their governments for prompt redress, had far fewer problems. On the positive side, the unrest guaranteed to the police that their problems would remain under constant review and that they would be assured of representation in grievance-redressal machinery.

The issue of police unrest would be examined in depth by the National Police Commission (NPC) set up soon after to examine a whole range of structural and functional issues relating to the Indian police—which had remained frozen since its reorganization in the mid-nineteenth century—and to make proposals for its modernization and democratization. The NPC was remarkably gifted with an eminent civilian as chairman, two of India's brightest police leaders, a top social scientist and a former high court judge as members. It produced eight very useful reports, which addressed most facets of policing and law enforcement in an effort to restructure and modernize a colonial police system. A study group, under former chief secretary R.P. Noronha and comprising an IG and two eminent public men, was set up by the MP government to frame its response to the NPC's terms of reference. I was its member secretary. Within a couple of months, we submitted a detailed report to the NPC which accepted several of our proposals. Unfortunately, halfway through its labours, the NPC lost the trust of the new PM, Indira Gandhi, who considered it a ploy by the Janata government to discredit her, much like the Shah Commission. So, the NPC was asked to pack up and its reports were sidelined. A historic opportunity to restructure and modernize an antiquated system of policing was thus lost due to party politics. Ironically, Pakistan incorporated some of the NPC's salient proposals in its Police Order 2002, which replaced the 150-year-old Indian Police Act that was locally known as the Pakistan Police Act.

The likes of Charan Singh and Raj Narain—petty provincial-level politicians—had a field day in the ragtag Janata government. Narain's visit to Gwalior stands out due to his bizarre behaviour. While inspecting the police guard, he warmly embraced the cops, much to their discomfort. Two constables happened to have the same names as the minister, a coincidence that pleased the latter no end and he proceeded to hug his namesakes once again with renewed zest. At an election meeting in Gwalior, Charan Singh waxed eloquent on the subject of toilet facilities for rural women and promised to get many lavatories constructed in villages if his party came to power. He often visited the BSF academy at Tekanpur, near Gwalior, mostly for rest and recreation. Since his special assistant was an IPS officer, we fondly believed that this was the time to put pressure on the Union government for expediting the process of reforms in the Indian police. We held several meetings with the man but to no effect, mainly because he lacked the intellectual depth to think beyond *daroga*s and kotwals, familiar figures to him in rural UP.

Morarji Desai, who visited Gwalior for electioneering, had some odd food habits to say the least. He would drink only cow's milk and that too from a black cow. Since a black cow was not readily available, a cow of an indeterminate colour was procured and painted black to satisfy the great man's whim. Such operations come naturally to that multipurpose arm of Indian administration, the tahsildar–thanedar duo. Fortunately, Desai did not insist upon personally feeding *this* cow, which he was often in the habit of doing. Indira Gandhi too visited the area, starting with Datia, where she worshipped a goddess, believed to cause discord and disunity in the enemy camp. She stayed the night at the Gwalior circuit house and left by road early next morning for Etawah in UP. No one except Congress workers met her.

Soon the Janata government, which had come to power largely as a reaction by the voters to the hardships suffered by them during the Emergency, got involved in squabbling and infighting. Home Minister Charan Singh ousted the PM, Morarji Desai, and occupied the prime ministerial chair with support from the Congress. Unable to secure a vote of confidence in Parliament, Charan Singh went down in history as the only Indian PM never to face the legislature. Fresh elections were called and the Congress came back to power with Indira Gandhi as the PM. Sanjay, her younger son, resumed his earlier dominant role in the corridors of power to emerge as an extra-constitutional authority, a concept that would henceforth become firmly entrenched in the Indian version of democracy. The Congress returned to power in MP and Arjun Singh was elected leader of the Congress legislature party by 'consensus', a term used by the Congress high command to foist their favourites as state CMs. In fact, Shivbhanu Singh Solanki, a senior tribal leader, had secured the majority of votes, but the high command prevailed upon him to withdraw in favour of Arjun Singh, a Sanjay loyalist.

I had now completed three years in Gwalior, the normal tenure in such postings; it was time to move on and possibly look for a Central deputation. Although I was now on the panel for promotion as an IG, an early promotion in my state seemed most unlikely. Some windows of opportunity were, however, available in Delhi. During a visit to Gwalior, Srinivasa Varadan, an MP cadre officer, then the Union home secretary, asked me if I would like to go to Manipur as IGP. In the meanwhile, P.S. Bhinder, appointed police commissioner of Delhi after superseding a number of his seniors, rang up to caution me against accepting the Manipur job. For I would get stuck in that difficult position for years since no IPS officer in his right senses would opt to replace me.

He advised me, instead, to look for some Delhi posting, which would also ensure that my daughters' higher studies were not disrupted. Two such positions were then available:

director, civil aviation security, and director, police training. He even arranged for me to meet the minister for civil aviation, but the minister's dubious reputation put me off. Nor did I find the job overly exciting. I, therefore, opted for the training job as this area of police had always been of deep interest to me. When I went to Delhi to follow up on the case, I ran into J.S. Bawa, director, CBI. Mr Bawa and I had been together in the first advanced course for IPS officers in Mount Abu, back in 1960. He suggested that I join the Central Bureau of Investigation (CBI) as joint director (JD). I was foolish enough to refuse the offer because the organization, earlier headed by D. Sen, a promoted UP officer of debatable credentials, had come in for much criticism for its style of functioning during Indira Gandhi's Emergency rule. So, I landed up in a decaying building off Curzon Road as director, training, in the Bureau of Police Research and Development (BPR&D), to look after the training and infrastructure needs of the Indian police force. Notionally, it was a huge charge but the office carried little weight in the corridors of power.

We left Gwalior for Delhi in June 1980 in my old Ambassador car, bought in an auction in Jabalpur as that was all I could afford. The send-off by the Gwalior police was indeed grand with a column of policemen and officers pulling my car in a ceremonial farewell march, in which all my SPs took part. In a farewell function at the kotwali, attended by the Gwalior city police, I received what I have always considered the ultimate compliment from the officers and the men with whom I had the privilege of working for three and a half decades. R.D. Mishra, the kotwali town inspector, sounded both surprised and happy when he stated inter alia that 'during the three years that the DIG sahib remained posted in Gwalior, not once did we see the *bai* sahib [meaning my wife] shopping in the *bada*'. Bada is the main shopping centre in the city, frequented by everyone of consequence in the local bureaucracy. I thought there could be no better testimony to the kind of regard that my wife and I enjoyed among my men and officers. I could look back with considerable satisfaction and pride on my tenure in Gwalior.

In Gwalior, dacoity had been brought under control and urban areas had generally remained free of law-and-order problems, except for a rather serious clash between lawyers and the police which had led to an inquiry by a judge of the Delhi High Court, who finally absolved the police of all wrongful action. The other major event was the police agitation which, too, had been handled well by my SPs The two IGPs, K.K. Dave and P.R. Khurana, with whom I had had the honour of serving as DIG, Gwalior, had appreciated and supported my performance. P.R. Khurana had often shared his thoughts and problems with me and consulted me frequently while dealing with various issues ranging from poor cadre management by the state bureaucracy to tackling some difficult politicians. He was disappointed with the political and the bureaucratic establishment for failing to address in time the roots of discontent in the police, and then for ignoring his advice in dealing with the resulting unrest and agitation. If the government had only been less obdurate and insensitive, the unrest could have been contained much earlier.

My friends had taken to referring to me as Khurana's Kissinger. Unfortunately, low-level intrigues by ambitious colleagues cut short his tenure and Kukreja again managed to make it to the IGP's chair. At a personal level, we had received abundant warmth and friendship from the local people. My eldest daughter got married and left us to live with her husband in distant Darjeeling. It was a traumatic episode in our life, and it took us quite some time to get used to her new commitments as a part of her husband's family. Separation from a daughter after her marriage is a most painful experience but, like the parents of all girl children in South Asia, we got over it in time.

12

Delhi: Serving the Federal Government

I joined BPR&D as director, training, in June 1980 and instantly started a hunt for a suitable house. This can be quite a problem in a system where housing facilities are scarce and entitlements are determined by seniority and pay scales. P.C. Sethi, a former MP CM and rather fond of me, was now the housing minister, responsible for allotment of houses in Delhi. So I promptly sought an appointment with him. He received me with his typical warmth and summoned his personal secretary, Bhatia, and the director, estates, to note down my requirements and get me a house on priority basis. I came out of his chamber, confident that this was the end of my housing worries. The director, estates, escorted me to his office to receive my official application for allotment. He told me in confidence that the minister had made so many promises that it would take several months for me to reach the top of the so-called priority list for house allotment. However, I could get a house one category below my entitlement in the normal course in about a fortnight, due to my seniority in that salary band.

I took his advice and got a three-bedroom flat on the sixth floor of a high-rise building on Delhi's Ring Road within a fortnight and we soon moved in. An added attraction was a set of tennis courts close by, where I landed up every morning to play my favourite game for a couple of hours before rushing back home to have a quick bath and to get ready for office in time for the chartered bus. This was the common mode of transport for officers in Delhi, except those at the very top, entitled to use staff cars. Since my office was located off Connaught Place, my bus was full of chattering salesgirls and telephone operators. This made the forty-minute journey quite exciting, if somewhat awkward, for a middle-aged IGP. Mercifully, I did not have to wear uniform and was thus able to travel in the company of those feisty young women without feeling too uneasy. Delhi proved to be something of a comedown after the kind of lifestyle we had got used to in Gwalior. Our spartan way of life in Delhi would have left any visiting MP officers greatly perplexed, not too sure whether I had indeed been promoted as an IGP.

Sanjay Gandhi, Indira Gandhi's younger son, died in an air crash just around the time we landed in Delhi. Since Sanjay had been involved in controversies of various kinds during his short life, his sudden death and his mother's reportedly odd behaviour, set off a cycle of rumours, uncomplimentary to her. The rumour mill was working overtime to hint at huge sums of money having been put away by the deceased and that Indira Gandhi had been seen frantically rummaging around the dead body of her son to get the keys to the treasured wealth. It was only natural for her to be heartbroken by the tragedy of having lost not only a son but also her anointed political heir. It was unfair to so uncharitably misconstrue her sense of loss and dejection. In a larger context, Sanjay's death at that juncture deeply impacted the course of political events and has kept students of Indian history engaged for years.

My job involved close interface with the state police authorities to appraise their training infrastructure and help them develop the requisite expertise and proficiency in those areas. As the convener of a monitoring committee of the home ministry, I was also responsible for ensuring that the funds allotted by the Union government for modernization and revitalization of state police forces were properly and optimally utilized. Both these tasks fitted very well into my framework of priorities in the area of policing, and I soon busied myself in diligently fulfilling my charter of duties. It required extensive touring across the country to meet police chiefs and directors of training, to inspect police training institutes and to liaise with state home departments. I was also the member-secretary of the NPA board of governors of which the Union home secretary was the chairman. This was a hugely exciting job in many ways and I did my best to restructure the training modules of the IPS by proposing several innovative changes in the training curricula, both for the induction and the in-service courses. Regrettably, the NPA board was reconstituted after I left the BPR&D: the director, training, was no longer its member-secretary, thus severing the vital link—through the director, police training—between the NPA and the state police training institutions. This kind of excessive fondness for creating autonomous turfs is quite common in Indian administration.

An important part of my functional charter was to arrange an annual conference of the heads of state training institutions. This enabled me to share my perception of the way Indian police forces had to develop in order to evolve into modern and responsive law-enforcement agencies for serving the people of a liberal, democratic polity. This also helped in the sharing of best practices between various state police forces. Having developed close links with top-level public-sector training institutes, such as the Administrative Staff College of India, and the State Bank of India Staff College, among others, which I often visited as guest faculty, I was able to arrange an inter-institutional exchange of ideas, strategies, faculty and course material, which was highly beneficial to both sides. It also helped me improve my own potential by using the research and training facilities available to me. I attended a number of generalist courses in national institutes of repute in order to develop a broader outlook on policing and administration. I even prepared a research proposal for a fellowship at the National Institute of Justice, Washington, D.C., which was duly endorsed by two of the three referees.

Soon after I joined the BPR&D, I had been nominated to attend a ten-day course on higher specialization in police in Messina in Italy. It gave me a whole lot of new ideas and a global perspective on policing and law enforcement. John Alderson, an eminent British officer and writer and a friend of long standing, was there as guest faculty, as was Dick Ward, then professor of criminal justice in Chicago. Dick had started life as a street cop in New York, drifted into academics and reached the very top in academia. Both John and Dick later wrote forewords for my books on the Indian police. The farewell dinner at a quaint little old-fashioned restaurant in Messina was a memorable event: we all got awfully drunk on the many kinds of exotic wines and spirits on the menu, sang songs in our native languages, made farewell speeches in some kind of Italian, and exchanged autographed menu cards that the restaurant had specially provided for the purpose. We finally parted with a heavy heart and abundant promises to keep in touch. Sadly, only a few of us were destined to run into each other again.

It was a well-conceived and well-organized course and though the course language was Italian, real-time English translation facilities were available. The guest faculty included both academics and police officers, carefully chosen for proficiency in their areas. Being the first-ever Indian officer in the course, I received a standing ovation on the first day. My presentation was on 'Police and the Media'. Local newspapers covered my talk and interaction with the participants at length though, of course, in Italian. The organizers told us when we joined that we should not leave any valuables in our rooms nor should we carry them on our person while going out. When we asked where then should we park our money, they just shrugged. My foreign allowance was so meagre that I had to go hunting every evening for the cheapest pizzas available. Notably, the most well-off among us were the Africans, who seemed always to have a lot of money to throw about and were also the best dressed. Mercifully, the hosts were considerate enough to arrange for a sumptuous lunch and plenty of fine wines for those of us who cared to join in.

For the concluding three days, we were taken to Rome for study visits to some key police establishments. This enabled me to explore the city leisurely, walking from one historical site to another, absorbing the delicate flavours and aromas of history. It was difficult to negotiate the language barrier, but there were always some English-speaking tourists in the same plight and one could get along fine. It was in Rome that I realized to my horror that the warnings repeatedly conveyed to us by the organizers to be careful with our money were not without reason. One would often come upon fetching young gypsy women with an infant clutching a bare breast while an older child walked closely by her side, keeping a sharp lookout for inattentive foreigners. And then, in a jiffy, while you were busy staring furtively at the young breast, the child would make a quick getaway with your shopping bag or wallet or whatever. A memorable event in Rome was a lunch hosted by the carabinieri at their wonderful clubhouse. An assortment of delectable wines and delicious dishes awaited us by the poolside that made me forget all my famished evenings in Messina. To an Indian policeman, accustomed to the miserable subsistence levels of the Indian police, this seemed to be truly a fairy-tale setting. Dominico Cucchiara and Giaconda Barletta, president and vice president, respectively, of the host institute, became close friends and invited me twice again as a guest speaker for their courses: in Cyprus in 1990 and the US in 2001. I could not attend the US course due to what has come to be known as 9/11.

By scrounging on food, I had saved enough lire to undertake a journey across Europe by train, visiting several charming places, among them, Geneva, Vienna and Budapest. Europe has always fascinated me because of its cultural diversity and literary traditions that had left a deep imprint on my mind ever since my introduction to French, German, Russian and other European writers and thinkers in English translations. Even when posted in the remote and culturally barren districts of MP, I had kept up my interest in literature and art through postal delivery of books of my choice. The Messina course opened a welcome window on Italy and Rome while my visits to Geneva, Vienna and Budapest after the course significantly enlarged my perspective on that charming continent. Hungary was still under communist rule and it would have been impossible to visit Budapest but for a high party official attending the course, who actually suggested that I undertake the journey and arranged a visa. And the visit was well worth it.

All three cities, each offering a different kind of experience, were small in size, even by European standards and one could do them on foot in a couple of days. On reaching Geneva after a long train journey from Rome, I headed for Sanjoy Bagchi's house for a quick bath and some food before looking for suitable lodgings. Sanjoy, an IAS batchmate of mine and an outstanding officer, was then a UN official. His wife made a delicious omelette for breakfast. While strolling through the many corridors of the League of Nations building in Geneva, now housing some UN offices, I came upon a typical Indian restaurant where I had my first Indian meal in many days. The old city beyond the famed Lake Geneva was typical of old towns all over the world. Hardip Puri, my probationer in Mussoorie, surprised me in the foyer of the Indian embassy, while I was looking at old Indian newspapers. He took me home to his beautiful flat for a delicious meal in the company of several young diplomats. On offer were a choice of great wines and an exquisite cuisine. Hardip had always been a man of taste and a gracious host.

Vienna, at one time the cultural and political hub of Central Europe and abounding in museums, opera houses, art galleries and imperial palaces, suggestive of past grandeur and splendour, presented a different kind of experience. I sat spellbound in the Vienna State Opera House, where Mozart had given some of his most memorable performances, and spent a whole morning sitting by the Danube, humming to myself the few tunes that called to mind the mystery of that great European river. The daily tram rides offered a quiet retreat from the noise and commotion of the city. I could quietly watch the traffic go by and reflect on the splendid objets d'art on display at the many museums and art galleries, some of which were way beyond my reach due to costly entry tickets. Old horse carts plying on cobbled streets marked the old city—redolent with whiffs of a past which was fading fast—where one could spend a leisurely afternoon. The Viennese regard Mozart as virtually their property. A charming garden, with a marble statue of him, in front of the State Opera House, marks his association with the place. A number of coffee and pastry shops dot the town's inner ring road. I visited one such shop, which projected on to the pavement, sipped Turkish black coffee and watched people move around. On offer were twenty-two different kinds of coffee, a rather difficult collection to choose from. Schönbrunn Palace, at the end of the tram route, was later to provide the model for Versailles. Its art gallery houses a remarkable collection of paintings by Rembrandt and other Dutch masters.

Once back in Delhi, I was drafted on to the 1982 Asian Games Organising Committee. Part of my job was to brief the media on hockey fixtures. The highlight of the meet was the finals between India and Pakistan in which India secured an early lead but then visibly wilted, allowing Pakistani forwards to score goal after goal, defeating Indians by seven goals to two. The crowd was livid with anger, blaming the goalkeeper for the humiliation. Decades later, a moving film, *Chak De! India*, was made on the theme, with the popular actor Shah Rukh Khan playing the role of the disgraced goalkeeper, now transformed into a dedicated coach of the Indian women's team. The team goes on to win the World Cup against all odds, thus, in a way, vindicating his position among his countrymen. I was also in charge of the march past by the participating teams at the closing ceremony where the teams were to march in alphabetical order. Iraq was to follow Iran. The two nations absolutely refused to march together. Finally, we had to place the team of another nation—I forget which—between the two Arab nations, which were at war back home, while simultaneously competing in Delhi.

In October 1983, I was invited to Messina as guest faculty where I spoke on the human rights of policemen, a subject rarely discussed in conferences on police and law enforcement. My presentation evoked a lot of interest and debate. Since I was already halfway to the US—where I was bound and where I had never been—I decided to have a brief stopover in London and then fly to New York. Airlines were much kinder to passengers those days and a dollar cost only eight rupees. What drew me to the UK this time was not London but an invitation from Brian Morgan, acting chief constable of Devon & Cornwall Police, to address his officers on policing and law-enforcement issues in South Asia. Meanwhile, he briefed me about the various reforms carried out by Alderson in the force that he had led for several years. I also flew with him in the police chopper over the moors, the scene of many a crime in that wild land.

The next day I flew to Milan, on the way to New York. In Milan, my diplomatic passport caused quite a stir when the young man at the check-in counter saw a traveller with a diplomatic passport stuck in a long queue. He left his seat and came to me, tendering in his native tongue what I presumed were profuse apologies for failing to clear me on a priority basis. While duly appreciating his concern, I asked him to get on with his job as the other passengers were giving me dirty looks. New York was an alien land for me in more senses than one. Even the pace of life was many times faster than anything I had known so far. I had to strain hard to follow the American drawl at the information desk. I did manage, though, to get to the domestic terminal to catch the shuttle service that took off every few minutes for Washington, D.C., my final destination. That was the first time I saw passengers walk straight into the aircraft directly from the street and buy their tickets after boarding. After a long transatlantic flight and a rather bewildering experience at the first point of entry into an alien land, I heaved a deep sigh of relief on seeing my cousin Dharam waiting for me at Washington airport to relieve me of all my worries.

Dharam was working with the World Bank in Washington. I accompanied him to the city every morning, wandered around the capital city and came back home with him. Dick Ward arranged for me to visit the National Institute of Justice in Washington and the FBI Academy in Quantico, Virginia. Both the visits provided a great learning experience. Dick also set up an interactive session with graduate students and faculty in the Department of Public Administration at the University of Illinois in Chicago, where he was then serving as VC for administration. This was my very first exposure to the American student community and I found it odd that they casually strolled into the classroom carrying cups of coffee and talking loudly. A few years later, I visited Chicago again to present a paper on transnational crime at an international conference, where I met several very learned and interesting people.

Back in my job after a glorious visit to Europe and the US, I became increasingly uneasy over the total apathy with which my nodal ministry was treating my carefully prepared proposals, which remained buried deep in red tape. I had drawn up a proposal in consultation with a friend in the IFS, who was then posted as high commissioner to Uganda, for extending to some African nations training facilities in our police institutions. My proposal just lay around, gathering dust in the ministry, while China readily took on the job. We could have created a clutch of friendly police bureaucracies in many African countries if only the proposal had been accepted. I decided to seek a transfer, although I would have stuck to the job despite its lack of many perks that my colleagues in other CPOs enjoyed. The CBI was still willing to ask for my services by name, which they soon did. After pulling some strings, I got a posting as JD in the CBI. I soon found that it enjoyed far more clout in the corridors of power than many other departments of the Union government, and for good reason.

After a few months, we shifted to the up-scale area of Bapa Nagar. Located close to India Gate and Rajpath as our new house was, several parks and some of the city's best shopping areas were within easy reach, as were all the beautiful roads around these historical sites. New Delhi is, in any case, a walker's paradise and, besides the bungalow area of Lutyens's Delhi, Bapa Nagar was indeed one of the best locations. Close by was Lodhi Gardens, where many of the high and mighty of the city came for their morning constitutional, mostly in huge cars. The famed India International Centre and the posh Khan Market were not far off either. I found this entire setting an ideal place for long walks, my favourite pastime. Twice a week, I drove for a game of tennis to the Delhi Gymkhana Club, where one could hope to share the court with some of the best tennis players around. Khushwant Singh, then a sprightly sixty, was often seen there in full action.

The CBI has a wide-ranging charter of duties under the IPC and the Prevention of Corruption Act, 1988. No wonder then that CBI officers of my rank were much sought after in several different ways. I was made in charge of two divisions, one covering eastern India and the other dealing with highly sensitive criminal cases from all over the country. This was a huge charge but I had some very competent officers to assist me, among them, C.M. Sharma from UP and A.S. Bal, formerly my SP in Jabalpur. Commuting still remained a problem. Bal and I tried a car pool but our ancient cars often left us stranded. I tried using a scooter, but did not have the heart to drive through the busy Connaught Place to reach my office in Sardar Patel Bhawan, located midway between Connaught Place and the Parliament complex. Finally, I took to walking the two-odd miles to my office, an ordeal in Delhi summers. So, when I opted for the very challenging job of DGP in a Punjab severely affected by militancy, my friends attributed it to my commuting problems in Delhi!

The CBI is often accused of being a tool in the hands of the ruling party for use against rival politicians or party dissidents. Such accusations have grown manifold over the last two decades since I left the CBI. As a JD, I was not privy to how such misuse occurred. I suppose discreet suggestions were made at meetings between the PM and the director, or conveyed through a trusted confidant. In South Asia, no one dares question the close confidant of a high dignitary to confirm whether the instructions did indeed emanate from the latter. So, there is always the possibility of a personal secretary or a personal assistant acting on his own. Again, in the still very colonial administrative culture of South Asia, the desires of the heads of government are tantamount to commands, and are rarely challenged. But, it is not as if only the CBI is used for such purposes. All enforcement departments—vested with powers of inquiry and prosecution under various laws—are open to such misuse.

When in power, the Congress—like all political parties—drew on intelligence agencies to keep tabs on its CMs and used the inputs so obtained to prepare detailed dossiers against them, which were put to good use to contain dissent and deter defections. So, when a popular CM of Sikkim seemed to be getting a little out of hand, a CBI team led by DIG C.M. Sharma was deputed to bring him around. It took just one fortnight for the team to collect enough material to prepare a charge sheet under several provisions of the law against the feisty CM. The dossier thus compiled was too potent for the impetuous CM not to fall in line. The same procedure had to be followed in the case of a former CM of Bihar, belonging to the ruling Congress party, when he showed signs of becoming too opinionated for the party's comfort.

Such distortions apart, the CBI, as a nodal investigation agency, handles its charter of duties most impartially when not hamstrung by political dictates. Central government departments, states and even the higher judiciary often requisition its services for investigations and inquiries into sensitive and intricate cases. Investigations are handled by inspectors and deputy superintendents, closely supervised by senior officers and vetted by designated law officers. This ensures good results.

An intricate and sensitive case that I supervised was the murder of a senior Punjab cadre IPS officer, closely related to the Gandhi family, thus inviting wide publicity. The deceased and I had been colleagues in the IHF and had worked together in the 1982 Asian Games. It was both awkward and painful to subject his wife, the prime suspect, to sustained interrogation. Our inquiries revealed that relations between the husband and wife had been difficult for some time as the suspicious wife often made loaded insinuations about her husband's marital infidelity. This had led to constant squabbling, taunts and sarcastic remarks. Although friends and neighbours were aware of the strained relations between the two, no one thought that things would take such a grave turn. Unable to bear the tension any longer, the wife won over an orderly to her side and late one night when the husband came home sozzled and enfeebled, the wife scoffed at his masculinity. One thing led to another and, exhausted as he was, he was overpowered by the orderly and the woman who, in the heat of the moment, struck a blow at his head. He fell to the ground in a heap and died soon after. In the scuffle, his belt came undone and his trousers slipped down from his waist. When things took such a critical turn, both of them panicked and stuffed the body in the boot of the small family car, with an arm partly sticking out, carried it by a side road to Sukhna Lake, and dumped the half-naked body into the lake sometime after midnight.

The body was first noticed by early-morning walkers on the lake promenade, causing a near-stampede of curious spectators. There was widespread shock and disbelief when the identity of the dead man became known. The reports reached the corridors of power in Chandigarh and Delhi. The local police took up the investigation but the case was soon entrusted to the Special Crimes Division of the CBI under my charge. All available evidence pointed to the wife as the guilty party. So she was charge-sheeted, the orderly having turned approver. A lengthy trial later, she was convicted, but was released on bail, pending finalization of her several appeals in higher courts. An accused with deep pockets can escape judicial reprisal by filing multiple appeals and, in any case, court trials take decades to conclude.

A rather intriguing case from Bihar, rooted in intense political rivalry between the CM and the Speaker of the legislative assembly, both senior Congress leaders, also landed on my table. It was not unusual for the Congress leadership to promote rivalries among state leaders to keep them in a state of insecurity. While both the Bihar leaders swore eternal loyalty to the high command, they were bent upon damaging each other's political credibility. The CM sought to exploit the death, in suspicious circumstances, of a pretty nurse, aptly named Bobby, by implicating the Speaker in the crime with the help of a pliable SP of Patna, brought on deputation from Gujarat. The SP also wielded a great deal of influence in the state as his father was close to the CM. When the Speaker complained to the PM, the CBI was asked to take over. I flew to Patna to look into the case. The SP, CBI, in Patna was a Bihari and thus had good relations with local politicians and bureaucrats. Allegations and insinuations flew thick and fast in both camps, but no one could provide a definite lead.

Finally, it was the range DIG who described to me the whole sequence of events and how all the district police were manipulating the case to fix the Speaker, who was angling for the post of the CM. Since caste was central to political and service loyalties in Bihar, the CM was being actively helped by the Brahmin police and forensic officials to hit at his rival, a Bhumihar. Not only was material evidence being manipulated by swapping of blood samples and other forensic exhibits, witnesses too were being tutored to depose in a certain manner. To my uninitiated mind, the extent of collusion between the politicians and the local police at all levels was beyond belief. We collected enough evidence to bring out the real sequence of events as far as it was possible at that stage and put up charge sheets against the real culprits.

Another interesting case involved a former minister from my own state of MP. He often called me to complain against the local police for flawed investigation in the case of the murder of his nephew. When I told him that the case was not with the CBI, he promptly had the case assigned to my division by some smart string-pulling in the ministry. Our inquiries revealed that the man himself was involved in the conspiracy to get his nephew killed because the young man had been indulging in activities that gave his family a bad name. Shocked to find the matter take this turn, the worthy man met me one last time to upbraid me severely for what he considered sheer cussedness on my part.

Then there were the many scams in the coal belt of Dhanbad and other areas in Bihar, where powerful mafia groups colluded with politicians, labour unions and officials to siphon off huge sums of money from Central revenues. Any local official who was seen to be an impediment was simply liquidated, either physically or figuratively. I too was warned by telephone and otherwise to keep away from the sinister world of the Bihar coal belt, dominated by the Indian version of the Italian Mafiosi. It was an interesting tenure and I learnt a great deal about the way Indian political parties kept their flocks together, and the wheeler-dealing which goes on in the power games that political parties play to secure and to cling to power.

Life in Delhi was fun in many ways though, of course, the cost of living was too high. It was simply impossible to see all the excellent plays and films on offer, and to avail of a hundred other amenities of big-city life, not to mention eating out except, occasionally, at the Gymkhana Club and the India International Centre, still considerably cheaper than restaurants. As an IGP, I received a monthly salary of 2250 rupees, which translated into about 1600 rupees after the usual deductions. No dearness allowance was admissible to officers in super-time scale of pay. With two daughters studying at University and my old mother to look after, we were indeed very hard put to afford a decent standard of living. Incredible as it may sound, I had to sell off my revolver and a first-rate golf set, which my sister had brought from the US, to balance my budget.

I carry very happy memories of my Delhi tenure though we could not fully enjoy the many delights that Delhi offers, thanks largely to the fickleness of my ancient car. An interesting episode concerns Rajiv Gandhi, then being put through his paces by his mother and her close confidants to inherit her political legacy after Sanjay's tragic death. After the 1982 Asian Games ended, the organizing committee, headed by Rajiv, arranged several functions to mark the successful conclusion of such a major undertaking. At one such party, I found a rather handsome man, who somehow looked familiar, standing all by himself in a corner. Arun Singh told me that the handsome guy was indeed Rajiv, probably the most powerful Indian after Indira Gandhi. I approached him and tried to start a conversation but received only perfunctory responses. Then I happened to mention Gwalior where I had been DIG some years earlier. The mention of Gwalior at once brought a smile to his handsome face. 'Oh, Gwalior!' he said. 'I used to fly that sector and often refused to land there because the runway was so frequently overrun by cattle.' No wonder he was loath to leave his preferred profession and join politics, even though his new career was bound to lead to the prime ministerial chair one day.

13

Punjab: The Ultimate Challenge

Operation Blue Star of June 1984 was widely covered by the Indian and the foreign media, setting off chilling rumours about the desecration and defacement of the Golden Temple by the Indian army. An air of anxiety and unease prevailed in the corridors of power in New Delhi over the anguish and hurt caused in the Sikh community by the operation. Among other measures being considered by the Union government for damage control was to post an ex-cadre officer to head the Punjab police, mainly because the Punjab IPS cadre had become deeply politicized over the years. Out of the three officers shortlisted by the ministry, I was finally chosen. This was as much a surprise to me as to others. For one, though my personal and official relations with politicians had always been correct and proper, I had never been what is called a 'politically convenient' officer. Even so, within the limits of legitimacy, propriety and decorum, I shared a mutually respectful relationship with several political leaders—among them P.C. Sethi and S.C. Shukla, two very supportive CMs of my state of MP, and Madhavrao Scindia, then an up-and-coming Congress leader—whom I had had the privilege to serve.

My selection for the crucial Punjab job must have been made after careful processing at many tiers in the government and at the highest political level. Perhaps, J.S. Bawa, director,

CBI, where I was then posted as a JD, had suggested my name, and the redoubtable R.N. Kao, the PM's security advisor and former director of RAW, India's external intelligence agency, had gone through my dossiers with a microscope. The meetings with the PM's top aides, ostensibly for advice, must also have been intended as a subtle way of vetting my credentials for the top job in that problematic state. My forthright and low-profile functional style and good service record were probably my strongest reference points.

Before finally approving my name, however, the PM herself interviewed me twice to satisfy herself about my credentials for the post in Punjab, then in the grip of a burgeoning militancy. She also used the occasion to brief me on the intricacies of my upcoming assignment, asking me specifically about why I thought I would be able to handle competently the grave situation then developing in the state. After describing as best as I could my perception of the Punjab situation, I asked her how the Government of India expected me to discharge my duties in my new job. Apparently satisfied with her assessment of my aptitude, she smilingly remarked, 'But people tell me that you are a very decent man.' The expression she used in Hindi was, 'Lekin log kehte hain ki aap bahut shareef hain.' Shareef or not, I continued to enjoy the privilege of being ushered into her presence whenever I sought an appointment to brief her on some vital issue concerning my charter of duties as DGP, Punjab, ahead of the CMs and other VIPs who would be waiting in the antechamber.

Interestingly, when I met Union Home Minister P.C. Sethi, a former CM of MP, after my appointment as DGP, Punjab, he innocently remarked, 'I knew it must be our own Dhillon sahib when I read about your posting *in the newspapers* [emphasis mine].' This bland remark most aptly depicted the decision-making processes in the Union government where the home minister learnt about a crucial posting from the newspapers. The media hype accompanying my posting to Punjab created the impression that I had been selected for the key assignment by the PM herself and so enjoyed a certain degree of proximity to her. Though I had free access to her whenever it became necessary for me to seek her counsel, I met her simply as the police chief of a severely disturbed state, seeking guidance and direction. I always found in her a willing and perceptive listener, ready with advice, often accompanied by an anecdote or two in a lighter vein. This was in marked contrast to my experience with Narasimha Rao, who succeeded the ailing P.C. Sethi as home minister. The sphinx-like Rao would give no inkling of whether he was even listening to what you were so earnestly trying to bring to his attention. Ironically, Rao succeeded Rajiv Gandhi as leader of the Congress party and as the PM after the latter was assassinated in a suicide-bomb attack. Rao will go down in history as the head of a modern, secular polity, who failed to prevent the demolition by Hindu fanatics of a historic mosque in Ayodhya, in the presence of television cameras and thousands of armed police.

I flew to Chandigarh on 3 July 1984 to take over as DGP, Punjab, within a month of Operation Blue Star, replacing an embittered P.S. Bhinder. K.T. Satarawala succeeded the other fall guy, B.D. Pande, as the governor in the post–Operation Blue Star change of guard in the border state. It is typical of Indian politicians and bureaucrats to look for scapegoats among field-level officers when things go wrong even when they themselves have been, in fact, responsible for botching a situation. That is why, in those days, governors and police chiefs of Punjab were given marching orders in quick succession. A few weeks later, S.S. Dhanoa of the Bihar cadre was brought in as the chief secretary. He and I had earlier served together as deputy directors at LBSNAA, Mussoorie.

My meetings with Indira Gandhi were typically short and to the point. Only once did I have the privilege of having a long meeting with her when she spoke rather wryly about how difficult it was to engage meaningfully with the Akali leaders for the resolution of the many complex issues that eventually led to Punjab militancy. That was when she was waiting in her Parliament office to intervene, if necessary, in an important debate, because, as she told me, the home minister P.C. Sethi, then not in good health, might not be able to face the Opposition attack. As it happened, there was no need for her to intervene in the debate, and as there were no other appointments, our meeting lasted for a full forty minutes. She was particularly dismissive of Balwant Singh, a junior Akali leader, who later played a major role in helping the Punjab governor Arjun Singh clinch the Rajiv Gandhi–Harcharan Singh Longowal Accord. When Surjit Singh Barnala became CM of Punjab after the September 1985 elections, Balwant Singh was allocated the powerful finance portfolio. His proximity to Arjun Singh lent him extra clout in the new Punjab administration.

Believing that I enjoyed some clout with the PM, Akali *jathedars* often approached me to intercede on their behalf. A minor Akali leader, on the run for some time fearing the usual third-degree treatment from the Punjab police, came to meet me late one evening rather furtively, his face carefully covered with a part of his turban to avoid identification. He wanted me to arrange for him a meeting with the PM so that he could personally assure her of his loyalty to her. The more I protested my inability to oblige him in the matter, the more insistent he became in his plea. It is a measure of the state of demoralization that had then gripped many Akali leaders that my visitor refused even to occupy a chair and preferred to sit on the floor. Seeing that I was not of much help, he apparently found a more amenable patron and secured an appointment as a member of the National Commission for Minorities with huge perks and creature comforts, no doubt flaunting his nationalist credentials.

A well-known Akali leader pleaded with me several times to arrange a meeting with Indira Gandhi: he wanted to make up with her because *he did not want to go to jail again*. He later broke away from his parent party to float his own organization, alleging that the parent party was too mild in its fight for Sikh demands. Several self-styled babas and *sants* of well-known Sikh deras, attired in typical flowing robes, much revered by the Jutt peasantry, also sought my good offices to make peace with the authorities. This was not unique to the Akalis, though. There were many others, mortally scared and running for cover for fear of the militants. They would wait for hours outside my office to meet me but would later pretend as though they had never known me. A senior Congress leader of Amritsar was seriously injured in a militant attack for alleged overpricing of wheat flour that he supplied to the Golden Temple for use in the *langar*. I found him utterly shattered and terrified when I went to see him in the hospital; he tearfully implored me to save his life from the militants who were determined to kill him. We provided him with the requisite security cover, and he lived on to adorn many a ministerial chair. But by then he had given himself a complete makeover with an angular pipe always hanging limply from the left side of his mouth. At a chance meeting in Delhi a few years later, he refused even to recognize me.

I was fully aware of the nature of my mandate in my new job. It seemed to me to be fourfold, namely, to contain the ongoing violence as early as possible; to examine the causes of the failure of the Punjab police to deal effectively with militancy in the initial stages; to address the immediate causes for the growing militant sentiment within the Sikh community, such as police atrocities and fake encounters; and to minimize the fear and panic among Hindus, many of whom were fleeing the countryside to find safety in cities. I was also aware of the formidable task ahead, which could hardly be accomplished without the full backing of my officers, especially those at the cutting-edge level in the districts and the battalions. I knew from experience that those tiers would not be in a hurry to shed their misgivings about an imported boss. As for the restoration of normal political and administrative institutions in the state, it was for politicians to find suitable solutions to the complex issues of governance that had become even more intricate in the absence of a clear-cut counterterrorism policy.

For too long a time, the Indian state had been treating grave issues of minority dissent and discontent as mere law-and-order problems, seeking to address them through the use of sheer force, often resorting to state terror. I believed it was possible to reverse the course of events in Punjab by adopting an affirmative and positive approach. This, and a few others of my assumptions, however, turned out to be incompatible with the priorities of the post–Indira Gandhi establishment in Delhi, as also in Punjab after Arjun Singh arrived as governor in March 1985, ostensibly to initiate the so-called peace process in the problem state. Although he belonged to MP, which was also my parent cadre, I had never served under him nor did he have anything to do with my Punjab posting where I had preceded him by a good eight months. We will revert to the subject a little later.

I thought it was important for me to share my ideas about the gravity of the problems which we in the security establishment were facing, and the possible approaches and strategies that I had in mind to meet the challenge of growing militancy. So, the first thing I did after taking over my new charge was to put across my views to the public and the police through radio and television. I also made use of the police radio network to share my thoughts with my officers and men all over the state. My next port of call was Amritsar—the main centre of activity during all those calamitous months since the time Sikh militancy had emerged as a major challenge to the Indian state. I am not a religious person, but I did believe that a visit to the Golden Temple would give me the moral strength to remain faithful to my calling as head of the state police, mandated to stabilize the alarming situation. It would also help me make a personal assessment of the extent of collateral damage caused to the holiest Sikh shrine during the army operations and to verify personally reports in the media that a number of Sikh men, women and children—picked up during army raids in gurdwaras and other places of worship—had still been kept confined in the cantonment. Since most senior army officers who had been involved in Operation Blue Star were then stationed in Amritsar, I utilized the opportunity to ascertain their views about the whole gamut of issues, relating to various army operations. They were fairly cooperative as most army officers are and had no problem relating whatever had happened during the operation and later, although, under the laws of the land, there was much to explain and tidy up.

Since the Indian Constitution contains no provision for martial law, all acts undertaken by the armed forces to quell civil disorder, when normal law-and-order systems fail to do so, are governed by the manual of military aid to civil authority. No such army action can be carried out except on receipt of a specific requisition from a competent civil authority, namely a DM if the call-out is limited in scope or the state home secretary if army aid is needed in more than one district. Also, the primacy of the DM remains intact even when the army is deployed to handle a situation beyond the control of the magistracy and the police. The army had apparently launched Operation Blue Star without any such requisition from the state government in the belief that the fact that the operation had the implicit or explicit approval of the Central government was enough. Then there was the belief—a colonial hangover—that the army was supreme in conditions of civil unrest such as what Punjab was facing, and no one's permission was needed to set things in order, which the 'bloody civilians' had failed to do. Army officers are generally unaware of key amendments made in the relevant rules since the supreme authority now rests undoubtedly with the civilian government.

There were also other slip-ups, mainly due to ignorance of law and procedure, which needed to be addressed. All those rounded up during and after the operations had to be produced before a competent magistrate within twenty four-hours of their arrest for remand if they were required to be detained for a longer period. This was not done and the detainees had been simply picked up and confined in improvised detention camps instead of police lock-ups or notified jails, as required under the law. These were indeed grave lapses that could have led to some very awkward situations. It required the security advisor, the state governor, Lieutenant General Gowri Shankar ('Gowri, the bloody Shankar', as he used to call himself), and me to fly to Amritsar several times to fix the many legal infirmities in the conduct of the operations. The detention camps were duly notified as jails.

Some state institutions can go wrong occasionally but the state always has to intervene positively to set things right. We did exactly what was called for under the peculiar circumstances then prevailing in Punjab and keeping in view the very sensitive context in which we were then operating. The army brass had obviously been too zealous in carrying out what they thought was the mandate given to them by the Union government and, in doing so, had ignored the updated version of the standing orders about aid to civil authority. Lieutenant General Sunderji, the general officer commanding (GOC), Western Army Command, and, thus, in overall charge of Operation Blue Star, was indeed a widely read and thinking general with a deep understanding of defence and security matters. But, like all handsome, eclectic men, he suffered from a high degree of intellectual arrogance that could possibly explain why the operation went wrong.

Curiously, though people across Punjab, especially Sikhs, were in a state of shock, the powers that be in Delhi and Chandigarh seemed impervious to the collective hurt felt by the Sikh people caused by the defilement of their holiest shrine, a profanity unheard of since the Afghan invasions. I personally saw the agony of ordinary Sikh men and women, ignorant of any extremist ideology, when they saw the bullet marks on the walls and doors of the Harimandir. They reverently ran their hands over what were, to them, real wounds inflicted on what they regarded as the incarnation of their gurus, and silently wept and sobbed. The thana lock-ups were packed with grim old men, picked up by military patrols during seize-and-search operations; all young men had fled their homes, fearing execution in fake encounters. Aided by the army, we quickly had all such cases screened, and released those not accused of grave offences.

I am sure if the Indian state had been more sensitive to the hurt running through the Sikh community at the time, Bhindranwale's storm troopers would not have succeeded in sowing the seeds of a long drawn-out militancy. The White Paper, so painstakingly put together by the Union home ministry, merely put forward the version that the establishment wanted to convey and not what had really happened. Expectedly, it failed to carry conviction, not only with the Sikhs but also with large sections of the liberal-minded public except those who believed in the rightist Hindu nationalist ideology, openly or otherwise. It is a measure of the widespread attention drawn by the operation and its aftermath that almost the entire world media covered my posting in post–Operation Blue Star Punjab. Television and radio reporters from far-off places and obscure networks accosted me on all possible occasions to seek my views on various key issues and to request interview sessions. It was difficult to accommodate all of them because of the sheer lack of time though I did my best to oblige most of them even if it was during my long road travels.

My visits to police units all over the state and my intensive interaction with my officers and men in the field, as well as sections of concerned and socially aware citizens, indicated that indeed much had gone wrong with the force, mainly due to rampant politicization and other corrupting influences all along its hierarchical spread from the police chief downwards, thereby critically denting the very basics of law enforcement, namely, neutrality and detachment. The Punjab police also suffered from a serious crisis of leadership because of flawed cadre-management policies. Chief ministers preferred to have a promoted officer as district SP rather than a direct IPS officer. Therefore, the IPS just did not have enough space to grow in the profession. Acute organizational decay—dating back to Pratap Singh Kairon's rule—had spawned an effete, politicized and brutalized law-enforcement structure, which proved woefully inept to face the militant onslaught. Managing a burgeoning militancy grew even more challenging when sundry politicians and officials in Delhi sought to rule by remote control, a classic case of exercising power without responsibility.

The Punjab administration had been virtually split into two warring camps due to the infamous political feud between Giani Zail Singh, a former CM of Punjab—now the Union home minister—and his successor and bête noire, Darbara Singh, each determined to undercut the other. And since Giani was closer to the seat of power in Delhi and far more Machiavellian than any of his contemporaries in Punjab, he ensured that the Punjab police functioned in a manner that would strengthen, rather than weaken, the forces of disorder. This was easy to accomplish through several officers who were loyal to him for favours received in the past or expected in the future, and who held important posts in the state. My first priority, therefore, was to work out a time-bound agenda for urgent and optimal reforms in the state police. This became easier as the Union government decided to set up a panel of experts to suggest a framework for such reforms within a period of about six months, with R.V. Subramaniam, a former IAS officer, as chairman and some eminent police leaders as members. I was appointed member-secretary.

The Subramaniam committee approached its task with remarkable alacrity and produced a most useful report in just about three months. The Punjab government then formed an empowered committee to implement the committee's proposals, with Subramaniam, now the governor's senior advisor, as chairman, and the home and the finance secretaries as members. I was again appointed as member-secretary. We were able to implement the bulk of the proposals on the ground in another three months. The undertaking involved immense hard work and quality input, backed by first-rate secretarial support by Chaman Lal, the new DIG, administration. This required the preparation of detailed agenda notes for the committee's weekly meetings; the recording of minutes; and the conversion of the decisions taken into office notes and orders in the files for executing on the ground. Police reform and reorganization is a highly complex task, involving as it does the reconciliation of many conflicting claims and imperatives. By the end of 1984, we had a fairly competent set-up at the police headquarters in Chandigarh, with a refurbished and expanded intelligence network and enough capacity fallback at the headquarters and in the districts to process, collate and dispense actionable intelligence to the field-level staff, the adequate crime and investigation wings, and a logistics division, apart from a reinforced administration section.

All these reforms were vital in order to invigorate the district and the thana police to meet the huge militant challenge, not only in Amritsar and Gurdaspur—which then formed the hub of the rising tide of militancy—but also all over the state and beyond. The reorganization schemes at lower levels took some more time, as they involved several district and sub-district units, which were even more central to grass-roots policing and to seizing the initiative from lawless elements, and re-establishing a measure of peace and order in the state. These broad-based reforms in the Punjab police proved immensely helpful in coming to grips with the very alarming militancy situation in the post-1986 period. However, in the confusion and chaos that marked the handling of terrorist violence towards the end, the close linkage between the success of the Punjab police and the post–Blue Star reforms were overlooked. Later, as IG, BSF, Chaman came to be known for his humane and positive policing style at a time of heightened militancy. He had to, however, ask for a posting out of Punjab due to serious differences with the then DGP, K.P.S. Gill, in conducting counterterrorism operations.

The feeling of grief and disgruntlement in the community was aggravated by the slow pace at which the joint teams of the army, the IB and the Punjab CID were screening the cases of Sikh detainees, who had been picked up by the armed forces during Blue Star and allied operations and kept in detention centres in Punjab and elsewhere. The process entailed elaborate scrutiny of the detained persons' dossiers, prepared by intelligence agencies. After a careful scrutiny of his or her dossier, each individual was placed into one of three categories—white, grey or black. Those placed in the white category were assessed as being the least likely to be hazardous to the state, if set free; the black were rated as the most dangerous and unlikely to be considered for release in the near future. The grey needed to be vetted again after some time. Such screening could take months to conclude, causing much avoidable suffering and discontent for the families of even the white-category detainees, since a mere placement in that category did not assure immediate freedom.

A high-level committee under the state governor met regularly to consider key issues bearing on the management and control of militancy and the many problems linked to it. Like all such panels, this committee too tended to be insensitive in its approach at times. Symbolic protests, such as the donning of saffron turbans and dupattas by Sikh men and women, respectively, to show their resentment at the desecration of their holy shrine, were sought to be handled by banning them. Only when I explained the significance of the saffron colour in Sikh tradition was it decided that the practice would be ignored. As expected, the silent protest soon petered out. When Arjun Singh initiated the so-called peace process, the pendulum swung to the other extreme. He wanted us to recommend the release of more and more detainees in order to meet the arbitrarily set targets, which we found hard to do without jeopardizing peace and security. Despite clear signs that Operation Blue Star had failed in its goal, the authorities persisted in sustaining the myth that it had indeed succeeded in breaking the back of militancy, an appraisal simply not borne out by ground realities. Anyway, the temple once again turned into a safe haven for militants, and another operation, Black Thunder, had to be launched to clear the temple of terrorist gangs.

Some Punjab officers had been shifted out of Punjab for poor performance and I was asked to select their replacements from other state cadres. Four officers—two IGs and two DIGs—came on deputation to Punjab on my advice. But I soon realized that I had erred in having placed more trust in ex-cadre officers than in Punjab officers. The latter had grown with the rank and file of the state police and thus were more aware of the nuts and bolts of policing in their home state than any of us from other cadres. Luckily, I was soon able to build an equation of trust and confidence with the local officers, thereby enabling me to appreciate better the unique cultural and functional milieu of the Punjab police. As for the two imported IGs, they continued to pursue their own agendas, not always conforming to mine. I realized also that, though the standards of policing and law enforcement had indeed significantly dipped, it was unfair to hold the Punjab police alone responsible for the eruption of militancy and for failing to respond adequately to it.

South Asian police forces routinely detain suspects without making a formal arrest in order to avoid producing them before a magistrate within twenty-four hours, as legally incumbent. In case a suspect fails to present himself before the police for inquiry, various kinds of pressures, such as detaining his male relatives as hostages, are employed to secure his surrender. The Punjab police adopt even severer measures, like detaining female relatives, seizing the suspect's bullocks, his diesel pump set, tractor and other agricultural implements, until the absconder gives himself up. Since senior officers seemed unwilling to view such misconduct seriously, citizens no longer relied on them for relief. Instead, they approached the high court, which then commissioned a district judge to *raid* the police unit where the illegally detained persons were allegedly confined. In one case, a number of men and women were *rescued* from a police station in Amritsar district by such a commission. When I received the inquiry report, my immediate reaction was to place the concerned officers under suspension and order departmental action against the district SP and the subdivisional officer of police (SDOP). The range DIG, a UP officer, agreed with me.

Before passing final orders, however, I thought it prudent to consult a Punjab cadre officer. So I walked into the adjacent room to consult Harjit Randhawa, IG, crime, regarding the action that I intended to take. 'Don't do any such thing, sir,' he said. 'It will dishearten our officers, and the extant legal provisions are just not enough to deal with hardened Punjab criminals.' This was a strange argument but, coming from Harjit, it could not be swept aside either. 'But what do we do about the high court directions?' I asked him. 'That is a minor matter, sir,' he said with a twinkle in his eye. 'The same people who are supposed to have been recovered from illegal detention will present an affidavit that they were never detained nor rescued from any detention.' And, believe it or not, that is exactly what they did and the cases were finally disposed of in accordance with time-tested local policing traditions. I knew that my action was not right in strictly legalistic terms, but I went along with the advice of a colleague who had a lifelong experience of dealing with such cases. I did try sincerely, though, to enhance the credibility quotient of higher officers by ensuring fair and speedy disposal of complaints. Despite their many limitations, South Asian police forces are genuinely responsive to the subtle gestures and signals emanating from the force leadership. Thus, a well-meaning and forthright police chief will typically draw a similar set of men and officers around him to carry out his programmes and agendas. Though I was an ex-cadre chief, my acceptability quotient with the district and the police station staff was fairly satisfactory. The few pockets of resistance that still remained did not matter in view of the total support of the ruling establishment and the local army brass, which I enjoyed then, both in Delhi and Chandigarh. While I had no problem in carrying the Punjab officers with me, I could not say the same about the two IGs on deputation, K.P.S. Gill and M.C. Trikha.

I had posted Gill as IG, Punjab Armed Police (PAP) and Operations, and with good reason. Over the years the PAP had been reduced to no more than a watch-and-ward unit, providing security guards and orderlies to sundry VIPs and holding scores of sportspersons on its strength for purposes of pay and allowances. It was, thus, incapable of operating as an effective armed police to combat militancy and extremism. I wanted Gill to reorganize the PAP to turn it into a top counterterrorist force. This would also have lessened our dependence on Central forces, which are less mindful of public sensitivities since they lack local knowledge. Gill wasn't pleased, however, since he wanted the key post of IG, law and order, which is traditionally the domain of the police chief himself as it involves control over the entire district police force. Unfortunately for me, he enjoyed the support of the senior advisor, R.V. Subramaniam, having worked with him earlier in Assam, about which I was then unaware. The other imported IG, M.C. Trikha, IG, intelligence, was a little too close to Governor Arjun Singh for comfort, having earlier served as JD, IB, in Bhopal when Arjun was MP CM. I believed in all innocence that Trikha would maintain the age-old positive equation between the police chief and his intelligence aide. When I discovered that I was wrong, it was far too late.

I wanted the Punjab police to function as a motivated and efficient force to effectively meet the very grave challenges confronting the state, but I did not want it to lose its sense of proportion and fairness in its public dealings. So, I interacted intensively with all ranks of police through frequent visits to police stations, police lines, training institutions and sports grounds. Inspection and supervision schedules—long-neglected by senior officers on the pretext of being too busy with law-and-order problems—were enforced, thereby improving rapport between officers and men. Politicization of state organs, especially those dealing with law enforcement, was a common enough malady all over the country, but the Punjab police, having been subjected to manipulative politics for ages, had emerged over the years as probably the most politicized. Even police chiefs were chosen on the basis of political loyalties. These links were more difficult to address, but it helped that the state was then under President's Rule.

I also thought that unless the army ended its active involvement in the districts, civilian officers would not come into their own. In any case, with a lieutenant general in overall charge of the home department as the governor's security advisor, the army should have no problem withdrawing from the districts. So, I put up a note to Lt General Gowri Shankar, who promptly issued the necessary orders. He was a good friend and a great general and ever-willing to lend his support for any good idea that I floated. When I mentioned to him that his majors general tended to avoid saluting me even though I wore a higher rank, he pulled them up in no uncertain terms in a joint civil–military conference at Jalandhar soon after. As security advisor, he was frank and forthright in his approach to all matters that came up for his orders. Unfortunately, he died soon after his retirement from the army.

It was not enough to talk only to the police. The public too had to be sensitized to the perils of anarchism towards which the state was heading. So, I toured scores of villages in areas most exposed to Bhindranwale's extremist sermons, which were being disseminated through cassettes, and spoke in detail at all the forums which I could reach in order to create robust public opinion against the looming threat of disorder and social turbulence. There was simply too much to do and too little time available. I don't recall a single day when I returned home from work before sunset or when I enjoyed a full day off duty. Much of what I had set out to accomplish, however, lost its edge when Arjun Singh took over as governor in March 1985. He had no interest in any viewpoints other than his own, and he took into his own hands all the strategic and tactical planning to battle militancy. In India, it is the generalist administrators, not police chiefs, who are central to decision-making, even where such decisions relate to the state's security functions. Also, the Indian police, who enjoy no functional autonomy, remain peripheral to policy formulation for containing disorder, terrorism and extremism. So, such flare-ups remain uncontrolled for decades.

The Union government realized that a major eyesore and the cause of much distress to the Sikh community was the demolished Akal Takht. It acted as a grim reminder of the many painful episodes linked to Operation Blue Star. So, it decided to rebuild it through its own resources in order to lessen somewhat the collective hurt of the community. Buta Singh, a Sikh cabinet minister, was entrusted with the task of restoration, under the mistaken belief that, being a Sikh, he would carry the necessary credibility with his community. This was a miscalculation as, being a member of the oppressive state structure, he was unacceptable to the Sikh masses. Anyway, Buta Singh arrived on the scene, armed with an official mandate and promises of enormous financial resources in money and gold. This was like adding insult to injury as Sikh tradition debars outside help and, instead, favours building religious structures with voluntary labour, called *kar sewa*. He further offended Sikh sensitivities by entrusting the work to Santa Singh, the head of a Nihang dera, the Buddha Dal, which was at that time on rather hostile terms with the Sikh clergy.

Facing opposition from the Sikh high priests and to somehow legitimize his mission, Buta Singh called a Sarbat Khalsa (grand assembly of Sikhs) in Amritsar on 11 August 1984, which approved the rebuilding of the Akal Takht with help from Santa Singh. The gathering also held the Akali leadership responsible for the desecration of Sikh shrines. Perceived to be a state-sponsored show, the event did not evoke much enthusiasm among the Sikh masses, though Buta Singh managed to bring the head of a Sikh shrine in Patna for it. A few weeks later, the Sikh high priests held a rival convention at a major gurdwara in Amritsar—the government having disallowed the gathering in the Golden Temple—and called it the World Sikh Conference. Buta Singh considered the Sarbat Khalsa decisions as sufficient endorsement of his plans and, assured of ample state funding, started the reconstruction right away.

All the money spent by Buta Singh was, however, destined to go down the drain as the restored Akal Takht was pulled down by the Sikhs. It was rebuilt some years later through donations and voluntary labour under the supervision of Baba Thakur Singh of the Damdami Taksal, the seminary once headed by Bhindranwale, thus, in a way, linking the rebuilding of the demolished Takht with the late militant leader. A dead Bhindranwale continued to fire the imagination of the Sikh masses as legends and myths grew around him, according him the status of *sant-sipahi*, saint-soldier, which is a hallowed concept in Sikh tradition. Bhindranwale thus acquired an image much larger than that of the Akali leaders, who thenceforth found it expedient to use some of his militant vocabulary.

This adversely affected the course of events in Punjab for years to come. Delhi too decided to withdraw the army from the Golden Temple complex and hand over its administration to the SGPC. Senior advisor R.V. Subramaniam was Delhi's pointsman for negotiations with the high priests for the purpose. This took months as he had to contend with P.C. Alexander, who was secretary to the prime minister and who claimed to be her conscience-keeper, looking into every little procedural detail. As for Santa Singh, he had to be virtually kicked out as he had taken to making money by meddling in police investigations and inquiries.

In the meanwhile, Giani Zail Singh was elected the first Sikh President of India, thanks largely to his oft-avowed loyalty to Indira Gandhi, who probably also wanted to use his elevation to the presidency as a sop to the Sikhs. Since the President is notionally also the supreme commander of Indian defence forces, the Sikh community held him responsible for Operation Blue Star and all the various acts of defilement during that operation, despite his assertions that he had had no prior information about the army action, and that he had not given his approval for it. He was probably right but the Sikh religious leadership, who were never very fond of him anyway, warned him of excommunication from the panth unless he personally rendered an apology to the Sikh *qaum* through the collegium of five high priests. It is a measure of the pull the collegium enjoys in Sikh tradition that, when summoned before them for violating Sikh *maryada*, no Sikh dares disobey. So Zail Singh too presented himself before the high priests soon after Operation Blue Star to expiate for his alleged misconduct.

While the collegium was busy pondering over the issue in its office and the President of India sat with hands folded on the floor outside, awaiting the ruling, media persons from India and abroad flitted around excitedly, trying to glean bits and pieces of news. Interestingly, the hymn from the Sikh holy book, *Kutta raj bahaliye chakki chattan jaye* (Put the dog on a throne, it will still lick the flour mill), heard all through the temple premises, openly lampooned the President for his failure to safeguard his community's holiest shrine. He often shared with me his anguish about the event, even asserting that he had considered resigning the presidency so as to re-establish his credibility with his qaum, though it is unusual for Indian politicians to give up high office. Buta Singh, too, had to face the Sikh collegium for entrusting the task of rebuilding the Akal Takht to Santa Singh and for dyeing his hair, forbidden in Sikhism. He had to undertake due penitence.

Within a month's time, the police had acquired a fair degree of control over the situation, though there were occasional setbacks. Some militants waylaid a police party on a busy road near Moga, escorting under-trial prisoners for a court *peshi*, and succeeded in freeing three hardcore militants. I rushed to the spot and was shocked to find that the standing orders for assigning escorts from the police lines had not been updated for years, and that this important duty was left entirely to the junior officers. Not even the RI personally checked such assignments, much less the SP or his deputies. I had the entire set of standing orders revised and updated in view of the vastly changed law-and-order situation. On the positive side, the Amritsar police nabbed two criminals when they attempted to kill a police informant after a hot pursuit across many villages. I personally visited the thana to compliment the staff.

There were other signs of revival of morale at the field level as I remained in close personal contact with the rank and file through regular visits to field units, easy enough in a small state like Punjab. We even organized a state-level sports meet, an area in which the Punjab police excelled. The week-long meet was meant to send a strong message that the state police had overcome their sense of despondence, and that they were ready to meet head-on the grave challenges confronting them. I made no major changes in the districts as I believe that most officers are capable of achieving the desired goals if led by professionally capable, morally clean and well-motivated leaders, who also have the capacity to shield them from undesirable political and other pressures. As for some hard nuts in the inspectorate—long notorious for their criminal and corrupt track records—I dealt with them ruthlessly so as to make an example of them. The Punjab police were now in a much better position to handle both militant violence and the tendency of politicians to fish in troubled waters. My plan to reorganize and modernize the PAP, however, did not go far. So, we had to continue to rely largely on Central forces for counter-militant operations, a compulsion that had its drawbacks.

Having been victims of state repression during a large part of their brief history, the Sikhs have developed a unique way of expressing their collective sense of anger and outrage through evocative tales of religious devotion displayed by their heroes in times of suffering in the past. This helps call to mind past eras of brutalizing regimes and subconsciously links them to contemporary events. Such recitals always hold veiled suggestions on how to cope with state oppression and how to organize resistance. Gurdwaras provide a safe haven for the purpose as they have traditionally been out of bounds for the police right from the days of the Raj. So, the gory tales of atrocities upon Sikhs during army operations and by security forces thereafter were being widely publicized in Punjab by folk singers, *ragi*s and *dhadhi*s (balladeers). Especially popular and active in this respect, during kirtans and religious functions in gurdwaras, and often clothed in compelling emotional imagery, was a group of young women known as *nabhe walian bibian*. The growing extremist sentiment among the Sikh masses was amply reflected by the large crowds that flocked to the *bhog* ceremonies of slain militants, their last rites of passage. Such gatherings also strengthened the militant movement by widening its recruitment base. We could not stop this glorification of slain militants due to conflicting signals from Delhi and Chandigarh.

The talks to transfer control of the Golden Temple proved time-consuming as the high priests were asked to give a written undertaking that the temple would not again revert to militant control, which the priests were in no position to do. Finally, the high priests agreed to recruit a posse of guards for the purpose and also allow police deployment in the vicinity. The army moved out in September 1984, thus putting an end to an unfortunate episode in the history of the Indian army. The protective measures put in place, however, soon broke down and, on 1 October, some 200 extremists gathered in the temple premises, made seditious speeches and raised pro-Khalistan slogans. We had to fortify police presence significantly around the shrine to prevent a recurrence of such incidents. We later found that the gathering was the work of an Akali faction, close to Zail Singh and his supporters in the Punjab Congress. Amusingly, all the major players in the momentous episode—Bhindranwale, Blue Star commander General Brar, Santa Singh and I—belonged to Moga in Punjab's Malwa region, as did President Zail Singh.

Due to the rampant politicization in the police, professional aptitude was not a major factor in postings and promotions. Thus, of the three range DIGs, two failed to provide adequate support to their officers; this included DIG, Jalandhar range, which covered the militancy epicentre districts of Amritsar and Gurdaspur. This officer just did not move out of his heavily fortified official residence to provide hands-on guidance to his officers. The DIG, Ferozepur range, did not leave his bungalow even to visit his office except under a heavy escort of the Central Reserve Police Force (CRPF). I too was provided with a driver and gunmen from the CRPF on my arrival in Chandigarh but I refused any security cover except from the Punjab police, and I never had occasion to regret my decision. Since there were only twelve districts in the state, only twelve officers could be posted as district SPs out of about 100 officers holding the rank. Unseemly lobbying to secure one of those twelve fancied posts was, therefore, common. This prompted talebearing, infighting and indiscipline of a high degree.

The news of Prime Minister Indira Gandhi's assassination by her Sikh security guards flashed on my office ticker early on 31 October 1984. The lurid manner in which the sad event was covered by television, highlighting visuals of incensed Hindu mobs shouting anti-Sikh slogans, was not a good omen and we, in Punjab, seemed to be in for hard times because we now had to fight not only Sikh militancy but also the impact of a likely Hindu backlash against the Sikhs in Delhi, signs of which were only too evident. I called an urgent meeting of the IGs' committee to take stock of the situation and put in place fail-safe preventive measures. As feared, Indira Gandhi's assassination set off an orgy of killings, plunder and arson directed against the Sikhs, which was savage, brutal, merciless and seemingly well-planned, with Congress leaders directing the rampaging mobs to target Sikh colonies with the help of electoral rolls, not unlike the Nazis going after the Jews half a century earlier. As for the police, mandated to act firmly in such cases, they simply vanished from the scene, much as the Gujarat police did eighteen years later, to facilitate the slaughter of Muslims by goons of the ruling party.

In Punjab, rumour-mongers and talebearers had a field day due to strict censorship of news and the banning of the entry of Delhi newspapers. The magnitude of the killings of Sikhs in Delhi and other places deeply angered the Sikh community, but overt protests or agitations could not be held in view of the stringent laws in force. Instead, the Sikhs expressed their resentment in religious gatherings in gurdwaras all over the state following the age-old tradition in times of adversity. Since the political leadership was either in confinement or stood disgraced or enfeebled, it was the militant groups that seized the initiative to whip up Sikh passions against the establishment. But, through rigorous security measures, we successfully pre-empted all possible adverse fallout in Punjab resulting from the gory events in Delhi. Notwithstanding this, Delhi was thick with rumours about trains coming out of Punjab with dead bodies of Hindu victims of Sikh reprisal killings, though not a single such incident had taken place in the entire state. In Chandigarh, directly under Central control, Hindus and Sikhs, long known for cordial relations between them, stood sharply divided with frequent spells of mass slogan-shouting against each other, undoubtedly an expression of a mounting sense of insecurity and distrust.

Central government officials were constantly on the phone seeking information about the many startling rumours circulating in Delhi. In one case, I was asked to comment on a report lodged by an Indian Airlines pilot that he had seen vast areas burning in the Punjab plains. The fact was that farmers routinely set the leftovers of the previous year's crop on fire before preparing the fields for fresh sowing. It was impossible to answer all the queries coming from the armchair babus in Delhi when they picked up scraps of news from national newspapers available to them early morning, even before my officers had finished briefing me on the previous night's happenings. Obviously, the authorities in Delhi were excessively and needlessly panicky, fearing the worst in Punjab. Their fears did not abate even when nothing untoward happened and the situation remained stable and under control. Pawan Sharma, a petty Congressman, set up what he called a Hindu Suraksha Samiti in Ludhiana. He had to be detained under the National Security Act, 1980, when he persisted in disrupting peace and order in the city.

Apart from the information provided by the Punjab CID, I also had to call up the Delhi police control room frequently to verify reports received from my sources in Delhi. The Indian state seemed to have withdrawn its protection to its Sikh citizens, a stigma the Delhi police will never be able to live down. Sikh policemen were withdrawn from field duties and Sikh officers remained deployed in staff jobs. When I called the Delhi police control room to help rescue my nephew and his wife from a flat in the up-scale New Friends Colony, under siege by a rampaging mob, R.S. Sahai, a young Sikh deputy commissioner of police (DCP), who had remained posted in the control room all through that critical period, updated me on the appalling situation in the city. Scores of Sikh policemen, I was told, their beards and long hair forcibly trimmed by lawless mobs—aided by policemen who shared their faith, to avenge the murder of their leader—remained stranded in the control room, certainly a safer place than their homes. My nephew, with his hair let loose like a woman's, and his wife had to be smuggled out of their locality in true filmy style, behind curtained car windows, and escorted to the airport to board a flight to Chandigarh.

There must have been several such cases in those troubled times. As the Sikh community in Delhi and Punjab grew more disillusioned and agitated with the government and its policy of masterly inactivity against the killer gangs and its apathy towards the victims, the Indian state and the Sikh people now seemed to be virtually at loggerheads. The Sikh political leadership—either in prison or in hiding out of fear of militant groups—was now assured of implicit support by an outraged community and plentiful supply of weaponry by Pakistan which was fast engulfing large parts of Punjab. Sikh militancy continued to grow and became, after 1986, virtually invincible and slowly engulfed not only entire Punjab but also parts of Haryana, Rajasthan and UP, also striking at will in the national capital and many far-off places.

From a conscious recasting of the past to linking the 1984 Delhi carnage with similar episodes in Sikh history, such as the *ghallugharas*, the great massacres, is but one short step. Together with Operation Blue Star, the 1984 Sikh massacres contributed significantly to the sharpening of separate identities and agendas between Hindus and Sikhs in the country. Although they still had much in common in social and familial terms, the gulf between the two communities was growing fast. They thenceforth looked at every major event in the country, starting with Operation Blue Star itself, in a sharply hostile manner.

Thus, while Sikhs began to perceive themselves in terms of a 'marked' minority—not unlike Muslims—most Hindus viewed the whole chain of events from Blue Star onwards as asserting their rightful place as the dominant majority with an unquestionable right to primacy in the country's polity. Sikhs also developed a more empathetic perception of the problems faced by Muslims and other minorities in a polity which was fast turning into a virtual Hindu *rashtra*, despite constitutionally being a secular state. With Hindus forming over 83 per cent of its population, electoral compulsions would ensure that it could not be otherwise. Having suffered two critical jolts to their sense of uniqueness at the hands of the Indian army during Blue Star in June and by Hindu mobs in November of 1984, the Sikhs were deeply upset. They could not but look back into the past to construct a response, in keeping with their historical experience, to defend themselves against what they perceived as an oppressive and unjust state structure. Since the Sikh tradition authorizes taking up arms to fight injustice and tyranny, the pre–Blue Star rhetoric of a dead Bhindranwale now acquired a fresh significance and worked as a powerful catalyst to galvanize the entire community into assuming a confrontational stance.

The question that deeply troubled the Sikhs was why no one—neither the actual offenders nor the political leaders who guided them, not even the negligent and colluding police officers—was ever brought to justice, though the killers of Indira Gandhi had been promptly hanged. The subsequent course of Sikh militancy redefined, in many different ways, the social and political equations between Sikhs and Hindus at one level, and between the Sikhs and the Indian state at another. While Indira Gandhi's assassination was perceived by sections of Sikhs as not an unjust retribution for the army assault on the Golden Temple, the Sikh pogroms of November 1984 were viewed by most Hindus as a justified retaliation for her killing. Though Sikhs resumed their normal life in the capital city in the course of time, traces of the bitterness stayed festering for a long time. During a visit to a friend's house in Delhi's up-scale Golf Links colony the day after Bhindranwale was killed in Operation Blue Star, every Hindu guest loudly and cheerfully ridiculed the 'Sikhras'—as Sikhs were now derisively referred to—who had been well and truly put in their place, much as the host tried to curb their zeal in view of my presence.

Sikh killings in Delhi and other Indian towns considerably galvanized the militancy in Punjab, leading to attacks on Hindus in villages, triggering their exodus to the cities. In some shocking incidents, Hindus were brutally done to death in public buses. But that was after I had left and the new Akali government had appointed a Punjab cadre officer, Baljit Dhaliwal, then on long leave in the UK, much against his wishes. Having no interest in a job virtually thrust upon him, Dhaliwal just withdrew himself from hands-on police leadership, leaving the force to fend for itself. In the event, the force lost its élan and motivation, painstakingly built over a period of time, enabling the militant groups to extend vastly the sweep and span of their criminal activities. Dhaliwal was, in fact, one of the Punjab officers who had been proposed for being sent out of Punjab for poor service record. No Central organization was willing to accept him on deputation, so he had taken long leave and proceeded to the UK to tide over the critical situation.

Indira Gandhi's son Rajiv, a reluctant politician at best, was sworn in as the new PM—without even being elected as leader of his parliamentary party—by a beleaguered President Zail Singh, himself under attack for being a Sikh in those highly charged times. This was apparently done to pre-empt Pranab Mukherjee, a senior cabinet minister, from laying claim to the office. Soon thereafter, Rajiv, promising to defend the nation's integrity against diverse separatist forces, led his party to win a record majority in Parliament. His resolve to do so was unmistakably demonstrated by the brutal Sikh killings in the national capital itself under the very eyes of the new government. Surrounded by friends from the corporate world, more at home with computers than the nitty-gritty of street politics that can often turn awfully dirty, the young Gandhi set about governing a vast land and a messy and fragmented polity in deep crisis. The new government—somewhat flippantly called a *baba log* government—started off well by introducing major changes in governance, with the new PM showing a special flair for infusing a brand new culture of innovation and modernism in administration, not only in the area of economic policies but also in the management of minority discontent in the north-east and Punjab.

Passionate about his self-professed mission to reshape radically the style and manner of governance in the country, the youthful, if impetuous, Rajiv Gandhi went about his business with singular zeal to clean the Augean stables of governmental corruption. Unfortunately, however, the systems and institutions of governance—rendered dysfunctional since long—proved too much for him and it was only a matter of time before he too got embroiled in charges of sleaze and venality, though the charges remained unproven. Surrounded as they are by hordes of sycophants, even the most forthright of Indian prime ministers are liable to grow arrogant and dictatorial in their disposition, though Rajiv proved somewhat more resilient. Since a new set of advisors in Delhi was now shaping the Punjab policy, I found myself greatly handicapped in even day-to-day functioning. For the first time since my posting to Punjab, I found that I had no access to the PM or his close advisors. Though I did not realize it then, Indira Gandhi's death was to prove an acute personal loss to me. In my periodical meetings with her, I had been able to build up a relationship of trust and confidence, which had given me the self-assurance to implement my ideas boldly. With her demise, the entire power equation in the prime minister's office (PMO), where all vital decisions were taken, radically changed. Her long-time aide and confidant, R.K. Dhawan, not only found himself thrown out of the PMO but was also obliquely accused of having been part of the so-called conspiracy leading to her assassination. In the true oriental tradition of medieval-era court intrigues, the Kashmiri lobby sought to use the assassination by consolidating its position in the new power structure. Dhawan's frame-up was also designed to eliminate the Punjabi influence in the PMO, a major feature since the time Sanjay Gandhi had married a Punjabi.

Arun Nehru, Arun Singh and Satish Sharma were part of the informal but powerful group around Rajiv that played a significant role in handling many crucial issues of governance, including Punjab, after Indira Gandhi's death. While Nehru and Singh had a legitimate role in Punjab as Central ministers, Sharma was brought in to advise on specific problems in his capacity as the PM's close friend. In the initial few months of Rajiv's tenure, Arun Singh was his closest aide and often accompanied him during his visits to Punjab. I found it much easier to seek his counsel, rather than Arjun Singh's, in dealing with some of the more difficult issues. Unfortunately for me, however, as Arun Singh was noticeably more upfront than the PM's other friends, he did not last long in the Byzantine environment—intricate, complex, manipulative—of the new dispensation, and left Delhi to enjoy the peace and tranquillity of nature at his farm in the UP hills.

The Thakkar Commission of Inquiry, appointed to inquire into Indira Gandhi's assassination, obliquely suggested that the slain PM's long-time aide, R.K. Dhawan, was a prime suspect in the conspiracy. I too was called by the judge to provide some information. The quaint phrase actually used by the judge—which soon became the butt of many a joke in South Delhi drawing rooms—was the 'needle of suspicion', which the learned judge sought laboriously to prove, pointed to the hapless Dhawan. Dhawan, who had wielded enormous power and prestige for decades as Indira Gandhi's personal assistant, now found himself consigned to total obscurity. A man who had devoted his entire life to serve her and had risen from a stenographer to become her confidant and advisor on many matters of state and political management, was now a virtual recluse, having retired to his rented house in Golf Links. He was repeatedly grilled by Central enforcement agencies but not once did he speak a word against Indira Gandhi. No one ever thought of calling on him to inquire about his version of the case, much less empathize with him. Congress CMs, who used to wait patiently to meet him, now avoided his very shadow. When I met him at a friend's house in Delhi, he cautioned me against being seen with him as it was likely to be regarded as an anti-establishment act. As expected, that one meeting and my telephone calls to him to ask after his welfare did not go unobserved. Another formal inquiry was instituted later, this time by Anand Ram, a former DGP, Andhra Pradesh, besides secret inquiries by several other organizations, including the IB, RAW and the CBI. Dhawan was ultimately cleared of all charges and reinstalled for a brief period in his old South Block office, though never to enjoy the same level of understanding with the son as he had with the mother.

In the first few months of his regime, Rajiv displayed remarkable ingenuity in breaking with the past to pursue a policy of peace through negotiations and entering into what was called in corporate culture a 'memorandum of understanding' with local leaders. This was the genesis of the Assam Accord in the north-east and the Rajiv–Longowal Accord in Punjab. The Indian people, long fed on a diet of trite homilies by jaded politicians, were greatly excited over the initiatives taken by the new PM to bring peace to the troubled regions, generating a heady sense of optimism all around. Unfortunately, however, the optimism proved to be short-lived because the so-called accords came unstuck one by one as they were found to be flawed in many respects. In the event, the much-vaunted policy of peaceful resolution of conflicts between an all-powerful Indian state and its myriad minority peoples received a big setback. As the efficacy and appeal of different accords in ending insurgencies and extremist violence in the disturbed areas faded and a sense of disillusionment set in among the affected peoples, the government once again reverted to its earlier strategy of using suppressive policies to contain minority dissent and agitation. The challenges posed by the various movements they spawned were met through overwhelming, brutal, illegitimate and inept force. As the British statesman William Pitt the Elder had noted in a different age and context, 'Where law ends, tyranny begins.'

In order to initiate the so-called peace process in Punjab, it was necessary to place an astute political operator to head the state administration, which had been under direct Central rule since 1983. So, the then governor, the suave and upright K.T. Satarawala, formerly of the IAS, was replaced in mid-March of 1985, by Arjun Singh, who had only recently taken over as CM of MP. Arjun had never been known to be under consideration for the crucial assignment, and we had all thought it would be Air Chief Marshal Arjan Singh, a former Indian Air Force chief and respected Sikh elder. We soon came to know, however, the full background of the relocation of the wily Arjun from Bhopal to Chandigarh, obviously the result of a well-orchestrated plan, although his abrupt removal from MP had set off several rumours, mostly unflattering to him. K.T. Satarawala had not even been informed of the impending change, much less consulted about it. Chief Secretary Dhanoa and I had to break the news to an incredulous governor. He had to wait in Delhi for months before securing his next assignment as Indian ambassador to Mexico.

Arjun Singh was an uneasy heir to at least one highly unsavoury skeleton in the family cupboard that his father, minister of industries in Vindhya Pradesh, had bequeathed to him, along with a petty estate in the princely state of Rewa in central India. The honourable minister had been nabbed by the Delhi special police establishment for demanding a bribe from a Bombay industrialist, close to Sardar Patel, then Union home minister, to let him set up an industry in Rewa. The minister had had to spend a few years in jail for the offence and the son was to carry this infamy with him all his life. As it was, despite his oft-professed devotion to the Nehru–Gandhi dynasty, he was always under a certain degree of suspicion on this count. A persistent rumour had it that the young Arjun had been so outraged at his father's incarceration during Jawaharlal Nehru's rule that he had vowed to ruin the dynasty some day. While electioneering in Rewa, Nehru had also allegedly urged the electorate not to vote for the corrupt minister. The story—probably apocryphal—refused to die down even with the passage of time. Recently, during a visit to India International Centre in Delhi for lunch, I heard the story being related gleefully at an adjacent table. Among the occupants of that table were a civil servant turned politician, once a Sanjay Gandhi acolyte, and governor of a state during Congress rule who had later also served as a Union minister in the BJP-led National Democratic Alliance (NDA) government.

Arjun Singh was initiated into the craft of politics by D.P. Mishra, a contemporary of Jawaharlal Nehru's and widely acclaimed as a modern-day Chanakya. Mishra took good care of young Arjun and groomed him well and proper to emerge as a powerful rival to the fresh generation of politicians from different regions of the new state of MP. The disciple exhibited an uncanny talent to absorb readily the varied nuances and shades of the art of political manoeuvring, for which his mentor was universally known and feared. Elected CM of MP in 1980 in a questionable manner, Arjun Singh was re-elected CM in March 1985. But he was moved to Chandigarh soon after, allegedly for the maladroit manner in which he had handled the critical situation following the world's worst industrial mishap in the Union Carbide Corporation (UCC) factory in Bhopal, which had resulted in thousands of deaths and collateral damage on a mammoth scale. The state government was widely blamed for its slackness in enforcing strict industrial safety laws in return for favours shown by the UCC to top officials and politicians, including a hefty donation to a charity, floated by Arjun Singh's family. Also, the Indian government was put to grave diplomatic embarrassment when a police party, led by the DM and the SP of Bhopal, placed UCC chairman, Walter Anderson, in custody when he landed in Bhopal soon after the disaster, evidently to see for himself what had gone wrong with the plant. Such a high-profile arrest could not have been made except on the CM's express orders. When the Americans lodged a strong protest with the Indian government, Anderson was hastily released from custody, put on the state aircraft and flown to Delhi, apparently after the CM was pulled up by the Congress bosses in New Delhi.

The baffling arrest and release of Anderson continued to cause embarrassment to the Congress party every time the matter cropped up, especially when it later transpired that Anderson had been assured of safe passage by India for his flight to Bhopal and back to the US. It remains unclear whether Arjun Singh was privy to this information or not. He continued to prevaricate whenever questioned on the subject. Decades later, when pressed to make a statement in the Indian parliament, he blamed the then chief secretary, Brahma Swaroop, no longer alive to contest the allegation. Arjun Singh's placement in Chandigarh may also have been due to his good personal relations with some top Akali leaders, who had spent a few years in detention in Pachmarhi, a salubrious hill station in MP. This was expected to help in opening a dialogue with them. Another view was that the Congress leadership wanted to kill two birds with one stone, namely, to ease him out of MP, where he had become a liability, and to charge him with managing the rising militancy situation in Punjab. If he succeeded in his new assignment, the Congress party would take the credit, but if he failed, he could be sidelined.

Master tactician that he was, Arjun Singh promptly set about exploring possible policy options for unravelling the tangled mess that he confronted in the state. A keen sense of history led him to draw upon a major episode in the Indian freedom struggle, which also carried deep emotional appeal for the Sikhs. It may be recalled that Bhagat Singh, the legendary Sikh revolutionary, and his two associates were hanged in Lahore central jail in March 1930 and their dead bodies covertly transported to Hussainiwala near Ferozepur for cremation so as to pre-empt violent protests in Punjab's capital. Arjun Singh thought that the observance of the anniversary of that historic episode would remind the Sikh youths of the immense sacrifices made by their people in India's freedom struggle, hoping thereby to wean them away from extremism. Collecting massive crowds for such rallies in India poses no great problem, especially when the state itself is the sponsor and a VVIP presence is assured. Even the prospect of a helicopter sighting would attract hordes of curious spectators. District officers would ensure maximum turnout from their districts and tell truck and bus owners to ferry for free large numbers of travellers to the meeting place, for which they would be allowed to flout many legal limitations to cover the losses suffered. The rally attracted a huge gathering of rural Sikhs to listen to the many VVIPs make impassioned speeches in praise of Bhagat Singh and, of course, Nehru, Indira and Rajiv.

As the PM's chopper landed on the makeshift helipad, the turban of Union minister Buta Singh was blown away by a strong draught of air. This caused a great deal of mirth among the small crowd waiting for the PM at the expense of Buta who, being a member of Parliament from Rajasthan, was wearing a Rajasthani– not a Sikh-style turban. The irony of the situation was not lost on the young PM since, unlike Rajasthani headgear, Sikh turbans rest on the wearer's head much more securely. On sighting his cabinet colleague chasing his turban across wheat fields, a visibly amused PM could not help making a dig at his uneasy minister. '*Buta Singh ji, apni pagri sambhaliay, kahin udh na jaey*.' (Buta Singhji, take care of your turban lest it fly away.) The remark all but ruined the rest of the day for Buta. The rally lasted until late evening, ending only after every VIP worth his salt had had his say. The audience listened to the speeches and sermons somewhat grimly, waiting for the event to conclude so that they could trudge back home to resume their dreary life. The rally made no difference to the alienation of the Sikh people from the Indian state, though it did provide a unique platform to the new governor to showcase his political dexterity to the Delhi establishment. As for the promised compensation for acres of ripe wheat crop that had been destroyed in the process of clearing the land for constructing the helipad, preparing the meeting grounds and laying the approach roads, it remained a distant dream even months after the attempt to bring Sikh youths into the so-called national mainstream by invoking historical legacies. But then, the Indian masses are long used to suffer such losses and indignities in silence.

Along with Arjun Singh had come several officers from MP, including his two special assistants, his security officer, his personal staff and almost a battalion of MP SAF. A close relative, an IG, CRPF, was often seen at Raj Bhavan and undertaking extensive touring in the state, as was another promoted IPS officer from MP, reputedly a smooth operator and a 'fixer', with a long experience in intelligence. It is not unusual for Indian politicians to surround themselves with loyalists for two reasons: one, they can freely pursue their chosen agendas, secure in the knowledge that their minions will cover the tracks; and two, they will not have to deal with a new set of officers, unfamiliar with their functioning style and personal agendas, who might raise uncomfortable questions. However, when such practices undermine the established norms of administrative propriety, they end up destroying the unity and effectiveness of the entire system of command and control. Despite his professed modernity, Arjun Singh remained a prisoner to his feudal and imperious background in his personal and professional preferences. I think it necessary to draw attention to this aspect of his functioning style because the institutional damage that resulted from his personalized mode of decision-making seriously dented the capacity of the Punjab police, painstakingly built over the previous months, to cope with the emergent situation in the state.

Contrary to the high hopes that the new governor had led the PM to set on the Hussainiwala rally, it did not materially alter the overall situation in Punjab nor did it alleviate the collective hurt that Operation Blue Star and the November 1984 killings had caused to the Sikh people. Unfazed by the setback at Hussainiwala, Arjun Singh sought to accelerate the 'peace process' by promising that all Sikh detainees not charged with sedition, murder, dacoity or arson would be released; that compensation would be paid for all those killed in Punjab since 1 August 1982; and that a committee would soon be appointed to review the status of rehabilitation of the victims of the Delhi killings. Several Akali leaders, interned since Operation Blue Star, were also released and the ban on the All India Sikh Students Federation (AISSF), lifted. We were required to periodically compile lists of internees, whom the governor could release for creating a *climate* conducive for furthering the supposed peace process, never mind if his arbitrarily set targets gravely upset our law-and-order imperatives. Ground realities, however, did not support the loud claims made by the governor about the positive outcome of these policy initiatives. When I voiced my misgivings, I was simply sidelined and the governor started dealing directly with Trikha and the new security advisor, a former DG, CRPF, appointed on the advice of a close relative. Being ignorant of the historical processes leading to Sikh militancy in the first place and unconcerned with the adverse fallout of the manipulative agendas being pursued by the governor, the new set of his advisors—official and unofficial—had no problem going the extra mile to keep the boss happy.

Apart from feeling increasingly uneasy in this kind of setting, I also found it hard to comply with his terse notes on slips of paper, embossed with the legend 'From the Governor's Desk', instructing me inter alia to transfer my officers without assigning reasons. These brusque directions covered all ranks of police from inspectors and sub-inspectors to DIGs. I was not used to such whimsical exercise of power in violation of due process, especially when such directions were not prompted by administrative or security reasons. So, I stuck to what I considered right and proper, and it must be added to their credit that both Home Secretary N.N. Vohra and Security Advisor Lt General Gowri Shankar fully supported me in this regard. I need give just one example to elucidate my point. Arjun Singh once asked me to transfer the SDOP, Khanna subdivision in Ludhiana district, and followed it soon after with similar demands in respect of SSP, Ludhiana, and then, the DIG of Patiala range of which Ludhiana was a part. What is more, he suggested the name of a controversial DIG to be posted to Patiala. While I had no problem in moving out the SDOP, who was, in any case, due for promotion, I expressed my inability to comply with his other directions. Vohra and I together put up our reasons for opposing these directions and the governor had to drop his demand, for which he never forgave me. I later learnt why he was so insistent on the transfers of various levels of police hierarchy in Ludhiana.

A rich landlord in Khanna had married a UP woman late in life, deserting his first wife but without a formal separation. On his death, a legal battle ensued over his huge estate and dragged on for years, as such cases are wont to do. Both parties had now approached the police for help in settling the matter in their favour through coercive and illegal measures, clearly for a consideration. Naturally, the UP woman being an outsider, lost out in the game against her husband's first wife. When things did not work out in her favour, she approached the governor for help on the strength of a claimed close relationship with a powerful aide of the PM. The whole matter unfolded when the woman finally came to plead with me about her case, and I told her plainly that her case was of a civil nature and the police could not intervene. It was then that I requested the governor to recommend my name for a posting with the Union government. His short answer was, 'We will leave Punjab together.'

The release of Akali leaders failed to improve in any significant way the prospects of peace in the state because the moderate Akali voices were fast losing ground to extremist ideologues. Barring Longowal, no prominent Akali leader was prepared to join issue with the advocates of a militant stand.

While Tohra was openly critical of the Longowal approach, Badal preferred to prevaricate in view of the fast-changing political scenario in the state. In the event, he alone among all his colleagues survived the process of the huge churning then taking place in Punjab politics to emerge as India's top Akali leader. While all Akali leaders favoured talks with the government, there were serious differences of approach between Longowal, who favoured talks with the government within the Constitution, and Tohra, who maintained that no resolution of Sikh grievances was possible that way. The Congress continued to promote its usual cynical designs to seek to demolish the Akali Party as a long-term political voice of the Sikh people. So, they once again chose to tread the path they had taken in 1978, when Bhindranwale was projected as a counterfoil to the Akali leadership, with disastrous results as India came to realize only too well.

They now zeroed in on Joginder Singh, Bhindranwale's father, to serve the same purpose. The latter was persuaded by emissaries, allegedly close to Zail Singh, to float a new party, the United Akali Dal (UAD), become its president and dissolve all other factions, including the one headed by Longowal, though the Indian government was still in dialogue with the latter. This process of periodical fragmentation and reunification of the Akali Party subsequently became a routine affair and severely damaged the credibility of the premier medium of Sikh political assertion. Soon thereafter, Jagjit Singh, Bhindranwale's brother, was released on bail, reportedly at Buta Singh's behest, something that we had been opposing all along. Joginder Singh named several extremist sympathizers on his party's executive committee and chose to publicize it to coincide with Longowal's return to Punjab after signing what came to be known as the Rajiv–Longowal Accord in Delhi. This could not have been a mere coincidence.

Longowal appeared to enjoy a fair degree of credibility both with Sikhs and Hindus. This did not suit the Zail Singh–Buta Singh duo and their supporters in the Punjab Congress, who had been playing a dubious game from the very beginning, which was sure to negate whatever Longowal and Rajiv Gandhi were trying to achieve, by weakening Longowal and strengthening the militant forces. I am not sure, however, whether Arjun Singh was a part of this game plan or had his own distinct agenda. Until then, neither Joginder Singh nor Jagjit Singh had exhibited any political ambitions. What goals had inspired the Central leadership, driven now by the Zail Singh and the Buta Singh cabals—not to mention sundry intelligence agencies responsible for messing up the situation in the first place—suddenly to develop such fondness for the late Bhindranwale's family, can hardly be called the best-kept secret of the times. Almost every male member of his family was wooed and inducted into Sikh religio-political institutions. This included his father, Joginder Singh, his brother Jagjit Singh, his nephews Gurjit Singh and Jasbir Singh, and his uncle Harcharan Singh, a former Indian army JCO. Such concern for the family members of the dead 'sant', whom the ruling establishment had branded the principal architect of the decade-long terrorist upsurge in Punjab not long ago, would, indeed, have been most touching, if it were not so patently Machiavellian in its conception. Gurjit later joined a major militant group, while Jasbir Singh was installed as the head of the Akal Takht after his mysterious release from prison. Jasbir had been cooling his heels in prison after being nabbed by Indian security forces in a dramatic chase across many continents.

Sant Longowal was constantly on the move to reach out to the Hindus, many of whom were planning to migrate out of Punjab. Since most other Akali leaders, including his principal associates, Tohra and Badal, preferred to sit on the fence at this most critical stage in the state's history, the full responsibility for normalization of the situation had devolved on Longowal, of which he was only too well aware. Along with insinuations against some top Punjab Congress leaders about their covert links with Sikh militants, media reports also spoke of the overt links that other Congress leaders had with the latter. Clearly, a battle royal to gain maximum political space in Punjab was raging between Congress leaders and Sant Longowal, now seen as the only Sikh leader genuinely interested in promoting a durable process of peace, and accepted as such among both Hindus and Sikhs. He should, in fact, have been recognized as the best bet for ushering in an era of peace and communal harmony in the state and should have been duly supported in his endeavours. But, the ruling Congress party now realized that Bhindranwale had earned a hallowed status in the collective Sikh psyche for having sacrificed his life during Operation Blue Star as compared to the Akali leaders, who had meekly surrendered to the invading army. Regrettably, it once again chose to disregard overall national interests by adopting manipulative policies, freely using intelligence and other state institutions to disparage a political adversary. It also proceeded to co-opt almost every male member of Bhindranwale's family for the purpose.

On 30 April 1985, at Anandpur, Akali leaders held their first formal meeting after Operation Blue Star to discuss what Badal called the past, present and future of Punjab. All those present supported a realistic approach to find a lasting solution to the turmoil and to the restoration of the dignity, honour and self-assurance of the Sikhs. However, with the official backing enjoyed by Joginder Singh's UAD, and the dissolution of all other Akali Dals under his edict—including Longowal's—it became difficult for the mainstream Akali leadership to pursue their political agenda vigorously. It must be said to Longowal's credit that he did not give up even under intense multiple pressures and soon emerged as the most influential contemporary Sikh leader. Later, in the same month, a meeting of district jathedars pressed both Longowal and Badal to withdraw their resignations, which they soon did. Nevertheless, the formidable challenge posed by the Joginder Singh phenomenon could not but critically corrode the confidence of these veteran Akali leaders. UAD organized a *panthic* convention in the Golden Temple to observe the first anniversary of Operation Blue Star on 6 June 1985, which was heavily suffused with 'the spirit of Bhindranwale', as noted by the media.

Three days later, the Longowal Akali Dal too held a convention in the Golden Temple, which attracted a much larger audience than the UAD meeting. This assembly, while supporting the revival of Akali–Centre talks to resolve the Punjab crisis, asked for the release of all detained Sikhs, the repeal of suppressive laws and special courts, and the withdrawal of the army from Punjab. Some people tried to disturb the proceedings by shouting pro-Bhindranwale and pro-Khalistan slogans, and accusing the Akali leaders of being in league with the government and betraying the panth. The miscreants were driven out by Longowal supporters. The Akali leaders met again at Anandpur on 8 July to draw up their future plan of action. They also reiterated their earlier demands and wanted an assurance from New Delhi that their demands would be addressed before further talks. By this time, however, the relations between Longowal on the one hand and Tohra and Badal on the other were getting increasingly strained for various reasons.

Longowal then decided to devote most of his time to touring the state to re-establish his contact with the Hindu community to help create a climate of peace and goodwill. Rajiv Gandhi, too, seemed to appreciate the changed situation, and a ray of hope lightened the popular mood as a reasonable formula seemed to have been worked out between the government and the Akali leadership. There were even suggestions for Rajiv Gandhi to visit the Golden Temple to express regret at the unfortunate events of June and November 1984 and to reassure the Sikhs that the government was indeed keen to move on. Though not unaware of the grave risks involved in such a visit, we did not oppose it and were fully prepared to provide him with fail-safe security, including the deployment of carefully chosen officers for ring-round duty with the PM during all his public functions. All these officers would be inches taller than the PM and thus shield him from any attack. The proposal was shot down by the IB.

Unfortunately, however, all hopes for peace and security vanished soon as militant sentiment in the Sikh community intensified and terrorist violence escalated exponentially. A series of bomb blasts in Delhi in early May 1985 left eighty persons dead. Another major terrorist act was the bombing of Air India flight 182 on 23 June off the Irish coast, in which 239 persons perished. The crime was traced to a Babbar Khalsa International cell in Winnipeg and Vancouver in Canada, set up by some Canadian Sikhs of Indian and Malaysian origin. In

Punjab, militants were becoming bolder and more organized in their operations, despite the continuing accretion to the operational capacity of Central security forces on deputation with us and the strengthening of the arsenal of repressive laws. Arjun Singh arrogated to himself all authority in planning and implementation of counterterrorism strategies, including the personal safety of Sant Longowal, with the help of his security advisor and IG, intelligence. Feeling isolated even within my special area of responsibility, I repeated my earlier request to the governor to let me seek a posting with the Centre. This time, the post of director, NPA, was available and the Union home secretary was prepared to sponsor my name for it. The governor, however, again chose to ignore my request. It was becoming increasingly difficult for me to go along with the policies and agendas that the governor was setting before my officers without taking me into confidence. This was a situation tailor-made for the two imported IGs to embarrass me further in various ways. However, as it is not in my nature to complain or keep on protesting—which I consider a sign of weakness—I let things be.

In July 1985, Arjun Singh succeeded in persuading Longowal to visit Delhi for a meeting with the PM and enter into an agreement with the government, aimed at resolving all the various problems that had been afflicting the region for years. Obviously, it was not easy for the Sant to take such a crucial decision all by himself as none of his senior colleagues was prepared to back him in case the move misfired. The only Akali leader who offered his counsel to the Sant at the time and who, in due course, accompanied him to Delhi, was the shifty-eyed Balwant Singh. Being a devout believer in the scriptures and faced with strong opposition from his colleagues,

Longowal decided to seek guidance and direction in the Sikh holy book to overcome his sense of unease and irresolution. As per Sikh tradition, after offering *ardas*, he opened the holy book randomly. The first stanza on the page read: '*Duvidha chhad, Guru tere ang-sang.*' (Abandon indecision, the Guru is with you.) When he left for Delhi that day, accompanied by Surjit Singh Barnala and Balwant Singh, both of whom had been in touch with Arjun Singh for some time, he seemed to have made up his mind: to negotiate peace with New Delhi.

Longowal, Barnala and Balwant Singh were lodged in Kapurthala House, a Punjab government guest house in Delhi. The art of equivocation did not come easily to Longowal who was basically a man of religion, and, in any case, he could never have matched the manipulative skills of an Arjun Singh, now determined to create history by bringing about an agreement between the Akali Dal and the PM. Cut off from his senior colleagues and deprived of their counsel, with only Barnala and Balwant as his sole advisors, Longowal must have felt trapped in a rather tricky situation. Having come all the way from Chandigarh in search of a final solution to the Punjab tangle, armed with what he naively believed to be divine intercession, he would have felt deeply committed to reach a settlement. Even then, he would have very much liked to consult his key colleagues, rather than rely solely on Balwant Singh, apparently more loyal to Arjun Singh than to the Sant. Longowal was fidgety and unsure during the talks, desiring to go back to Punjab to consult his colleagues. Arjun Singh subtly ruled out any such move as it would have meant the end of the entire exercise, so adroitly worked out by him and his close advisors. Finally, Longowal put his signature to the so-called Rajiv–Longowal Accord on 24 July 1985.

Longowal returned to Chandigarh right away to face an inquisitive media, eager to learn all about the document he had signed in Delhi earlier that day. They informed me at my late-evening press briefing that the Sant was deeply depressed and troubled. After spending the night in Chandigarh, he left for his village where he engaged himself in prayers. The governor's game plan seemed to have been to get the accord signed as early as possible, hold legislative elections and manipulate the electoral process so as to ensure an Akali victory. Then, to transfer power to an Akali government and let them battle the militant forces, while the Centre watched the Sikh premier party fail miserably to contain the rising tide of militancy, and intelligence agencies discreetly stoked up extremist violence. Following Longowal's assassination, Badal told me that the former had wanted him to take over as CM after the elections. Badal sounded clearly unhappy because now that the Sant was no more, his promise meant nothing. This sounded somewhat strange because, how could the Sant have presaged an Akali victory in the upcoming elections unless there was a tacit understanding between the Sant and the Centre that elections to the Punjab legislature would be managed in such a way that an Akali government would assume office in the state?

Subsequent events seemed to confirm that there had, indeed, been such a deal. The game plan, in fact, went further. It had also to be ensured that the selection of Akali candidates was made in such a way that Barnala—not Badal—would emerge as the leader of the Akali Party since Arjun Singh found the former easier to manage. Apparently, Arjun Singh had a hand in selecting the candidates, in the legislative elections of September 1985, both for the Congress and the Akali parties. As it happened, Barnala took over as CM and remained so deeply beholden to Arjun Singh that, even as an elected head of government with a huge legislative majority, he continued to abide by his advice in every matter of import. What is more, Arjun's crony, Balwant Singh, emerged as the power behind the throne, so to speak. Thenceforth, Barnala remained a hot favourite with the Congress party and he continued to occupy gubernatorial posts for decades.

The accord, which purported to 'bring to an end a period of confrontation and usher in an era of amity, goodwill and co-operation, which will promote and strengthen the unity and integrity of India', was widely applauded as a young prime minister's welcome initiative to reach out to the agitated Sikh community. The media was upbeat about peace and order returning to the region because of the accord. This was strange because, barring Longowal, Barnala and Balwant Singh, nearly the entire Sikh religio-political establishment—ranging from Joginder Singh's UAD to minor Akali leaders—was openly critical of the Sant for signing a dubious accord and that too without the government accepting any of the terms that the Akalis had for a long time set as preconditions. Not even Badal and Tohra—Longowal's two key associates—were prepared to support it, claiming that they were not aware of the secret negotiations between Longowal and New Delhi and, therefore, were not a party to it. The accord, which had not been endorsed by a vast majority of the Sikh leadership and which was condemned in no uncertain terms by the swelling ranks of militant groups, soon lost its sheen among the Sikhs.

Further, the document itself turned out to be seriously flawed in many respects in the major clauses, especially those relating to territorial claims and sharing of river waters. It proved to be virtually impossible to implement, due mainly to its vague phraseology, hedged in by inbuilt contradictions, the result either of poor draftsmanship or intended obfuscation. Who actually prepared the draft and who vetted it at various stages remained unclear, though many conjectures were then in circulation. One can be sure, though, that the final product must have received the most careful attention of Arjun Singh and, if the failure of the accord were to be attributed to its interpretative ambiguity, it must have been drawn up with precisely that purpose in view. For it is inconceivable that a meticulous draftsman like him would let a poorly drafted document pass through his hands, unless he meant it to be so. To add to the confusion, the neighbouring states of Haryana and Rajasthan, ruled by the Congress party and affected by the terms of the accord in a major way, had not been made a party to it. As if on cue, Haryana soon refused to cooperate and the much-acclaimed peace process came unstuck. This considerably strengthened the militant lobby in the Sikh community, leading to a substantial accretion to the militant ranks. The Indian establishment was hard put to evolve a suitable and effective response; all that the wise men in Delhi could think of was to change governors and police chiefs from time to time and enact a battery of repressive laws, which proved woefully unequal to the challenge of militancy. All such draconian laws were, in fact, used by the police to harass innocent citizens.

It did not take long for Sant Longowal to realize that he had been tricked into signing a document that inspired little enthusiasm in his community. Moreover, the militants had found in the accord and its likely failure a strong impetus to revive their activities with greater vigour and to get more assured support in the countryside. With all major Akali leaders— except Barnala and Balwant Singh—distancing themselves from the accord, the primary responsibility to push it among the Sikh masses fell exclusively upon Longowal. So, he set about seriously promoting it as the only peaceful alternative to the unending violence and terrorism by embarking on an extensive mass of contact tours all over the state. An extremely devout Sikh, he intuitively turned to scriptural sources for solace and inspiration, frequently visiting gurdwaras, prominent among them being his own dera at Longowal village in Punjab's Sangrur district. In an effort to establish a degree of rapport with the militants, he also started attending the bhog ceremonies of militants, slain in police encounters. However, despite the outward calm and poise, the Sant was clearly a sad and troubled man, shunned by his colleagues and berated by militants for signing a phoney accord with the despotic Delhi durbar.

Longowal now came under increasing threat from the many militant groups, who were steadily gaining support within the community and thereby getting stronger and bolder in their reach and thrust in the region. Those groups blamed the Sant for having signed away the vital interests of the community by entering into an inequitable agreement with an oppressive Centre—a line of reasoning that fitted in admirably with the collective perception of the community. In view of the enormity of the threat perception to Longowal's life, the Punjab government, in consultation with the Union home ministry, decided to provide him a high level of personal security, though he firmly refused any state security cover and understandably so. The matter needed to be handled very tactfully in view of the highly sensitive nature of the task and the kind of situation then developing in the state.

I asked Trikha, IG, intelligence, to carefully examine the entire issue in consultation with local officers, keeping in view all the relevant factors. Trikha held a meeting at Sangrur with IG and DIG, PAP, DIG, security, SP, Sangrur, and other concerned officers to draw up a comprehensive security plan for the Sant, who was discreetly briefed about the scheme to which he grudgingly assented. Gurbachan Singh Mann, an SP-rank PAP officer, who enjoyed the Sant's confidence, was placed in overall charge of the security arrangements. A small but reliable group of officials in plain clothes along with a uniformed detachment was placed at his disposal for the purpose. The unit was also provided with advanced communication and other logistical equipment to remain in touch with each other as well as with Chandigarh. This entire unit was placed under the supervisory charge of IG, intelligence, and DIG, security, who were also responsible for their postings, transfers, replacements, training, briefings and the necessary security clearance. Thus, the entire set of functions pertaining to the Sant's security was to be closely monitored by IG, intelligence, under the overall direction and control of the DGP, who was also to be kept informed about any significant development. According to the practice prevalent then, the bulk of this security force was borne on the strength of the PAP at Jalandhar.

As it happened, within a month of his signing the accord, Longowal was assassinated while attending a religious function in a gurdwara in Sherpur village, near Longowal, where he belonged. Who actually killed him and for what reason, was never conclusively established. An inquiry was conducted by Lieutenant General Gowri Shankar, security advisor to the governor, within days of the murder, but his report was never made public, although some PAP officials were suspended or dismissed in the process. The general demitted office soon thereafter, whether on his own initiative or otherwise remained unclear. I received a call from him shortly before he left Chandigarh for Madras, where he finally settled, to share some information with me, but we were unable to set up a meeting. I have a feeling that it was about Longowal's killing that he wished to talk to me. Unfortunately, he did not live long after his retirement. At a farewell function arranged for me by the state civil services association, I too picked up bits and pieces of the alleged plot by certain interested parties to kill the Sant but without any verifiable kernel.

The gravest of many lapses that most likely led to Longowal's killing was the replacement of Gurbachan Singh Mann by another officer, Jit Singh, by IG, PAP, within days of the security scheme coming into force, without clearing it with IG, intelligence, as was claimed by the latter. Jit Singh had only recently faced a departmental inquiry for having militant links, and his dismissal from service had been recommended to the governor with whom the file was pending for final orders. To assign such a crucial job to an officer whose very credentials were in serious doubt was a highly reckless act, to say the least. Sadly for the late Sant and the prospects of peace in Punjab, this grave lapse did not come to notice until after the foul deed had been done. Neither IG, intelligence, nor IG, PAP, could offer any plausible explanation for such a serious act of negligence or worse. The governor now hastily ordered Jit Singh's dismissal. Was the undue delay in disposing of such an explosive case a mere coincidence, considering that Arjun Singh was universally acclaimed as an astute politician and a clever administrator, who remained in constant touch with IG, intelligence, on the situation developing in the state?

A one-man inquiry commission, presided over by Justice Gurnam Singh, was set up by the Akali government after assumption of office in September 1985. The commission summoned me to clarify some points regarding the role of IG and DIG, PAP, in the chain of events that had led to Longowal's assassination. K.T.S. Tulsi, a senior Supreme Court advocate, cross-examined me on behalf of the IG, PAP, K.P.S. Gill, whose part in implementing the Sant's security scheme was under inquiry. Jit Singh, the dismissed PAP SP, under whose watch the Sant's killing had taken place, cross-examined me himself. This officer had at one time served under the controversial former IPS officer Simranjit Singh Mann in Faridkot district, where Bhindranwale had organized an *amrit prachar* (Sikh baptism) camp in the district police lines. After dismissal from service, he had joined as personal secretary to Mann, who had floated a radical Akali faction of his own after his removal from the IPS, allegedly for being a part of the conspiracy to assassinate Indira Gandhi.

G.I.S. Bhuller, SSP of the adjacent Patiala district, told me what actually happened on that fateful morning when the Sant was killed. Some stunned members of the congregation, eyewitnesses to the foul deed, had narrated shocking details of the sequence of events during interrogation by the local police right after the incident. It seemed that two young Sikhs sitting behind the Sant whipped out their revolvers and shot at the Sant as he bowed in prayer after the ardas. Predictably, the firing led to much commotion among the worshippers, though some of them had the presence of mind to lie on top of the Sant, thus shielding his body from further attack. A police officer then apparently appeared and asked those protecting the Sant to let him get up as the alleged assailants had been caught. It was then that the Sant was fatally shot again. True to form, these details could hardly have formed part of the recorded evidence, as neither the local police nor the witnesses would be too keen to place themselves in a situation pregnant with awkward possibilities. The authorities sought to gloss over all such revelations though some of them must have come to the notice of the Justice Gurnam Singh commission of inquiry and been reflected in its report.

No one then in power in Chandigarh or Delhi—least of all Arjun Singh—was overly interested in ascertaining the real position, and understandably so. All adverse inferences were, therefore, resolutely suppressed. Who was really behind the crucial replacement in the proximate security set-up of Sant Longowal, which had apparently facilitated the foul deed? What could have been the motive for elimination of the Sant, who was poised to play a historic role at that critical stage in the history of Punjab? Was it a plain and simple act of negligence or was there something more to it than met the eye? It is not as if the IG or the DIG, PAP, were unaware of the antecedents of Jit Singh, the officer they had posted to guard the Sant. The inquiry leading to his dismissal from service was conducted by the same IG and DIG who had made the questionable replacement. More importantly, why did they not seek clearance from IG, intelligence, and if they had, why had the latter not kept me in the picture? And why did the governor keep the file pending for so long? These are not merely rhetorical questions; they seek to ascertain the logic behind and the raison d'être of a militant movement and many catastrophic events—alien to Sant Longowal's philosophy—that followed his slaying. A wireless message sent to IG, PAP, on the subject immediately after the killing remained unanswered.

Though an Akali government did come to power, the legislative elections of September 1985 failed to bring peace to the state. Not all Akali leaders were able to see through the governor's astute game plan of the installation of Barnala as CM, though many did, and soon started distancing themselves from the new government. Since the Akali leadership was able neither to provide quality governance to the oppressed citizens nor to prevail upon the Union government to address Sikh grievances, the elections could achieve none of the goals of a democratic exercise. On the contrary, militant violence rose critically; even Akali leaders now became favourite targets of terrorist guns, many of them losing their lives, including several ministers, among them Finance Minister Balwant Singh, chief promoter of the accord. Even Tohra, with known militant links, narrowly escaped a deadly attack. Most Akali leaders went into hiding, leaving their people to fend for themselves as best as they could. Not trusting the Indian security agencies to protect his family members from militant attacks, Badal sent his only son abroad and stopped visiting his vast estates in Punjab.

While the gross mismanagement of the situation by the establishment played a significant part in fanning the flames of Sikh militancy, the growing interest exhibited by Pakistan in the fast-moving events in Indian Punjab aggravated an already complex problem. Also, the large expatriate Sikh community was only too willing to provide the community with a wider transnational base to plan, conduct and sustain terrorist activities. By now, many overseas Sikh organizations and individuals—prominent among them being Ganga Singh Dhillon in the US and Jagjit Singh Chauhan in the UK—had joined to lend support to militant groups, both in financial and logistical terms. Chauhan had set up a Republic of Khalistan-in-exile as early as 1971 and the National Council of Khalistan shortly thereafter. The council continued to canvass support and collect funds in Germany, Canada, the US and the UK, countries with sizeable Sikh populations. Chauhan quietly surfaced in Punjab in 2001, apparently with the tacit approval of Indian authorities. After lying low for a while, he tried overt political action by floating an outfit, Khalsa Raj Party, which soon died an unmourned death along with its founder, having achieved little in securing a Sikh homeland, to be called Khalistan, a highly unviable unit that has fired the imagination of many Sikh theoreticians for decades.

Chauhan had earlier founded the Dal Khalsa, a radical Sikh group, allegedly inspired by some Congress leaders (Zail Singh for one) in order to split the Akali Dal, which was then holding office in Punjab. Notably, it was the Dal Khalsa that claimed responsibility for the 1986 murder of General A.S. Vaidya, Indian army chief at the time of Operation Blue Star. Gurbachan Singh Manochahal, a prominent leader who later headed a most vicious militant group and, still later, one of the panthic committees, was for long on the list of the most wanted men in India. Another group, the Dashmesh Regiment, responsible for a large number of killings, cases of arson and bombings, was founded around 1982 by Bhindranwale's close associate, Major General Shabeg Singh, a highly decorated Indian army general with wide experience of guerrilla warfare, who was later cashiered for professional misconduct. Many other militant groups cropped up with the passage of time. At one time, even the Punjab police had allegedly floated a militant group called the Khalistan Armed Force, doubtless in a no-holds-barred attempt to battle the fast-growing militant violence. There were also at least two all-women militant groups.

More importantly, the AISSF, representing the Akali youth

wing and involved in some terrorist acts, acted as a breeding ground for extremists. In the years following Sant Longowal's assassination, the political and militant situation in Punjab turned more and more confused and murky with the blurring of the zones of authority and the fudging of channels of command and control in the government. The dismissal of the Barnala government a few months later greatly aggravated the situation in the troubled state. With no visible signs of decline in militant violence in the foreseeable future, the situation was tailor-made for devious political players to fish freely in troubled waters. There was no state agency to enforce accountability and that role was finally appropriated by an all-powerful Punjab police, which now took full control of the chaotic state of affairs while all other state institutions became dysfunctional.

With the removal of Sant Longowal from the scene, the only sane voice at that critical juncture in the history of Punjab stood silenced, offering free rein to radical Akali leaders to inflame passions in the community, still seething with anger at the Indian establishment for its utter apathy to their plight. This immensely reinforced the extremist sentiment within the community and set off a deadly wave of militant violence in the region. At a personal level, this assassination affected me as well and my career prospects in a major way, just as Indira Gandhi's had done in another context earlier.

On the day the Sant was shot dead, I was in Delhi for a meeting with the Union home secretary to work out the logistics for holding legislative elections under the shadow of a rising tide of militancy and the threatened boycott of the electoral process by all Akali factions except the one carrying Longowal's name. I rushed back to Chandigarh and found that the governor had already left for the scene of crime. When I called him, he asked me to stay at the headquarters to put in place the necessary security measures and also to keep a close watch on the likely fallout of the assassination in the major centres of militant activity. Home Secretary N.N.Vohra and I stayed on in my office all through the night, tackling a very grave situation indeed and attending to telephone calls from the PMO, the home ministry, the IB and sundry officials in Delhi, not to speak of a host of media persons. A large variety of VIPs, eager to register their concern for the dead leader, were flying in from Delhi and they had to be provided transport and security for the road journey to Longowal village. I deputed K.P.S. Gill to stay put at the airport for the purpose. By early morning, however, he too had proceeded to Longowal without my knowledge or permission.

All this while, I was in constant touch with the governor and feeding him with all the necessary information about the developing situation in the state. The governor flew to Delhi after the funeral with a brief halt at Chandigarh but without giving me a chance to meet him. I learnt later that he had had a detailed discussion with his security advisor, the IG, intelligence, and IG, PAP, at Sangrur near Longowal village, where he was camping, and that he had issued certain orders, again without taking me into confidence. He seemed to have already come to some conclusions regarding the assassination on the basis of information fed to him by the very officers whose negligence or worse was actually responsible for the shocking event. Neither IG, intelligence, who was responsible for providing foolproof security to the Sant nor IG, PAP, who had posted Jit Singh as head of the security detail for the Sant, could escape the blame for what had happened. What was worse, IG, intelligence, did not consider it necessary to keep me informed about the swift developments taking place in Longowal village.

I have already described at length the detailed security scheme for Longowal and its operational nitty-gritty, as also the minutiae of the catastrophic event that I could access then and later. It needed no great intellect to deduce from the course of events outlined above that all the governor's men were, in some way or the other, aware of a critical breach of the security scheme which had been drawn up so carefully just a few weeks earlier, and who were thus constructively accountable for the dastardly crime. The studied manner in which I was excluded from the decision-making process at that crucial stage by the governor could not have been fortuitous. And why had he wanted me to stay on in Chandigarh if not to preclude any chance of the specifics of the tragic act being uncovered? If I had not been specifically asked by Arjun Singh to stay put in my office on that fateful day, I would surely have determined the full facts of this murder most foul and the grave acts of omission and commission on the part of both IG, intelligence, and IG, PAP; and I would have been able to prepare a comprehensive report for the Union government. This was precisely what the governor presumably did not want. He wanted to pre-empt any action by me as head of the state police to inquire into the lapses by my officers, who had been assigned to provide fail-safe security to the Sant, a job that they had miserably failed to carry out. I am sure that if the governor had not excluded me from the decision-making processes at that critical time, it would not have been very difficult to establish more or less conclusively whether the assassination was the result of grave negligence by those entrusted with protecting the Sant or of a sinister design to get rid of the only Sikh leader then carrying credibility with his community.

Though the governor had not considered it necessary even to ask for my views before making up his mind about the subsequent actions to be taken, I did send a detailed report to the director, IB, the next morning, setting down the exact sequence of events of that fateful morning. I doubt if my report was put up to the PM or even seriously considered by the decision-makers in Delhi. After a couple of days, I learnt that Arjun Singh was pressing the PM for my removal on account of Longowal's murder. I tried to contact him in Delhi but he refused to take my calls. I also learnt that the PM wanted to know from Arjun Singh how the DGP had now become so incompetent when, just a month earlier, the governor had refused to spare him for a posting in Delhi. Finally, however, the views of the governor prevailed and I was repatriated to my home state of MP. It was not only the ultimate humiliation of being blamed for a failure to prevent a dastardly crime that had occurred primarily because of manifest negligence, or worse, of the IG, PAP and IG, intelligence—both of whom Arjun Singh was in regular contact with; what was most hurtful was the manner in which this was done. I recall that searing episode with deep distress and can never get over the sheer crudity of it all.

Arjun Singh returned to Chandigarh after a couple of days, armed with a semi-official letter from the Union home secretary addressed to himself, asking him to relieve me with immediate effect on repatriation to my parent cadre. I met him at the airport as I had to seek his permission to go to the Punjab police academy at Phillaur for the passing-out parade of a batch of officers but I found him oddly unresponsive.

When I asked him specifically for permission, he asked me to follow him to Raj Bhavan. There, too, he refused to see me and sent word through his aide-de-camp that I could meet him on my return from tour. I returned home, packed my bags and left for Phillaur. I had covered just about twenty miles when I was stopped by an officer to inform me that my presence was required at an urgent meeting at senior advisor Subramaniam's house. When I arrived there, a sombre home secretary, N.N.Vohra, handed me a state government order that I hand over my charge to the IG headquarters and report to the MP government without availing of joining time. I had half-expected some such action, but only Arjun Singh could have given that spiteful and malicious blow to my self-esteem. Vohra invited me home for a drink after which I came home and informed my wife about what had happened. She admitted that she, too, had been on edge the whole evening. I suppose women possess some extrasensory perception that enables them to presage calamitous events likely to befall their families. We spent a restless night, trying to come to terms with the baffling turn that events had taken within just a few days and planning our future course of action.

Sudip Banerjee, Arjun's long-time aide, briefed an overly curious media about what had led to the removal of the DGP who, until recently, had been considered indispensable. Clearly, such stern action needed to be backed by sufficient evidence of his culpability. That was not difficult, given the evil genius at work and the denial of any opportunity to me to refute whatever blame was sought to be pinned on me. By early next morning, the news was all over the national and international media, and a stream of anxious calls from friends and well-wishers kept my telephone busy for the rest of the day. My sister called from the US, asking me to quit a service which treated sincere and diligent officers so shabbily. Badal came to commiserate and asked me to resign from the IPS, join politics and contest the upcoming legislative elections, adding that his party would back my candidature. I was, however, not political material and did not wish to abandon my service career merely because of this one heartbreak. The deputy commissioner of my home district of Faridkot had casually remarked at a high-level meeting in Chandigarh, chaired by the governor, that I would win hands down in any election if I ever decided to join politics. I still recall with amusement the way a startled Arjun Singh had reacted to the stray remark with a tentative grin and promptly moved to the next item on the agenda.

It is not unusual for Indian politicians who wish to escape blame to find scapegoats in the civil service for botched policies and actions. As civil service conduct rules debar officers from going public with their side of the story, politicians literally get away with murder in an uneven contest, in which one party is denied the right to question the alleged malfeasance. With a young and still-gullible PM intent upon cleansing the Augean stables of a moribund polity, several high functionaries were removed around that time, including the governor of Tamil Nadu and the lieutenant governor of Delhi. Arjun Singh found it easy, therefore, to give me the same treatment except that the blow had to be particularly hard so that I would be in no position to protest the absurdity of it all. Even so, it caused me intense mental agony as nothing like this had ever before happened to me. I carried the hurt for weeks until K.F. Rustamji, who had been rather fond of me from the time I was an SP in MP, where he was IGP, told me over a delicious meal at his Delhi home to stop brooding and get on with my life since I had done nothing wrong.

What was even more comforting was his firm belief that I could not have done anything which could even remotely be construed as failure to do my duty to the best of my ability, adding that my positive approach in coping with the Punjab militancy would one day find its proper place in history. His counsel went a long way in restoring my self-esteem and my faith in the values of decency and integrity that had guided my wife and me all these years, and helped me reacquire my customary poise and sangfroid. Moti Lal Vora, then MP CM, responded positively to my request for a posting on my return to the state, when I spoke to him on telephone from Delhi. Before leaving for Bhopal, I paid a farewell visit to Arjun Singh, who was once again at his deceptive best, promising to help find me a posting in Delhi, where we planned to live after my retirement. It would also resolve the problem of moving my seriously ill mother to Bhopal. He said I should see him in Delhi but, whenever I went to see him after fixing an appointment through his long-time assistant, Baby, he would slip away from the back door!

In utter contrast to Arjun Singh, Vora was every inch a gentleman and it was a pleasure to work with him. He and two other former MP CMs, Shyama Charan Shukla and P.C. Sethi, with whom I had had the privilege to serve earlier, seemed to be genuinely concerned by the shabby manner in which I had been treated by Arjun Singh. P.C. Sethi, in fact, suggested to Vora that I would be an ideal state DGP, but after the thrill and sense of fulfilment of the Punjab posting—notwithstanding the shabby treatment Arjun Singh had dealt me—I was no longer interested in heading another police force. P.H. Vaishnav, who succeeded Dhanoa as the Punjab chief secretary, proposed my name for appointment as chairman of the Punjab Public Service Commission as I still had to complete my term of deputation to Punjab. CM Surjit Singh Barnala was, however, too afraid of Arjun Singh to approve the proposal.

Two and a half decades down the line and with the benefit of much deeper insight gained into the wellspring of human behaviour, my Punjab tenure comes across to me as a classic case of conflicting intents between a shrewd politician—who was a past master in the art of simulation and dissimulation—and a forthright and principled officer who took too seriously his duty to restore normalcy in a troubled state through lawful and legitimate means. Before Arjun Singh arrived on the scene in March 1985, we were doing fairly well, with militant violence markedly under control. The ugly incidents in the Golden Temple in October 1984 were not unexpected, given the implicit support extended to Bhindranwale's father and other close relatives by senior Congress leaders with political stakes in Punjab. I am sure we would have dealt with this problem, too, if the new governor had not actively pursued policies that were clearly determined by goals other than plain and simple containment of militancy. All his programmes and agendas were clearly driven by goals that did not include the restoring of a sense of dignity to a traumatized people and of assuaging their many hurts and grievances. What it did include was coercing a simple man of religion to sign a phoney accord with a still-naive PM, knowing well that the so-called peace process had no chance of success. Sant Longowal's assassination—apparently an outcome of the failure of the accord—further aggravated an already fragile situation in the state. All these factors combined to set off probably the world's deadliest terrorist violence in north India.

In retrospect, I often recall Indira Gandhi's remark when she approved my posting to Punjab, '*Lekin log kehte hain ki aap bahut shareef hain*.' Indeed, I had been too shareef for the wily governor and all his chosen men and advisors. I did sincerely believe, though, in the rule of law and humane policing policies and, given half a chance to follow my approach to the containment of Punjab militancy, the state would have been spared a decade-long dance of death and destruction, leaving thousands of innocent people traumatized at the hands of the fanatical militants—who indulged in mindless terrorist violence in the pursuit of unattainable goals—and a brutalized, lawless police who enjoyed absolute impunity from accountability processes, and who were believed to be armed with an unusual mandate from the PM, no less, namely, to get rid of terrorism within the law, if possible; outside it, if necessary. Given the well-known propensity of the Indian police to cut corners in dealing with crime and disorder even in normal times, the heightened militancy conditions in post-1986 Punjab was a God-given opportunity to indulge in some of the most shocking misconduct in combating the fast-escalating terrorist violence.

Social activists and human rights defenders have chronicled the course of events in Punjab during those extraordinary times, when the police reigned supreme, with all other government agencies having abdicated their obligations, leaving the police alone to hold the fort as best as they could. Neither the judiciary nor the magistracy, and least of all the political executive, was in a position to hold the police accountable to law or propriety, a situation that the police—under the leadership of their all-powerful chief, christened a 'super cop' by an awestruck media—exploited in its worst sense. One is not quite sure whether they fully realized that the expression 'super cop' derives from David Greenberg and Robert Hantz, two cops of the New York Police Department, who typically stepped outside the confines of law to deal with drug-runners and other hardened criminals at a time when police accountability processes had still not fully evolved. Or perhaps they did, for that is exactly what the Punjab police were doing at the time. It was not long before even the media stood silenced with the fear of God put into them by a no-holds-barred police. Corruption, extrajudicial killings, extortion, abductions and other such illicit practices throve; many officers acquired huge properties around Chandigarh and other cities overnight.

Such abysmal misuse of autonomy by the Punjab police during those horrible times thenceforth became an irrefutable argument against the very idea of functional autonomy for the Indian police, as is provided for in all police departments around the developed world. Many middle-level officers were later arraigned before the courts for their criminal acts though the police chief and his principal staff officers—primarily responsible for allowing dubious and unlawful policing activities to flourish—eluded the due process of law. The punitive action against a few wrongdoers was, however, of little solace to all those innocent men, women and children who had suffered unspeakable atrocities and indignities during that period.

Postscript

Arjun Singh took the earliest opportunity to leave the hot seat in Chandigarh for more promising political prospects in the national capital. His formidable skills in managing the media even secured for him a rather triumphal return to Delhi after what was portrayed as a landmark settlement of the Punjab problem, never mind clear evidence to the contrary. Interestingly, his autobiography, rather pompously titled *A Grain of Sand in the Hourglass of Time*, published posthumously in July 2012, devotes just a couple of pages to his Punjab tenure, from where he had returned in triumph in November 1985. His autobiography confirms what was already widely known that in crafting his anti-terrorist strategies and policing policies, he was guided, not by the state police chief but by his wife's uncle, then an IG in the CRPF, who was often seen frequenting the governor's residence and touring the state without my knowledge or permission. Also, it was he, not the state police chief, who the governor trusted in the matter of postings and transfers of police officials and other crucial issues relating to day-to-day policing.

The luckless Barnala government, which had come to power in the legislative elections of September 1985, failed to achieve any success in containing the forces of extremism. So, the ministry was dismissed and President's Rule was imposed once again in early 1986, this time to last for some seven years. My friend and batchmate Julio Ribeiro, a distinguished IPS officer from the Maharashtra cadre, was now posted as DGP. Julio did his best to bring the increasingly worsening militancy situation under some control but failed to stem the rising tide of militant violence for reasons already recounted. The post-1986 phase of Sikh militancy in India, in fact, set new records in this dubious area. Militant groups were now striking freely in many hitherto-unaffected areas, venturing far into other states from their base in Punjab. The sundry panthic committees, which provided religious and community support and guidance to the militants, gained added acceptance in popular Sikh perception. Soon it became clear that an effectual response to the Punjab militancy must also take into account larger historical and ideological factors that had fuelled discontent and alienation in the community in the first place.

To make this happen, the Indian state had to evolve, on a priority basis, strategies and a mindset that sought to address the key concerns and grievances that had bred a sense of estrangement among the mass of the Sikh people. Mere deployment of huge forces and enactment of a battery of suppressive laws were not enough. It is not in the nature of postcolonial administrations, however, to accept this reality, readily and willingly. Ribeiro too was kicked upstairs as advisor to the governor and K.P.S. Gill was brought in as the new DGP from CRPF, against Ribeiro's advice. Gill had been in and out of Punjab for years ever since I had first inducted him into the state as IG, PAP, in 1984, an assignment that he did not much like. S.S. Ray, known for his brutal handling of the Naxalite violence in West Bengal in the late 1960s, where he was then CM, was appointed governor. He was expected to provide protection and alibi to the police in their no-holds-barred approach to 'eliminate terrorism at any cost, within the law, if possible; outside it, if necessary', believed to be the mandate given to Gill by the powers that be.

In November 1990, K.F. Rustamji called me to Delhi to meet the then PM, Chandrashekhar, for a discussion on the worsening terrorist position in Punjab. The PM asked me to study the Punjab situation and suggest realistic policy options to deal with the growing militant violence without alienating the already estranged Sikh community. It was suggested that I undertake an extensive visit to the state; meet a cross section of civil society and members of the Sikh religio-political establishment; and interact with the police and share my findings with Rustamji so that he could go to the PM with a set of concrete and optimal proposals. In the meanwhile, Gill had got embroiled in the pat-on-the-back controversy at a dinner hosted by the state home secretary, involving a senior woman IAS officer. Ever on the lookout for juicy stories, the media gleefully played the story up all over the country. When the woman officer lodged a complaint with the governor, he asked Ribeiro to hold an inquiry. However, the governor chose not to act on Ribeiro's report on the ground that since Gill was then involved in fighting the nation's war against secessionist forces, nothing should be done to disturb him. After a while, though, Gill was posted out and D.S. Mangat of the Punjab cadre was appointed DGP.

I visited Punjab in November 1990, toured the more seriously affected districts, and met a number of public men, including some Sikh leaders, representing a range of political opinion, willing to talk frankly despite likely reprisals from the Punjab police. One of the more vocal of my interlocutors was the veteran communist leader Satya Pal Dang, who offered several very positive suggestions for handling Sikh militancy in a humane, lawful and transparent manner. I prepared a comprehensive report on the subject and sent it to K.F. Rustamji on 4 December 1990. An update on the earlier report was given to him on 29 January 1991. I made specific suggestions for several political, administrative and religious initiatives that needed to be undertaken to facilitate a peaceful resolution of the many issues that were troubling the Sikh community, a process that would, in turn, minimize the militant support base in the community.

Rustamji wrote back saying that my notes had been handed over to the PM. I learnt later that some of my suggestions had been accepted. The process, however, could not be fully followed through because the parliamentary elections that followed soon after brought a new PM to office and, as usually happens in such cases, my suggestions lost their importance with the new circle of advisors around the PM. When nothing else seemed to be working, the powers that be once again chose the tyrannical route to combat the forces of disorder, even though it was to cause huge collateral suffering to the innocent civilian population of the affected areas. Gill was brought back as police chief. Somewhat mysteriously, the Punjab militancy, which had seemed unbeatable until as late as March 1991, came to an abrupt end by 1992 amidst the showering of fulsome praise on a triumphant Punjab police. No one spared a thought for the thousands of innocent men, women and children, victims of an all-powerful and unaccountable security apparatus.

14

Back to Academics

A couple of months before my retirement from the IPS, Home Secretary Vinay Shankar told me that the government of India had allotted some All India Services courses to the MP Academy of Administration, and the CM wanted me to handle those courses in view of my earlier experience at LBSNAA, Mussoorie. I was also given an extension in service so that I would be available for posting to the academy as soon as the scheme was finalized. In due course of time, several courses for IAS and IPS officers were allotted to the MP Academy and I joined as officer on special duty-cum-senior faculty to handle those courses. This was an eminently enjoyable charge as it enabled me to relive my Mussoorie experience. It was doubly satisfying since I was now in a position to weave into my new job all the knowledge and insights that I had acquired during the intervening years in Jabalpur, Gwalior, Delhi and Punjab. I was given a two-year tenure, which would have been extended further if the functioning of Bhopal University had not come to a standstill due to unruly conduct by students and staff members alike. I knew that the university was in some trouble but had never expected to be asked to sort out the mess. The realization came one evening when a surprise visitor, CM Moti Lal Vora's secretary, dropped in.

Even before settling down, he told me somewhat hesitantly that the CM would like me to take charge of the troubled university. This was a most unexpected proposal and my wife quickly made a negative response in view of the rather dismal finale to my Punjab tenure. However, it is not in my nature to refuse challenges and I hated to say no to a man who had been so good to me. I asked my visitor to convey my gratitude to the CM for reposing confidence in me but requested that I be permitted to take a day or two to make up my mind. He said the situation was so grave that I would have to take over charge the very next morning. This was indeed a challenge that I simply had to accept and without further hesitation I said yes to the proposal. My wife wasn't happy about it but she was used to such precipitate decisions by her husband. Earlier, when I had accepted the Punjab posting, she had been away in Calcutta. By the time she learnt about it, it was too late to back out. I did ask my visitor to inform the CM that Railway Minister Madhavrao Scindia had already sounded me about my appointment as VC, Gwalior University. He told me that the proposal had been cleared with Mr Scindia. Late the same evening, my appointment order as VC, Bhopal University, was delivered to me by the office of the chancellor.

I proceeded to the university to take over charge the next morning after calling on the CM. Since my predecessor and the registrar had left town fearing the worst from unruly students, and all sections of the university community were on strike, I took up my new position in something of a solitary splendour. Groups of students and non-teaching staff tried to block my way, raising slogans against the chancellor and the government. Gradually, some student leaders started trickling in, seeking a meeting with me, followed soon after by similar signals from teachers and the non-teaching staff. I agreed to meet all of them provided they withdrew the strike so that we could start with a clean slate. I met the students first. It was a motley group of mostly politicized students, the kind who stay on in the educational stream for years to further the interests of different political parties. As good students shun such disorderly ways, most Indian universities end up being held hostage by toughs and bullies who have little interest in studies. Most of these student leaders set up schools or colleges of their own, adding to the scores of poorly equipped institutions owned by influential individuals out to make a fast buck in an environment of stark commercialization of education. Realizing that as a former IPS officer, I could always call on the local police to promptly quell any disorder, they avoided all conflict.

I promised to look into all the students' demands right away, provided they refrained from unruly conduct for the next two months to which they agreed. The non-teaching staff union was the next to fall in line when they called off their strike unconditionally. The teachers were a little more difficult to deal with, as Indian policemen are held in near-contempt by the so-called intelligentsia, and for good reason, I suppose. Most Indians who come into contact with thana-level police do not carry happy memories of such encounters. Also, the teachers probably regarded me as something of a gatecrasher. I held a meeting with the teachers in one of the larger classrooms as there was then no proper conference hall on the campus. It was a novel sight, a former DGP addressing a gathering of professors, readers and lecturers who held doctoral and postdoctoral degrees, several of them with unruly grey hair and unshaven chins, sported by Indian intellectuals as a mark of erudition, crowding a classroom designed for students! I am sure the irony of the situation was not lost on them as indeed it was not lost on me.

I started by making two confessions and two promises. The confessions were that I certainly did not consider myself the best candidate for the VC's post, which rightfully belonged to one of them. Also, that I did not wish to stay on beyond the minimum time needed to fulfil my mandate, which was to restore normal functioning in the university. The two promises were: one, that in implementing my academic charter, I would be guided by a council of professors, which I intended to set up right away, and two, that I would never allow the police to enter the campus as long as I was there. That was what really took them by surprise and made a profound impression on them. They had probably been looking at some version of

Police Raj on the campus with a former chief of the dreaded Punjab police as vice chancellor. I found them visibly relieved, reassured and fully at ease with me thereafter. By the afternoon, everyone was back at work, including the registrar, who had gone into hiding for fear of violence. By next morning, the campus regained its normal poise and decorum. Once free of their reservations and uncertainties, the academic community was more than willing to cooperate and assist me in my efforts to run the university in a fair, just and transparent manner.

I found the academics easy to get along with; a few of them remained lifelong associates in some projects that I later took up in the academic field. In a few difficult cases, stern measures had to be adopted. But they soon fell in line when they realized that I could be pretty tough when needed. A head of department and the president of the non-teaching union had to be placed under suspension and departmental inquiries ordered against them for misconduct. There was no trouble thereafter and we were able to take many academic and administrative steps to strengthen university functioning. Improper conduct and indiscipline—whether among students or staff—were handled strictly and speedily. Sports and cultural activities were revived to redirect youthful energy into positive channels. The professors' council, set up as promised, met every Monday to advise me in matters falling under their individual areas of expertise.

The only organized forum for vice chancellors to thrash out their problems was the universities coordination committee, which met periodically with the chancellor in the chair to go over an agenda prepared by his office and the education department, which generally ended up as a command performance with most vice chancellors feeling unsatisfied with the outcome. I persuaded my colleagues to set up an MP Forum of Vice Chancellors to provide an alternative and autonomous forum to address this problem. Around that time, legislative elections in the state brought the BJP to power and, soon after, a new governor-chancellor. I did not find the new government overly interested in university reforms. So, all the proposals we had discussed in the first meeting of the VCs' forum, held in my office, lost their edge and remained unimplemented.

Although the building grants were meagre, we were able to scrounge enough resources to build an auditorium in the physics department which was to host an international conference on quantum physics. That was the first time a major event was held on the campus and not in a rented building. The administrative wing was housed in tin sheds, which got unbearably hot during summer months, leading to absenteeism and shoddy work. An administrative block, part of the original plan, had remained incomplete for decades due to lack of funds. A foundation stone, laid by a former chancellor some two decades earlier, stood as a grim reminder of the poor financial health of the university. I thought the completion of the administrative block was of immediate importance and put all our resources into this task. When the work was completed in record time, I wanted the outstanding effort put in by our engineers to be publicly recognized. My colleagues in the university suggested that we invite the CM to do the honours.

In India, anyone holding high office is ipso facto regarded as the repository of all wisdom and knowledge and is much sought after for formal ceremonies of whatever nature, from blessing married couples to inaugurating new buildings and institutions. So, we invited the great man for the function and left no stone unturned, literally and figuratively, to make it a grand affair. However, far from appreciating our initiative, the honourable CM proceeded to draw on his well-known sardonic wit and sarcasm to ridicule the excellent job done by the university staff in providing a much-needed facility. The CM was apparently miffed at my refusal to change the name of the building from Satya Bhavan to Deen Dayal Upadhyaya Bhavan after the much-vaunted BJP ideologue. My suggestion that the new library building could be named after the BJP icon as a more fitting tribute to his highly extolled erudition was summarily dismissed. The episode left a bad taste in the mouth and prompted me not to seek reappointment much as I prized the academic environment and the many creative opportunities it offered.

Most vice chancellors of this university in its formative years had come from the cadre of college principals, who imported a typical classroom culture, assigning little value to research and publications that rightly constitute the building blocks of a good university. There were only twelve teaching departments on campus and they did not include such core subjects as mathematics, chemistry and English. I sounded the University Grants Commission, which agreed to sanction these departments in the next Five-Year Plan but the proposal fell through due to the indifference shown by my successor and the state government. Canteens and coffee houses are traditionally vibrant centres of intellectual contestations that go to make university life a treasured interlude in the transition from youth to maturity. In the absence of a decent place for social interaction, the students flocked to roadside dhabas. We persuaded the India Coffee House people to open a canteen on campus. After the classrooms, the library is the most frequented place in a well-run university, or so I thought before I visited the library on this campus. It presented a jail-like look with locked cabinets and barricaded windows to guard against the filching of books and costly journals. It required a huge effort from me to get the cabinets unlocked for free use by the students even if it involved losing some books.

The political fallout of the change of government started impacting the university, working in many negative ways with the new ministers constantly intruding into my domain. Soon this tug of war became a major headache, sidetracking my reformist agenda. This was unfortunate but not rare in heavily politicized institutions of higher learning in India. The new governor-chancellor, only moderately blessed with intellectual acumen, was of little help. It seemed the right time for me to leave but, before that, the normal functioning of the university had to be restored. This required the formation of various university bodies, which had remained suspended for long due to disturbed conditions. We speeded up the process of holding elections to the syndicate and other university bodies, and completed the job in record time with ample help from all university employees, led by professors Chauhan, Bisen and Gautam. Having achieved my mandate, I hastened to submit my resignation to the chancellor, requesting to be relieved early. Looking back on my tenure in a difficult university, I often wonder at the ease with which I was able to adjust to a wholly new role in a hostile setting, at least to begin with.

Although I left the university with an uneasy feeling of not having been able to fully accomplish the agenda that I had set for myself, I recall my efforts in that direction with a distinct sense of fulfilment and pride. Since the new government was not overly fond of me, for I had failed to carry out their political dictates, it was easier for me to quit at the right time. The university posting had given me an opportunity to meet and interact with eminent scholars and educationists at national and international conferences, an experience that helped me greatly in growing away from a constricted frame of concepts and values, typical of police forces the world over, but especially so in South Asia. Professor Amrik Singh, a former vice chancellor and secretary of the Association of Indian Universities, described me in an article in the *Tribune*, Chandigarh, as 'more academic than many academic vice chancellors' that he had known, and that was before he had even met me. 'Mr. Dhillon started his career as a college lecturer and ended up as a vice chancellor, in between he also did some three and a half decades of policing' was how Professor J.S. Grewal, director, IIAS Shimla, introduced me once. Thenceforth, this become a regular feature of introductory remarks about me, something that I value above everything else.

My tenure as a VC was something of a catalyst in setting my post-IPS career graph. I had a flair for writing right from the beginning and was a regular invitee to sessions of the All India Police Science Congress, where I presented several papers. I also occasionally wrote for newspapers and magazines. A 'middle' on the edit page of the *Times of India* had led the incomparable V.D. Trivadi, then editor middles, to compliment me personally. A paper on traffic engineering presented by me in Bombay in 1960 remained a reference document for years in many a police department. All such papers, I now realize, must have reflected limited perspectives, although some courses in IIPA and the Administrative Staff College of India had helped me develop a wider appreciation of social reality. Post-IPS, the nature and thrust of my writings changed markedly, displaying a heightened awareness of wider social, political and economic issues. It was around that time that I got an invitation from the IIAS, Shimla, to speak at a seminar, organized by them, on the anatomy of violence in the Indian context.

The paper, based largely on my Punjab experience, generated a lot of interest and lively discussion. When the seminar concluded, the director suggested that I apply for a fellowship at the institute. I readily agreed and submitted the prescribed application along with a research proposal, prepared then and there with help from the director's stenographer, defining the outlines of a research project on the history of Indian, or what was now the South Asian, police. Soon after my return to Bhopal, I received intimation from the IIAS that my proposal had been accepted and that I should join the institute as a fellow from the next session. This turned out to be a wonderful opportunity to enter a new world of learning and scholarship that would offer me the kind of intellectual fulfilment that the IPS could not.

The IIAS is housed in a magnificent mansion with vast grassy lawns and exquisite gardens, built in the mid-nineteenth century for British viceroys to escape the dust and heat of Indian summers. My wife and I would take off for Shimla early March each year in my small car to arrive at the charming hill station in a week, travelling in short stages. We would return to Bhopal at the end of November in the same manner, to enjoy the brief Bhopal winter and revive our contacts with the town and a host of friends. It was all so romantic and energizing, starting a new career in late middle age. The institute provided a lovely cottage with a breathtaking view of the hills for our stay and a cosy room for study and research. The magnificent ballroom of the mansion housed a very well-stocked library. As all IIAS fellows held doctorate degrees, I too was addressed as 'Doctor sahib', much to the amusement of my wife. One of us would present his paper at the Monday meeting, with all the other fellows and the director in attendance, for peer review. The presenter would then revise or modify his findings and come back to the group for a second review. All this went into making the fellowship a great learning experience. Playwright Bhisham Sahni, novelist Krishna Sobti, television critic Amita Malik and the legendary Professor Randhir Singh of Delhi University were among my colleagues at the IIAS. Randhir Singh, a leftist of the older variety, maintained that no genuine thinker could be anything but a leftist. All of them were very friendly people and exceedingly pleasant company. Sobti gifted me the Punjabi version of her evocative magnum opus, *Zindaginama*, because my Hindi was so weak.

Policemen were something of a rarity among IIAS fellows and while my selection for the fellowship could be considered an honour of sorts, it made me overly self-conscious since Indian scholars regard policemen as arrogant, crude, bossy and uninformed, even boorish. Though my colleagues soon realized that I did not fall into the stereotype, I still had to compete with the best products of academia. A notable event during my IIAS term was a seminar on 'Redefining the Good Society', organized by the Rajiv Gandhi Foundation, in which a galaxy of scholars, administrators and politicians took part. Sonia Gandhi, chairperson of the foundation, presided over the seminar sessions. She came across as a woman of great charm, integrity of intent and sincerity of purpose, though basically a shy and reticent person. She would quietly queue up for lunch along with the participants, firmly ignoring fawning ministers and high officials. She would also neatly dodge those who were keen to get themselves photographed with her. Inside the seminar room, it was Natwar Singh, then a close family friend, who acted as the principal anchor on her behalf. The seminar concluded with a grand dinner in the imperial ballroom in the true tradition of the Raj days. The seminar possibly had a political dimension as some Congress leaders were then trying to persuade Sonia to distance herself from Narasimha Rao's government. Arjun Singh, the key promoter of the exercise, was certainly around a great deal.

It took me some six months of study and research before I could get down to writing my book on the history of the Indian police. The peer review of the chapters that I presented in the weekly meetings helped me greatly in refining the style and content of my work. It also broadened my frame of reference and the way I looked at police and society, and police and the state. I submitted the manuscript of my book soon after I left Shimla, one of the few fellows who did actually complete their projects. The study was published by the IIAS a few years later under the title *Defenders of the Establishment: Ruler-Supportive Police Forces of South Asia* and was released by Prime Minster I.K. Gujral in 1998, along with other IIAS publications. It remains an authentic history of South Asian police from ancient times to 1947, the year of the Partition of India. My book questioned, for the first time, the ruler-supportive role of the Indian police as compared to the citizen-friendly police forces in mature democracies. The initial title of the book was *Twin Legacies of the Indian Police: Servility and Oppression*, because Indian policemen are overly servile to the rulers and excessively harsh towards the underprivileged classes. However, K.F. Rustamji advised me not to be so uncharitable because our police served under very difficult conditions. A few years later this book was followed by a history of the Indian police from 1947 to 2002 titled *Police and Politics in India*. Both these works are used as important reference books in South Asian police and administrative training institutions, as also in some universities in the US.

I have always known that I am a rather indifferent poet but that has never prevented me from indulging in my profound passion for the muse. A poem titled 'The Temple of Learning', which I wrote in Shimla, almost sums up my take on the institution and the small-minded people who, at times, stray into positions of power in the IIAS, a brainchild of S. Radhakrishnan. Here it goes:

From far and near they gather
To savour and partake of the fruits of knowledge.
Some with a demonstrative, stylized swagger,
Others with the diffidence of a fresher in college.
Seminars, study groups and library sessions,
Interaction, scholarly powwow and contentious situations
Constitute the sole springs of learning, while passions
Rising, sparkling and boiling over, morph into disputations.
Neither ripe maturity nor callow youth would preclude
Argumentative posturing, gesticulations and sharp attitudes,
To deconstruct a postmodernist construct to deduce,
Converse, contrary but attractive platitudes.
Open collars, unbuttoned cuffs and a studied neglect
Of accepted dress modes proclaim scholarly credentials.
High drama unfolds during visits of the select
Band of super scholars to assess aptitude in all essentials.
Super scholars, like super cops, hold in sharp contempt

Conflicting beliefs and perceptions to reach mysterious
  decisions,
Leaving a shocked campus engaged in a vain attempt
To decode the super-scholarly visions and revisions.

My book *Defenders of the Establishment* was a pioneer
in highlighting the many flaws of the Indian Police Act of
1861 and its failure to serve a modern democratic polity. So
far, all similar studies have used that act as a reference point
to critique the Indian police in many ways, but have never
questioned its raison d'être in a democracy. Apart from the core
thrust of my book, the phrases 'ruler-supportive' and 'citizen-
friendly' became integral to police reforms advocacy by social
activists. More notably, this book caught the attention of the
Commonwealth Human Rights Initiative (CHRI), mandated
to protect human rights in the Commonwealth. CHRI had
found that most human rights violations in South Asia were
committed by the police. My book highlighted the reasons
why this was so. Thereafter, they made advocacy for multi-
layered structural reforms in the Indian police an important
part of their agenda. As a member of CHRI's executive
council, I remained deeply involved in police reforms for
years, highlighting the many shortfalls in law enforcement and
policing in India. It was a long and protracted campaign, since,
ranged against any systemic police reforms, were the powerful
political and bureaucratic classes, who were loath to give up
their control over the police as had been provided in the 1861
Act. Even the police leadership disfavoured any plan to make
the police democratic and citizen-friendly. In April 2002, a top
Bombay NGO wanted me to serve on the Citizens' Tribunal
under Justice Krishna Iyer, a former chief justice of India, to

probe the role of the Gujarat government in the mass massacre of Muslims following the Godhra incident. I had to decline the honour because I was scheduled to go abroad for an important conference.

I remained involved in the affairs of Indian hockey from 1976 to 1994, first as president of MP and Punjab hockey associations and then as senior vice president and chairman of the selection committee of the IHF. I opted out in 1994 to devote more time to reading and writing. I lost the only election I have contested for the office of IHF president to M.A.M. Ramaswamy ('call me Ramu', he would insist), a wealthy race horse owner from south India, by three votes in 1985, mainly because Vidya Charan Shukla, then president of the Indian Olympic Association, chose to work actively against me. Many state hockey associations, unhappy with the moribund state of the game for lack of sincere leadership, were with me. Sensing that he was on a weak wicket, Ramaswamy offered to nominate me permanent delegate to the International Hockey Federation (FIH) if I withdrew from the contest. This was an attractive proposal as it implied immense scope for foreign travel and lavish hospitality at the expense of the IHF. Since I was sure of my position I made a similar offer to him. As the evening came to an end and the rival camps geared up for their campaigns, Shukla set about nibbling at my support base and by morning had succeeded in taking away a couple of my votes. As chief of the Indian Olympic Association, he had enormous powers of patronage, and Ramaswamy was an enormously rich man. Dhanraj Pillay and Ashish Ballal could not have lasted long in the national team but for my firm support.

I twice accompanied the Indian national teams overseas as manager for fixtures. In 1987, I took the junior men's team for playing two matches in Moscow and another two in Minsk, the capital of Byelorussia. When we landed in Moscow after a long flight, we found the ambience rather frigid, both in letter and spirit. The young cop at the immigration counter could understand no other language except his native Russian with the result that every now and then he had to go inside the cabin to consult his boss; so, it took ages to clear the long queue at the counter. To add further to our woes there was just one horribly filthy toilet in the waiting area. The Soviet Union was still intact though party control was noticeably slipping. Glasnost and perestroika were much in the news though no one then thought that the break-up of the mighty Soviet Union was so imminent. The rouble was artificially pegged at a high exchange rate against the dollar though illicit trading in dollars was common all over the city. Despite the visible signs of economic and political decline, however, the Lenin theatre still attracted high society, very European in sartorial and cultural preferences. Addiction to alcohol and abject poverty drove many men to beggary and women to prostitution.

Most items of daily use were virtually unavailable to the people. One saw long queues at food stalls with those at the back not even aware of what was being sold and often the supplies ran out before everyone in the queue had been served, leaving many disappointed shoppers, who would then wander away to join another queue, again unaware of what was on offer. Pilots flying in from Central Asian airports, like Tashkent, could be seen proudly carrying huge water melons tucked under their arms. Minsk was a brand new city, built on the ruins of the old city destroyed by the Germans during the Second World War, and it was a pleasure to walk along the wide avenues, lined with beautiful flowering trees and acres of green lawns. Communist party officials would vociferously assert that their country was not a Soviet satellite but a sovereign UN member. We won all the four matches, though not without some questionable decisions by the umpire, ostensibly out of kindness to a foreign team. When I expressed my reservations to our coach, he quietly and somewhat smugly told me that such things were common in international hockey. At formal receptions, we received fulsome warmth accompanied by bear hugs and extended kisses, with me as a favourite target, which left me red in the face.

In 1990, I had to miss a rare chance of visiting Lahore as manager of our team for the World Cup due to my commitments in Bhopal University. In 1992, I accompanied our national team to Europe for a five-nation tour, which took us to Belgium, England, Germany, Spain and Holland, to play thirteen matches. In Brussels, some Sikh extremists tried to lure away our Sikh players but were firmly put in their place by Pargat Singh and Jagbir Singh, while the local police did the rest. In England, we spent a few days in a beautiful old mansion, converted into a hockey academy, upstream of Thames River and near a quaint little village with an archaic pub adding greatly to its attraction. We played two matches against the English at the boom town of Milton Keynes and won both, thereby greatly enthusing the very voluble crowd of Indian-origin spectators, who exploded with joy every time we scored a goal, gleefully jeering at the few white people at the site. They flocked to our hotel every morning, carrying costly gifts with offers of lavish hospitality for the boys, telling me cheerfully that they were immensely happy to see that the haughty English had been well and truly put in their place. My old friend John Alderson came to see me in Cardiff, where we played two matches against the Welsh team, winning both. In Madrid, we played a four-nation tournament, Egypt and Argentina being the other teams besides the hosts, Spain, and us. Again, we came out on top.

Our ace player, Dhanraj Pillay, a strict vegetarian, often had to subsist on bread and cheese. His endurance finally wore out in Madrid where he refused to eat anything but a good old south Indian meal. This seemed an impossible demand but soon the word got around and several local Indians appeared with baskets of dosas, idlis and other such delicacies. Dhanraj and his teammates had a hearty meal for the first time in many days. Next morning, baskets of parathas and omelettes materialized in the same manner. I had to stop this gluttony because it could cost us the afternoon match. Douglas Grey, a very affable Irishman and the FIH observer at the tournament, got along famously with me and remained a lifelong friend. Our Spanish bus driver shared his countrymen's lethargy. So, when our bus broke down on the way to the stadium where we had an important match, he remained unperturbed, muttering, 'Tranquilo, tranquilo.'

That was a remarkably successful tour as we won eleven out of thirteen fixtures, lost one and drew one. The loss and draw were against the German team that eventually went on to win the championship at Barcelona Olympics two months later. German media and local authorities were most effusive and warm, recalling the 1936 Berlin Olympics where the Indians led by Dhyan Chand had won all fixtures by huge margins and finally won the gold by defeating the hosts. 'Our masters from India have come' read one headline in a prominent German daily. Despite our many inadequacies in resources (we did not have even a movie camera to film our and our opponents' games so as to study and analyse each other's weaknesses and strengths), we had done extremely well in this tour and yet, in the Summer Olympics in Barcelona in September, we finished close to the bottom. That was because the coach and the manager were not on talking terms with each other, and team selection was not free from regional biases. At the post-match cocktails in Amsterdam, the Dutch hotly contested my observation that the greatest beer drinkers in the world were the Germans. They vociferously claimed that distinction for themselves.

By the time we arrived in Frankfurt to board a flight to Delhi, we were grossly overweight in terms of our baggage, what with all the shopping and the gifts amassed by the boys. It required the charm and guile of centre forward Jagbir to get around the comely girl at the check-in counter to let our luggage be loaded into the aircraft without being weighed. We were carrying scores of miniature hockey sticks for presentation on just such occasions. All the airlines staff simply adored our little gifts. But then those were still laid-back times and flying had not become the nightmare that it is these days. I am sure it would be impossible to achieve such a feat in these terror-obsessed days. We landed in Delhi to an enthusiastic welcome by an ecstatic crowd even at that unearthly hour. In my report to the IHF and the sports ministry, I highlighted the many inadequacies in our training infrastructure, stressing the need to arm our teams with all the tools our rivals had in their possession since long. The near-collapse of our team in Barcelona attracted a lot of criticism and the IHF was hard put to defend its policies and practices.

In 1997, P.R. Chari of the IAS, and an old friend, asked me to join him in a project to put together a number of essays on various aspects of Indian administration in the form of a book, to coincide with the fiftieth anniversary of Indian independence. I readily agreed to write the chapter on internal security and law enforcement. The book was published under the title *India towards Millennium* and was formally released by the President of India at the presidential mansion. I later expanded the essay to compile a detailed history of the Indian police from 1947 to 2002. I chose to extend my study to 2002 because that year witnessed a most deplorable episode in the history of sectarian relations in the country, when hundreds of Muslim men, women and children were mercilessly slain by violent Hindu mobs, aided and abetted by the police in Gujarat, allegedly under the CM's instructions. The carnage remained under inquiry for years before the Supreme Court constituted a special investigation team to ensure a fair inquiry and secure justice for the persecuted Muslim community. What happened to Muslims in Gujarat was, in many ways, a replication of what the Sikhs had had to go through in 1984 in Delhi, except that the Delhi massacres had occurred under a Congress government. And just as the Delhi killings had led to the intensification of Sikh militancy, Indian Muslims, who had so far refrained from joining the Islamist terror outfits, were now often found to be involved in jihadi activities. Soon, home-grown Muslim terrorist modules sprang up in several parts of the country.

This book was published in 2005 under the title *Police and Politics in India: Colonial Concepts, Democratic Compulsions*. In between, I contributed an essay, 'White Sahibs: Brown Sahibs', to an edited volume on several aspects of the Indian Constitution, published under the title *Social Justice and the Constitution*. I also contributed essays to some half a dozen other volumes, on various topics, like extremist violence, minority rights and police reforms. In 2006, my book on Sikh militancy was published by Penguin India under the title *Identity and Survival: Sikh Militancy in India*. I also participated in a number of conferences in India and abroad and presented papers on a wide range of subjects, mainly relating to policing, public order, human rights and police reforms. An Indo-French collaborative effort resulted in the production of a comparative study of Indian and French systems of criminal justice under the title *The Police, State and Society: Perspectives from India and France*, in 2011, for which I wrote the lead essay, 'The Police and the Criminal Justice System in India'. My paper on 'Accountability Mechanisms in the Indian Police', presented by me at an international conference in Prague in 2006, is part of a book published in September 2012, *Global Environment of Policing*.

Dick Ward, a distinguished professor of criminal justice, who finds mention in this book more than once, went on to head criminal justice departments in a range of American universities and institutions of higher learning. He also continued to produce valuable studies in areas of his specialization. While still teaching at the University of Illinois at Chicago, he had set up the office of international criminal justice as a transnational centre for studies in policing and law enforcement. I was a permanent invitee to all his conferences, seminars and workshops, whether in the US or abroad, though, of course, I could not avail of many such opportunities due to the high travel costs involved. Given the volume and variety of my writing, and the partaking in seminars, workshops and conferences in India and abroad on a regular basis, apart from several positive engagements with civil-society issues—in the years after my retirement from the IPS—I often debate with myself whether it had been worth my while to stick to my police career for so long. Or, would it have been better for me to quit the IPS and seek a full-time but more fulfilling career in academic study, research and writing? Maybe, thereby, I would have gained a deeper insight into the art and craft of writing and acquired a more refined sensitivity to social concerns so as to mature into a full-time writer and activist. But would I have been able to develop the heightened awareness and sense of discernment if I had not experienced first-hand the myriad iniquities and indignities to which ordinary Indians are exposed, day in and day out, in a still largely feudal social set-up and a callously unfeeling postcolonial state structure, and if I had not been an integral part of that very system? And then, of course, there was the sheer thrill of working in hazardous and risky assignments in dacoity areas and facing deadly mobs while tackling sectarian riots and urban mafia gangs.

Indian police leadership had acquired considerable importance in administrative matters during the last decades of British rule, which visibly diminished after Independence with the government becoming more concerned with development. The IPS, however, later regained its centrality to governance, especially in areas of national and internal security as the dangers of the republic coming apart at the peripheries did not abate for reasons mentioned earlier in this book. Service in the IPS, therefore, opened windows of opportunity to observe at close quarters the realities of India and to participate in substantial measure in the exciting enterprise of administering and governing this vast land. This would in itself provide enough reason to have remained a part of the state apparatus even if I had not been picked up at some crucial stages in my career to hold some very difficult and sensitive positions, with the Punjab appointment surely at the top of such assignments. That is why I have named the Punjab chapter 'The Ultimate Challenge'. Also, the Punjab posting brought out the best in me and provided me with fresh insights into policing and management of crisis situations in a context of highly destabilizing political and administrative intrigues, where nearly all state and non-state players had their own individual agendas, regardless of the interests of the citizen or the state. On the whole, the experience and inputs that a career in the IPS made available to me were invaluable and, but for that, I would have been much less qualified to write this kind of book.

Appendix: Dhillons of Buttar Village from the Seventeenth Century to the Present

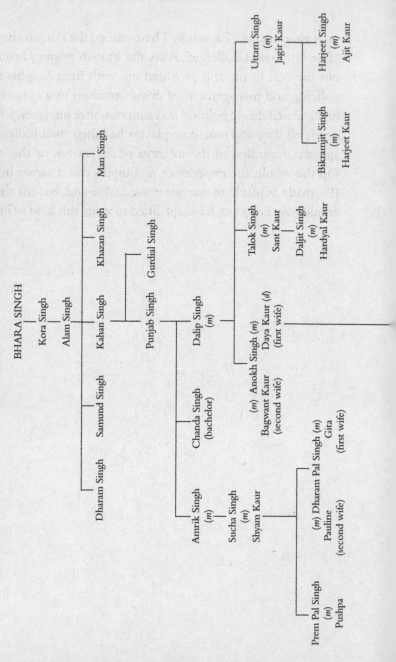

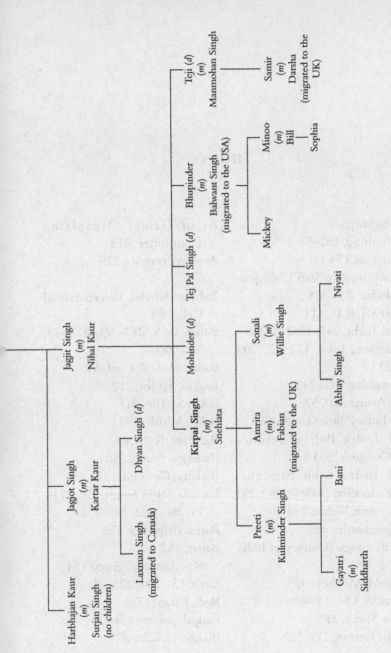

Note: This has been reconstructed from old family documents

Index